WATCH YOU DIE

P. A. GODDEN

Published by New Generation Publishing in 2023

Copyright © P. A. Godden 2023

First Edition

ISBN   978-1-80369-028-5

www.newgeneration-publishing.com

New Generation Publishing

In memory of George a wonderful storyteller

JULY 2000

With a bunch of white roses in one hand and secateurs in the other, she walks in from the garden. She sees the plastic sheet covering the floor and calls out, 'I thought we were going out, not doing DIY.'

She puts the secateurs down beside the sink and reaches for a blue pottery vase from the shelf above. At the sound of footsteps, she turns ready with a smile.

The sun shining in her eyes catches the glint of steel on a long kitchen knife held in steady hands.

Her eyes widen, her mouth opens and the knife plunges. The silence broken only by a whimper, as fingers loosen and flowers fall.

Blood mingles with white petals on the plastic beneath her. 'Why?' she murmurs as her eyes close. The last sound she hears is a whispered reply.

'I want to watch you die.'

TUESDAY 4TH OCTOBER 2005

'Damn, where's the light? Louise fumbled in her handbag for her small torch and groaned as shopping bags slipped from her grasp and emptied some of the contents at her feet. 'Damn, damn and more damn. Bet that's the tomatoes ruined.' The torch beam caught flashes of small red balls as they rolled across the path. 'I knew it' she moaned and swooped up as many as she could but the squelch as she stepped gingerly towards her door, caused another loud 'Damn.'

As she groped for the light switch, the sound of claws scrabbling on the wood alerted her to what would happen next. 'Whoa Buster' she shouted while she deftly turned to avoid a full body onslaught of her huge brown bear of a dog. She shooed him past her and out into the front garden.

Shopping safely on the kitchen worktop, she glanced at her watch. It was well after six. She pulled out a half empty bottle of white wine from the fridge and filled a glass almost to the brim. Nectar, she thought as she licked her lips and let out a long slow breath as the effect of her challenging day lessened. It always seemed worse when she'd had to commute to Bristol to the GP practice where she worked two days a week. It was much easier the days she worked privately from her home.

All her life people had brought problems to her for advice, so she'd taken it a step further and become a counsellor. Once she'd trained it had become easier to set professional boundaries and avoid being cornered for lengthy outpourings. Now in her fifties and after working for many years, she still loved it. She'd found it challenging at times and was sure it had added more than a few grey hairs to her auburn mop but wasn't ready to stop just yet. Friends told her she still looked younger than her years and was pleased that a size twelve still fitted her as well as it always did, although finding trousers for her tall frame could be difficult.

As she wandered up the stairs with wine clutched in one hand and feet cold on the bare rough boards she thought longingly about a hot bath she could relax in but if George has started work as he said, there'd be no chance. She peeked into the space that, until today, had been a fully functioning bathroom. He'd started! Scattered about the floor were old fixtures and fittings mixed in with his work tools and the dust and rubble gave the impression that a hand grenade had been thrown into the room and she groaned and hoped this untidiness wasn't a reflection of his work.

She had to admit, the thought of George made her smile. They'd met at the gym in the village, an unlikely place for her, as exercise was not something she had ever felt driven to do. Henry must have felt it was a son's duty to keep her fit and he'd bought her the sessions for Christmas. It was an unwanted gift but the amount it had cost led her to choose a weekly class. She'd liked riding a bike when she was younger, so chose a spin class but it wasn't bike riding as she had ever known it, and even the thumping music didn't seem to make it feel like fun. However, if she hadn't gone she'd never have met George, the cyclist next to her. It was refreshing to meet a man in his fifties who wasn't a client.

There was never time to talk during the class, but they'd started to chat after and a while ago she'd agreed to have a coffee at the small café on the premises. Despite her initial hesitation she had grown to like these meetings.

She smiled as she remembered his reaction after she'd told him she was a counsellor. "What, as in solving worries or as in working for the Council?" She wished at the time she'd invented a different job. People often stopped talking to her when she told them what she did but, for some reason, he didn't. He just asked some pertinent questions.

When eventually she learned he was a builder, she suggested he give her a quote to update her bathroom. She'd surprised herself by her lack of caution; she would normally have checked out his work and asked for references. Now, after a few months, he'd finally started and the state of the bathroom made her question her decision for a moment.

Buster's whine interrupted her thoughts and she returned downstairs to let him in but he didn't settle. He paced around, looked at his lead and whined some more. She didn't want to go for a walk but knew she wasn't being fair; after all he hadn't asked to be shut up all day. The rescue centre had told her the puppy was an unknown mixed breed and she'd guessed from his big feet he might get large but hadn't quite expected this enormous shaggy dog, whose affinity for water made her think perhaps there was some Newfoundland in him.

'Come on then, let's go.' She took a last swig of wine from her half empty glass, clipped the lead on him, grabbed her phone and set off. She'd only gone a couple of steps from the door when her foot landed on something soft and squelchy. 'Blast – I'd forgotten the tomatoes. Hang on, Buster.' She dropped his lead and got her torch out of her pocket. She gathered the ones she could see into a pile on her doorstep so she could take them in on her return. 'Now we can go,' she murmured, as she picked up his lead.

Some of the houses had their lights on and this always reassured her on her night walks. She didn't know all of the people who lived in her road but her good friend Caroline lived in the last house at the far end of the terrace. She wondered what sort of a day she'd had at the local infant school where she worked as a teaching assistant. Perhaps I might call in on the way back, she thought but then shook her head slightly. She was tired and they'd be meeting up on Friday anyway for their regular G & T night.

At the top of the hill she could see the city lights of Bath, well within walking distance but far enough away from Weston, which although now a suburb still had the feel of a village as it once was.

The old iron kissing gate that led to the church squeaked as she opened it. The vicar didn't seem to mind dogs, as long as people cleared up their mess. Since some people found the churchyard eerie after dark, she mostly found herself on her own. It had become her usual evening walk as the path, which wound around the church, was long enough for her to feel Buster had stretched his legs.

On their return Buster snuffled at most of the lamp posts and tree trunks. The night gave no colour to the trees and it was hard to imagine the brilliant red, amber and copper leaves that would light up the morning. It wouldn't be long before they'd cover the streets and she'd hear the autumnal shuffle of leaves as she walked. She gulped and brushed her hand across her eyes as she remembered autumn and winter night walks with James through the streets of Bristol. This memory still caused pain even though his death was now years ago. 'Come on Buster, I think this will do, it's cold and I need something to eat and I don't feel like being sad tonight.'

Buster guzzled his food, while she put baked beans in the microwave and made some toast. She picked up her glass of wine from where she'd left it and wandered across the hall into her counselling room. She loved this room, chosen as her therapy room. It was conveniently next to the front door and she'd painted it a soft calm green. It felt comfortable and safe to her and hoped it did to her clients too.

She glanced around to make sure it looked tidy, that the wastepaper baskets were empty and not filled with sodden tissues. She checked to make sure there were enough boxes of these and the two clocks on the walls opposite each comfortable chair showed the right time. She remembered the arguments she'd had with a colleague over this. Like many, her colleague liked to be the only one that could see a clock but she liked her clients to have the freedom to manage time in their sessions. It also allowed her to give them the choice of seats. Most seemed to prefer the chair furthest from the door with its back to the window. This left her in the one nearest the door, which she preferred and which was thought to be the safest if you needed to get out fast. She'd never needed to but there had been some dodgy moments.

After she'd eaten she settled herself on her comfortable sofa and wondered about the new client she'd agreed to see the next day. He'd sounded pleasant but clearly troubled. She'd need to gain his trust quickly to give him an idea of what it would be like to work with her, which was sometimes a challenge. She flicked stations on the television and once settled on one, promptly fell asleep until a wet tongue licked her face and she jerked awake. 'Ugh. Get off Buster. You're right it's time for bed.'

Since James had died, she'd found talking out loud to Buster was comforting. Perhaps it made the house feel more alive as she'd suffered from empty nest when Henry and Katy left home. Caroline constantly reminded her she was lucky because Katy and family lived nearby but she wished Henry lived nearer than London.

WEDNESDAY 5TH OCTOBER 2005

The view from her therapy room always gave her great pleasure as she watched the ebb and flow of the seasons. Goldfinches bickered over Niger seeds on feeders in her small front garden and the sun illuminated the flash of gold feathers and gave an autumn polish to the plane trees outside.

Still at the window when Tim loped up the path, she couldn't help a grin. What a quirky guy, she thought. He looks like a university lecturer from the 50's with his floppy grey hair, horn rimmed glasses, corduroy trousers, a long coat, and scarf. His serious face probably belied his age, which she guessed was early sixties. She'd been his supervisor for a while and often wondered what his clients made of him.

She opened the door with a smile, murmured a greeting and indicated he should go into her therapy room. Once he was sitting, she began the session with a question she always asked to establish how he was, and what clients he wanted supervision on.

He screwed his eyes up in thought before he answered. 'I'm fine thanks though work is quite busy.' He paused and added. 'I have been pondering about retirement as I do get tired sometimes.'

'Is that what you'd like to do or is it a break you need?'

He scratched his head. 'I'm not sure, I still feel I have a lot to offer.' He hesitated. 'It could be good although perhaps it is just a break I need. I'll give it some thought.'

Louise nodded and picked up her notepad, 'You say you're busy, so tell me what you would like to talk about today? Is there a client or a particular issue causing you concern or one you would just like to explore?'

He shifted in his seat and slowly unwound his scarf, frowned, placed his fingertips together and sat in thought for a moment before answering. Louise noted these

7

movements and wondered what he was about to bring which had caused anxiety.

When she wrote up her notes afterwards, she wondered why he was having such difficulty with this guy Paul. Yes, he'd been convicted for killing his wife, which might throw some people but Tim had worked in the prison for a while so that shouldn't be a problem. The fact he believed Paul's protestation of innocence and formed a relationship with him, was more worrying. Tim wasn't naïve but this man had somehow managed to manipulate him. Perhaps he really did need a break or retirement.

When Buster leapt up to greet her after the session, she felt pleased he had finally got used to the idea of strangers in the house and stopped barking every time someone knocked on the door. She left the kitchen door open that led into the garden so he could go out while she made a cup of coffee and put an apple and cheese on a plate.

She had several texts. The first from George. *Hi Lou, sorry about the mess, I got called away and didn't have time to clear up properly – see you at the gym tonight? XX.* He always ended with two kisses and she wondered if he did this with everyone.

She quickly replied. *No problem, not as if I was going to use the bathroom! Yes, hopefully will be at the gym, if not too tired that is!* She hesitated with her finger above the X, unsure whether she should add two kisses. Thought for a moment and added XX.

The other message was obviously from her new client; *Just confirming - meeting tonight 5.00.* She never stored names of clients in her contacts list so felt irritated by the assumption he would automatically know who he was. She tapped back *Confirmed - Look forward to meeting you. Louise.*

One client cancelled, so she saw only one person before the new client was due; altogether an easy afternoon. She wondered what he would be like and what issues he might have.

She jumped at the loud, rather imperious, knock on the door. She guessed he was confident and perhaps a little angry, then remembered his appointment was at the suggestion of his office, so possibly an unwilling client.

She glanced in the hall mirror before she opened the door and checked her hair wasn't too much of a mess and the red lipstick she liked to wear was not on her teeth. With her wild auburn hair and a face covered in freckles she'd realised a long while ago she either had to find a way to hide or be defiantly obvious, and she'd chosen the latter. She sighed at the streaks of grey in her hair but at the age of fifty-seven didn't feel ready to colour it.

'Hello. You must be Mr Sewell.' A tall, blond, handsome and blue-eyed man stood in front of her. He wore a smart dark grey suit partially covered by an equally tailored black overcoat. Both looked expensive. Louise gave what she hoped was a welcoming smile and he returned it with an extraordinarily broad one. He stepped through the door and put his hand out. She hesitated before she shook it, and he raised an eyebrow. She guessed he'd noted her hesitation.

His handshake was firm, almost aggressive, but accompanied by an incongruous wide smile. It was mostly men who wanted to shake hands; particularly those whose belief in politeness was a sacred creed. She wondered if people realised how much it gave away about themselves.

His handshake felt like a power handshake and the attached smile indicated he felt in control. As he removed his hand, he wiped his shoes on the mat just inside the door and looked down. She followed his eyes and saw the red stain on her doormat. His demeanour changed and he snorted in disgust.

'Oh no. I'm so sorry, I must have missed one.' Her face grew hot as she explained about the tomatoes. He must think her a bit weird, if not a complete idiot. Not a great way to start a session.

She led him into her therapy room and hoped he hadn't noticed her discomfort. She pointed out the hook on the back of the door for coats. He ignored her and just stood where he was and scanned the room. His gaze hovered over the unlit candle in the fireplace for a moment longer than it had with other things. She wondered if she should explain she only lit it when the weather was grim to make the room feel more welcoming.

She indicated he could sit where he wished and waved her hand between the two armchairs to show him. He looked at them for a moment and threw his coat over the back of the one that faced the window and was nearest the door; her usual seat. She had no right to feel irritated, but she did. She prided herself on giving clients the choice of chair. Yet somehow when he chose that seat, she felt wrong-footed and irrationally it crossed her mind he had done it on purpose.

She sat down opposite him, aware her heart rate had accelerated and her hands felt clammy. He focused his blue eyes on her and smiled again. I'm right, she thought, he's feeling in control and it's made me feel nervous. She decided it was important to clear up the handshake moment.

'I believe you noticed my hesitancy in shaking your hand but in most therapeutic models it is seen as best avoided. It may seem strange but it can interfere with the start of the therapeutic relationship, and sometimes trigger memories of unwanted touch.'

His eyebrows moved again but he said nothing. She picked up the forms she had beside her and cleared her throat.

'Before I hear details of why you've decided to come for counselling, there are just a few admin things I need to do, so if you are happy for me to go ahead, I would like to start with these now.' He gave a slight nod, so she continued. 'Firstly, what do you like to be called? It's Edward, isn't it?

He shook his head and said he preferred to be called Ed which surprised her; she'd not seen him as an Ed.

'Okay Ed. First I need to explain about confidentiality and the few exceptions.' He watched her intently while she spoke and frowned when she got to the part that mentioned the exceptions. She ignored the frown and carried on. She paused for a moment after speaking but he made no response. 'Do you understand?'

He nodded, but she hadn't forgotten the frown. She told him she wrote notes during the first session, whilst collecting basic information. In other sessions she made notes after the session had ended. 'More like an aide memoire.' He still frowned, so she added. 'Of course, you are welcome to see them at any time.'

She also explained about a therapeutic supervisor; it being another therapist with whom client issues could be discussed confidentially.

'Not really confidential, is it, then? he snorted. There was anger in his eyes but he immediately laughed and said, 'I guess nothing ever is, though, is it? You mentioned notes. Where do you keep those then?' He looked round the room to see if there was a possible place for them.

'No, they're not here. I keep them in a locked filing cabinet in my study.' Louise pointed towards the room above using the pen in her hand.

He gave her a look she couldn't interpret. 'If I want to see what you've written about me, I can see them?' She nodded in response then paused for a moment. He added nothing further so she handed him her usual Contract and asked him to sign it.

He studied it in detail but then he had told her he was a lawyer when he made the appointment. She remembered he had virtually demanded he be seen at the end of his working day and when she had explained her latest appointment was at five, he had pressurised her to alter it to a later time. She had remained firm but he hadn't been happy. She thought perhaps he was still irritated, which might explain the slightly hostile undercurrent she felt.

Once he'd perused it, he looked up and said with a sneer, 'I hope your cheap charging rate isn't a reflection of the service I'll get.' Her shoulders tensed. She kept her private rates low as she hated the thought of disqualifying some members of society. Think I'm right he's still irritated by not getting his own way.

He gave a half-smile as he said, 'Only joking, our Senior Partner Michael recommended you, so I guess you must be all right. I'd like to think I'm seeing the best.' She ignored the smile and asked for his full address and doctor's details.

She had begun to wonder why she found him so difficult and then a face popped into her mind of a distant member of her family who looked vaguely similar and had been abusive to her as a child. Probably just a case of transference and I'm reacting to him as if he is that person, she thought. I must keep this in mind when I work with him. She took a deep, silent breath before she continued.

She asked about his present family. He told her he had no living relatives but she noticed a slight hesitation before he had answered.

'Do you have a partner, Ed?'

This time the reply was instant. 'Not at the moment, no but I am starting to see someone and so far, so good.'

As a response Louise smiled and then asked, 'What about past relationships?' No hesitation this time. 'Yes, there was someone but it didn't work out.' He shifted in his chair.

She saw that question had made him uneasy so let it go and went to the next question. 'You might feel this is a bit intrusive but I find if I don't ask, then the information is rarely given.'

Ed stared at her and pulled down the corners of his mouth as if preparing to make an angry retort. She carried on before he had the chance. 'Is there anything you use to help you get through a difficult time? This could be alcohol and/or what some people might call recreational drugs. It could even be chocolate, or sex. The point is we use things sometimes in the belief it will make us feel better and although they might be good in the moment, they rarely help in the long run and can even become a problem in themselves.'

He looked over her shoulder into the distance before he replied. 'Well, I like a glass of wine with my meal and perhaps a whisky or two before but not more than that and I'm not a great fan of chocolate. Sex is quite another matter though; quite another matter!' He gave a smutty laugh and Louise shifted her body. He either had large a sexual appetite or wanted to pretend he did. She had spotted the look in his eye when she had mentioned drugs and suspected that, like many professionals, there was probably the odd snort of coke, if not more.

Next she asked whether he'd had any counselling before. His reaction to such a simple question surprised her. He crossed his arms and stumbled over his reply, which was in the negative. It felt as if he hadn't expected to be asked this and she felt sure, for some obscure reason, he hadn't told the truth. His knee jerked up and down and she was sure he wanted the questions to end.

'I don't have much more to ask you Ed, but the information you are giving me will help me work with you if you decide that is what you want.'

He sighed but nodded his head.

'This question helps me understand how you manage your emotional life. What do you do, if anything, that makes you feel better when you are feeling low? It may possibly relate to the question I asked just now.'

He coughed loudly which she could have sworn hid a choked laugh.

Once he'd recovered, he spoke out clearly and firmly. I listen to music and go to the gym or out running.'

Louise made a note of this but somehow didn't believe it. She was sure he'd said it because he felt it was the answer she wanted. However, she smiled and gave a small nod of her head. 'So, is there anything you find yourself doing that definitely doesn't work? Again, this might relate to the earlier question.'

He grinned and almost flirtatiously, replied. 'Now, you're trying to catch me out. No, if I choose to make myself feel better it always works.' Then teased, 'I mean running; running definitely works.'

Louise was sure that wasn't what he'd meant at all but continued. 'This is the last question. Who would you turn to if you needed support? I know you said you have no family but it might be a friend perhaps.'

The question clearly disturbed him and he was quiet while he searched for an answer. When he gave one it did not surprise her.

'I've never had time to make friends, so there's no-one really. I've always made my own decisions and so I suppose the answer is that it's me. I'm the one that supports me.' There was no laugh and he sank into the chair.

This felt like an honest answer to Louise and she felt sorry for him.

'Thank you. Just one final question though. If you decide to start some sessions with me, what would you like to have happened or changed by the time we finish?'

His forehead puckered but he told her he wanted to change and to learn how to stop losing his temper so quickly or easily.

'I see. I know you said on the phone your company had asked you to come, so I guess this is the reason why?'

'Yep, afraid I was a bit of a naughty boy.' He chuckled to highlight the last two words. 'I completely lost it with another member of staff. Management thought I should do something to get my anger under control.'

He clearly thought women liked this sort of banter but she wasn't fooled by it. It was an odd way to behave but guessed he had never learned how to be around women.

'Ok but what about you? Do you want this or would you just be doing it for your firm?'

'Oh no not just the firm, although that would help but I do want to make some positive changes, particularly if I am to start a new relationship and it might stop my boss getting at me.'

Another of those smiles! He obviously uses his charm to get what he wants and loses it when things don't go his way. I think he won't be the easiest of clients. She returned the smile and with his agreement made some appointments in her diary.

As Louise took him to the door, he shook her hand again. 'Thank you so much, Louise, I feel as if I am in safe hands already. I am so glad the firm recommended you. I can see you will sort me out in no time at all.' He gave her arm a small squeeze as he passed her.

She closed the door after he'd gone and gave a long and deep breath out. The session had unsettled her but when she ran through it in her head, couldn't quite put her finger on what it was. He was arrogant and thought a lot of himself but he was also rather a sad character.

She looked at her watch. She would have to be quick writing up her notes, if she was to get to the gym on time and give Buster a quick walk.

Her son's old bedroom was now her study. It always felt a good place to be as it was the sunniest room in the house and she'd painted the walls a cheerful yellow so it was always bright, even on rainy days. She kept the key to her filing cabinet where she kept her notes, in a pot on her bookcase; it was one James had given her and had an owl on the lid. She'd already prepared a folder for Ed so, as she had made notes during the session, only needed to write a quick resume, file the notes and then lock them away.

While she walked, she remembered a couple of things that bothered her. When she'd asked the question about having had therapy before, Ed denied he'd had any but she'd noticed the crossed arms and guarded look in his eyes. Then there was the question about what made him feel better and his cough and smothered laugh. There would certainly be a lot of things to unravel.

She asked herself the same question she'd put to Tim earlier. What would it be like to be stuck in a lift with him? She stood still, imagined it for a moment and shivered slightly. She would need to talk to Jasper about transference and her abusive Cousin Craig that Ed reminded her of, at her next supervision.

It was just a short walk down into the village to the gym, which was in a rather dilapidated old Victorian building. The spin class was held in a large room on the first floor and she was pleased to find that she could still run up a flight of stairs without being out of breath. Louise waved hello to those she recognised on her way in. George was already there and smiled and mouthed hello as she got onto the bike next to him.

She thought he was quite a handsome man. He had just a few streaks of grey in his otherwise dark hair, and deep brown eyes that twinkled out of his rugged face. She wasn't sure of his exact age but would have placed him as perhaps a bit older than she was. He had wrinkles which deepened into interesting crevasses when he smiled or laughed. He was dressed as usual in a T-shirt that showed off his toned arm muscles, no doubt gleaned through building work and some awful old shorts that had definitely seen better days. Perhaps his building work didn't pay that much.

The music started up at a resounding volume, which prevented any conversation, even if they'd had the breath for it. Her mood rose and by the time they finished she felt exhausted but happy.

'How about something stronger than coffee tonight Lou?'

The thought of a proper drink made her feel less tired. 'Okay, you're on. Where shall we go?'

'The pub just down the road is okay - The Bunch of Grapes, I think it's called.'

In all the time Louise had lived in Weston she'd never been in it and, in her opinion, thought it looked slightly seedy but she didn't want to lose the chance of developing their friendship, so agreed.

He'd told her he'd wait outside the gym and she found him propped against the doorpost in his thick jacket with the collar pulled up. He looked a bit furtive and she felt a flicker of anxiety.

It was a pleasant surprise to find her impression of the pub had been wrong. The furniture was perhaps a bit worn but the walls had been fairly freshly painted and the room had a real fire and some unoccupied comfy chairs beside it.

'Why don't you sit down and I'll get the drinks?'

She returned his smile and walked towards the chairs by the fire. She had almost reached them when he caught up with her to ask what she wanted to drink.

'Cheers'. She clinked her wine glass against his beer mug, took a large swig and licked her lips. 'Mm thanks, that's really good. What did you think of the workout tonight? Was it tougher than usual or have I just had a long and tiring day?'

'I didn't find it too bad, so it's maybe because you're tired but I do think it's getting tougher on the whole though.' His eyes met hers and he grinned. 'Don't know why we haven't done this before.'

He managed to make the statement sound flirty and his smile showed off his beautifully aligned teeth, which made her think of Ed who was also good looking but had more of a cosmetic smile. There was a warmth about George that enveloped her and she no longer felt any anxiety; just protected and safe.

He interrupted her thoughts and asked her to tell him about her day. This was always a difficult one. Her work being confidential she couldn't really say much except, it was not a bad day and she had taken on a new client.

He waited for her to say more but when she didn't, added, 'And?'

'And what?'

'Oh, I don't know it was just the way you said it. I thought you were going to say something more.'

'No, I can't say anything; it's confidential.'

He nodded, 'So, who can you talk to? I'm only a bloke and may be wrong but I think that look you gave meant you'd have loved to have said more.'

She couldn't help thinking how good it was to talk to a perceptive man! 'Clever of you. Yes, you're right, I would have liked to say more but I can't. All I can say is I thought he was arrogant and reminded me of someone I didn't like.'

'Hmm. I can see that might make it hard to work with but tell me something; I was wondering, how do you keep yourself safe? Supposing you have a man or a woman who is a bit of a nutter, what do you do then?'

'I am fairly careful who I take, and if I don't like the sound of someone on the phone then I would think of an excuse and decline to see them.

George frowned. 'Doesn't sound a particularly good system to me'.

Louise felt a need to defend herself. 'I have been doing it for a long time and I've been okay so far.'

He frowned again at her defensive answer, so she quickly said. 'I'm sorry that was a bit sharp. I have a great counselling supervisor I talk to for an hour and a half once a month. I can speak about anyone or any issue I want. I've seen him for a long time and I know he would pick up on a client that might pose a threat. However, I do sometimes see people with severe anger issues and when I know I have a client like that, I let a friend know and we agree that I will text at the end of the session. If she doesn't hear from me then she checks I'm alright or phones the police. Caroline is a very good friend and she lives at the end of the terrace so very close.'

George didn't look impressed by this answer and opened his mouth as if he might add something but instead looked at their empty glasses. 'How about another one before we disappear into the night?'

She shook her head. 'Sorry I'd have loved to but I need to get home to feed a hungry dog. She knew if she had another without anything to eat, she would go off the idea of food and end up staying and that wouldn't be fair on Buster. 'Thanks for the drink but I really must go. It's been a hard day, but I promise it'll be my round first next time.'

'Sure, that's fine. I'll look forward to it. I need to go too but it was good sitting here with you. Let's do it again soon and not necessarily just after a spin class.'

Louise disguised the rush of heat to her face, with a quick retort. 'Well, as you're my builder I hope to see you on

Friday at work on the bathroom.' She laughed and gave him a quick kiss on each cheek. This had now begun to feel more and more like the start of something special.

She walked off towards her home and thought how lucky it was that George had agreed to work on the days that fitted her work hours. He'd agreed Friday, when she had no clients and Monday and Tuesday when she worked at a surgery in Kingswood. He even said he might work some weekends.

THURSDAY 6TH OCTOBER 2005

Weird dreams had disturbed her night, so Louise turned off the alarm as soon as it sounded and went back to sleep. When she eventually woke it was no longer dark and the time was an hour later than she had intended to get up. Buster would just have to make do with a wander round the garden. There'd be no time for breakfast as her first client was due at eight.

The clients she was due to see were ones she knew well so had no need to refer to her notes. One was a woman married to an alcoholic who, to Louise's frustration, hadn't grasped he would soon have drunk all the money she'd recently inherited, and would leave her destitute if she didn't leave him soon.

It was difficult not to yawn as she waited for her first client and wished she'd gone to bed earlier and not spent the first hours of the night thinking about George and the dreams hadn't helped. I'm no better than a teenager really, she thought, as she remembered how the kiss on his cheek last night had affected her. It's crazy I'm not even sure whether I actually want a relationship. She shrugged as if trying to shift the anxiety of the dilemma and made a mental note to fit in some meditation. I just need to take it a day at a time.

In the end she'd coped with her tiredness and her clients hadn't been difficult. Even the woman with the alcoholic husband had at last started to question the wisdom of remaining in a place where she wasn't safe and their money just disappeared down his throat.

She clasped her hands around a hot cup of soup and gazed into the garden where the few remaining flowers threw up the last remnants of colour. She loved to spend her break with a view of her garden but her thoughts soon turned to George. She was so caught up in these that when she glanced up at the clock, she leapt to her feet, 'Only a few minutes to my next client and I need the loo.'

The afternoon proved to be more of a struggle and at one point had pressed her fingernails into her hand to try and prevent being overcome by tiredness. Even the several quick trips into the fresh air between each person didn't make much difference and she dreaded her last session with an exuberant supervisee whose energy always seemed to sap her own.

Amanda strode into the room and threw her thick padded jacket over the arm of her usual chair and unwound the long brightly coloured silk scarf from her neck. 'Oh no, I've managed to unhook one of my ear-rings.' she moaned as she fumbled through the scarf to find it. 'Yes, got it. Sorry, Louise, I shouldn't wear dangly earrings when I am wearing a scarf. I'm always doing this.'

Amanda pulled one of the cushions from behind her and hugged it close. Her blonde hair around her elfin face made her look eighteen, rather than nearer forty.

She worked in an agency dealing with domestic abuse and Louise knew how challenging that could be. It was frustrating and confusing when a client continued to stay with a partner when they were consistently either emotionally or physically abused. Amanda was a good counsellor and they had worked together on some difficult cases but Louise saw today she looked particularly troubled.

Amanda stammered the words out, 'I'm seeing a client similar to Julia.' Louise tried hard not to gasp but Julia was a client of Amanda's that she would never forget.

'Tell me more? What makes you feel there are similarities?'

Amanda took a deep breath. 'Well, like Julia, Melanie has been with her partner for several years. He seemed kind and loving at first but now she realises he has gradually taken away any autonomy she had and his caring is really control. Although it is difficult to understand why she put up with him for so long, there is a pay-off.'

Louise nodded, she understood exactly the type of man Amanda described. 'What is the pay-off? Is it presents, or the kindness that often follows violent or manipulative and controlling behaviour or is it fear of losing status?'

Amanda nodded, 'I actually think the main thing is status. He is extremely wealthy and has a position in the local community and she fears losing what she has, especially as he keeps reinforcing the idea; she is nothing without him and would end up on the streets, homeless and begging, if she ever dared to leave.'

Louise leaned forward towards Amanda and knew she felt fearful of the answer to her next question. 'Why do you feel it's similar to Julia?'

Amanda took a sip of water from the glass on the table beside her. 'It's the whole situation really. What makes it difficult, is she has now missed two sessions without any word from her. If she misses another one, then the organisation will take her off their list and she will have to wait to be seen again and it may not be me she sees.'

Louise knew this was a complex problem when working with an agency where waiting lists were long and appointments hard to get. She asked again why Amanda connected this client to Julia.

'I'm not sure but I have this horrible feeling. When I saw Julia five years ago she had a very similar story and a partner who used coercive control. The only difference being, although she denied physical violence, I suspected this wasn't true as I'd seen some bruises. I'm sure you remember me bringing her to you at that time.'

Louise shivered. How could she forget the many discussions they'd had over what action needed to be taken given the complexity of the situation. They'd made the decision together and with input from the agency Amanda worked for. It haunted her still because she wasn't sure the decision they'd made had been right.

'Yes, of course I remember. Julia stopped attending sessions and several months later was found dead.' Louise remembered she had only been found because the water level in Chew Valley Lake was low due to the drought and a fisherman spotted a large amount of plastic which clearly shouldn't have been there. 'What specifically reminds you of Julia though?'

'I guess it's mainly because their stories seem similar and Melanie has stopped coming. The only difference I can see is Melanie had made no plans to leave.'

Louise gave a small sigh while she thought and then said, 'I sincerely hope it's not the same but that is a big difference. As you know the most dangerous time can be when a person makes plans to leave and you say she did not intend to do that. Did you put the safety measures in place that we devised after Julia was found dead?'

'Yes, I did. I have the number of a friend of Melanie's and she gave me permission to speak to her if I needed to contact her for any reason. I rang the friend yesterday but could only leave a message. So far she hasn't returned my call but may not have listened to her messages. I will ring her again today if I haven't heard anything.'

Louise went through Amanda's last sessions with Melanie in detail and when they had finished thought for a moment before she spoke.

'Julia's murder was horrific but it doesn't mean a similar thing has happened to Melanie. I don't think any further action is needed at the moment but let me know when you hear from her friend. As you know missing appointments is not unusual.'

Once Amanda had gone, Louise let Buster out of the kitchen and returned to her therapy room. The situation with Julia had thrown her off balance at the time and she'd been relieved when the culprit had been caught, charged and imprisoned. She hoped they had made the right decision about Melanie and sat with those thoughts while she idly stroked Buster, who'd nuzzled into her.

She didn't sit long as Buster agitated for a walk. 'Think we'll go a bit further today and go along to Victoria Park,' she muttered once she had him on his lead.

There were always a lot of dog walkers around in the park at night, so she usually felt safe but this time it felt different. The dark trees looked ominous and scary. She knew it was the last session and the reminder of Julia's fate which made her uneasy but turned for home earlier than she'd meant to.Her cheeks stung where the crispy cold wind bit into them and plumes of smoke like breath hung in the air before they disappeared into silky blackness. Other dog walkers passed her and the dogs seemed excited by the cold as they pranced by. 'I'm just being silly' she murmured and thought she'd ring Katy later and cheer herself up.

A good time to ring her daughter was usually after she'd fed herself and Buster. Dave, Katy's husband, often worked late and her two grandchildren were in bed. She often wondered what it would be like to be a detective but wasn't sure she'd enjoy it, although clearly Dave did.

The phone rang for a while before Katy answered and Louise wondered if she should have rung her mobile but thought a mobile was more intrusive than a land line.

'Hello?'

'Oh hi, Mum. Are you OK?'

Louise's face broke into a silent smile. 'Yes, I am fine. I hope this is a good time to call. I haven't spoken to you this week and felt like contact.'

'Bad day?'

Louise smiled again. Katy had always been intuitive to her moods and it made her feel good, just to hear her empathy.

'Yes, not great but I'm all right.   Tell me about the children. What have they been up to?'

'Mmm. Funny you should ask. Max came back today with a story about someone at his school and is clearly troubled by it.'

'Oh dear, what happened?'

'I'm not sure really but it seems one the boys in his class has been bullying others.'

Louise started to speak but Katy quickly jumped in, *'No Max hasn't been bullied but the boy who was wasn't in*

*school today. The bully boards at the school, although I
think his home is local too. I guess they may have sent him
home. Max says he is not particularly friendly with either
of them but whatever happened has definitely upset him. He
doesn't seem keen to talk about it.'*

*'I'm sure he will tell you everything in time; you have a
lovely relationship with him. Just be there for him and he
will tell you when he's ready.'*

'Yes, you're right, he often opens up when I go to into
his room to say good night when he can chat without Milly
being around.'

Katy then turned the conversation towards Louise and
asked her what she had been up to. Louise wondered if she
should tell Katy about George but there really was nothing
to tell at the moment, so decided against saying anything
apart from the fact that work had begun on the bathroom.

*'It must be difficult for you without a bathroom. Do come
to us if it gets you down and of course come for a shower.
Actually, I was going to ring you myself later to ask whether
you wanted to come over for Sunday lunch. It would also be
a good opportunity for you to have a shower.'*

Louise heard the warmth in Katy's voice and gratefully
accepted. Their lives were so busy she wouldn't have
bothered them for a shower but the offer of lunch raised her
spirits. Katy never forgot that she had found Sundays
difficult after James had died and although that was a long
time ago now Louise still sometimes found a Sunday
troublesome. She tried to make it a day to go out for walks
either with a group or with friends and generally keep
herself busy but her favourite was a family day.

*'Good, it's a date then and Max might open up to you
about what happened. I know he hates to worry us.'*

After they'd ended the call, Louise thought about Max
and wondered what this bully could have done that so upset
him. She settled down in front of the television and
watched a recording of a Nordic thriller. Not sure why I
like them so much, she thought, I'd be terrified if what I saw

in them happened to me. Julia popped into her mind and she wound the sofa throw tightly around herself.

FRIDAY 7TH OCTOBER 2005

What on earth's going on? The constant thud on the door eventually seeped into Louise's consciousness. Disorientated and unsure whether she was dreaming, she screwed up her eyes and peered at the clock beside the bed. Hell, it's past seven, the alarm can't have gone off again. She flung the covers back and leapt out of bed. 'I'm coming, hang on,' she shouted and grabbed a dressing gown and ran down the stairs. 'Fine guard dog you are Buster, why aren't you barking your head off?'

She unlocked the door, managed a muttered apology and a rather limp smile. George strode in, his mouth in a wide grin.

'Morning, Lou. Over-slept, did we?' She heard the chortle as he walked into the hall, tools in hand.

She turned her back on him and walked towards the kitchen, hoping he hadn't noticed the flush of her cheeks.

'Coffee or tea George?' she shouted as he was already half up the stairs.

'Tea please, strong as you like with three sugars.'

She raised her eyebrows and made a mental note to buy more sugar when she went out later.

She put the tea down on the bathroom floor and muttered she'd had a late night. 'What I mean is, I couldn't sleep. I had a few things on my mind. I'm usually up by six as Buster is often desperate to go out but for some reason, he didn't wake either.' George smirked at her. He probably did think she'd been out but then it was none of his business was it and with this thought she turned to leave.

As if he'd read her thoughts he answered, 'Not my business, Lou.' and laughed out loud. She loved his big rich laugh and couldn't be cross, even if it was at her expense.

'Hope it's not going to be too noisy for you today. I have to get under the floor and there will be a lot of hammering.'

Pleased at his consideration she said, 'Don't worry, I'm out most of the day. I have to go into Bath for a group supervision meeting at ten. I'll probably shop or meet a friend after, so won't get back until near the end of the day. I wonder if you'd mind letting Buster out when you stop for your lunch?'

'Course, I'm happy to. Glad you'll be out though; thought I might drive you nuts and then you wouldn't come for a drink with me later.'

She thought there was nothing she'd have liked better but before she changed her mind said, 'Sorry I can't; not tonight. Friday is the night I meet a friend who lives at the end of the street; it's a regular commitment. We meet for a G & T and put the world to rights.'

The smile he'd had on his face faded. 'Okay then but what about tomorrow? I'll be here anyway most of the day. I said I could work some weekends. Perhaps we could go for a drink after I've finished work?'

She realised the drink the other night had changed things between them and left them both wanting more. The uncertainty in her head returned but if she didn't give it a go, she would never know and couldn't go on behaving like some lovesick lunatic in her late fifties.

'You're on. A drink would be great. I'll try to remember to set an alarm for the morning, so you don't have to face me before I've had my breakfast and start being nice to the world.'

He gave a large smile. 'Don't worry, I like a lie in too, so won't start until after nine.' He bent to pick up his hammer but turned back. 'Actually, I don't mind seeing you at any time of the day.'

Her face felt hot and was convinced it was bright red too. She hurried off to get dressed and cursed to herself and her body for allowing such a cheesy line to affect her.

In her bedroom she picked up the photo of James on her bedside table. It was taken on their last holiday before they knew what was ahead of them. It was taken by someone sitting at the next table in a small taverna in Greece. James had been fooling around with the camera and she had been doing some pretend poses when someone asked if they wanted one of them both. The result summed up so much of their life together and it had been their first holiday without any children. She had it framed as soon as they had returned home and it now both cheered and upset her. She wiped away a tear, got dressed and headed downstairs to wash.

She shouted up the stairs. 'I'm off now George. Help yourself to tea and coffee; it's on the kitchen unit and chocolate biscuits to keep you going. I've given Buster a quick walk round the block so he should be alright for a while.'

George shouted back 'Don't worry I won't forget to let him out. Have a good day. Oh, and yes, thanks for the biscuits; much appreciated.'

The cold blustery wind meant the walk into Bath might take a bit longer but Louise thought she'd make the meeting on time. It was held in a flat in St James Square which wasn't too far away.

A young girl stood on the corner by the row of shops at the entrance to the square. She held up a *Big Issue* in one hand and in the other, held a few more. Louise saw her fingers were white and her legs were bare under a skimpy skirt, with a thin jumper and a knitted wrap on top. She shivered; the girl wasn't dressed for the cold.

She had always supported *The Big Issue* and tried to have a quick chat with the seller. She hadn't seen this girl before and thought she must be new. She obviously hadn't enough cash to buy many magazines to sell, so Louise hoped the money from her purchase would help her buy more. She didn't have time for a chat but thought she would if she was still there when the meeting ended.

Frances had a flat in the basement of a large Georgian house on the square. The old iron handrail led down steep and treacherous steps and as Louise clasped it she was glad she had put on flat boots with a good sole. How on earth Frances copes in bad weather I can't imagine, she thought as she caught hold of the old-fashioned bell pull and heard it's jangle somewhere inside.

It wasn't Frances whose face appeared as the door opened. 'Hi Louise' smiled Harriet. 'I'm opening the door this morning as Frances is in the kitchen making drinks. Katherine's already here'.

Louise gave her apology for being a bit late as Harriet ushered her in and a voice shouted from the kitchen. 'No, you're not late, come on through. I'm guessing you want your usual strong coffee.'

She walked through to join Frances, taking in yet again the ambiance of Frances' old basement flat which had once been the kitchen area of the big Georgian house above. The one large living room was painted a rich yellow and hung with modern paintings and prints in various sizes. Louise particularly liked a large Bob Dylan print of a rather blousy woman resting on a bed. She hadn't realised he was also an artist until she'd seen this print. There were also some brightly coloured glazed pots and sculptures on shelves she knew Frances had done herself, and the old bread oven housed a vast and eclectic collection of CDs. Each of the chairs and a large comfortable sofa were draped in warm throws with a variety of rainbow coloured cushions placed randomly on them. The whole place reflected Frances's personality and that of her psychologist partner, Sasha.

When they'd had their drinks and been unable to resist the chocolate biscuits on the pine chest in front of them, they began their session.

Louise glanced at her peers. Katherine was older than the rest of them, with a hairstyle that had more than a little in common with the once powerful Margaret Thatcher. She looked tired but it might have something to do with her husband, who was a senior partner in a large law firm in Bath. She'd mentioned on several occasions he could be a difficult man. Louise knew her the least and thought she probably didn't have much in common with her, but respected her work.

Harriet sat next to Katherine and was unusually young for a therapist but competent and insightful. Louise admired her as she couldn't imagine how as a single mother with two small children could also manage a full-time job.

Finally, there was Frances, always a vibrant member of the group, probably in her forties. She was known in the therapy world in Bath for her competent and creative work with children.

Louise loved this supervision group primarily for the work they did with children and with no group supervisor they were able to run it as they wished. They always started with a quick personal check-in, then individual requests were made for space to speak about a client.

Harriet wanted to talk about a boy she saw at the school where she had just started work. She had only been there for a short while and said she'd felt supported and valued by the school.

'For the sake of confidentiality, I'll call the boy Tom. He is ten years old and because of some unacceptable behaviour, the school have referred him to me. I don't know much about him other than he boards at the school. He is a sad boy who I believe has already had a great deal of loss in his life.'

Louise noticed Harriet's voice dropped and she had sighed when she mentioned him being sad.

'Can you tell us why he's sad and what do the school mean by unacceptable behaviour?'

'I understand he's from a one parent family. I think he lost his mother when he was quite small, which probably would account for the sadness but there is something about this boy that doesn't feel right. He's polite but has this large defensive wall around him and I'm not confident I will ever manage to break through it.'

'Why was the school worried?' asked Frances.'

'Oh yes, sorry I didn't answer that. He loses his temper quickly and apparently once tried to throw a chair at a teacher but the incident that alarmed them was when it was discovered he'd hurt another boy. It was very nasty. He'd picked nettles on the edge of the playing field, having protected his own hands with a tissue and then grabbed a boy and lashed the nettles across his legs. When someone came to see what all the fuss was about, the other boy was in a terrible state with large nettle rashes all over his skin. It took ages to calm him down and when they heard how it had happened, Tom was sent to the headmaster. He declared he was sorry, but the Head wasn't convinced, and it was decided to ask for help.'

In a strange way Louise envied Harriet. She loved the challenges working with children brought and the huge emotional reward when she was able to help them. She encouraged Harriet to continue.

'I've only had a couple of sessions with him. Both times I've felt totally inadequate. As I said he's polite but apart from hello at the beginning of the session, he says virtually nothing at all. If I ask him how he is doing or what is happening he just shrugs and says, *"Nothing, I'm fine. There's nothing wrong"* and asks to go. I did let him go early the last session as I felt at a total loss and couldn't think what to do next. I usually find the game Jenga gets boys talking but he just looked scornful and folded his arms when I suggested it.'

Louise knew from her work that this was a common enough scenario and encouraged Harriet to keep trying. She told her of a young client she'd had who said nothing for several sessions before finally trusting her enough to talk and then didn't want to end the sessions when he was better. Frances also gave examples and ideas of how she worked with troubled children.

'I have wondered' continued Harriet, 'If there is some form of abuse as it would explain his behaviour. I noticed a strong negative reaction when I mentioned his father, or stepfather as I think he is. Also of course there is the loss of his mother.'

Louise spoke as soon as Harriet had finished. 'I agree with you. I would also have thought about abuse. It would be helpful to know more about his losses and what happened to his mother.'

Katherine asked Harriet whether she had managed to ask him about the things he had done and whether he showed any remorse for hurting the other child.

'Well, in a way he did. It has been the only thing I have been able to draw him out on. It was such a random thing to do and he said he knew how much it had hurt the other boy. I asked him if anyone had ever hurt him like that but he said not. I'm not sure I believe him. He told me the other boy was a friend and when I suggested what he'd done wasn't something a friend would do he muttered something I had to ask him to repeat. It was, "*You would if he'd let you down.*" I think I also need to look at how he sees friendship and how often he's been let down.'

'He does sound a sad and perhaps frightened boy,' said Louise. 'I'm sure though with your help and understanding he will soon start talking more.'

'I hope you're right. I feel sorry for him but he can make me feel uncomfortable and has a look that scares me. Ridiculous I know. I'll let you know at our next meeting how I get on.'

Apart from some other small issues with clients, no-one else had much to say and after they'd finished and taken their mugs to the kitchen to wash up, it was time to go.

Katherine was the first to leave and hurried off down the road muttering she had to get something from a shop nearby and had organised to meet a friend for lunch.

Harriet followed Louise up the steps. As they reached the top Louise felt a hand touch her on the shoulder. 'Is there any chance you could come and have a coffee with me? There are just a few things I'd like to check out with you. There is this great Italian place at the bottom of the road.'

She sensed Harriet's anxiety and agreed with the proviso they had something to eat, as she was hungry and needed to feel strong enough to face the shops afterwards.

The wind whirled around the square and found its way under Louise's coat. She stopped to fasten it properly and was glad the café was not far away. They were met by the warm nutty smell you only get with freshly ground coffee.

They found their way to one of the few tables at the end of the room by the window. They surveyed the array of delicious salads, quiches, pies and cakes under the glass counter. Louise opted for a goat cheese quiche and salad. Harriet chose the soup of the day; squash and coconut. To her delight it came with hot bread on the side.

Once settled, Harriet looked at Louise. 'I know we shouldn't talk about clients in a public place but there is only one person here and they are sitting at the other end of the room. I do want to say a bit more about the boy I was discussing. I feel completely unnerved about something that happened yesterday when I'd finished work and I would like to run it past you before I mention it to the group.'

Louise was horrified when she saw Harriet's hands shook and wondered what she was going to say.

'I'd seen my last client, collected my bag and bits and pieces and walked to my car parked in the school car park. I opened the door and was about to get in when an arm came from nowhere, lent behind me and slammed the door. I turned around and there was this man. He smiled at me but there was no smile in his eyes. They were cold and dead. I asked him what he thought he was doing. In a menacing way he hissed, "*I'm wondering what exactly you think you're doing?*" I didn't understand what he was talking about but I happened to look away from his face for a moment and caught sight of Tom in the distance looking extremely scared.

Louise frowned, 'That's horrendous and it was definitely his father?'

Harriet gave a brief nod. 'I just stared at him. I didn't know what to say. It was obvious to me who he was and that he knew I was seeing Tom. I guess he'd heard from the Head. He then put his face close to mine, so Tom couldn't hear, and whispered in my ear. *"I hate and loath counsellors. You're just phoney time wasters."* He said he'd been forced to agree Tom could see me, or he would be excluded. Then he pushed closer and his lips touched my ear and he hissed. *"Don't you dare believe any lies and nonsense he might tell you, or it will not go well for you."* Then stood up and backed away, smiling as though we had just had a pleasant conversation. Then said loudly, I guess in case anyone was watching. *"Really lovely to meet you, Ms Jackson, keep up the good work."* He turned and grabbed his son roughly by the hand and walked away. The look Tom gave me was easy to read; he was frightened.'

Harriet took a deep breath and a sip of water and then the waitress turned up with the food. They both muttered thanks and acknowledged it looked really good, but Louise could see Harriet had lost her appetite.

'Oh, Harriet, what a horrible experience. It does sound as if abuse is the most likely explanation for Tom's behaviour.'

'Yes, it was horrible and when I got into the car I was shaking all over and couldn't drive for a while. Then I had to rush to pick up Jem and Toby from nursery. What do you think I should do? I was tempted to go to the police but don't want to make things worse for Tom.'

Louise put out a hand and touched her arm. 'He sounds a right piece of work and he threatened you. It's serious enough to go to the police but you need to speak to the School Safeguarding team and say what happened and they can talk to Social Services.

Harriet nodded. 'The trouble is, to most people he comes across as a charming man, so I'm not sure anyone would believe he threatened me.'

'I don't agree. I think anyone could tell you are not someone who would make up a story. Do you get on with the school head?'

'Yes, I get on fine with Mr Wood, who is a very fair man so I think you're right. I'll get the school involved.'

'That's good but don't stop working with Tom, who is clearly intimidated if not terrorised. He needs you, even though he might not realise it. You might need some extra supervision too. I know I would and of course, you can bring him to our group as well.

'Thanks, Louise, you've been so helpful, and I'll go and see the Mr Wood after the weekend. I don't know why I didn't talk about it today. I suppose I felt intimidated and frightened and perhaps I thought I might be judged but I knew it would feel right to talk to you. I will also speak to my personal supervisor when I see her next week.'

They finished their lunch, paid the bill and went their separate ways. Louise wandered around town and visited various of her favourite shops, including the small fashion shop she'd loved from the moment she'd spotted some crazy patterned shoes in it years before. She'd danced about in front of James and persuaded him to buy them for her. She smiled as she remembered the evening they'd had when she wore them for the first time and how pleasantly it had ended. She tried on several tops and in the end bought a patterned velvet one, in a deep blue colour with swirls of purple, which she thought she might wear when she went out with George tomorrow night.

George greeted her at the door, 'Just finishing, Lou. I've left it a bit tidier than I did before. Thanks for the biscuits. I did manage not to eat all of them! By the way, Buster was a bit difficult to get back into the house, so I let him roam your back garden for a bit. I hope that was all right.'

'Yes, great, thanks. I'm afraid he is sometimes a bit difficult, especially if he hasn't had a proper walk so you did just the right thing. I'll see you tomorrow then, will I?'

'Yeah, that's for sure and I'm looking forward to tomorrow evening already!' He went to go past her, and he pecked her on the cheek. Then smiled and laughed as he ran down the path. Louise couldn't get her breath for a minute and her heart raced. 'Oh Buster, what a clown I am,' she muttered and then laughed as she realised she had enjoyed the light kiss. 'Come on, I'll have a quick cup of coffee and take you for a run before I head over to Caroline's.'

Louise shut her front door and immediately couldn't see much. 'Damn! Bloody light - why do I keep forgetting to get it fixed?' She got out her torch so she could see until she reached where the streetlights lit up the pavement. She only had to walk three houses down the road as Caroline had the fourth house at the end of the terrace. It was slightly larger than hers and benefited from a bigger garden, which Louise always envied.

As soon as Louise had rung the bell, the door was flung open and Caroline thrust a large gin and tonic into her hand.

'My word, Caroline, were you standing there waiting for me? Let me get my coat off, you crazy woman.' She had a quick sip of the gin and gave it back while she removed her thick winter coat.

A real fire burned in the grate and its warm glow lit up the beautiful, Victorian-style, lounge. She had large comfortable armchairs and a sofa Louise just wanted to sink into and never leave. On the polished coffee table in front of the fire there were glass bowls full of nibbles. Louise grabbed a handful of nuts and another sip of gin before she settled herself down on the nearest chair to the fire and started to question Caroline.

'OK, tell me everything and I mean everything.' Caroline didn't reply immediately, so Louise carried on. 'I know you said you'd met someone on a dating site and I'm guessing, by the way you greeted me, you have a lot to say and wanted to do away with social niceties!' Louise couldn't help a chuckle and Caroline grinned in acknowledgement.

'Right, here goes. I've met him once, last weekend in fact. For a start he is absolutely drop dead gorgeous. He's also charming, has lovely manners and makes me feel the most beautiful woman ever.'

'Well, firstly you are a very beautiful woman and secondly, wow is he actually real? I didn't think there were men like that, at least not any on the free market so to speak.' It had always annoyed Louise when Caroline put herself down. She seemed to have no idea how attractive she was and her wretched ex-husband had done nothing to help matters. Her shoulder length blonde hair always shone with a vibrancy that matched her smile and with her blue eyes, which now sparkled with excitement, she looked beautiful. She looks at least twenty years younger than me, rather than the ten she is, thought Louise and urged her to tell her more and where they met.

Caroline's smile stretched as wide as a smile could. 'We met in a bar in town; the one which you didn't like because of the way they'd redecorated. I chose it because I knew the layout of the place, in case I wanted to make a quick getaway! I spotted this attractive man from the doorway and hoped it was him and it was. I walked in and he got up and came straight towards me, saying my name in a sort of questioning way. He led me to his table and asked what I wanted to drink. I can tell you I was so nervous I couldn't think. If you remember, Phil ordered my drinks for me. I wanted to say a double vodka or something as I thought it might steady my nerves but instead asked for a white wine. Of course, he wanted to know what sort and gave me a choice but again I couldn't think, so just said I wasn't fussy. He explained he had come straight from work which was why he was dressed rather formally in a suit.'

Louise smiled. 'Slow down, Caroline! Give me a moment to take it in. However, it all sounds good so far.' Louise thought it typical of Phil that he'd always chosen what Caroline drank.

'I know I'm gabbling, but Louise, I really liked him and never expected my first date on this site would be so good. We talked and talked and what's more he was interested in me and seemed to like me.'

Louise hoped he was a genuine guy and not someone just out to get what he wanted and then leave. 'Tell me what you learned about him? You said he wore a suit, but do you know what he does? Where does he live, was he married, and does he have children? You know what I mean, I'd like to hear his back story.'

Caroline twisted her hands together, 'You sound like my mother used to sound. Don't you think he's genuine? I couldn't bear it if he turned out to be like Phil.'

'No. I am not thinking anything bad but I am keen to know more about him.' Phil had been an ineffectual and weak man who was also mean and controlling. He'd managed to make a young and very beautiful woman feel ugly and worthless and Louise had hated him for it. She was relieved when he'd gone off with someone he worked with, who hadn't yet realised what a sleaze bag he was. However, it had devastated Caroline and so Louise hoped this was the start of something good for her.

'We didn't really talk about his work, he just wanted to know about me and what I did. He told me his wife died and he'd been left with a small child. Louise, believe me, he seems such a kind and lovely man. It's like a breath of fresh air meeting someone like him. We are going to meet again tomorrow evening, so I can tell you more afterwards.'

'I'm glad. You really deserve to meet someone special and I hope this is 'the one' but please don't ask him to your house until you are really sure, will you? By the way, you haven't told me his name.'

'No, I won't ask him here yet. I'm not an idiot, you know!   But, I do feel it could be good. His name is John. Now tell me about you and this George fellow, how's it going?'

Now Louise felt awkward.   'Funnily enough, we're having a proper first date tomorrow, so I'll let you know more when I next see you but I think it's going well. He's very much my sort of guy and it would be lovely to have a partner who could renovate my house!' A laugh burst out of Louise and they both giggled. 'Let's have another drink while we delve deeper.'

When she came back with the drinks, she nodded at Louise and urged her to go on.

'It's a bit similar to you. I really like him. He's not exactly handsome but has rugged good looks. He has an amazing smile and kind face. He's a similar age to me I think. I'd guess mid to late fifties. He seems caring and is fun and although he is very different to James, I feel comfortable in his presence.'

'There is a but though isn't there?'

'You're right in a way. It isn't a big one. I'm just not sure whether I do want a relationship. I have a busy life and I have got used to being on my own. I've got Buster for company and he's good for cuddles.' She hesitates. 'Perhaps, if I am being honest, I am a bit worried about having sex with someone else. I haven't had a relationship with anyone since James died. It was a good and fulfilling marriage and I can't help feeling I'd be betraying him. We talked about it my having another relationship when he was ill, but once he'd died it felt different.'

'I can understand how you feel. I always felt jealous of your marriage and relationship. You seemed to be so in tune, and I know his death devastated you, but it has been a long time now and you do deserve happiness. I know it's hard being on your own. It is even for me, who lived with an abominable man. I think we both should just give it a go, don't you?'

Louise grinned and then, because she felt they had talked enough about men, changed the subject. 'Tell me what good films I've missed or what I should be watching and also the latest music which has probably passed me by. You are so clever at finding things I enjoy and so in tune with all the latest trends in music. I can never remember the names of any of the songs nor the artists. Just an old fogey me!'

They chatted for the rest of the evening until Louise looked at her watch and realised it was late and Buster would need to go out.

She gave Caroline a big hug and said, 'Let's get in touch after we've both had our evenings out so we can compare notes.'

Caroline nodded, 'Yes, let's and we'll have loads to share next Friday.'

Louise thought about their very different situations as she walked home. As far as she knew, Caroline had never experienced what it was like to be really loved by a man. She knew she had and would never want anything less. This made a new relationship seem even more risky.

SATURDAY 8TH OCTOBER 2005

Louise heard the key in the lock. 'My goodness, George, did you oversleep? I've already had breakfast and been out for a walk.' She had a grin on her face when he appeared in the kitchen doorway and was pleased to see that, for once, he was the one who had gone a bit red in the face.

'Sorry I'm late Lou. I was deliberating over something and I do hope it will be all right with you. Anyway, the upshot is I've booked a restaurant for us this evening.' There was a short pause while he took a breath. 'I know I only said a drink but it seemed such a good opportunity for us to get to know each other better over a meal.' He searched her face. 'What do you think, have I done the wrong thing or is that something you would be happy with? It would give us a chance to get to know each other more.'

George hopped from foot to foot like a lovesick schoolboy but Louise stifled a laugh. 'I'd love that, it's a great idea. It's quite a while since I've been asked out for a meal.' Then added, 'As long as it isn't somewhere too smart as I wouldn't have the wardrobe for it!'

His face spread into a large grin, 'Fantastic! That's really great. I didn't know whether you'd agree, after all it's a step further than a drink after work. It isn't anywhere you would have to dress up for; just a small bistro in Bath. I did a job for them once and always liked the look of it and thought we could try it out.'

'Sounds perfect. Now do you want a tea with a revolting amount of sugar before you start and I get started on some gardening?'

She had a long and productive day there and hoped the satisfying sounds of hammering in her house meant it was the same for George. She was glad that Mr Braithwaite was a bit deaf though or he might have complained but the students were unlikely to care what noise she made. She was lucky to have good neighbours.

As soon as she came in from the garden she heard George on the stairs and called out. 'You leaving already? I was going to have a cuppa and perhaps even a chocolate biscuit.'

'If you think I can be bought with a chocolate biscuit you've misjudged me Lou.' He gave her a wink. 'No, I'm joking but I need to have a shower and change as I'm taking out some posh bird tonight! Pick you up at seven.' He shouted as he left the house.

What have I got myself into and do I want it? The warm glow she'd felt when he teased her answered her question. She ignored the tickle of anxiety.

She needed time to decide what to wear and to get ready, so Buster only got a short walk that evening. Her bed disappeared under numerous outfits, including the top she'd bought yesterday, before she decided on something.

The bistro had a glorious garlicy smell she always associated with France. Louise liked it immediately and felt the evening was off to a good start. It had a counter at one end and tables set close together in the rest of the small room. When full would probably only seat twenty or so people. There was a single candle and a small glass bottle filled with a few real flowers on each table. The green shabby paint and yellow aged French posters on the wall made it feel cosy and intimate. She loved the mellow sound of the woman's voice on the CD that played quietly in the background and thought it was Madeline Peyroux. The ambiance was perfect and anticipated a wonderful evening.

George looked completely different. He'd tidied his unruly hair and his stylish blue jeans, shirt and thin woollen jumper made him look a bit French as well. He didn't look the same man who she'd known only in his work outfit or in those terrible shorts and track suit. He really is quite good looking, Louise mused as he saw her to her seat and helped her off with her coat. She swallowed and took a deep breath. Her reaction surprised her, as it was unusual for her to feel uncertain, but this George seemed quite different than the builder one.

He glanced at the menu he'd picked up and looked up at Louise. 'You look fantastic Lou, thanks for coming out. I wasn't sure if you would'.

Her grin must have reassured him as she replied. 'It wasn't really a difficult decision to make, I'm always up for a meal out.' The waiter arrived at that point with the wine and she was able to hide the discomfort she'd felt at her slightly flirtatious answer. She ordered a pasta dish which sounded interesting and George chose a steak, which she'd imagined he might choose.

Once they started to eat Louise asked him to tell her more about himself. 'I really don't know much about you, other than what we've talked about at the gym. Have you always been a builder and how did you get into it? I know you are well known around the village and you have clearly built up a good reputation.'

He laughed. 'Is this the inquisition then? Am I worthy of taking you out?' He quickly added, 'Don't worry, I'm not serious. Actually, it was my dad who was the builder and I worked as his mate and learned the trade from him. It wasn't what I really wanted to do though and I joined the army. I did quite well and on the whole, enjoyed it. Then I got injured in a rather nasty accident whilst on a training exercise. It was something that should never have happened and I was invalided out shortly after. I think I probably had PTSD, but anyway it put an end to what was a rather unhappy marriage, followed by a nasty divorce. I was in a very bad place for a while and didn't want to do anything or see anyone.'

Louise guessed by the speed with which he had covered his life, he wasn't used to talking about it and found it difficult. She leant across, lightly touched his upper arm and encouraged him to continue.

'I have two sons, that sadly I have lost touch with. I don't think I was a particularly good father and they supported their mother, quite rightly I think, as I was being a bit of a bastard.'

Louise found it hard to believe he could have been as bad as he said but realised he wanted to be honest and had done it so she would go into whatever happens next with her eyes open. 'It sounds as though you've had a rough time of it. PTSD is not something to pass off lightly. Did anyone help you with that?' Louise wondered if she'd pushed the questioning too far but he carried on.

'Yes, they did eventually. I couldn't go on like I was and my money was running out, so I started doing odd jobs for people locally and it sort of grew and in the end, found I was doing people's extensions and much bigger building projects. I discovered I enjoyed it and it was good to get back to some physical work. I think it helped me mentally as well. Then one day I was chatting to a bloke I was doing some work for and found myself telling him about what happened. He said he had been in a nightmare car crash and had seen a doctor who put him in touch with a counsellor. He said it helped enormously and encouraged me to get in touch with my GP, which I did and was referred to a fantastic guy who I saw for a while.'

'Lucky you don't belong to my practice or you'd have been referred to me and then we wouldn't be sitting here together.' They laughed and the atmosphere lightened.

'I think that's why I am interested in what you do, Lou. I had never really thought about counsellors or therapists before but after seeing one, I realised how valuable it was and just what an amazing job it is. I am sure it must be hard but I guess also very rewarding.'

This is a new experience, talking to someone who actually gets what I do, she thought and then said,. 'Yes, it is all of those things. I love it and always wanted to do it but it wasn't until James died, I sort of felt free to go off and do something that was for no-one else other than me, although it might sound strange given the nature of the job!'

'I think I do understand. How long have you been on your own?'

'About ten years but because James was ill for two years before he died, it somehow feels longer.

I've been working as a professional therapist for eight years. I threw myself into my training immediately after his death and devoted nearly all my spare time to my work; learning new methods and training.' She swallowed and tried not to remember how hard it had been. 'Guess you might think I am a sorry sort of person without a life.' George started to open his mouth. 'But I've never seen it that way,' Louise said quickly. 'Being on my own has given me a lot of freedom.'

'Yes, I found that too but on the other hand, I have missed doing things like this.' He put his hand out and played with the edges of her fingers lying on the table. His touch burned her fingers and the shock of it raced through her body. So, this is what going weak at the knees means, she thought. Thank goodness they are under the table or he might spot the wobble and gave a small cough to hide the giggle that threatened to emerge.

He pulled his arm back and they continued with the meal as if nothing had happened. It took a while before her heart steadied or she could control her thoughts. These feelings were more like ones she had felt when she was twenty-six, not fifty-seven and the effect of that touch was like nothing she'd felt in years. All she knew was she wanted more, a lot more and this thought surprised her. For the first time in many years she felt her sexuality.

The waiter cleared the plates but she was so wrapped up in her thoughts, she jumped when George asked whether she'd like a dessert or more to drink or go somewhere else to drink. Louise looked at the empty wine bottle on the table before she replied.

'No, don't think I want a dessert but you have one if you want. I think I've probably had enough to drink, so no, I don't think I want to go anywhere else but why don't you come back to me and have a coffee or something stronger?'

He gave her a deep look and Louise wondered if he had read her mind. She'd not felt like this in years and perhaps it was too soon to ask him back. That seemed a ridiculous thought though as he already knew the house like the back of his hand.

He made no indication he had read her mind. 'Yeah, why don't we do that, I guess Buster doesn't like being left on his own too much anyway.'

Buster careered down the hall as soon as Louise opened the door and leapt at her. Unable to help herself she stumbled back into George. 'Get back in your basket.' she shouted as she tried to disentangle herself, but George tightened his grip on her waist. His hands moved to her shoulders and he turned her gently round and pushed the door closed behind him. He leant forward and kissed her softly on the lips. It was a sweet and loving kiss and she couldn't remember when she'd felt such tenderness. He pulled away and searched her face. 'You're gorgeous, Louise. I've wanted to do this ever since I saw you at the gym, almost a year ago.' He pulled her towards him and this time their kisses were harder and more frantic. Louise no longer cared where this might lead and any fears she'd had floated away.

It had all happened so fast and Louise knew that if she hadn't had all that wine, she would have at least made an effort to resist but she didn't want to. She pulled her hand free, put it around his shoulders onto the back of his neck and kissed him again. His hands roamed her body and she felt the moan as it escaped from her lips. He scooped her into his arms and carried her up the stairs to her bedroom and placed her gently on the bed. He crawled up beside her, undid the buttons on the front of her top and used his lips to touch every spot he uncovered. As his hands moved down her body, she caught hold of his wrists.

'Stop, George please. I don't think I can do this.'

He stopped immediately and helped her sit up. 'Sorry Lou, it seemed so right and so good but maybe it was too fast.'

She felt guilty when she saw the look of concern on his face. What had stopped her, she was enjoying it wasn't she?

The voice of a client who had told her about a relationship she'd started in her early sixties came into her head. She hadn't hesitated, she'd told her; just felt lucky that her body still responded as it should and had gone for it.

Louise felt the giggle start in her tummy. It was so ridiculous. She was lying beside a gorgeous man and now she dithered. How many times had she encouraged clients to go for it in a similar situation? What on earth was the matter with her? The giggle escaped and once she'd started, she couldn't stop. George looked surprised for a moment and then started to laugh as well.

The laughter gave the space needed. Louise pulled him towards her, gave him a wide smile and unbuttoned his shirt. 'Ok, let's go for it then' and gave another giggle.

Each article of clothing was removed and thrown far into the room with a flourish, as if it was a javelin contest. Gone was the slow seductive route George had followed and instead there was laughter and abandonment.

Finally, they lay naked and for a moment Louise felt the awkwardness of this new situation she'd found herself in. George seemed to read her mind; pulled her to him and held her tight with one arm while the other explored the shapes and curves of her body. She'd almost forgotten the joy of sex and like her client was relieved her body remembered and responded.

They woke several hours later, slipped under the duvet to get warm and dealt with the cold in a passionate and enjoyable way.

SUNDAY 9TH OCTOBER 2005

She woke just as the door opened. Heat rose to her face and she pulled the sheet up around her. This is such a cliché, she thought, the morning after the night before. She wondered how they would manage what had the potential to be, an embarrassing moment. However, in the end humour again sorted it for her as George minced into the room with coffee in his hand and she laughed at the sight of him.

'Ooh, how lovely. Don't know when I last had a seasoned drag artist bring me an early morning cuppa!'

George responded with a twirl and a laugh as the silk of her dressing gown floated around him. 'I couldn't find anything to cover myself up with and didn't want to frighten Buster! Anyway, I rather think this silk dressing gown suits me.'

'Well, what do you think in the cold light of day and more sober?' she said with just a glimmer of a smile. She realised the embarrassment she had felt was not one sided, so put down her coffee and pulled him towards her.

Louise stirred first. 'Oh, my goodness - the time! I really think perhaps we had better get up and go and do something, I don't think I've stayed in bed until after midday on Sunday for about a hundred years!'

'OK, let's go for a walk,' said George. 'We still have a few hours of daylight left, so perhaps we could walk round the park and then why don't you come back to mine for tea and perhaps a shower, since you can't have one here.' Louise accepted the invitation but while they dressed the phone rang,

'Where are you, Mum? Are you Okay? You usually come up late morning when you're coming to lunch.' There was a pause and Louise's heart quickened. *'You haven't*

forgotten, have you? Only I wanted you to talk to Max and I know you wanted to use the shower too.'

Louise glanced at her watch and thought quickly. *'Sorry love, I got caught up in something.'* George smirked at her from across the bedroom. *'Is it too late to come now, I could get there in half an hour.'*

'No that's fine, I was just worried about you. I thought perhaps you'd tripped over your lazy builder's tools! See you soon. Bye.'

Louise turned to George. 'I am so sorry. I can't believe I forgot.' Then smiled as of course she knew why everything had left her mind. 'I said I'd have lunch with my daughter and family. I must go as she will have cooked for me and we had agreed I would talk to my grandson, who is having a bit of difficulty at school.'

George pulled the sort of face which was supposed to look as if everything was all right but left Louise in no doubt he was fed up. 'No, of course you must go. I am desperately disappointed but really I do understand.' He added with a grin, 'and I do realise you might want to get away from your lazy builder!'

Hands on her hip, she said, 'You weren't meant to hear that and anyway I only told her you'd left the room in a mess that first day.'

He laughed. 'That's fine, you go off and get your lunch and you can come to me another time.' He caught hold of her and gave her an enormous hug and a long kiss. Her face relaxed into a smile.

'That was mean, you are just trying to make me stay and perhaps prove you're not a lazy lover! Tell you what though, I'll ring when I get home and you could come over for the evening and stay the night and be ready at your place of work in the morning!'

On the way to her daughter's, Louise reflected on the speed the relationship had developed. She wondered if she'd been reckless. More than reckless, but it felt good and she smiled to herself. *I never asked him about other relationships, it's difficult to believe there have been none* since his marriage broke up and she felt again a touch of anxiety.

It was lovely to see her family and Katy had cooked lasagne, one of her favourite dishes and the children's too, judging by the scraped plates. Katy suggested she and Max take Buster out for a walk while Milly stayed and helped her wash up. Max readily agreed as he would have loved a dog of his own. 'That's great, Granny, I have a ball I found the other day we can take for him.'

'That's not fair, Granny I want to go too.' Milly caught hold of Louise's hand and pulled her along. Katy gave her a look and Milly stamped her foot, 'But why can't I? I want to. I like throwing things for Buster too.'

Louise picked her up and gave her a cuddle. 'I love you, Milly, and it will be your turn next. Sometimes it is lovely to see each one of you on your own and then I can give you all my attention, but today it is Max's turn and it is your job to stay and help your mum.' Milly gave a big pout and flounced off.

'Don't worry, she'll be fine.' Katy reassured her. 'I'll do something special with her while you are out.'

Katy's house was not far from the canal towpath, so they walked along it for a while until they reached a footpath which led across fields, where there was plenty of space for Buster to run and chase the ball. Max was a good thrower and she judged Buster's panting and tongue that dripped in saliva meant he had got tired and Louise suspected Max had too.

'It's getting late, Max, so I think we should head back now.' Max nodded as he threw the ball once more.

Once they were on the towpath, she had a chance to talk. 'I've been wondering how school's going. Mum told me there was some sort of trouble the other day.'

Max kept his eyes on his shoes as he scuffed along the gravel on the path. Before he spoke, he took a quick glance at her, 'Yes. There's this boy and he's not nice'.

'What do you mean, not nice? Is he mean? Does he bully you?'

Max continued to look down so Louise put her arm around him and pulled him close.

'Not me but he is a bully and he did something horrible the other day and then was found out and got into a lot of trouble. He deserved to get told off but not...' His voice tailed away.

'Not what, Max? What were you going to say, did something else happen?'

Again, there was a long silence. Louise heard a gulp and saw what an effort it was for him not to cry. She spotted a log on the edge of the towpath. 'Come on, let's sit on this for a while,' and waited until he had sat beside her and become calmer before she said anything else.

'I think you were going to say something more but I wonder if the memory is so horrible it's difficult to talk about. Perhaps you've been trying to forget what happened but the more you try to forget, the more you think about it. A bit like pink elephants.'

Max looked up. 'Pink elephants, Granny, what do you mean?'

'Well if I asked you not to think about pink elephants, even if your life depended on it, you would find it impossible because the minute I say the words, that is what your mind conjures up. So perhaps if something horrible happened and you are trying not to think about it, then it becomes almost impossible not to.'

Max put his head on one side. 'Yes, I think you are right, Granny; it is just like pink elephants.'

She gave him a squeeze, 'So when a memory is really horrible sometimes it helps just to tell it to someone else and then it often stops being so horrible.'

He swallowed and nodded. 'It wasn't because Ben got told off, that wasn't it. It was when his father came to collect him. I wasn't supposed to be where I was. I was there because I was getting late for the next lesson.' He swallowed again and tears had formed in his eyes so she gave him another squeeze by way of encouragement. He sniffed before he went on, 'I took a short cut through the

Orchard playground, which is really out of bounds during lesson times. The car park is just beside it so I saw, I saw Ben's father and what he did.'

'Go on, Max, what did you see him do?'

Max hesitated and gulped. 'He, he, he caught hold of him and slapped him so hard he nearly fell over and then he shook him and all the time he was shouting at him. I couldn't hear all of it but it was something about drawing attention to himself.' Max finally allowed the tears to fall and he clung to Louise and sobbed. 'It was so horrible; I can't stop thinking about it and about Ben and what it must have been like. I think he was hurt because he was shouting and crying and it doesn't matter how bad he had been, no-one ought to be hit like that.'

Louise pulled out a tissue, handed it to him and waited while he wiped his eyes and his nose. 'What happened next?'

Max gave another gulp and continued. 'He pushed him into the car, slammed the door and drove off.'

'You said his name was Ben, didn't you?'

'Yes, why?'

'Just wanted to make sure I remembered it right, in case you get any more problems. Now I think we'd better get going, Max, or your mum and dad will wonder where we are and the light is beginning to fade. But I am so glad you managed to tell me what was worrying you and I hope it will make you feel better.'

The story she'd just heard sounded familiar and she wondered if there was any connection to the child Harriet was working with called Tom. Harriet hadn't given the name of the school she worked in and her client wasn't actually called Tom, so it could possibly be the boy Max had talked about.

As they walked she wondered how she could put something he might not want to hear. 'Max, this story you've told me is the sort of thing adults do need to know about, so they can decide what needs to be done. I think, I am going to have to tell your parents what you've told me.

You are right, it was a very horrible thing you saw, whatever the boy had done and no father, has a right to behave that way.'

Max nodded, murmured, 'Fine' and ran off to where Buster sat patiently, picked up his lead and walked towards their home as if the matter was now over and done with. Louise smiled and knew she needn't have worried.

When they got back Max rushed off to play and Louise took the opportunity to explain to Katy and Dave what Max had said and why he'd been so sad recently. They were both shocked. Dave thought he should deal with it officially but Louise suggested they first tell the Head Teacher so he could inform the appropriate authorities.

On the journey back she thought about that poor child living with an abusive father. She yawned and realised how tired she felt and decided she would ring George to suggest they don't meet up again today. She'd been so caught up in the excitement of it all but it had been a bit of whirlwind and she could do with getting her breath back.

MONDAY 10TH OCTOBER 2005

It had been a long and tiring day in Bristol. Several clients hadn't shown up and unusually, possibly because of her long waiting list, this had irritated her but it was equally possible she was just not in the right space to work.

Louise put the key in the lock and waited for the usual greeting from Buster but the house was silent and felt strangely empty. Puzzled, she walked into the kitchen and saw the table had been laid for a meal and there was a small vase of purple Michaelmas Daisy heads in the middle, which she recognised were from her garden. She smiled and walked upstairs, wondering where they both could be. She looked into her bedroom and the spare one opposite and then made her way to the bathroom. George was not there. She saw he'd made a great deal of progress and the new shower cabinet was now in place. She walked back into her bedroom and changed out of her work clothes. She had just pulled on some comfortable trousers when she heard the door go.

'Sorry Lou,' shouted George from the hall, 'I thought we'd make it back before you, there were a few things I needed and I could see Buster also wanted a walk.'

'It's fine. I'm just changing, be down in a minute.'

Before she made it out of the room, hands encircled her waist and George pulled her towards him and kissed her gently on the neck. 'No, I'm not letting you go down yet.' He pulled her onto the bed and there followed a glorious repeat of Saturday night.

George was first to move. 'Take your time, Lou, have a bit of rest. I'll bring you a cuppa, while I cook some food for us.'

'You never stop surprising me. I think you are far too good to be true. Surely you must have some deep dark secrets that you might feel fearful I'll discover?' This was a joke but she still hadn't dared ask him about other relationships. How could a man this good not have a string of attachments hidden away? He'd made no secret about the ex-wife and his two boys but that was a considerably long time ago. There must have been other women surely. Never mind I'm sure he'll tell me at some point. She thought that he might be thinking the same about her but in fact, although she'd been out on some rather hilarious dates, there never had been another proper relationship since James. He made no reply to her comments and had left the room before she could tell him she wasn't in need of a rest but wanted to make a couple of phone calls.'

Katy's land line rang a few times before she answered. *'Hello. Oh, hello Mum. You Okay?'*

'Yes, I'm fine, just got back from the surgery but I was thinking about Max and wondered how he was after yesterday?'

'Of course, yes. I was going to ring you later, to thank you for your help. We saw the Head this morning and he said to leave it with him and he would keep an eye on Max. We will tell Max what we've done later, when Dave gets back from work. Actually, he seemed to be a lot happier last night after speaking to you. I asked him about Ben and he feels he might try to be more friendly towards him.'

Louise wasn't sure she liked the idea of him becoming friendly with a child who had such a violent father but said, *'Well done to Max then. I am sure someone being friendly is just what this boy needs. Katy, I won't chat now as I have just got back from work.'*

She looked at her watch; Caroline would be home now and she probably had just enough time to ring her as well and hear how her date went.

Caroline picked the phone up straight away. *'Hi it's Louise. I was just wondering how Saturday night went and whether you found John as lovely as you thought?'*

There was a slight pause and Caroline gave a long sigh. *'It was fabulous, much better than I could have imagined and what's more, he has suggested we go away together this weekend, so I'm sorry but won't be able to do our gin Friday this week. I'll ring you after the weekend and then we can meet again next week.'*

Louise was pleased to hear she had enjoyed her second date but the idea of her friend going away for a weekend after only a couple of dates worried her. Caroline's history with men left her a bit vulnerable but decided not to spoil the moment.

'I'm so pleased, I really am and I'll look forward to hearing all about it. Where is he taking you, I hope it is somewhere nice?'

Louise could almost hear the purr in Caroline's voice. *'Cornwall. He says he knows a good place and is going to book it.'* There was a silence and Louise thought Caroline probably already imagined herself there with the new love of her life. She then asked how things were with George.

'Yes good. Very good.' She wondered if Caroline could sense the smile on her face.

There was a slight gasp at the end of the phone, *'You didn't, did you?'*

Louise chuckled, *'Actually we did, and I must say, I need never have worried. I think this relationship could turn into something special.'*

Caroline let out a long sigh, *'Oh I do hope so, that's wonderful. After all the people you've helped and the rough times you've had, you so deserve to have some happiness for a change.'*

'I have to go now as I am having a meal cooked for me, which is another thing I can't quite believe, but then I haven't tried it yet! I'll look forward to catching up next week.'

The meal was delicious and so was the wine they drank with it. Afterwards they took the remains of the bottle and settled down together on the large comfortable sofa.

Louise told George about Max's schoolfriend and explained that's why she'd phoned Katy earlier as she wanted to hear what had happened.

George was still for a minute. 'That sounds awful and must have been tough for Max. No wonder he was upset. I guess the school will deal with it now and I think you said Dave is in the police, so he would know if anything further needs to be done.'

'You're right it has already been dealt with and yes Dave is in the police but I think even he was uncertain as it was his child involved.

Thanks for listening though. I'm not used to having someone to mull things over with and it feels really good, so thank you.' George gave her a tight squeeze in response.

She had to leave early on Tuesday morning and left George to walk Buster, which was an added bonus as she usually had to fit it in before going to the surgery. She reflected on how well he had got on with the bathroom and how lovely it would be when done. I shall miss him today though, she thought.

WEDNESDAY 12TH OCTOBER 2005

Work was nearly over for the day and Louise thought it had gone reasonably well. All the clients had turned up and she'd managed to keep her mind totally on the job. She just had one more left to see and wondered whether he might be the one exception, as Ed hadn't seemed particularly keen in his first session.

Her thoughts were interrupted by a loud knock at the door. Ed had a large smile when he stepped through the door but it didn't quite reach his eyes. She returned the smile and led him through the hall into her therapy room. When she'd opened the door she was sure she'd caught sight of a face full of anger which had changed to a smile immediately he saw her. She supposed she could have imagined it but it made her wonder what the session would be like.

'Make yourself comfortable, Ed. As I said before, there is a hook on the back of the door if you want to hang your coat up.' He eased himself out of his heavy winter overcoat but once again ignored what she'd just said and flung it over the back of the chair. Obviously not a man open to suggestions.

'I'm glad you've decided to continue and I wonder how you've been since our last session? As it was an assessment, I spent a lot of the session asking you questions. Today I will take a step back, in order to hear more of what has brought you here. Before we start though, is there anything that came to your mind over the week or anything you need to say about your last session?' He smiled but didn't look at her.

'No, no questions but I may have misled you. I think I was nervous because when I said I'd had a partner previously and it didn't work out it was only partly true.'

Louise doubted he had been nervous but was interested to hear what he meant.

'In fact, when I said partner, I meant my wife. It's true that it didn't work out and we separated but she became ill and then died unexpectedly.'

'I am sorry Ed. I'm guessing that was reason you only told me a half truth. It must be hard to talk about, but this is what these sessions are for. You said it was unexpected but also she was ill. I assume that was why she died.'

He looked away before he replied and she thought perhaps the emotion had got to him. 'Yes, it was. It was a very rapid form of cancer and quite horrible so I don't want to talk about it.' He pursed his lips and Louise knew he'd said as much as he was going to but then he added. 'The other thing I should have said was, I was left with her child. He was only six when it happened. I got a nanny to help with his care, as that side of things are not really my scene.'

'Thanks for telling me. I'm sure it was hard to do but good that I know. I think we'll need to return to it at some point but I'll leave it for now as you'd rather not talk about it at the moment.

Last week you said you had come because of anger issues. Tell me what anger issues mean to you and give me some examples of times you've been angry.'

'There is not a lot to tell, but I don't suffer fools lightly.' Louise noticed he clenched his hands and thought, I bet you don't.

She paused then said. 'I wonder then if there is a particular fool you're thinking of?'

He continued to clench and unclench his fingers. 'There's this idiot at work. He's a complete and utter thicko and he really shouldn't be doing the job he does. He's very disrespectful to people in general but I think in particular to me, which he ought not to be, given my position.'

Louise let the judgmental word go but noted his air of superiority and asked him to clarify what he meant by his position. In response one hand formed a fist with knuckles stretched and white but he said nothing.

'Perhaps it would help if I heard about the incident that got you sent here to me.'

His eyes strayed to the corner of the room and he crossed his legs and shifted around in his chair before he replied. 'Oh, all right, I'll tell you, but it's ridiculous really. This idiot; this tosser, is one of the paralegals and he was assigned to help me. I asked him to fetch some files. He turned up at my desk and in an incredibly sloppy way, threw them down in a heap. This was irritating enough but they were not the files I had asked for. The whole thing was maddening so I lost it and shouted at him. It was probably a bit over the top but he is such an idiot and a wimp. On top of that, he rushed off and told our senior partner.'

Louise listened and imagined this was not the first time he had done this; it would be unusual to send someone for counselling on a first offence but thanked him for telling her. 'Now, if you can, tell me what you felt before you shouted?'

'What do you mean? I just lost it. Stupid man just stood there gaping at me; I wanted to punch him but I didn't. I just shouted and that's not a crime, everyone gets angry now and again.

'Yes, they do, but there's a very big difference between anger and rage. Anger is not necessarily a bad emotion as it can be a shifter and a mover. A lot of injustices in this life are put right by people who have utilised their anger and put it to good use. Rage though, is an entirely different thing.'

Ed now sat like an enigmatic statue and Louise found it difficult to read what was going on. 'I think we probably need to work in two ways; first to help you manage your feelings in a way which would be more socially acceptable and second to find out what lies beneath your angry outbursts.'

Louise noticed a shift in his eyes. They appeared to have become an icy blue and reminded her of the shielded eyes of a snake.

His response too was as sharp as a snake bite. 'I think Louise, I just need you to concentrate on helping me with my anger and we can leave the other stuff. I'm not really interested in the how and why, I just want to get done here as quickly as possible.' He gave her a defiant stare but she suspected he then saw this was not the reply she wanted. He added, 'Or let's just keep the why stuff for another time.'

She had found this session more challenging than she would have expected which might explain why she chose to let this remark go and just said, 'OK, we'll just deal with the anger for now and I will give you some tools to help.'

'Great thanks, that would be really helpful.' Louise realised he'd slipped his cloak of charm on again.

She talked him through a simple way of looking at anger, using a traffic light approach to manage it. 'Green is when you feel fine. Then if something happens which irritates, you might slip into the orange. It is very important to be aware of this change. Within the orange emotional space there is a possibility of dealing with the irritation/anger in a controlled and manageable way. But if you allow yourself to get into the red stage or the rage, it can be too late to take the necessary avoidance action or be able to contemplate the consequences of an action taken while in this position.'

He was clearly intelligent but she was not sure he had emotional intelligence. It was hard to get him to understand this system or see that there is a progression through stages from irritation to anger.

'Sorry, Louise, I don't really get what you're saying. I'm fine, when you might say I'm in the green. Then if someone does something stupid, I get angry and in your words go into the red. It's as simple as that. There's no progression at all, it is just like a switch and then I react. You know, the old red mist just comes down.' He ended with a grin and added, 'Anyway it's not my fault some people are complete idiots.'

Louise clenched her teeth. He seemed to purposely misunderstand or avoid what she tried to explore. It didn't seem to bother him that once he was in the red and angry, he just unleashed his anger at whoever or whatever had made him feel that way. He took no responsibility for anything and placed all the blame on them for his actions. Louise decided to change tack for a while as she felt it wasn't wise at this moment to push him anymore, so instead asked him about his new relationship.

He unclenched his hands and sat back in his chair and gave a broad smile. 'Thanks for asking. I've met her a few times now and I think it's going rather well. Actually, very well. She is my type of women and very attractive too.'

Apparently now on a safer subject and nearly at the end of the session Louise felt her jaw relax. 'I'm pleased for you and do hope it works out. Hopefully you will be able to confirm all is going well when we meet next week. Remember to try and have a go at the technique we talked about. If you don't recognise when you go into the orange, then at least try and be aware of any feelings during the week, both pleasant and unpleasant and we can do some more work on your response next week.'

As she wrote up her notes Louise ran through the session in her head; yawned and flopped back in her chair. There was definitely something he had left unsaid.

George was already at the gym when she arrived and cheekily called out. 'Hi babe' as she walked in. Nearly all the other bikes were full and everyone looked up when he shouted. Louise put her head down and walked fast towards her bike. He grinned at her and as ruffled as she felt, couldn't resist grinning back. 'Goodness, George, if you are going to shout things out like that it had better be when there is a real babe walking across the room. Did you see the sniggers when they saw who you shouted at?'

'Oh, come on now, you are my babe and they'd better get used to it.'

Louise gave a half-hearted laugh as she climbed onto her bike and then the music drowned any further conversation.

They opted for the pub again and as Louise went towards the seats by the fire she remembered she owed George a round from last time and got out her purse. He put his hand up. 'No worries, Lou, put it away, wouldn't dream of letting you pay.'

He settled himself down opposite her and took a long drink of his beer. 'Ah, that's better. I think you're right, I swear Joss is making his training sessions much harder than they used to be.'

Louise nodded and took a large gulp of the water she'd asked for as well as the wine.

He put his glass down, reached forward to touch her hand, looked into her eyes and smiled 'Who'd have thought a week or so ago we would be here together?' He squeezed her hand tight as he gave her one of his broad smiles which spread up his face to his eyes.

She reflected how very different he was to the man she'd seen earlier in her counselling room and frowned.

'What's the matter? Bored already?'

'Sorry, no. I mean no certainly not,' and squeezed his hand. 'I was just thinking about my last client today, you know the one I talked to you about the first evening we went to the pub.'

'Ah yes, the one that worried you. Is there anything I can do?'

'Yes, I think perhaps you could, if you wouldn't mind. Do you remember I told you, I sometimes ask Caroline to ring me after I'd seen a client that I thought might be a bit dodgy? '

'Yes, I do remember, and also remember I didn't think it was a particularly good way of protecting yourself. What do you want me to do?'

'Perhaps if I am not able to get hold of Caroline, could I ask you to be my safety phone call?'

George sat back in his chair and thought for a moment. To Louise it felt like rather too long a hesitation; perhaps she was wrong to have asked him.

He smiled and leant forward again. 'Sorry, I didn't give you an instant reply, but you took me by surprise. Of course, I will. It feels like quite a big deal, so I had to think about it. I'm glad you trust me enough to ask.'

Louise relaxed and leant over and kissed him. 'Thanks. I think I read your hesitation as a rejection and then I felt anxious because I am already feeling this....' and she waved her hand at him, 'is something really special and I don't want it to end.'

His eyes widened and he grasped her hand, 'I hope all my reactions are not going to be read and re-read; not sure I could manage that. Going out with, what my family would have called, a Divi doctor is a new experience and one I can see now could be quite complicated.' He laughed which showed Louise this wasn't too serious a problem but there was probably some truth in it.

'What on earth is a Divi doctor?'

He looked uncomfortable, 'Oh you know, someone who sorts out people who are not right in the head!'

Louise's mouth fell open. 'Not sure I would have got on with your folks then.'

'Just as well they are not around anymore. I think I come from quite a different background to you. I don't mean I was underprivileged but perhaps they weren't the most sensitive people. I think it is not really an expression they would have thought twice about using and it is used a lot in Devon where I originally come from.' He looked thoughtful. 'I don't think my gran would have liked it. She was where I got most of my cuddles and the ability to view the world in a much kinder way than I got at home. I felt very lost when she died.'

Outside, Louise clung to him. She would have liked him to come back to her house but as she had clients in the morning, agreed it was far more sensible for him to go to his. They planned he would then come over on Thursday after she'd finished work. She knew she would find it hard to wait.

THURSDAY 13th OCTOBER 2005

The distant sound of her mobile reached her just as she'd swallowed the last mouthful of porridge. The sound came from her study so rushed up the stairs and just managed a rather breathless, 'hello' before it clicked into her answerphone.

'*Louise, is that you? It's Amanda.*'

'*Hi Amanda, yes it's me. Sorry, just a bit out of breath. How can I help?*'

'*Oh didn't mean to make you run. I just thought I'd let you know Melanie has turned up again and all is well.*'

Louise had to think quickly who she was talking about and remembered that Melanie was the client that had reminded Amanda of Julia who'd been murdered.

'*She said it was all getting too much for her and decided not to come for a couple of weeks but then realised she was being childish and rang to see if she could re-start. Actually, the break seems to have done the trick as her head is in a much better place.*'

Louise heaved a sigh of relief. '*I'm so glad. It's so lovely that the process continues even if the client isn't seeing you. Thanks for ringing and letting me know. I was left with very vivid thoughts of what happened to Julia after our last session.*'

'*Yes, me as well,*' agreed Amanda, '*Even her partner's obsession about what she wore. If the fisherman hadn't spotted the plastic she might never have been found.*'

'*Yes, poor man - not something you'd expect to find while out fishing.*' Then Louise thanked her for letting her know and said she'd see her at her next supervision in a few weeks.

WEDNESDAY 19TH OCTOBER 2005

Life had taken on a different rhythm and Louise saw George at every possible moment. She recognised a significant change, the most obvious being she felt happy. She had started singing in the house, something she hadn't done for a long while and started to listen to more music.

Although it was warm in her counselling room, outside the wind howled and leaves tumbled from the trees that lined the pavement. At this time of year after a day of clients, she felt soporific and longed for a soft sofa and a cup of coffee. The streetlights were already lit and seen through the glass looked quite eerie. She shivered and walked to the window to close the curtains. She had her hand on one curtain when a movement across the road caught her eye. She screwed up her eyes to try to get a clearer picture and saw it was the figure of a man. She frowned and continued to close the curtains. It was possibly Ed, who was her next and last client and felt irritated because if it was, why couldn't he just have walked straight up to the door. He was already late.

When Ed eventually arrived, his mood seemed as cold as the weather outside. He strode ahead into her room, threw his coat over the back of the chair and sat down.

She left him to settle and wondered if he'd offer an explanation but he didn't. 'Is everything all right Ed? I'm guessing by the way you entered it might not be.'

He scowled then gave a rather forced smile. 'Yes, you're right. I'm afraid I've arrived in a bit of a black mood. I've had a dreadful day at work and that idiot does my head in.' She visualised steam rising from his head. His body was rigid and his hands were tightly clenched. 'You wouldn't want to know what he has done now.'

'Actually, I think I would and as it was the theme of our last session I am pleased you recognise you're in a black mood. So, tell me what is upsetting you. Perhaps tell me about it and then say how you handled the situation. I'm hoping you've been able to use some of the anger tools we'd discussed.'

He said nothing and sat in silence. Louise mirrored his silence and wondered what was going on in his head and what he had got up to. She had an image in her head of a panther ready to spring and wished she had put her usual safety precautions in place. She hadn't seen or spoken to Caroline since she'd been away and although she had mentioned it to George in the pub, she hadn't followed it up. She made a mental note to do so before Ed's next session. She was sure he wasn't a threat and her feeling of anxiety was because she was being reminded of her abusive cousin.

She was so deep in her thought she almost jumped when he finally spoke. The panther had become a domestic cat.

'Sorry, think I've been rude, the way I came in. I know I was late and I apologise. I admit I was angry; you certainly picked up on that quickly but I'm fine now. To answer your question, your method did help me this week and so I didn't lose control. My goodness though, it was very hard; the man is such a fool. I don't think I want to tell you what happened as, with reflection, it is not something I need to discuss. The man's an idiot and that's about all there is to say. Do you know he actually went again to the Senior Partner in the Practice but Michael and I had a word and as a result he's promised to attach this guy to somebody else and so it's now sorted.'

Louise sensed that he hadn't told her the whole truth. 'I am pleased you managed your anger. Not everyone can in such a short time; you're obviously a fast learner.' As soon as she spoke she wished she hadn't added the last sentence as it sounded a bit sarcastic or patronising, then noticed he had straightened his back and puffed himself up on the praise. Obviously a man used to success whatever the task.

'So how did it feel to have managed that scenario in a more acceptable way?'

'Yes, good. Very good, particularly as Michael has now placed the guy somewhere else. It's had a much better outcome than I ever thought possible.'

'Great, that's good. You now have evidence that controlling your anger can resolve a problem in a much more civilised way.'

He smiled, but Louise caught something in his eyes and decided to pick him up on it. 'I wonder if you could tell me what happened just then? I saw something change in your eyes and wonder what you were feeling?'

In an instant he became more animal than man and snarled. 'What the hell do you mean what happened?' He clenched his hands again and with a voice that would cut glass. 'Nothing happened. What the fuck are you insinuating you…'

He stopped and Louise was sure he had been about to add some derogatory word about her but felt she needed to pursue it. He'd just illustrated how quickly he could turn and knew it was important for her to remain calm, even if her muscles had tightened.

'I'm sorry if you feel I was insinuating something, but when I said you had controlled your anger, I saw a flash of something in your eyes and I just wondered what feeling had caused that. If you remember I've been trying to help you recognise your feelings.' She paused before adding, 'And you've just shown me how quickly you can leap into the red.'

He took a large breath and pursed his lips. Louise was then certain he wasn't going to allow her any glimpse of what had happened in that moment or make any comment about his flash of anger, so wasn't surprised by his change of tone.

'I wasn't really feeling anything.' He frowned, 'Apart from being pleased you thought I had done well, I suppose and yes, I got angry but didn't understand what you were getting at.'

Louise knew she should explore this example of his loss of control but whether it was anxiety or lack of energy, decided to leave it at present but would return to it later in another session. 'Right, let's move on. How's your new relationship going?'

Ed gave a long sigh and shifted position in his chair. 'Brilliantly. She's a lovely woman and we get on like a house on fire.'

Louise smiled. 'That's lovely, I'm glad for you.' It seemed an ideal moment to ask about his child and what he thought. 'In our last session, you told me about your son and I wonder what he thinks about you starting a new relationship? I know it can be tricky sometimes introducing someone new.'

Ed frowned. 'Probably but I haven't told him yet. He's away at school but it's half term in about a week and I intend to talk to him then. I don't expect a problem. He has always liked the women I've employed to look after him, so I'm sure he'll like someone I am going out with too.'

Louise thought he was being slightly ingenuous. 'I hope you are right but it can be hard for a child. Tell me, how did he manage when his mother died?'

His eyes flickered and he turned his head away for a moment before he replied. 'Children are very resilient. He was fine and I don't think he ever really thinks about her now. He certainly doesn't talk about her.' He paused and looked into the distance again. 'There were a few nightmares in the beginning, naturally, but not anymore.'

Louise wondered what images his mind saw when he looked away. She was sad to hear this rather glib account of how children deal with bereavement. In her experience adults more often saw the child's apparent continuation of normality and lack of visible grief as an acceptance of the situation. Adults rarely asked the right questions and children don't find it easy to find words to express their feelings. Poor boy. She wondered if he'd had any help at all.

'It must have been extremely difficult for both of you. Despite your complicated relationship with his mother, you would have been dealing with your own grief. It must have made it even harder to start bringing up a child on your own.' This was probably not the right moment but her concerns made her ask anyway. 'Given we are talking about your anger issues, I wonder whether you ever go into the red when you are with him?'

Ed gave a look which she was certain meant he was going to lie. 'What! No, never - that wouldn't be right. I mean I do get cross sometimes but I never lose it in front of him or with him.'

Convinced she was right about the lie, tried to clarify what he meant. 'You get cross but you never lose it with him?'

'I just said so, didn't I? No, absolutely never, it would be wrong. Not that he isn't a pain in the arse sometimes and I have to tell him off but that's different.' She supposed she had no choice at the moment but accept what he said.

'What about you though? I understand your wife died very suddenly. I think you said you were already separated, but I wonder how it was for you? It still must have been very painful, especially as you say it was very sudden.'

He sighed and lowered his eyes. There was a long silence before he spoke again. 'Yes, I didn't expect it to be so soon. As I said things weren't great between us and she left to stay with; well a friend. I don't think it worked out as she hoped. When she discovered she had cancer, she asked if she could move back with me. I agreed and looked after her while she was; well she was basically dying.'

He gave an enormous sigh and Louise waited for him to fill the silence.

'She had an operation but when they saw what was there, just closed her up and said there was nothing further they could do. The chemo hadn't worked and she died within a couple of weeks. It was a huge shock.' He looked up and then lowered his eyes.

Touched by this story Louise told him she was sorry he'd had such a sad and difficult time.

He didn't immediately respond and kept his head bowed. Ready to hand tissues to him if there were tears, she watched him carefully but after a while he lifted his head, shifted his position and she felt able to continue.

'Where was your son when this was happening? Was he at home with you?'

He drew his eyebrows together and looked puzzled. 'Well, yes of course he was but I hired a nanny for him when his mother wasn't fit enough to look after him.'

It must have been incredibly difficult and again Louise wondered how the little boy had coped. She realised Ed irritated her less now, despite his rages. Even those seemed more understandable given the circumstances. He certainly deserved to meet someone to share his life with.

'I can only imagine how difficult it was for you and for him. He's lucky he has a good father.'

Ed smiled and his good looks almost startled her; he was so different when he wasn't glowering.

She glanced at the clock. 'We've only a few minutes left and I wonder if there is anything you need to say before we finish?' He shook his head, so she continued, 'We've covered quite a few difficult life events today and I know some of it has been hard. I'm not surprised you have some anger issues but am so pleased you managed to avert a problem this week. Hopefully you will be able to remember and keep those methods of managing in your head until they become a natural way of coping in the future. We'll stop now and I'll see you next week. I'm glad you feel you have met someone and I hope the discussions with your son go well this weekend.'

As the closed the door after him, she heaved a sigh of relief. A very complex client but at least she felt more empathy; he really had experienced a terrible and difficult early life. She looked forward to being able to talk to Jasper, her supervisor, about him on Friday.

Buster needed a quick walk before she got ready for the gym so her session notes were rather hurried. She wasn't the slightest bit interested in keeping fit any more but longed to see George.

'Hey, Lou, your bike is all warmed up and ready for you' he shouted. Now she was certain everyone there knew they were together.

They opted for a pizza after the gym and made their way back to her house for wine and whatever! A part Louise couldn't quite get her head round.

'You know, George, young clients sometime talk about older people they know having new relationships and they are horrified at the idea of it.'

George let out one of his glorious deep belly laughs. 'Yes, truly horrifying, isn't it?' And with those words he clasped her to him and yet again the sofa offered a soft and welcoming harbour.

THURSDAY 20TH OCTOBER 2005

Louise couldn't help her irritation when Tim phoned and asked for an extra session. Her day was already busy and it meant that she'd had to squeeze him in after what she'd thought was her last client.

Once he was seated he seemed to find it difficult to find the words and ran his hand through his hair several times before he started to talk about Paul, the wife killer.

'I can't believe I said I liked him; could even have been a friend in different circumstances. He's a nasty piece of work and although he still protests his innocence, there's no doubt in my mind now he murdered his wife.'

Louise had never questioned the guilt of this man, despite what Tim had said but asked him what had changed his mind.

'I believed our sessions had gone well and despite his apparent adoration of his wife, thought he was beginning to see his relationship could not have been as good as he portrayed; after all it had ended in divorce.'

His fingers played with the buttons on his shirt and Louise waited for a moment before she encouraged him to continue.

'Halfway through the session, without any warning, his mood changed. He had been talking about how beautiful his wife had been; how proud of her he was and how he loved having her at his side when they went out. I then simply asked when things had changed. He started to look agitated and gripped the sides of the chair so hard I could see blood drain from his knuckles.

It was apparently when his son was born that everything changed. She became someone he didn't relate to. She no longer wanted to wear the clothes he liked to see her in and was often out when he got back after work. She had friendships with people she'd met at toddler groups and spent more and more time away from the house, sometimes in the evening too. He felt totally betrayed but even worse, felt she showed more love to their son than to him.

He didn't try to make things work and told me dreadful things he had done to try and get her to "toe the line". He'd also taken her phone away from her and put locks on the door that only he had a key to.'

Tim told Louise Paul's wife had no other family and he had successfully got rid of the new friends she'd made, so she was even more vulnerable.

Louise thought he must be a man used to control and guessed he'd used his manipulative techniques on Tim initially. 'Murder wouldn't be an inevitable outcome though.' Louise commented. 'So, what was it made you change your mind and think he did kill her after all?'

'I think it was his vehemence when he talked about her and the violent rage which he exposed when he described the betrayal as he saw it. He had been agitated when he started to talk but then without warning he jumped up and shouted, "Filthy rotten bitch, she had it coming; finally got what she deserved. I hope she'll rot in hell."

'That must have been hard to listen to, particularly as you hadn't experienced his rage before.' As she spoke Louise noticed the colour had left Tim's face and suggested he have a drink of water and take a moment.

She waited while Tim sipped some water and had put the glass down before she spoke again.

'He must have hated her rejection and seen her marriage to someone else as a complete betrayal. All of this would have increased the rage he already had but I find it a bit odd that he didn't kill her when he first discovered she might leave him, which is usually the most dangerous time. I wonder what led him to kill her so long after and what that trigger was.'

Tim nodded, 'Yes, I wondered that too, especially when he told me he had suspected she was having an affair and planning to leave. He'd even bought a surveillance camera to watch her movements but I guess his anger had just built up over a period of time. Paul keeps telling me he is innocent and suspects the man who later became her husband but his explosive reaction has left me in no doubt he is guilty. At the end of the session just as we were about to finish, he laughed and said at least he'd managed to take her down a peg or two.'

Louise shuddered. Many women would have left as soon as they thought they were being spied upon but women with exceptionally low self-esteem often felt they deserved to be treated in this way.

'I wonder what he meant when he said he'd brought her down a peg or two. I think that would be worth exploring when you next see him. This work seems to be veering away from bereavement counselling, which was why you were asked to see him, so I wouldn't offer too many more sessions. A bit strange to think he could grieve the person he killed but it's not unknown.'

We have to stop now but don't blame yourself for being misled in the beginning. He is clearly manipulative with the ability to be pleasant and charming and engages well with people. It's why it's so hard to detect psychopaths or sociopaths. I'm sure he deserves to be where he is. After all, if he could lose his temper when he was talking about it, what must it have been like for his wife when she was within the situation?

Tim nodded. 'Thank you, Louise, it has been a great help. Shall I see you in a month's time as usual?'

'Yes, let's book it for a month but if you need to ring or see me in the meantime, then let me know.'

The coffee left in the cafetière hadn't taken long to reheat in the microwave and her efforts to resist opening the biscuit tin failed and she grabbed a couple to enjoy with her coffee while she wrote up her notes. Poor Tim was obviously shaken up by the session. She was still surprised he'd been so taken in; clearly Paul was a very manipulative man.

The walk to the Co-op wasn't long but it cleared her head after a day of work. She had planned to cook for George and needed some necessary ingredients. She had reached the check-out when she saw a smartly dressed woman walk in. She looked familiar but was too far away to identify. She had her hair up, heeled shoes, a short straight skirt and what looked like an expensive yellow coat, most likely with a designer label attached. She'd never be as sophisticated as that.

As the woman turned to walk down the first aisle, Louise gasped. It looked like Caroline. She craned her neck around to see if she could get another look but she'd disappeared. 'Surely it can't be her' she mumbled. She'd never seen her dress like that and she's always said she couldn't afford expensive clothes. She told herself she must be mistaken; it couldn't have been her.

'You planning to buy these items?' The cashier interrupted her thoughts.

'Sorry, yes .. in a dream.'

Buster had already had a walk and Louise had almost finished cooking when George walked in.

'Mmm, what's that I smell? Certainly, one to light up a man's stomach.' He grinned as he caught her round the waist and gave her a kiss that lingered on her mouth for more time than she'd taken a breath for.

She shook him off; 'For goodness sake, George you're acting as if we're in some old movie and in our twenties?' She laughed. 'I loved that time though, didn't you, when sex was had at every opportunity wherever you were and whatever time it was.' She had in her mind a field by a wood when she and James were first going out.

'I'd have loved to have known you then Lou, don't think any of my girlfriends were that liberated.'

She laughed again, turned back to the stove and made sure the rice had not gone mushy. He had told her the one thing he absolutely loved was a chilli. She hoped he'd like it but you never knew with chilli. She smiled as she remembered James being absolutely silenced by the heat when she'd first cooked it for him. She held her breath until

George had taken a mouthful and then let it out again when he licked his lips and murmured 'Mmm.'

Afterwards when Louise loaded the dishwasher, she remembered what she'd seen in the co-op and the likeness to Caroline. 'It was odd George because if it was Caroline, she looked quite different. She had her hair up and was wearing BBC clothes.'

'What on earth do you mean? BBC clothes, I've never heard that expression before, what are they?'

'Sorry, of course you wouldn't. It's an expression I made up a long time ago. Katy would have known what I meant. It's just I think presenters on the BBC always wear high heels and short skirts and I have always thought the corporation to be a bit controlling. I've never seen Caroline dress like that. It would be totally unlike her and impractical, especially as she works with young children.'

She'd stopped loading the dishwasher to talk, so George took the plate out of her hands. 'Here, Lou, let me take over, you've obviously got your mind on something else!' He laughed as he finished what she'd started and didn't reply until he had closed the door and started the machine.

'Of course, I don't know Caroline but perhaps it wasn't her or maybe she was going somewhere special. You can ask her tomorrow night, can't you?'

Yes, I can but I think I'm right. She laughed as he caught hold of her and pulled her into the sitting-room and onto the sofa.

FRIDAY 21st OCTOBER 2005

'Don't think I'll ever get used to waking up next to you,' murmured Louise as she cuddled into him, 'Especially as it's a dark morning and a Friday and I don't have anything planned until my supervision later this afternoon. We can stay here as long as we like.'

George emerged from beneath the duvet and pushed her away. 'Sorry sweet pea, I can't lounge about today. I have work to do and I have an exacting and strict employer who insists not a moment is wasted and definitely would not like me to be skiving on the job.'

'You'd better get on the job then, hadn't you?' Louise whispered as she leapt on him and left him in no doubt that she was the priority job at that moment.

Even though it was now the middle of October the weather was still brilliant, so Louise decided Buster deserved a longer walk. She thought a trip up to the golf course near the Battlefields would be a good place to go. She fetched his lead and after several attempts clipped it onto an excited dog.

The air was crisp and bright and there were still enough leaves on the trees to make it a painter's landscape, with hues of crimson, orange, yellow and brown. Buster gambled like a young puppy on fallen leaves and sniffed everything he found. The wind ruffled his long shaggy coat and Louise thought what a handsome dog he was and giggled as she thought her boyfriend wasn't bad either.

The hill was hard going and when her phone rang, she was glad of an opportunity to stop. *'Got you at last.'* The deep voice resonated in her ear. She grinned, *'Henry. How lovely, aren't you in the middle of work, or have you decided to give up earning a living?'*

'No Mum, I haven't given up work, just taken a day off and thought I would have a chat with the old dear.'

'*Not too much of the old if you don't mind, but it's lovely to hear from you. I have been meaning to ring you and Emma for a few weeks now but life just got a bit busy.*'

'*Really? I know you are working hard but surely not every evening. It is why I have been trying to ring you as I was worried, you don't usually let me loose for this length of time! What's up? Is something wrong, something you're not telling me? You're not ill are you?*'

'*No, I am not ill in fact far from it but I wasn't sure I was ready to talk about it and haven't even said anything to Kate yet.*' Louise coughed and tried to clear her throat, which had gone dry. 'Well, I've met someone'.

It was now Henry's turn to be silent for a moment before he urged her to tell him more.

'*Actually, it is through you that I met him. It was at the gym you paid for me to join. I've known him for about a year but recently we got talking and I found out he is a builder and asked him if he could do bathrooms.*'

Henry chortled, '*That was handy then.*'

'*He's a lovely man, as well as being a good builder and he's fun and interesting too. He was in the army for a while and when he came out, started helping people. He did odd jobs and it sort of went from there. I have begun to see a lot more of him socially and we get on well. He's been renovating the bathroom, which I have wanted to have done for ages and it's going to be fantastic. Actually, I haven't felt this good for ages, so don't bring me down.*'

Henry gave a rich laugh, '*Oh Mum I'd never bring you down. If you like the man that's all that matters. It would be so lovely to see you properly happy again and I know Emma will feel the same way. I am thinking of coming down to visit in a couple of weeks so we can meet him then.*'

Louise sighed in relief. '*Oh, that's great and it will be lovely to see you anyway. Tell me how's your work going? How are the worried well at your clinic?*'

'*As you know very well, they are far from the worried well. Those are the ones you see. I see the range of schizophrenics, bi-polar and those that are as crazy as a box of frogs.'*

Louise thought it was funny psychiatrists could be so disparaging and disrespectful in the way they talked but so caring in reality.

She saw Buster had turned around and run back down the hill after some real or imagined scent. *'Sorry, Henry, I have to go. I am up on Lansdown and Buster has disappeared into the distance. Let me know if you do decide to come down, lovely to speak to you, Lots of love, Bye.'* She'd ended the call abruptly but Henry would understand. She hurried back down the hill and found Buster at the bottom having rolled in something smelly and disgusting!

George was in the hallway when she got home and it looked as though he'd stopped work for the day.

'Looks like I've got back at just the right time. Bread and cheese okay for you?'

'No. I'm not stopping.' His eyes no longer held the look of romance that melted her heart and he was clearly distracted by something. 'Just had a phone call and something has come up so I'm sorry but I have to go now. I'll grab something to eat on the way or later.'

She tried not to let her disappointment show. 'That's a shame I'd fancied a lunch with you but don't worry, another day. Anyway, I'll see you soon, won't I?'

It wasn't supposed to be a question but George stopped when he got to the door and turned back to face her. 'I'll see you tomorrow. There is no point my coming over tonight as you will be at Caroline's until whatever hour and I'm sure good for nothing after that, I'll see you tomorrow.'

The door banged shut and Louise felt a twinge of loneliness. She knew what he said was true but wondered where he had to rush off to so suddenly. She had the feeling it was something he wasn't going to share with her. She'd seen the tension in his body while he had spoken to her and after he'd gone, she registered that she hadn't been given a goodbye kiss. Her chest felt tight and some of her initial doubts crept back into her head.

It wasn't too long a drive to her supervisor on the outskirts of Bradford-on-Avon and she went through lovely scenery on route so always enjoyed the journey. The sky was still a clear bright blue with a tinge of navy and the orange and red glow of the leaves on the trees reflected the last rays of the autumn sun.

The narrow country lane which led to his cottage was hardly used and even had grass down the middle. She wondered if she could ever live somewhere as remote as this. The cottage itself was old and always draughty, so had dressed appropriately and put on a thick winter coat and her favourite fair isle woollen jumper under it and leather boots.

'Come in, Louise, very nippy today even though the sun has been lovely.' Jasper grinned and his long grey beard which covered most of the lower half of his face seemed to add an energy to his welcome. Louise always thought this larger than life character looked a bit of a hippy with his long hair tied in a ponytail but he was one of the best therapists she knew and loved working with him. His work with bereaved children had inspired her way back in the beginning when she first met him on a training course.

She returned his greeting and shed her coat on the chair in the hall, while he hurried off in the direction of his therapy room.

'Ah,' She sighed as she sank into the old-fashioned winged armchair. 'I love this chair and I love this room. I always feel I've come home but then I feel I want to sleep, but I'd better get that idea out of my head or you'll be charging me for snoring!'

His laugh seemed to emerge from his enormous stomach and it echoed round the room. 'I'm not going to allow you to sleep as I need to hear what's been going on for you.'

Louise grinned. She remembered she had already disclosed to Jasper she'd met George at the gym and was someone she was rather drawn to. 'I'll start with the personal, shall I?'

Jasper grinned when Louise told her they were now together. 'That's great Louise. After all you've gone through you deserve to meet someone and be happy. Now tell me about the clients you want to bring.'

She pulled her supervision notebook out of her bag and glanced at the names she'd written and been thinking of in the car.

She described her first meeting with Ed and her first sessions with him. She said initially she'd had an unfavourable impression but thought this might be explained because he reminded her of one of her older cousins who appeared charming but had been abusive to her when she was young.

'So, you think there may be transference and perhaps because of this you're feeling a little uncertain about him?'

Louise thought for a moment. 'I think uncertain is the right word and on talking about it I'm sure that it is just transference. It's almost as if my cousin is sitting there and I'm responding as if he were.'

Jasper frowned. 'You said 'first impressions', which implies you feel differently now. What has changed?'

'I feel more empathic now because I've heard more of his story and have more understanding of what he's had to deal with. He hasn't finished telling me his life story but he seems to have had a difficult and abusive life. He's come to me for anger management, after several angry outbursts against a member of staff but I think the source of it goes deeper than that.'

Jasper stretched back into his chair. 'Sounds like your feelings towards him are due to transference but remember it is always worth taking a note of gut reactions. We learn a great deal by listening to what our gut says but we so often override these feelings by telling ourselves we are being silly or imagining things. Remind me of what safety precautions you have in place when you see clients at home?'

Louise reminded him she had previously had Caroline as back up but she was now in the throes of a new romance and was often out. She said George had agreed to do it and would be the one she would phone if she was concerned about an unpredictable client and he would check up on her after the session.

Jasper made a note of what she'd said before he asked her to talk about the supervisee she was concerned about. She recounted the situation between Tim and Paul.

He listened intently and murmured 'Interesting.' Then added, 'Bereavement counselling for the death of the client's victim! I can see why you say this is complex.'

'I'm not sure why I've brought this to you but Tim was in such a state when he talked about this client, I thought I would just flag him up. I think I may have more to hear about this man and may need to talk about how Tim is handling him in the future.'

'Yes, good to bring it but remember Tim's client was tried by a court and found guilty. It sounds as though Tim has forgotten that.'

Louise nodded agreement, 'Yes I agree but I certainly haven't forgotten but I think Tim realises now he made a mistake when he believed him.'

She then explained about the incident in the car park that Harriet had told her about and how she had advised her.

'I suppose with this, I just want to check you agree with my action and there was nothing further I ought to have done.'

Jasper agreed she'd taken the best course of action.

'One more thing that is a bit odd. My grandson, Max, witnessed an unpleasant and abusive scene in the school car park between a boy who had been caught bullying and his father. My daughter and husband have informed the school but the whole thing sounds so similar to the story Harriet told me I'm wondering if it could be the same man and the same boy. I can't be sure as Harriet used the pseudonym, Tom and Max said the name of the boy was Ben and I don't even know if it is the same school.'

Jasper screwed up his eyes as he thought about what she'd just said. 'Hmm that is strange and, as you know, I'm always suspicious of coincidences. I know there are many unhappy and abused children but I think you have to bear in mind that you may be right and they could just possibly be the same child.'

Louise waved back as Jasper stood and watched her walk to her car. As she drove home, her head was still full of the issues she'd spoken about and nearly forgot she was seeing Caroline later and needed to stop at the village supermarket and buy some chocolates to take with her. Whilst she was there she also bought a curry to microwave as she didn't want to bother to cook.

By the time she returned to her house it was nearly dark and her path was difficult to see because of the shadows made by the shrubs on either side of the path. She shivered and thought it felt like a setting for a gothic horror. She made a mental note to ask George what was happening about the electrics or perhaps she should just go ahead and ring an electrician herself.

Her phone pinged just as she'd put her coat on to go down the road to Caroline. *Hey, Sorry Louise not able to meet tonight - hope not messed up your evening, xx.*

Well of course you have. I was looking forward to seeing you. Why couldn't you have let me know earlier; I might have been able to see George. Louise recognised that the angry thoughts were more because she was disappointed. She'd wanted to hear about her new man and perhaps to discuss hers with her too. The text didn't even sound particularly friendly nor did she sound as if she was really sorry.

Still in her coat she reached into the fridge for a bottle of wine and poured herself a large glass. It was an odd text. Caroline usually started a text with Hi, not Hey and always ended with four xxxx, not the two that ended this text. There was no 'How are you' or 'I had an amazing weekend, how about you?' In all the time she'd know her she'd never had to question her friendship but this made her feel unsure.

They'd been friends from the first time they'd met when they were both suffering from life events. She from grief at losing James and Caroline from the wretchedness of being in a marriage with a man who was controlling and mean and from which she was trying escape. Despite the ten years difference in age they'd struck up a friendship and had supported each other through everything ever since. Once Caroline was on her own, they had met at her house every Friday for a G and T and a chat.

It was hard to settle and Louise knew that what she needed was company. She started to text the one person she most wanted to see. *Been blown out by Caroline, any chance you're free or are you settled at the pub with your mates, your very sad lonely friend! Xxx'.* A reply came back immediately, *What a pain! Sadly, can't, but you guessed right, I have a good pint of beer in front of me and more on the way. See you tomorrow.*

Oh well it's a night in with Buster. I guess with a good thriller, a large glass of wine or two and the box of chocolates I'd bought for Caroline. With these thoughts she finally removed her coat and tried to get comfortable on the sofa. She'd just put her feet up when she remembered she hadn't asked George to pick up the taps she'd ordered from the local hardware store on his way to hers in the morning. She pressed his number on her phone. It rang for a long time and she expected it to go into voice mail. He probably wouldn't even hear his phone with the noise of a pub but just as she thought this, he answered. It didn't sound like him. *'George, is that you?'*

There was a rather husky response but she was convinced he'd said yes, so continued to speak.

'*I forgot to say Hammonds on Chelsea Road have rung to say they now have the tap parts you ordered, so you need to pick them up on your way in tomorrow.*' He didn't answer but she waited. Then he thanked her and ended the call. It was odd and a bit abrupt but she supposed he wouldn't want to say anything endearing with his mates there.

She gulped down some more wine and thought about the call. It didn't sound as though he was in a pub, there were no pub sounds. In fact, there were no background sound at all and she felt a prickle in her spine.

SATURDAY 22ND OCTOBER 2005

As soon as she was awake, she thought about last night and the rather odd phone call she'd had with George but by the time she'd eaten breakfast and gone over it again in her head, she'd made herself believe there was a reasonable explanation.

She heard a key turning the lock in her front door followed by a shout. 'Lou, where are you, it's me.' Once he'd discovered her whereabouts, he rushed towards her and wrapped her tightly in his arms. She sighed in relief.

'Whatever time do you call this? She teased.

'Don't be like that, you asked me to pick up the taps and now I can fit them.'

Louise had forgotten about the taps. 'Oh, yes the taps. I had hoped we might do something together today.'

'No, I think I'd like to get the bathroom finished if I can but we've got the whole weekend and we can do something tomorrow if you like.'

His grin and the frown that accompanied it made her believe he would have liked to have gone off with her today. She'd have to make do with tomorrow and anyway the bathroom would then be done and they could celebrate.

She was glad he would be there the whole weekend but no longer felt as cheerful as she had done. She couldn't help the thought that something had changed. She'd noticed his bloodshot eyes and his clothes looked as though he might have slept in them. He'd done and said all the right things but something felt disturbingly different.

WEDNESDAY 26TH OCTOBER 2005

She looked over the notes she had written of Ed's last session. There was so much that puzzled her about him. She had begun to feel compassion for his unfortunate life but still found him a difficult one to sus out and thought about the snake. She knew she needed to ask more about his childhood and hoped she would get a clearer understanding in this session.

She was on her way downstairs when she heard the knock. He was early. She hurried the rest of the way and was breathing heavily when she answered the door. Ed's look swept her body and she lifted her hand to her neck as she felt heat rise towards her face.

'Sorry think I'm a bit early. You're out of breath Louise, are you all right?' Without waiting for an answer, he swept past her and into the counselling room. To her surprise he took off his coat, walked back and hung it on the back of the door. He then sat in the chair, made himself comfortable, removed some real or imagined bits of something on his trousers, and then looked up in a way that suggested to Louise he was now ready and in control.

She took a deep breath and tried to regain some composure. 'So how has this week gone for you?' Are you managing to keep things under control at work?'

'It's gone well, thanks. My relationship is good and work has been so much better since that idiot is no longer working for me and Michael isn't on my back all the time. He should have moved him a long time ago.'

'I'm glad to hear work is now going well and what you saw as the source of your anger has been removed. However, it is still useful to think about managing anger when it arises. Do you think you have got more understanding of the traffic light system?' Louise saw the frown and thought she could make it easier for him. 'I guess if your relationship is going well you have, at least, had the chance to notice what happens in your body when you feel good things.'

Ed gave, what might be described, as a dirty laugh. 'I know where I feel most excited; she really turns me on, if that's what you mean.'

Her jaw tensed. 'That wasn't quite what I meant, but if you're talking sexually then I'm glad it's going well. I was meaning more about noticing a response to an emotion. If you remember, I was wanting you to understand what happens between the 'green' and the 'orange'. Some people feel the beginning of anger in their stomach, or their feet; they might also feel hot or sweaty. I was asking you to notice good feelings because I thought they might to be easier for you to notice their progression. Perhaps as you connected my question to sex and arousal, then think of that progression. Perhaps if she comes into the room you might feel one thing and then if she hugged you, it would feel different again and then when you kissed, something else. Do you understand what I am saying?'

'You know what, I find this sort of questioning ridiculous. I don't get what you mean and as far as I am concerned, I'm fine and I think Michael is happy too, so perhaps we need to stop.'

Louise couldn't prevent the gasp that came when he mentioned not continuing. She wasn't quite sure how they had got to this position. She noticed his knuckles were white as he gripped the arms of the chair.

'I'm sorry if I haven't explained it well. I see you are upset, so perhaps tell me what you are feeling now? For instance, I see your hands have gripped the chair so I wonder what emotion made that happen?'

The look he gave was steely. 'If you want to know, I'm actually totally pissed off and I'll tell you what, Louise, I'm going into that bloody orange of yours and before you know it, will fucking well be in the red and then what happens, Louise, what happens then?' He half rose out of his chair but changed his mind and sat down again.

Louise tried to keep her breathing even and relaxed the muscles in her back. I should have insisted on sitting in my usual chair, now if I want to escape I will have to get past him to get to the door.

In a calm voice she continued. 'I'm sorry you feel like this, Ed, but what is happening now is exactly what I have been talking about and is something we can work on. I think it would be really helpful if we try to work through this now. Could you do that?'

Ed relaxed his hands into his lap and Louise took a silent but deep breath of relief. The moment of crisis seemed to have passed and his voice when he spoke had a normal rhythm and was much quieter.

'Yes, all right I'll stay. I'm sorry but you see what I mean, don't you? I don't know what comes over me but what I do know Louise, is you can help me.'

Louise smiled encouragingly but secretly thought it wasn't what he genuinely thought. He's as slippery as an eel and that charm he's put on won't wash.

'Okay, I believe I irritated you. You then wanted to get away from that feeling and blamed it on me and the questions I was asking. That was when you started to go into a rage and moved into the red. However, you didn't and so looking at what stopped you would be good, as you would then know what tools you need in 'the bloody orange' as you put it.'

Louise's glance towards him met with the snake eyes again and couldn't help seeing an image of herself as a vulnerable rat waiting to be devoured. Then quickly thought, no I'm an intelligent rat and I can outwit this snake.

Ed gave her a quizzical glance before he answered. 'Well it was you. It was you who stopped me actually. I didn't want you to think badly of me.' He shifted in his seat and stared at her. 'Do you know what Louise, when you get agitated those freckles on your face sort of disappear.'

She couldn't help the sigh. He'd just said something actually true for a change and then tried to divert the conversation. She ignored it his comment about her and tried to get him back on track. 'What is important is we discover what happened to you.'

'I think it was your disapproval, I hate that'.

'OK. You fear my disapproval but what happened earlier? I think you didn't understand what I was getting at and that irritated you. Does not understanding something make you feel angry?

Ed leaned back in his chair and looked up towards the ceiling. 'Yes, possibly … perhaps.'

'Can you remember how it felt, not understanding or being disapproved of as a child?'

'Yep, suppose I can. Nightmare stuff really.'

'Nightmare stuff? Can you say more about that?'

The bitterness of the reply was as sharp and as quick as a snake bite. 'I loathed them, what they put me through. Anyway, they don't matter now because they're dead and I can put them out of my mind for good.' He shrugged as if to throw them off.

'Who are you talking about, Ed? Is it your parents?'

'Yes, them. Cruel, mean and nasty but they got what they deserved in the end.'

Louise felt the snake slither up her spine. 'What do you mean, they got what they deserved?'

Ed grinned. 'Got killed in a car crash. Didn't care, it meant I was totally free and I got the house and all the cash my dad had stashed away. So, it turned out all right in the end.'

His voice seemed to have changed to that of a younger man and she knew she had been correct in thinking his childhood was where the work was needed.

'You're saying, it turned out all right for you at the end. I think that's what you mean. I am sorry, but we are getting to the end of the session and I know it's hard to stop just when I think we are getting to some of the reasons why your anger erupts, but we can continue with this next week.'

'Right, fine. See you next week.' He grabbed his coat off the hook and almost before she realised, he was out of the front door and gone.

She gathered up her diary and walked slowly upstairs, thinking she hadn't managed that as well as she could. *My goodness, he can turn but I'm glad he's decided to continue with the work. I can only imagine what he might have had to put up with as a child.*

She wrote up her notes and started to think about Caroline. She hadn't heard from her since her strange text and they had so much they needed to catch up on. Louise had tried to ring but she never picked up her phone and the situation was beginning to irritate her.

It's sad when a friend drops another as soon as they are in a relationship but I never thought she'd be like that. However, I guess she has never had a good relationship before so maybe she can't help herself. She decided to take Buster past her house when she took him for a walk after work and see if she could catch her in.

She picked up her phone and texted George. *Sorry, won't be at the gym tonight, trying to track Caroline down. C u later.* She got an instant reply: xxx

Louise put on her thick coat, scarf and hat and fetched Buster's lead, which was almost impossible to put on as he danced about in excitement. 'Sit still, you stupid mutt or we might never get out.' As she stepped out into inky darkness she switched on the torch she now kept by the front door. George had tried to mend the light but said it needed an electrician and he would arrange for one but hadn't done so yet.

Louise stood at the front of Caroline's house and saw no sign of life, so walked around to the side. There she spotted a light in a room upstairs and quickly pulled Buster back to the front door and rang the bell. Nobody appeared, even though she rang it several times. She peered through the letter box but could only see the foot of the stairs and no sign of life. *I guess the light was left on by mistake, so I'll bring a note to push through the door next time.* Buster pulled on his lead anxious to walk, so they continued around the corner and onto the road that ran behind Caroline's and led to the churchyard.

On her return home, she tried to put thoughts of Caroline out of her head and focused instead on the buzz she felt in anticipation of an evening with George.

'Lovely meal Lou.' George mumbled once they'd settled themselves on the sofa. 'Do you want to continue watching that Danish thing?'

Louise gave a half-hearted nod. 'I'm still worried about Caroline. She's never missed an evening without explanation or at least a text.' In an absent-minded way, she picked at some wool bobbles on his jumper.

George put his hand over hers to prevent her doing more damage and pulled her towards him. 'I'm sure she's fine. She's probably like us, immersed in a new relationship and not giving much thought to how life used to run before.'

Louise nodded, picked up the remote and pointed it at the television, but before she had time to press the start button the phone rang. She managed to answer just in time and with a large smile on her face, mouthed 'Caroline' at George. *'Hi Caroline, thank goodness. I'm so glad you've rung - I was worried. How are things? How is the lovely John and what was your weekend like? When were you ever going to phone me?'* Her words all came out in a rush but she then stopped and waited for Caroline to respond. George signalled to her he was going to get himself another beer from the kitchen and Louise nodded.

Caroline's voice had sounded different; quieter and softer and Louise felt she wasn't at home, so asked her where she was. Caroline laughed and Louise instantly relaxed.

'I'm so sorry Louise. No, I'm not at home I'm at John's. I know I've been terrible but I've had a wonderful time. The weekend was amazing. He took me to Cornwall and since then I've spent most of my time here at his house. I'll be back at my house on Friday and I hope we can meet up. I want to hear all about George.

'Good, that's great. I had hoped we could meet up on Friday as usual. I'm pleased you're having such a good time.'

'*Lovely. I'll see you then. I can't wait to see you and we can have our show and tell moments!*'

Louise laughed at Caroline's use of primary school language, said her goodbyes and put the phone down. George sat down beside her and gave her one of his enormous bear hugs.

'There you are, all is fine and sounds like she is enjoying life.'

'Yes, it does. I'm relieved. I hope you don't mind about Friday night?' And then added 'Not that it would matter if you did as I would still go' and laughed.

George made a face but joked, 'No I don't mind, it will be a relief, I might actually get to spend some time in my own house, or more important still, I might get to go to my local and meet up with some of the lads for a beer. They will be wondering what on earth has happened to me.' Then when he saw her look, added, 'but we've got tomorrow night anyway!'

Louise smiled, leaned forward to pour herself another glass of wine from the bottle on the table and snuggled back down. She ought to be feeling safe and warm, but she couldn't shift the worm of unease.

THURSDAY 27TH OCTOBER 2005

George left before she was up. She wasn't sure how he'd managed to leave without her knowing and hadn't even heard the front door bang. Damn, I wanted to ask him why his friends would wonder what had happened to him, she thought. After all I thought he saw them on Friday night. She mulled over this and then remembered he hadn't actually said he was with friends but just sitting with a glass of beer. If that was the case he could have asked her to join him.

When she got downstairs, she saw a note on the kitchen table.

Hope I didn't wake you but have to be somewhere early. See you tonight - perhaps get something to eat. Don't miss me too much!! Gxxx. Louise felt a glow of warmth but deep inside recognised an unmistakeable flutter of anxiety.

She buried herself in her work for the rest of the day and avoided any introspection as to why she felt anxious. Time seemed to go fast and before she knew it, she had closed the door on her last client.

'I'm coming, Buster, won't be a minute' she shouted. He'd been whining all the time she had been writing her notes. He'd been more of a nuisance than usual during the day and she was glad she'd finished and was free to walk him. Once in the kitchen she set the table so she wouldn't have that to do when she got home. She hoped he would enjoy her quick version of carbonara, remembering that some men are funny about pasta.

When she returned the house was silent and dark, which meant George was not back. Just as well, she thought, as at least I have time to prepare the sauce and then just have to put on the pasta when he arrives.

She'd lost count of the time when she finally heard the door open. She shouted from the sitting room to say where she was and then added. 'I wish you'd let me know when you were coming back, the meal was ready ages ago and now I've drunk much more wine than I meant to.' As soon as she'd said it, she regretted letting her frustration show and realised she sounded like a petulant teenager.

He stood in front of the sofa and looked down into her face. 'I am so sorry, I got held up and anyway I didn't know you were cooking.' He sat down beside her, put his arm around her and pulled her towards him. 'I wouldn't upset you for the world'. He took no notice of her rigid body and gave her a large sloppy kiss.

The alcohol on his lips was obvious even though she had also been drinking. 'Ugh, I think you made a bit of a detour, didn't you?' She tried to lighten the words with a laugh but she wanted him to know she knew. He removed himself from the sofa and stood stiffly with his back to her. She wondered if he was deliberating whether to tell her the truth or not. She so hoped he would opt for the truth.

'Actually, you're right Lou, I ran into a mate and stopped off at the pub. I really didn't know you were cooking for me and am sorry if I got that wrong but surely, we are not going to go down that road, are we?'

'And what road is that exactly?' Louise retaliated as the defence in his voice had surprised her.

'Well we haven't been going out for long and already you want to know what I am doing and where I've been. Doesn't bode well, does it?'

She gasped, 'That's not what I said. I'm sorry if I misinterpreted your last words to me but actually it was in the note you left. Remember? You said we'd get something to eat.' She realised they were having their first row and actually her professional self quickly realised it wasn't just about this evening, it was the way he'd been all week. She hoped he wasn't the sort of man that turns everything into someone else's fault.

George put a hand up to his head. 'Yes, I did. I remember now. Really, I'm sorry, Lou, my bad as they say,' and laughed. 'Let's put this behind us and go and eat whatever it is that you've cooked.'

Uncertain whether she wanted to pursue the reason behind her anxiety she decided in the end to let it go. 'Come on then, we can have a drink while I put on the pasta.' She noticed his reaction - so not a pasta man. Well he's going to have to lump it this time.

FRIDAY 28TH OCTOBER 2005

The rain on the window woke her and she stretched out an arm towards George as she remembered how well the evening had turned out. He gave a contented sigh and she curled close and rested her head on his shoulder with her hand on his chest.

A sleepy voice murmured, 'Come back for more, have you?' He touched her head and gently tipped her towards him so he could kiss her face. In reply her hand wandered round his body and touched every curve and shape with a gentle caress. Now completely awake he pulled her to him. After a wild and pleasant interlude, they both gasped for breath and collapsed with laughter at their unexpected energy.

'What a wonderful way to start the day.' Louise crooned. 'How about a cup of coffee?'

George nudged her side. 'Well, how about you make me one for a change. Thought you were an emancipated woman who wouldn't want a man waiting on her!' As she started to move he held her back. 'Only joking, I know how much you enjoy having a cuppa in bed and it's not something I would ever normally do.'

Louise snuggled back under the duvet. Maybe last night and his strange behaviour during the week was just him in a mood and she grinned at the thought of how right things were now.

There wasn't a lot more to do on her bathroom and George reckoned if he got started immediately after breakfast, it would be finished today.

Louise busied herself with some necessary housework until she realised the noise had stopped upstairs. 'Brought you your elevenses and a chocolate biscuit,' she said as she pushed the bathroom door with her knee. She saw he was on the phone, so put the mug and biscuits down beside the sink. He didn't look pleased with whoever it was that had rung him. She left the room quietly but heard him say, '*All right, all right, don't panic, I'll be there but probably not until after four.*'

Where was he was going? She thought he'd be here until he'd finished; that's what he said this morning. She felt irritated when he appeared downstairs later with his coat on and his overnight bag.

'I'm sorry Lou. Afraid I have to go. Something's turned up.'

She looked down at his bag. 'I take it this means you don't know when you'll get back?'

She thought he was going to explain but instead he said, 'I wasn't going to be here tonight anyway as I know you're seeing Caroline, so was sure you wouldn't really mind.' The door closed and he was gone.

Why does he keep everything so close to his chest? Where on earth can he be going when he promised to be here? What could have come up? It didn't sound like work. Somehow with all these thoughts whirling, Buster sensed her unease and pushed his nose up to her hand. 'Least you're always here for me, Buster, not sure I'm that certain about this man though.' She sighed again; it had been so perfect this morning but whatever that phone call was about and whoever it was, it had changed things. 'He didn't even give me a kiss as he left again.' she muttered.

Coffee in her hand she mulled over his strange disappearance. What do I really know about him? The sex is great, but I don't know a lot more about him other than he was in the army and had an accident. He hasn't even told me anything about that. We don't sit and discuss books and we've only had about two walks together. I have told myself and others we have a lot in common but what? I'm not sure now. Tears started to glide down her face and she reached across the kitchen counter for the kitchen roll.

Caroline didn't rush to answer the door as she usually did and Louise wondered if she could have made a mistake. 'Come on, Caroline, it's cold out here.' She rang the bell again. This time she heard footsteps and the door opened and Caroline peeped out. It wasn't like her usual greeting and Louise wondered what the matter could be. 'Caroline, are you all right? You usually rush to open the door. I was beginning to think I had the wrong day!' Louise handed her the replacement chocolates she'd bought and Caroline took them with a slight nod of the head. She gave a faint smile and led the way into the kitchen, where they usually fixed their drinks together. Louise automatically opened the freezer to get the ice and expected to rummage around for it as usual, but the freezer had been tidied and the ice was on the top. 'Wow, you've had a bit of a clean out!'

Louise found her strange. Even what she was wearing was different, she didn't usually wear a sloppy track suit. She hoped there would still be a fire as there was a definite chill in the air and not just because of the weather. The fire was lit but sadly, no sign of any nibbles, and Louise was glad she had managed to have something to eat earlier. She decided to ignore the strangeness for the moment and carried on as if she hadn't noticed anything.

'Cheers, Caroline.' Louise leant across and clinked her glass to hers. 'Now, tell me what's been going on for you. It is ages since we've met up and you've been away. I'm longing to hear how it went and from the sound of things you've been staying at John's a lot.'

Caroline looked up. There were dark circles under her eyes and the spark of excitement she had seen last time seemed to have disappeared. She sat and looked at Louise but didn't open her mouth.

'Are you positive you're all right? You don't look terribly well, and I am not sure you really want me here.'

Caroline forced a smile. 'Of course, I want you here. I've so looked forward to seeing you tonight but I didn't sleep at all well last night and I'll admit I'm tired. School finished early today as it's half term, so I came home and lounged about in these old clothes. I will probably try and have an early night.'

Louise felt slightly heartened it was nothing more than tiredness and knew what that felt like and in the early days of a relationship, sleep wasn't something you got a lot of, as she well knew.

'I'm glad that's all it is, I was worried when you weren't behaving at all like the Caroline I know. I'll only stay for this one gin and then you can get to bed. But I am not going until you tell me how it is for you. Is he as wonderful as you thought and is it as wonderful as you thought it was going to be?'

Caroline nodded vigorously as she shifted her position. 'It is, yes, absolutely wonderful. He's an amazing man. He lives in a fabulous house with a beautiful garden, so we have mainly stayed there. He has only been here once and I am not sure he thought much of it, and seeing it through his eyes, knowing where he lives, I think I agree with him.'

'Don't be silly, this is a wonderful home and I love coming here.'

'I know but if you could see his place, you'd know what I mean. Anyway, to answer your question, yes, the weekend was gorgeous, and we stayed in this beautiful cottage. We walked along the beach in the day and out for meals in the evenings. He keeps buying me presents and actually is altogether smartening me up.'

Although Caroline sounded more like the woman she loved, Louise bristled. 'Smartening you up, what do you mean? You always look lovely' but then she interrupted herself when a thought came into her mind. 'Ah, so it was you I saw in the Co-op the other day, with high heels and smart coat?'

Caroline frowned. 'Yes, possibly. I have been there this week and I think I was wearing my new coat and shoes, but I didn't see you. They were just a few of the presents he's bought me. I could never afford clothes or shoes like that.'

'That was kind. Though I wouldn't have ever seen that as your style. Did he choose them?'

'You're right it wasn't me. I would have thought they weren't my thing, but he was so thrilled to see me in them I couldn't say I didn't like them, and it is such a new experience for me to feel flattered.'

The conversation then turned to George and what Louise had been doing and before they knew it, the evening had become late after all. She didn't mention to Caroline how odd George was being at the moment.

'My goodness is that the time, I said I would leave you to go to bed early. I'll say goodbye and hope to see you soon. Perhaps we can meet again next Friday, as it will still be half-term but after that I guess you'll probably be more at John's house. However, I hope that won't mean we can't still get together on the odd Friday night. It would be a shame if either of our relationships prevented that.'

Caroline laughed nervously, 'Of course we can still meet and yes, next Friday should be fine as Ben will still be with John.'

Louise walked towards the front door but before leaving she turned and hugged Caroline. The squeal of pain raised goose bumps on Louise's body. 'What on earth's the matter, what did I do? I'm so sorry Caroline.' Then added apologetically, 'My hugs don't usually give people that reaction.'

Caroline quickly reassured her, 'No, it wasn't you. It wasn't the hug at all. I think I must have stepped on a drawing pin or something; I spilled some when I came in from work.' She bent down and massaged her foot.

Louise wasn't satisfied but went along with it. 'Ah, that explains it then. Do you want me to check your foot?'

'No, it's fine now. I don't think it's still in there, but I'll vacuum the hall after you've gone.' She held the door open and hurried Louise out.

Standing outside, Louise felt the strangeness of the whole evening overwhelm her. When she'd heard the name Ben, it had unnerved her. She reasoned that it's a common enough name and it would be too much of a coincidence for him to be the boy Max talked about.

It wasn't until she had snuggled down in her bed that she thought about it again. She remembered what Jasper had said about co-incidences and perhaps he was right. She found it hard to get to sleep and wished she had George to discuss it with. He hadn't answered her texts but as a last check she leant over and picked up her phone which was plugged in by her bed. Nothing. She quickly shot off a text to him, *Night night, miss you like mad, and the bed is really cold without you in it*! LOL xxxx. When she typed those letters, she wondered if he was up to date enough to know she meant Laugh Out Loud rather than Lots of Love.

SATURDAY 29TH OCTOBER 2005

Louise woke just before someone in her dream sprayed water on her face. It was still dark and the noise of the rain was clearly what had disturbed her. She sat up, turned on her bedside light and pressed her hands to her head. It felt gin heavy, although she'd only had two gins the night before. She marvelled and cursed at her internal body clock which woke her at this time every day, even if she had no work. As light flooded the room, so did memories of the previous day. She unplugged her phone and hoped she'd find a message.

Her throat constricted; there were none. She reminded herself it was only a day since she saw him but the silence felt strange and unnatural, even in the short time she'd known him. Perhaps it's all too fast for him, she mumbled. She shivered as she removed the warm duvet and grabbed her dressing gown. She looked for her slippers, but they weren't anywhere within sight. 'Damn, where are they?' She fumbled under the bed and then got down on her knees to look and she saw they'd managed to find their way right to the far side. As she stretched her arm to reach them, her phone pinged. She grabbed them then cursed as she hit her head on the frame as she wiggled a hasty retreat.

Louise felt a rush of disappointment. It wasn't George. It was a number she didn't recognise.

Not coming to the session next Wednesday. C u the week after. There was no apology for the early hour of the text, or the rather curt way the appointment was cancelled. More and more she found people seemed to text whenever they felt like it whatever the hour, day or night. It was unsigned but Louise saw from the previous curt message, that it was Ed.

Buster looked up from his bed in the kitchen and gave a faint wag in acknowledgement of her presence. She opened the back door to let him out, but he took one look at the rain and plodded back to his bed.   Louise carried her coffee upstairs to bed and drank it whilst she sifted through thoughts that had plagued her most of the night.   She drummed her fingers on the sheet while she thought what she should do; picked up her phone and started to text.

Lovely to see you last night. Just out of interest, I was wondering what school John's son goes to?   Is it by any chance the same as Max's? Then added - j*ust being nosey! xxxx*

Caroline didn't come back with an immediate reply as she would have done in the past, but this had become more of a norm in the last few weeks. Perhaps she's still asleep, especially as she had been so tired last night, and they had drunk rather a large amount of gin!

There was no message that morning from George and he didn't turn up for work, which was doubly frustrating as the bathroom was so nearly finished; yet another delay. He hadn't appeared by mid-afternoon and neither had he sent a message. Louise drifted around the house in a low mood, not helped by the dreariness of the day.

The rain had stopped but she didn't feel energetic enough to go for a long walk, so decided the churchyard would have to do.   On her return, to make it longer, she walked back on the road which took her past Caroline's house.

Since the rain, the leaves were no longer crisp under foot and the pavement was slippery, so she kept her head down most of the walk.   When she reached the front of Caroline's house, she looked across towards her sitting room window in case she was there but there was no light, and the curtains were open. Caroline had been so strange last night. If she'd caught sight of her she would have checked she was alright.

As she started to walk away from her house, along the terrace, she heard a car. She turned to look and it roared out from the parking spot at the side.   It looked an expensive one and although not someone who took much notice of that sort of thing, thought it was perhaps a Mercedes or a BMW.

There may have been a passenger but it was so dark she wasn't sure.

Perhaps John had come over to collect something, she thought as she tried to make sense of it but then Caroline had said he would be tied up with his son as it was half-term.

She had a lump in her throat when she thought of Caroline and John together; George had neither appeared nor contacted her. She felt a familiar darkness wash over her as her heart filled with the sadness and pain of losses she'd previously endured and they flowed through her head like magician's flags produced one after another. She'd helped so many people but when it came to her own life she'd found it hard to prevent negative thoughts ambushing her and carrying her off to unpleasant places.

Company would help and so Louise got out her phone. Who better to be with than your own grandchildren.

'Hi Katie, just wondering if I could pop round for a while and perhaps have that shower you promised. I'm just a little tired of strip washes!'

'Yes, sure, Mum, I thought you'd forgotten, as haven't seen anything of you since last weekend. Max would be thrilled I know and Milly too of course. Naturally we would love it as well. Why don't you stay and have something to eat with us?'

In an instant she felt better and told Katy she would be there within the hour, she only needed to get Buster home and then collect her wash things, shampoo etc.

By the time she reached her house, it had become dark. She found the light and shivered. Something felt different, almost alien. She'd lived in the house for so many years and had always felt nurtured by it but not now, not this evening.

She walked from room to room but saw nothing unusual. The sense of unease in her body hadn't left but Buster seemed oblivious to anything strange. She watched as he guzzled what leftover food there was in his bowl and felt reassured as she was certain he would have picked up anything untoward. She sighed; I must be going a bit dippy. I think my worry about both Caroline's and George's strange behaviour has put me on edge.

She checked the bathroom in case there was any sign of George having been there but nothing had changed. She stared at the mirror and murmured to herself. 'Louise, get a grip. It's only been a day and he can't just drop his life for you. There'll be a perfectly good explanation; I'm sure there will. As for Caroline she's a grown woman who has developed into a very assured woman in the last year or so and if there is a problem in her relationship, I'm sure she'll deal with it. She smeared some of her usual red lipstick onto her lips and gave herself a rather grim smile as she left the room.

It didn't take long to drive to Katy and on the way tried not to think of how miserable she felt and was cross she'd reawakened her own 'black dog'.

Katy answered the door and gave her a big hug. 'Good to see you, Mum, are you all right. You look a bit sad?'

Louise thought, once again, how lucky she was to have such an intuitive daughter. 'Oh, I am fine, just a bit tired. The weather's been dreadful and always brings me down.' She didn't want to discuss problems on the doorstep, if at all.

Katy nodded and gave her another hug, 'Do you want a drink, or do you want a shower first before joining the madhouse proper?' She waved towards her large kitchen where sounds of giggles and children shouting could be heard.

'Louise gave her a squeeze on the arm, 'Thanks, Katy. Think I'll have a shower and then join you in the kitchen and look forward to a drink after.'

The shower felt good. It had been difficult without one these last few weeks and it had always been good place to resolve problems and Louise was determined to put a stop to her irrational fears. The last weeks with George had been special but it didn't mean he should give up any life he had before and she began to feel a little guilty.

She felt more human once she'd showered and decided if he hadn't contacted her by Monday she would go to his house. Perhaps something was wrong and he hadn't been able to tell her about it.

As she'd heard on her arrival, the children were full of energy, giggles and mischief. She was reminded of a holiday she'd had abroad, where groups of monkeys gathered on the beach to steal clothes from tourists who had ventured into the water and then scampered off with them into the trees. Louise grinned and realised the children had done the trick; they'd cheered her up. After they'd eaten they played Monopoly together, although Milly wasn't really old enough and Katy took her off to bed before the game was over.

With Milly gone, Louise was able to ask Max something she'd avoided until now. 'I haven't asked you how school is going Max. How is it with Ben since the problem you had with him?' Louise knew talking to children while they were playing a game, often resulted in them telling you what was really going on, rather than saying what they thought you wanted to hear.

'Good; all good'. He said, while he was in the middle of a move and anxious to get on with the game. 'Quick Granny, here's the money. I want to put a hotel on Park Lane. Yes, Ben's coming over next week. Mum said I could invite a friend over and I thought I would ask him as he seems to be having a bad time.'

'That's kind, Max.' Louise raised her eyebrows, this wasn't what she'd expected.

'He's not a bad person, Granny, just a bit odd. Don't think he's ever had a proper friend.'

Dave joined in the conversation and suggested it might not be a good idea to drop other friends just because he felt sorry for Ben.

Max clearly thought he was being told off and defended his decision by saying he was also having two other good friends over on another day.

Louise offered to accompany Max upstairs and to read him a story if he wanted. She loved to read to the children and although Max could read perfectly well himself he loved to listen too. It also gave her a chance to reassure him that it was thoughtful and kind of him to invite Ben over.

Katy and Dave were settled in their lounge when Louise reappeared. 'Come in, Mum, come and sit and tell us what's going on for you, now we can talk without being interrupted.'

Louise told them about George. Initially they sounded delighted but weren't so happy when they heard it might not be working out. 'I've told you because I wanted you to know but don't want you to worry. I'm sure there is an explanation for his disappearance and he's got to come back to finish the bathroom, so it isn't as if I won't be seeing him again.'

Katy quickly said, 'I'm sure you will work it out and if not, just think of it as a pleasant time and perhaps it will encourage you to go out and look again.' Then gave a look that told Louise how much she loved her. She didn't want to argue with her but knew if it didn't work out with George she wouldn't be interested in looking elsewhere, at least not for a long while.

Louise changed the subject. 'Tell me about Max having Ben round, what do you think about that?' As she spoke Louise tried not to show her anxiety at the idea of her family becoming mixed up with that man. Neither answered so Louise continued, 'It was kind of Max, given what had happened but I hope you won't ever let him go back to his house. His father doesn't sound stable and there could be an investigation by social services because of what Max saw.'

'We know that and no, we won't be letting him go with him. We think it's good of Max to offer him a friendship that might help him, but we'll keep a good eye on things, you can be sure of that.' Dave looked at her intently as he spoke, and Louise interpreted this to mean he would keep a professional eye as well.

Louise hadn't meant to stay so long and was reluctant to leave the warmth of her family but said her goodbyes and shivered as she walked out into the cold.

This time the house felt the same as usual and as she hadn't taken Buster over to Kate's with her, she was welcomed by a friendly dog. Just before she turned out her bedside light, she noticed the picture of her and James wasn't where it usually was, on her bedside table. Panicked she sat up and looked around. It was now on the table on the other side. Surely, she hadn't moved it - it was always beside her on the side of the bed where she slept.

SUNDAY 30TH OCTOBER 2005

Buster greeted her in his usual enthusiasm when she appeared at the bottom of the stairs in her dressing gown. 'All right boy. Calm down.' She peered out of the backdoor. The sky was virtually clear of clouds, and it looked as if it would be a sunny day. Her geraniums had finished flowering but some of the leaves were still green. She noticed these had a smear of white on them and assumed there had been a frost. Great day for a walk, she thought, and started to hum.

As she waited for the kettle to boil, she had a thought. I'll give Caroline a ring and see if she would like a walk too. She did occasionally join her on longer walks and it would be good to have company and a distraction from thoughts about George.

It was still a bit early to phone, so texted her. *Hey, are you free to have a walk with me today as both our men are busy? Louise xx*

She balanced her plate of toast and marmalade and cup of coffee on a tray and carried it upstairs. Glad to grab some luxury time to read while she waited for an answer from Caroline.

She was engrossed in her book so when her phone pinged it made her jump. It wasn't from Caroline; it was George.

Sorry Lou can't c u for a bit. Can't finish the bathroom this week but hope to the next. Explain when I see you. xxx

No explanation of why he hadn't phoned or turned up since Friday. Her heart sank and disappointment turned to irritation at not being given the courtesy of some sort of explanation and for ruining her previously happy time with her book. She knew these thoughts were unreasonable but she guessed were probably because she'd started to open her heart to him.

By the time she'd got dressed and gone downstairs there was still no reply from Caroline. She wandered into the garden; untidy after the summer flurry of flowers. She replenished her bird feeders and looked about her. 'How lovely,' she exclaimed as she spotted one rose still in flower and it somehow brightened her day. There was a noise in the garden next door and saw her neighbour, old Mr Braithwaite, with a hoe in his hand. She called out a cheery hello and waved.

'Hello Louise. Did those students keep you awake last night?'

She shook her head. 'No, I didn't hear them, when was it?'

'Was early. Maybe around eight.'

Louise felt she needed to defend the students, who had never bothered her, and quickly responded. 'I wasn't back until fairly late as I visited my daughter. Expect it was someone's birthday or something, they are not too bad on the whole. It's not like they have a party every weekend, is it?'

As she turned away, Mr Braithwaite continued. 'Yes, although it was a bit odd as I thought I saw one of them in your garden a bit earlier. It was still light so must have been late afternoon.'

Louise turned back. 'What do you mean? Was there someone in my garden? What were they doing?'

'Dunno, just looked like they were searching for something, like they had thrown a ball over or somethin.'

There was a little alley which ran around the back of the terrace and each house had a back gate or, as in Caroline's case, a side gate.

'Yes, I expect you're right; they probably lost something, and I was out so they couldn't ask me.'

'Yeah, spec so.' Mr Braithwaite replied as he returned to whatever he'd been doing previously.

Louise shivered. Perhaps someone had been in the house but perhaps not, perhaps someone in the garden. She checked the garden gate was securely locked from her side before going back inside.

Mr Braithwaite had unsettled her and so the idea of a distant walk appealed. 'Come on Buster – can't wait for Caroline. How about we drive to the Mendips and have a really long walk.' He wagged his tail vigorously when he heard the word walk.

Despite her determination to forget her problems, she couldn't resist a slight detour past George's house. She slowed down but there was no sign of him and no sign of his car in the road, even though, unusually, there were spaces. He must have already gone out, or perhaps he wasn't even in Bath, perhaps he was somewhere else. Her thoughts raced again, and she cursed to herself as she left the town behind.

I love it here she thought as she walked up the rocky slopes from velvet bottom to the top of the Mendips. It was sometimes possible to see Wales in the distance across the river on a clear day and she scanned the horizon. She enjoyed the rest of the day as she strode across the ancient hills and her black mood left her.

There was no further word from George and when she got home the unfinished bathroom was a cruel reminder of his disappearance. There'd been no message from Caroline and Louise wondered how she would spend her week off from the school. Perhaps she had got together with John after all. This thought inexplicably sent a shiver down her spine.

She'd only just got into bed when she had a text message. Since his last message she was sure it wouldn't be George but hoped it might be Caroline and it was.

Sorry - just found yr. msg. Wd have loved a walk but not today - feeling rubbish and tired. I plan to rest this half term but let's meet Friday as usual. Ben's school is Brampton Hall, is that Max's? If so they are same age and must know each other. Must tell John. Sorry for long text, night night. Xxx

Louise was pleased Caroline was alright but alarmed to have her fears confirmed about Ben. It meant it was almost certainly John's son who was the boy Max had talked about and very possibly the man who had accosted Harriet. She'd now just need to find out Tom's real name. Poor Caroline but I can't say anything until I'm certain and then I'll need to find a way to tell her that John is not the man she thinks he is. She pulled the duvet over her and tried to get warm but her body was ice cold.

WEDNESDAY 2ND NOVEMBER 2005

Sleep deserted her until well into the early hours and so had slept long past her usual early start. For a moment she worried she would be late for work but then remembered she had no booked clients. Half term is a bit of a blessing, she thought, even if I don't have school age children and won't get paid.

Having given up the idea of more sleep she emerged from her duvet cocoon to the sight of a dirty grey sky. It took away the delight she'd felt at having two days off and was at a loss as to how to fill them. She would have asked Caroline to do something, but she'd been quite clear about how she wanted to spend her time off. Though I suppose if we had met, she thought, I would have had to deal with my dilemma about what to tell her about John. She contemplated contacting some of her counselling friends but dismissed that idea quickly, as most of them would be at work.

She felt more alone than she had for a long time and blamed this mood on George. She'd got used to time on her own but since she'd met him, she'd enjoyed the company. As if he'd guessed her mood, Buster rubbed his head against her. She bent down and ruffled his coat and murmured, 'I know Buster, I always have you to do things with.' The deep black hole where she kept all her sadness since James's death, beckoned and she didn't want to be pulled into it today. She realised socialising would have helped and berated herself for not having kept up with as many friends as she could have done.

She caught sight of *The Girl with the Dragon Tattoo* lying on the dresser. She'd just finished it; it had been one of those hard to put down books and had felt sad when she'd got to the end. Her face lit up. I know I'll go into Bath and have a bookshop browse and perhaps get the book by Kazuo

Ishiguro about the child organ donors that has caused big discussions with some of my colleagues. The idea of a trip to a bookshop felt a positive thing to do and she started to get ready.

Her phone rang in the distance and she raced up the stairs and grabbed it from beside her bed. It was George. Her heart leapt but before she could answer he'd rung off. She dialled the number straight back, but it just rang and rang. Damn - how could he ring one minute and not be there the next? She held the phone in her hand while she collected her bag and coat. She hoped he wasn't the sort of guy who played cat and mouse games.

As she walked from her house, she saw one of the students from next door. He had already started down the road, so quickened her pace. 'Luke,' she shouted. He stopped and waited for her to catch up.

'Sorry to hold you up but Mr Braithwaite said one of you came into my garden on Saturday evening and he thought you were searching for something. Did you find it?'

He wrinkled up his face. 'In your garden? Nope, I don't think so, in fact I'm sure not. We had some friends round and we were all in the house playing music, but I will check with the others. Anyway, how would we have got in? You keep your back gate locked, don't you?'

'Yes, I do but I sometimes forget and leave it open. Don't worry, probably old Mr Braithwaite just being a bit of a troublemaker.' She added, 'I'm not accusing you of anything - just wondered if you'd knocked a ball over the fence or something.'

Luke smiled and nodded before he strode off, clearly feeling the matter was closed. She followed him at a slower pace until their paths took them in opposite directions.

Without Buster she was able to add interest to her trip into Bath with a walk through the twisting and secret paths that meandered through the botanical garden. She loved it there, where rocks were piled up above the path and waves of plants tumbled down over them like a green waterfall.

The garden had so many beautiful and unusual plants and always remained peaceful even in high summer when there were more people. In the summer the herbaceous border with the blues of delphiniums and the gleaming yellow and white daisies was spectacular, although there was nothing to see there now but brown dead twigs. There were only a few trees with leaves left on them and the occasional remaining autumn flowers, but the borders had become dull and disappointing One of the trees she loved the best was an old Medlar tree, whose squelchy and nasty tasting fruits had ripened in early autumn and then dropped. She stopped and watched the squirrels as they raced about in the branches. Buster would have had a field day chasing them.

A chill ran through her body. The weather had changed and the grey day had become darker and colder. The trees felt menacing and ugly and she had a sudden feeling she was being watched. She peered into the trees and bushes but saw no-one. The dark shadows, made by the few evergreens, no longer looked interesting or beautiful; just threatening. She quickened her pace and moved as fast as she could towards the exit. When she reached the gate, she glanced back and could have sworn she saw a figure move out of the shadows but when she looked again there was nobody there; she persuaded herself it was just her imagination and she was being ridiculous.

She kept up a fast pace and was out of breath by the time she reached the end of St James Square. She was reminded of the delicious cakes the coffee shop made and found herself drawn towards it.

When she placed her hand on the door she glanced through the window to her left and gasped. Caroline sat at one of the tables side on to the window; at least she thought it was Caroline. She looked different and looked again to be sure. Although she could only see part of her face, she looked tired and drawn despite wearing makeup. She wore a short skirt and flung over her shoulders was the smart mustard coloured coat she'd seen when in the Co-op.

Louise had her hand on the latch but something made her stop. Caroline looked as though she was waiting for someone so probably wouldn't welcome an uninvited guest! Then thought it was odd as she said she wouldn't be seeing John this week because of half-term but then thought she could be waiting for someone else.

She gave up the idea of a cake, she could always try again on the way back. As she retreated, she almost knocked over a man behind her, who she assumed was wanting to enter. 'Oh, sorry, I'm so sorry. I'm afraid I wasn't looking.' She glanced back to see if Caroline had noticed but it looked as though she hadn't. The man grunted and walked away from her up the road. She frowned, that was weird and rude, I thought he wanted to go into the shop.

Going to this independent bookshop always felt a treat and it was no different today. There was never a time they didn't greet customers with a warm smile, and she told the man behind the counter how much she appreciated that.

'Great, glad to hear it.' The man behind the counter beamed back.

Her steps felt lighter as she walked home with a copy of *Never Let Me Go* tucked under her arm. It was always good having a new novel to read. She reached the road where the café was but the idea of the cake no longer appealed as Caroline might still be there with whoever she was going to meet.

Her phone went as she reached the start of her road.

'*Hi Mum, I've heard from Henry. He's coming down this weekend and so I wondered if you're able to come over for a family Sunday lunch and bring George as well if he is free.*'

'*That would be lovely, Katy. Can't wait to see Henry and Emma, seems ages since we caught up with them. Don't know about George though. He's not around much at the moment. Seems to have gone out of my life in the last week.*'

'*That's a shame, I'm sorry. You sounded as if you really liked him, and we'd have loved to have met him. Perhaps he'll reappear – you never know.*'

Louise said nothing for a moment. '*OK, well, we'll see, just maybe not the man for me after all but it all feels slightly strange and a bit mysterious. How is Max? Is he enjoying his half term? I have tomorrow off as well and was wondering if I could do something with the children?*'

'*Max is fine, in fact he has got Ben here today, they seem to be getting on well and he is a very polite boy, quite a pleasure actually. Quite different from some of Max's other rather rowdy friends!*'

Louise reached in her pocket for her keys. Hearing Ben was at Max's threw her for a moment. '*I'm in my house now Katy, please go on.*'

'*Well, I was just going to say, not quite sure about tomorrow as Max and Ben seem to want to meet up again, but Milly would love to do something with you, I'm sure, if you don't mind just having one of them.*'

Louise frowned but made no comment. '*Just Milly then. That'd be lovely.*'

Louise agreed to the arrangements and then thought again about Max and Ben. She felt anxious about their friendship, but it was impossible to express her fears to Katy. So much of what she knew was confidential. However, Dave and Katy both knew what happened with Max, so they ought to be wary and she was sure they would be.

She now had a possible explanation for Caroline waiting in the café. If John's Ben was in fact the Ben Max was friends with, it meant John would have been free to meet up with Caroline. She must have been waiting for him but then she didn't look like someone waiting for a boyfriend and her change of style was weird. Perhaps this new style made her feel glamourous and sexy; nothing wrong with that. Louise remembered she had felt anxiety about getting ready to meet George on their first proper date and had chosen her clothes carefully. She smiled at the thought of the chaos of clothes in the bedroom while she tried to find the right thing to put on.

Coffee and a book always go well together, she thought, as she snuggled into a chair. She'd only just reached the end of the first page when there was a bang at the door. She cursed silently and got up to see who it was.

'Luke, hi come in.' She led him into the kitchen. He refused the chair she offered, just stood and shifted from foot to foot.

'Just to let you know I've spoken to the others and none of them went into your garden, so Mr Braithwaite must be mistaken, or it was someone else.' Luke stared at Louise and she sensed he wanted to ask her a question. 'It couldn't be the builder bloke, could it? I know you've been having a lot of work done and he is around quite often, perhaps he'd forgotten his key.' She could tell by the way he said it, he was fishing and had probably seen them together when not behaving like a builder and his employer.

'Yes maybe, I'll check with him but thanks for letting me know. You sure you won't have a coffee?'

His refusal was a relief as he was the student she had once heard describing her as a 'bit of a looker even if she was probably as old as his mother.' She'd felt awkward with him ever since. She tried to think whether she had ever told George about the house key she kept hidden in the garden but knew she hadn't.

Later in the evening she remembered about Henry and the Sunday lunch. Suppose I'd better let George know and got out her phone. It went straight to his voicemail. *'Hey George, you have an invite to Sunday lunch at my daughters on Sunday, Henry and his wife are down from London and Katy and Dave would like to meet you.'* She paused, then added ... *'Guess you're tied up with whatever but let me know if you can.'* Bet he won't even reply she thought and added, *'Did you by any chance come in through my garden gate on Saturday? My neighbour says he saw someone - cd it be you?'*

SATURDAY 5th NOVEMBER 2005

How lovely, she thought, a lazy breakfast and the paper, perhaps it's good not to have George here, but knew she kidded herself. She'd, in the end, quite enjoyed her few days off and a highlight had been time alone with Milly. Pity Caroline had cancelled saying she was exhausted and wanted an early night. There was definitely something going on with her and it worried her.

She munched her toast and rather flippantly read the paper until a story caught her eye.

"BODY OF DIVER FOUND IN POOL OF DEATH.
The body of a diver was found yesterday in Dorothea Quarry in the Nantlle Valley, North Wales. Dorothea has taken many lives over the years and because of its depth, hidden caves and tunnels, usually only attempted by experienced divers. It is possible that the body could be that of a Sgt. Bannerman, who disappeared whilst on an army exercise eight years ago.

Louise's breath quickened as she read the account and knew a panic attack was looming. An old and terrible fear gripped her as the past rushed towards her. She couldn't stop it. She struggled to get her breath under control and focused on the picture of James beside her bed but was whirled towards the memory of the event she wanted to avoid; the terror of nearly drowning.

She remembered sitting on the rock dabbling her feet into the water unaware that a huge wave had risen up behind her. Then gulping for air as she was engulfed in water and thrown off the rock into the deep water. She remembered being under the water surrounded by white bubbles that merged with the foam of the wave and left the taste of salt forever in her nightmares. Louise screwed up her eyes in an effort to concentrate – she must stop this and breathe – prevent a full panic attack. She told herself she had helped many clients manage their panic attacks so she could surely master this one. The thought of clients helped her. She breathed out as hard as she could until her body responded and forced a deep intake of air. She steadied her breath and counted five in and five out – slow and steady.

Her fear subsided and another memory gave her a glimpse of her father's arm as it scooped her up and back to safety. She felt hot and sweaty but shivered; the fear of water had never left her, no matter how often she'd taken it to her own therapy. She'd learned to manage the panic but that story in the paper of a death in a quarry had triggered it again.

The panic left her exhausted and was not helped by another night where sleep had escaped her. Mr Braithwaite's tale had unnerved her and she had spent time trying to work out how someone could have got in. She decided it had to have been through the garden. If the garden gate had been unlocked or they'd found a way in somehow, they could well have been searching for the hidden spare house key.

She yawned and stretched out her arms. She'd love to have sunk back into the comfort of a second sleep but she knew Buster would need a walk and so reluctantly got up.

She had Buster's lead in her hand when there was a knock on the door.

'Dave! What a surprise, not often you call in on your mother-in-law! Come in and have a coffee, think Buster will cope with a delayed walk.'

Dave pulled up a chair at the kitchen table and sat while Louise made coffee. She saw he looked tired and drawn and for the first time she noticed that he had areas of grey sprinkled in his sandy coloured hair. He had always been a handsome man and it made him look perhaps more distinguished. She'd had reservations at the beginning but wasn't surprised her daughter had fallen for him, although she sometimes felt she wasn't his favourite person. Perhaps he'd recognised her earlier difficulties and found it hard to put it behind him.

Each with a full mug in front of them Louise searched his face for an explanation. 'Now we have coffee, I wonder what brings you to my door looking, if I may say, slightly grim?'

Dave's face shifted and he smiled. 'Sorry, I just wanted to run something past you. It's about Ben. I suspect you know more about him than the rest of us.' He raised his eyebrows.

Louise put her mug down while she thought. 'Mmm. I probably do know a little more but I'm afraid I can't tell you more than you know already.'

'I sort of guessed that but is it okay if I just talk, because I think there are things you ought to know?'

Her body tensed and wondered what he might come out with.

Dave cleared his throat. 'Ben came to our house last Wednesday and all went well. I was at work but Katy seemed pleased and thought he was a polite and altogether lovely boy.'

He stopped and Louise saw to her surprise he looked embarrassed. 'Go on.'

He shifted in his chair and had another sip of coffee before continuing. 'I do remember what you said but because they got on so well, Katy agreed Max could go to Ben's house the next day. He told her he had a huge garden and a fantastic den which he wanted Max to see. Without thinking about it Katy agreed. When I found out, it was too late to do anything. I wish now I had been able to stop it, after all, we knew enough about the stepdad and his quick temper.' He put his head into his hands.

Louise had felt more anxious by the minute. 'What happened Dave, just tell me.'

Dave shook his head. 'It wasn't what you were worried about, but Max said it was very strange. Let me tell you the full story.'

Louise nodded and Dave told her that Katy had dropped Max off after she'd dropped Milly.

So that's why Katy was happy to drop Milly off, she thought. She knew I wouldn't be happy with the plan.

Dave continued with the story. He said that Ben had come to the door and put his finger to his lips and whispered to Max to come in. Katy had hoped to meet the stepfather and to agree a time to pick Max up but he never appeared. She told the boys she would return at four o'clock for Max.

Dave paused and checked Louise was taking this in and when she nodded, he continued. 'Max told us that, despite the cold Ben took him straight to his den. Max had imagined it would be like a hut or summerhouse, but it was a homemade den at the bottom of the garden in a small wood. It was really a cave, with a tunnelled entrance under a fallen tree. In order to get in they had to push past some dying nettles and Max was stung. Max didn't particularly like the idea of going in but he followed Ben. Inside it was quite spacious and dry and not particularly cold.'

The nettles reminded Louise of the story Harriet had told her. This must be the same child and he must have got the idea of using nettles to hurt another boy by being stung going into his den. It looked more and more certain that Caroline's John was the father of this Ben. She gave a long sigh and before Dave could ask her what the matter was she leaned forward in her chair to ask what it was like inside the den.

'Max said Ben had made it reasonably cosy. There was an old chair and some bits of worn out carpet on the mud floor, and he had put a large camping light on an old box. When Ben first put it on, Max saw the cave had loads of pictures stuck to the walls.'

Dave stopped and had a gulp of coffee. 'The pictures were mostly of two women, although I think Max said there was also a picture of an animal. Max asked Ben about them. He wasn't that keen to talk but then told Max one woman was his mother, who had died when he was little and the other was his nanny, who left him. What gave Max the creeps and what he told me about when he got back, was the pictures had each been slashed across their faces. He didn't know what to say and Ben didn't explain.'

Louise wasn't sure what she could say, it all sounded very odd. She asked Dave if his stepfather ever appeared.

Dave shook his head. 'No, apparently he didn't and I wonder if he even knew that Ben had invited Max there. You need to hear the rest of the story and I apologise if it seems a bit longwinded.'

Louise wondered what was coming next and urged him to continue.

'Right. According to Max they were playing some sort of war game, hiding from one another and Max was hiding under a fallen log. Ben had apparently burrowed into a dip in the ground on the side of a slope.' Dave stopped but again Louise urged him to go on.

'This is the odd bit. Max heard Ben give a loud scream followed by a sob. Max thought he was injured but when he found him, he lay face down on the ground beating the earth with his fists and had something clenched in his hand. Max didn't quite know what to do but when he said he'd go and find his dad. Ben shouted, "Not him. No." I think Max was at a loss so just sat with him until he calmed down.'

'What was the thing he had in his hand?'

'That's strange too. When he unclenched his hand, Max said saw it was a dirty rag.'

'A rag?'

This sounded very odd to Louise and she wondered what the significance of the rag could be and asked Dave what he thought.

'Apparently, Ben was certain it was the scarf his nanny often wore, or what was left of it.'

'A scarf? Did Ben explain to Max what was going on?'

Dave nodded, 'Ben told Max when he saw it, he'd felt angry and sad. He had hated her leaving and felt angry she'd gone. Ben didn't understand how it had got there. It was her favourite scarf and he didn't think she would ever have left it behind. He said she wore it when they were playing. She used to put it over her mouth when she pretended to be a gangster or some such thing when they played in the woods.'

Dave stopped and Louise sat quietly for a moment and reflected on the rather complicated story she'd just heard. 'It does sound very odd but I suppose the Nanny could have lost it while they were playing.'

'Yes, I hope you're right. The stepfather makes me feel uneasy though.'

Louise couldn't say much to Dave as most of what she'd learned and suspected had been told to her in a confidential setting.

'Whatever the scarf means he is clearly a very disturbed boy. If he felt very upset when the nanny left, seeing the scarf could well have caused a strong reaction.'

Dave continued to look worried, so Louise asked him what he imagined might have happened.

'I dunno. I'm a policeman and hear and see so many awful things I tend to think the worst in some situations and as this involves my son, well... I suppose Ben's strong reaction made me immediately suspicious.'

Louise nodded, 'Several things could be going on here that are not necessarily sinister. It could be about the attachment this boy had for her. From what Max saw in the car park Ben's stepfather is not a nice character and not a good stepfather but it doesn't make him a killer, which I can tell is what you're thinking. I'm guessing the social services have now been involved and they will keep an eye. I think Ben is a disturbed boy who might be finding it hard dealing with the tragic life events that have been thrown at him. The simple explanation about the nanny is she left because she was dissatisfied with her employer. I don't think he's the sort of man that I would like to work for.'

The smile Dave gave was of relief. 'Yes, you're probably right. I think when Max came back distressed, it alarmed me and I immediately jumped into work mode. The pictures are odd though.'

Louise answered slowly and thoughtfully. 'Yes, I was just thinking about the slash across the pictures, and it probably ties into what I've just said. If the pictures were of his mother who died and the nanny that left, then both women he cared for left him, which would explain his anger. He probably blames himself in some way, perhaps thinking he was a bad person, and they didn't want to stay with him.'

'But I believe his mother died - she didn't leave him.'

'I know, but people do get angry at someone for leaving them when they die, and children often believe it was something they did wrong which caused the death. He may even feel it was his fault the nanny left, although it's far more likely to be his difficult stepfather as I said, and surely if anything untoward had happened you'd have had the nanny's relatives knocking at your door. Tell me, does Max want to continue to see Ben?'

'I think at first, he said he never wanted to see him again but now he thinks he might invite him to us in the school holidays. The stepfather never did show up. Katy went back at four and Max was waiting for her at the gate.'

Having reassured Dave, Louise wished she felt more at ease herself.

SUNDAY 6TH NOVEMBER 2005

Henry's Emma always wore stylish clothes and Louise often felt dowdy in comparison. Dissatisfied with what she saw in the wardrobe she wished she'd been more discerning with her shopping choices. In the end she pulled out a plain green dress that she'd always thought looked good with long boots and added a colourful scarf to brighten it up. She really needed a haircut and wondered if she should try something different now the red in her hair was softer and perhaps even something to hide the grey.

Her phone pinged. It was a message from George.

Sorry not replied sooner. Will do my best to get to you for the lunch. Wd love to meet your family. Just text me the postcode - will meet you there xxx.

Louise frowned as she read it and texted. *Wd be gd if you picked me up!* She waited a moment for the reply.

Yeah, but in case I get delayed – don't want you waiting around.

It wasn't the answer she had hoped for - she'd have liked to have gone together. She couldn't think of a reply that wouldn't sound petty so she put a couple of kisses followed by her daughter's address and postcode. She sighed – at least he'd said he'd come. She picked her phone up and sent another text to Katy to let her know there was now an extra person.

Max opened the door and immediately grabbed Buster's lead. 'Give him to me, Granny, I'll take care of him.' Having got rid of her coat, she walked into their lounge where she found Henry and Dave. When Henry saw her, he leapt up. 'Mum. Lovely to see you' – and he gave her an enormous hug.

Louise hugged him back and laughed. He had always been demonstrative in his affection, and she loved him for it.

'Come and sit next to me.' Henry patted the other side of the sofa. 'Now tell me all about your dastardly builder. Dave says he is not entirely the flavour of the month, but I hope we get to meet him. Are we?'

'Dave, you should know better than to gossip about your mother-in-law.' She smiled as she spoke. 'Actually, it was all going swimmingly but then he suddenly took off somewhere and I've hardly had any contact until this morning when he texted to say he would be here for lunch, so we'll wait and see!'

Dave murmured, 'Typical of a builder to disappear with no warning.' She ignored him as she spoke to Henry. 'Anyway, tell me what you've been up to. Seen any good psychopaths recently?'

Henry laughed. 'A few. What about you? Surely you get to see the odd few too?' This was the sort of banter they'd had ever since he became a psychiatrist. She knew he worked with some seriously unwell people.

Louise would have made a facetious remark, but Katy and Emma appeared from the kitchen.

Katy remained at the door and blew her a kiss before she returned the way she'd come. As Louise had anticipated, Emma was dressed immaculately and coincidentally, also in green. It was a woollen dress, well cut and obviously expensive. She went over to Louise and gave her a hug and a kiss.

'Hi Louise, good to see you. You look well. Must be the new boyfriend!'

Louise smiled; she was fond of Emma but wished she hadn't just said that. 'Oh, I suppose everyone knows. Can't keep anything secret nowadays.'

Emma let out a giggle. 'It's only because we are all so pleased. We would love it if you had found someone special.' With those words, she turned and went back into the kitchen.

Dave remembered Louise hadn't got a drink and he also disappeared into the kitchen.

'Seriously though, Henry, how is work going? I hope not too many complex patients?'

'No, all going well actually, and I enjoy my work immensely. How about you, Mum, you got any difficult ones?'

Louise thought for a moment. She knew Henry would never repeat anything he'd heard and she'd never give him any detail he could tie to a name but sometimes it was good to tell him a little.

'No not really but there's one I'm not particularly keen on. He's arrogant and difficult to like - a situation that isn't always easy, as I'm sure you know.'

Henry pursed his lips and nodded.

'However, now I've heard more of his history it is easier to empathise and I think my problem is mainly that he reminds me of someone I knew and disliked. There is something else however, I would love to chat to you about - a dilemma I've got.'

'Fire ahead, if you think I can help.' At this moment Dave came in with the white wine she'd requested, and Louise indicated to Henry she couldn't speak now. 'Sorry, Louise, have I interrupted something? Here's your drink. I can take myself off if you like?'

'No, of course not. I'll get a chance to talk to Henry later. Have you told him what has been going on with Max and Ben?'

'Yes, I have, in fact I had started to tell Henry a bit about Ben just before you arrived.'

Henry looked up. 'Yes, sounds as though he's a bit screwed up but I gather he has had, or is having quite a difficult life, which probably explains his behaviour at school. Don't like the sound of the dad though and I think it is good the school have got in touch with Social Services.'

Dave nodded. 'It's good to get your opinions and I am relieved because you've both said virtually the same about Ben; his behaviour being due to his losses. I think we'll just invite him here in the future. I don't think Max wants to go back to his house anyway.'

Emma bustled in from the kitchen again. 'Hey Louise, do you think George will get here, as lunch is nearly ready and we were wondering whether we should wait or not?'

'I'll text him but he was worried he might be late, so perhaps we can wait a bit longer and then start without him.'

Louise got out her phone but before she started to text, the doorbell went and Dave got up and returned with George, who held a large bunch of flowers and a bottle of wine in his hands.

'I'm so sorry if I'm late; the traffic on the motorway wasn't great, even though it's a Sunday.'

Kate joined them and put her hand out to him. 'Hi George, I'm Kate, Louise's daughter and it's great you could come, we've looked forward to meeting you. Oh, thanks - are those for me? That's kind.' and she took the flowers and the wine and went back to the kitchen.

Uncertain how she should greet him since his disappearance, Louise looked at his face for guidance. Heavens, he looks as if he doesn't know what to do either, she thought. She walked up to him, took him by the arm and pulled him forwards to introduce him to everyone. Dave offered a drink but Louise was pleased to see he shook his head. 'No, not for me thank you. I know I'm late and don't want to hold things up more than I have, but perhaps one with the meal? I think I have already upset your mother-in-law enough by being late!' They laughed and Dave led the way into the spacious kitchen.

After lunch they all went on a walk and when, at one point, Katy walked beside Louise, she whispered, 'I think he's lovely, Mum, don't know what the matter was but it all seems fine now.'

'Yes, it does but I do wonder where he's been. He said he was on a motorway somewhere.' She looked back over her shoulder and saw him in deep conversation with Milly who skipped along beside him.

Katy gave Louise a quick hug. 'I shouldn't worry about it, I'm sure he'll tell you when he wants to.'

Back at the house Dave made his apologies but said he needed to take Max back to school for the firework display and hoped everyone wouldn't have gone when he got back. Katy disappeared into the kitchen.

'I'm afraid Emma and I will have to make a move soon too - quite a long drive back to London.' Mumbled Henry. Louise pulled a face unable to hide her disappointment. 'Ok we'll stay for a cuppa and hopefully a slice of my sister's cake and maybe Dave will be back by then.'

Louise and Emma went to help Kate and returned with trays of cups, plates and a cake, and settled themselves on the sofa. 'See I've lost the comfy seat then.' Said Henry and walked towards the window. He picked up a newspaper that lay on a hardbacked chair and then moved the chair nearer to the others. Once seated he flipped through the paper.

Katy had just poured the first cup when Henry's voice broke into the conversation. 'God, what an awful way to die. Did you see this?' He waved the paper at the group. 'They've found the body of a diver in a quarry in Wales. It sounds as though it could be a diver who disappeared eight years ago. The quarry has a nickname too - the Pool of Death. Apparently, there are a few deaths every year, hence the name.'

Louise shuddered. 'I know, I saw it yesterday – just too awful to think about so please can you stop talking about it. When I read it I was reminded of what happened when I was little and I only just avoided having a full-on panic attack. You know how much I have a fear of going under water. In fact, I don't know what I'd do if anything like that happened to me again.' Henry mumbled an apology and put the paper down.

'Still with the horror of it in her head, Louise was startled by a crash and turned to see what had happened. George had dropped the cup of tea he'd just been handed - the cup had smashed and its contents had spilled onto the carpet. He leapt to his feet and apologised profusely but his clumsiness had irritated her. Katy asked Henry to fetch another cup and saucer and a cloth and reminded them that they were in the middle of tea and best not to talk about something so horrible. She glanced across at Milly who was in the corner of the room with a doll in her hand and hoped she hadn't heard.

Dave had not reappeared, and Henry and Emma said they had to go and Louise and George decided it was also time for them to take themselves off. They supposed that Dave was perhaps delayed because he had waited to see the display himself.

Once outside Louise turned to George, 'Are you coming back to mine or are you going to disappear off again?' Louise couldn't help the bite in her words.

In place of an answer, George wrapped her in his arms and kissed her soundly on the lips. 'Well, not if you're going to be a crabby witch.'

Louise struggled but the pleasure of being held broke her resistance. When she eventually freed herself, she suggested they make their way back to her house. She headed towards her car with a smile on her face. George waved when he got to his then turned back to say he needed to pick up some things from his house but wouldn't be long.

As soon as she walked into the house she noticed the smell. It wasn't the normal house smell, more earthy or perhaps flowery. It smelt familiar but she couldn't place it. Buster put his head down and sniffed around the ground floor, as though he too could sense something odd. She wandered around but nothing looked out of place either downstairs or up.

In her study her eyes tracked the desk, the chair, and the bookcase. Everything seemed to be as it should be. She hesitated when she reached the jar in which she kept the keys to the cabinet. A ripple of fear ran through her; it had been moved. She swung round and stared at the cabinet. The keys were in the lock; someone had been there. She would never have left them like that. She tried to remember when she had last locked the cabinet and wondered if she could have left them there without thinking? I've never done it before and I always leave the jar in the same place. No, I am sure this was done by someone else. When she thought of the unlocked cabinet and all her confidential notes, she felt sick. Who could possibly have been here? She wished George was here.

The large wine glass in front of her was half empty when George walked in. 'See you couldn't wait then' and he leant down and kissed her.

'What? No. Well, yes but....' Her voice quivered. 'I think someone was here, in the house. No, I'm certain someone was here.' Her voice went up an octave. 'In this house, George.' She brushed away the tears that had started to run down her face.

He sat down opposite her and took both her hands in his. 'You really think someone came in here? How do you know?'

'My keys were in my filing cabinet and not in the jar where I keep them, and the jar was in a different place.' He frowned and shook his head. 'Have you looked to see where they might have broken in?'

'Yes, I have but I couldn't see anything. You go, please, George, you go and look too.

'Okay, I'll go now'

But she put out her arm to stop him. 'Wait, there's something you don't know. My neighbour, Mr Braithwaite, thought he saw someone in the garden the other afternoon. I dismissed it but someone could have been here.'

Once George had gone, she sighed and murmured; 'I can't believe it. Surely, I've imagined it but that smell, flowery and familiar; definitely doesn't belong here.' The smell was fresh as if a door had been left open and let countryside in. She tried to think of when she last went to her cabinet. Possibly the last time she saw any clients, but that was before she'd had the days off. Then it came to her; she'd forgotten to add something to Amanda's notes and had opened it then. That was yesterday, so could she have just forgotten, but she wouldn't have moved the pot.

'I can't see any sign of a break-in, Lou, and as you say all the doors are locked.   Could it be you just forgot this once and maybe moved the pot?'

'I've never done it before but suppose it's possible but then there was that smell.' He raised his eyebrows and she realised she hadn't told him about the smell.'

He listened to her explanation. 'I didn't smell anything but I suppose it could have come in from outside when you opened the door. You say you checked you hadn't left any other door open, and I've just confirmed there's nothing open.'

Louise realised he was trying to calm things down and went along with it as she didn't feel she had the energy for anything else, and anyway he was probably right.

'Think I'll have another glass of wine.' She held out her empty glass.   George refilled it and at the same time poured himself a beer.

Louise moved towards the sitting room, but George stopped her.

'I think I know what will take your mind off things. Follow me.' He caught hold of the hand free of wine and led the way upstairs.

Louise had wanted to ask him so many things and especially where he'd been this last week. She had particularly wanted him to know how cross she'd been with him but somehow now it all seemed unimportant, and she followed him up the stairs.

WEDNESDAY 9TH NOVEMBER 2005

'You okay in there? Sounds like you've trapped a magpie.' George flung open the door to the shower.

'Hold on a minute, just because you built it, doesn't give you rights and if you don't like my singing, I suggest you leave right now, cause I'm not stopping. I'm far to ....' Her words were lost as he stepped in and pulled the door shut.

Later they towelled each other dry and giggled as they did so. 'Think we must have covered most of the Kama Sutra moves and in such a tight space too,' muttered Louise with not a little pride in her voice. 'Maybe even more' George murmured.

His footsteps clattered on the uncarpeted stairs as he went to make breakfast for them both and the joy of him being there with her spread warmth down to her toes. She pulled on her favourite cream Cashmere jumper, the one which kept her warm while she listened to clients. This is going to work; it's really going to work she thought. The last two evenings were glorious and the finished bathroom is perfect - just wish he would tell me more about where he's been.

George enveloped her in an enormous bear like hug followed by a long kiss as soon as she entered the kitchen, his hands smoothing the soft wool of her jumper. 'I'll just have my cup of tea, and I'll be off,' he murmured in her ear. 'See you tonight, same time, same place.' He made it sound like a secret assignation, so in the same vein she replied, 'I'm the one wearing a pink leotard'. She didn't want to change the tone of their banter but she couldn't stop herself. She wanted to know.

'George, I know you're in a hurry but is there any chance you could tell me where you've been and what is going on? Something doesn't feel right and it's making me anxious.'

He had his hand on the door handle ready to leave but turned back. His face creased up and showed worry lines Louise had never seen before. 'All I can say, Lou, is that it has nothing to do with us and please believe me, I don't want anything to spoil what we have. I'm just asking you to trust me for the moment. I will tell you as soon as I'm able to.' Then he was gone, and the door shut behind him.

She wanted to trust him; she really did but why wouldn't he tell her what was going on. With that thought she wandered into her counselling room to wait for her first client.

Tim certainly appeared less stressed than he was his last session and the way he replied to her usual opening question supported her view.

'I'm certainly feeling more centred than I was when I saw you last - everything seems to be going all right now.'

Louise asked him whether he'd thought more about retirement but he told her he'd put it on the back burner. She checked what he wanted to discuss and guessed correctly it was Paul.

She watched to see how he'd reacted when he mentioned Paul and was reassured his face showed no sign of anxiety or strain.

'As you know he and I were all over the place, but he has calmed down and even apologised for his behaviour.'

That's a surprise. Never thought he would, thought Louise. 'Tell me how the sessions have gone since, and did you explore the 'taking down a peg or two'?'

'Yes, I did. I feel we are beginning to get somewhere at last. I haven't changed my mind about him being a nasty piece of work and I think his relationship must have been hell for his wife and child, but I do question his guilt.'

'That's interesting, I'd like to hear how that's come about but you didn't fully answer my question about his taking her down a peg or two.'

'Oh yes, I'm sorry. It turns out it was something he'd referred to in earlier sessions. His wife had adored their dog and to take her down a peg he told her it had got run over and died. In fact, that wasn't true. He'd actually taken it to the dog rescue and told them he'd found it wandering about on the street. It wasn't chipped so they couldn't have traced it back to him.'

Louise imagined what it must have been like for Paul's wife and her son to lose a pet. She thought about Buster and what she would have felt if it had happened to her.

'That sounds very cruel Tim.'

'Yes, I agree. Apparently, both mother and child were devastated. Paul told them it must have wandered off and onto the road. Later he'd changed his story and told her he'd had it put down, and if she didn't 'toe the line' then other things she loved might go the same way.'

Louise felt the heat of anger flood her body. 'It does seem incredible that you are still unsure of his guilt. It sounds as though he was implying something might happen to the child.'

Tim agreed but reminded Louise she had said bad people were not necessarily killers and he had not actually killed the dog but taken it to a place it would have been looked after.

Louise pursed her lips but nodded as Tim continued.

'In subsequent sessions we spent time exploring the hate he felt towards his wife. It is not an uncommon scenario. He had an abusive mother, and his childhood was pretty horrific. I think now he sees the control he imposed over his wife and son is connected. He now seems to be using our sessions in a more positive way.'

Louise frowned. The reason for his behaviour sounded right but she wasn't sure there could have been enough sessions for genuine change to happen and asked Tim again why he doubted his guilt again.

Tim shifted in his chair, sat back and tried to look relaxed, but the way he ran his hands through his hair gave Louise the impression he was unsure she was going to accept his theory. 'He said they had found his DNA on her body but told me he hadn't seen her for months and believes it must have been planted.'

Louise couldn't help the sigh that escaped. 'This sounds like he's trying to manipulate you again and it doesn't sound credible this hadn't been fully explored during his trial.'

'Yes, I know and I agree but it would be hard to prove, I guess. He picked up the glass of water on the table beside him and took a sip before continuing. 'He seems determined to follow it up though. He tells me he's met a guy in prison who had been a private detective at one time. He got banged up for armed assault but is now out on parole and Paul has asked him if he would investigate further.'

Louise pursed her lips. 'This doesn't sound good and I'm not sure what he hopes to gain by it. It's important that you don't get involved in his schemes Tim and your therapy with him doesn't veer away from being therapeutic. You are there to help him manage his situation now and to help him deal with some of the hatred he feels, which has erupted into a severe grief reaction and not collude with him.

Tim nodded and admitted he found the case fascinating and had probably been manipulated a bit.

'Don't be hard on yourself, people with personality disorders can be deceptive and difficult to read and also, of course, be very charming.' She smiled to reassure him.

While she sipped a mug of coffee at the end of her day, she couldn't stop thinking about the story Tim had told her. What a crazy world they were dealing with.

WEDNESDAY 16TH NOVEMBER 2005

It was Ed's fifth session today. Louise no longer felt nervous about seeing him, despite his angry outburst last time. She realised the more she heard of his life story the sadder she felt for him.

'Hi Ed, come on in'. He strode past her, threw his coat over the back of the chair and slumped down. He waited until she was seated, looked directly at her and gave, what she thought was a false grin. She was reminded of a book where the key character found a drawing where the vicar had depicted himself as a wolf preaching to his congregation of sheep. Am I the sheep? This man always put such a variety of different animals into her mind; there was a panther, cat, snake and now a wolf.

Louise smiled, which she hoped did not look sheep like. 'Good to see you. I hope you had a pleasant half-term and you were able to tell your stepson about your girlfriend and it went well.'

There was a long pause and Louise wondered what was in his head.

'Yes, it went well, thanks. I did tell him and he seemed fine with it. In fact, we spent a day all together and he seemed happy.'

She said she was glad, but then wondered whether he had told the truth because his fingers played with the edge of his suit jacket in an agitated way, but she continued. 'At the end or our last session, we had started discussing your parents and you had begun to tell me what a terrible childhood you had. I wonder if you would like to explain what you mean by that?'

After another long pause, he opened his mouth to speak but instead leapt to his feet and in one movement he was in front of her. 'Sorry, Louise, could I possibly use your loo?' He towered over her and her heart started to beat at a faster rate. She took a deep breath, so her voice was steady, before she replied.

'Of course, it is just down the hallway, next door on the right.' Her heart pounded and she took an even deeper breath. That was awkward, I've never seen anyone move so fast. I wonder if he did need to go as urgently as he made out. Why can't I shake the feeling I'm walking across a frozen lake and the ice might crack at any moment.

She watched the clock tick the minutes away and wondered what could be the matter with him? After ten minutes she wondered if she should go and see if everything was okay. She started to get up, but he reappeared so she sat down again.

'Sorry I'd forgotten to go before I left the office.'

She gave a weak smile and nodded to show she understood but it wasn't what she felt. She was sure he'd used it as an excuse to avoid the subject she'd just brought up.

'Just before you left the room, I mentioned your childhood and your parents. Do you think you could manage to talk about them now?'

He stared out of the window for so long she thought he might never answer but she held the silence. She'd once held a silence for nearly a whole session with a client and it had been very productive and helpful, but this wasn't like that. She was about to speak when he finally replied.

'All right if you want. It's not a pretty story - in fact rather a boring one.' He shifted about and she held her breath, uncertain what he was going to do next but he settled down and started to speak.

'I don't think they really wanted to have a child and my mother gave me the impression my father had been pretty cruel to her while she was pregnant. I believe the beatings started as soon as I could toddle but it may have been before that. Anyway, I don't remember a day when I wasn't hit or beaten by him and as I got older, the beatings got worse and worse. My mother used to stand there like the pathetic creature she was.   I never forgave her for allowing it to happen.

After he'd beaten me, I'd be locked in the dark in the cupboard under the stairs. I was terrified and screamed for help. No help ever came, and I sort of got used to it and quite liked the fact I was shut well away from them.   I was in there all day sometimes and then when they had eaten, he would drag me out and force me to eat their leftovers.'

He paused and made eye contact and she felt he had just checked she was moved by what he said and felt a quiver of anxiety. He gave her one more glance and continued.

'I was at a local primary school but I think I became a nuisance to them and they finally sent me home. It was then my parents sent me to a boarding school. I was only six and it was worse than worse.   I know I was a difficult kid but no-one wanted to be my friend, apart from a teacher who came into our dorm each night and picked out one of us to take to his own bed.

Louise felt a tightness in her throat and she blinked to stop the tear that threatened to fall as he continued.

'I wasn't often picked out but what he did when we got to his room was frightening and disgusting.   There was no-one I could tell and none of the other children talked about it and so it just went on without anyone saying anything. As I grew older I knew I had to fight back. I started by taking control of my peers. I think they were quite frightened of me and it felt good to be the one calling the shots. I eventually managed to arrange it so it was always one of the others who was picked for his bedtime abuse.   On top of this, when I went home my father would continue with his beatings and then I would long to go back to school even though it was an unsafe place. Eventually I managed to get my own back.'

As the story unfolded, the various emotions which had swept through her had begun to make her feel sick. Hearing such awful abuse, it was no surprise he had anger issues. Whatever she said now would sound trite but she knew she needed to say something.

'Ed, this is an awful story and what happened to you sounds too terrible for words. It is extremely brave of you to tell me all this and I imagine it must have been very hard for you to do so. You do realise none of it was your fault? Sadly, abused children often feel it is, and I wonder if you perhaps thought it was?'

His head went down and his jaw moved as he clenched his teeth. She held her breath, then his head snapped up and he looked straight at her. 'Yes, I think I did at first but then I realised it was them and only them and I could see clearly what I needed to do.'

'You saw clearly what you needed to do?'

'Well…' he paused. Louise saw he watched her reactions carefully and realised he enjoyed telling her, perhaps even enjoyed making her feel ill. '…. with the teacher I let myself be taken to his room one night and watched as he got the part of his body ready, he wanted me to attend to. I pretended to comply but then I sunk my teeth in hard. He instantly pulled away, howling like a banshee. I ran out of the room and he didn't appear again that night or in the school for a long time. He obviously couldn't report it to anyone and when he returned to his teaching role after a period off sick, he was a different person and never bothered any of us in that way again.'

'That way?'

'Yes, well he did bother me I suppose because he reported me for disruptive and disturbing behaviour and as one of the boy's parents had also complained about me, they got Social Services involved and sent me to a counsellor.'

'I'm glad they did. Were you able to disclose what had been going on both at school and at home?'

'No, I didn't tell anyone, in fact I never have until today. The counsellor was hopeless, he just didn't have a clue and just treated me like an idiot, so I wasn't going to tell him a thing.'

Louise shifted in her chair. 'I'm glad you've been able to tell me and I wonder how it feels, if you have never told this story before?'

The snake peered out. 'I feel good about telling it and you are so easy to talk to, Louise, a great listener. I think you must have loads of friends, in fact the montage of photos in your toilet shows you do.'

She felt the jolt in her body – that must have been what he was doing for such a long time - looking at her photo montage. For a moment she couldn't think who the pictures were of, she had put it together such a long time ago. She decided not to comment about it as he hadn't really answered the question she'd asked.

'I'm glad you have managed to tell someone. It can't have been easy to hold onto such a huge amount of baggage for so long. What about your father, did he stop?' She tensed, as she realised there was more of this awful story to come.

'He did. When I next went home, I felt so strong I believed I could do anything and so when he got his belt out to hit me, I grabbed it and lashed out at him. I used the buckle against him and it hit his face and tore a chunk out of his chin. He never hit me again.'

His eyes glistened as if what he said gave him a thrill.

You said your mother just stood by and watched. Could you not have told her about what was going on at the school?'

'I tried once but she told me I was making things up. I think in a way, I feel most angry with her because she never ever came to my defence; just abandoned me to my fate. She kept telling me she loved me but never once showed me she did.'

'It must have been hard to feel abandoned by those meant to protect you. So, tell me what happened after you left school? It seems you completely turned your life around, which is amazing after such a bad beginning.'

He puffed himself up. 'Thank you. I suppose I was lucky; I've always had a mind which retained facts. I got a scholarship to Cambridge to study Law. I never lived at home again; I got work in Cambridge during the vac and then got articles with a firm in London. I stayed with them for a while and then came to Bath, where I am now.'

Louise told him again she was impressed by this and by his determination to change his life. She felt she now understood his arrogance and the way he postured when he got or knew he deserved praise. She suspected the only praise he'd ever received was from himself.

'I think you told me in the last session your parents died in a car accident. Did you ever see them again, after you'd become an independent man?' This question brought Ed back from wherever his mind had taken him and jerked upright when she spoke.

'Yes, I did but only once. It was just before they died. I was then living in Bath and I thought I'd visit my mother as I'd heard she hadn't been well and there were things I wanted to ask her. She did write the odd letter to me but I never answered them. I'd arranged to go when my Father wasn't around. She wasn't particularly pleased to see me and criticised me for not coming sooner. She seemed incapable of understanding my life as a child had been unbearable. She kept saying my father wasn't a bad man and I was a difficult child. I told her I'd had been disappointed in her and asked why she had never defended me. She told me she was too frightened and didn't think he was actually doing anything very harmful. I asked her about the time I tried to tell her what was happening in the school but again, said she thought I was making it up.'

Louise again felt heat spread through her body. How must it have been for a child to be subjected to such atrocious abuse with no protection from anyone at all. It was a story she had heard so many times from adults and children and it always sickened her.

'I imagine it must have been very hard for you to hear, Ed. I guess you were hoping to find answers and hear she loved you.' His face changed and it was as if all the animals she'd seen in him were tearing across his face but his eyes were those of the panther.

When he spoke again, she expected his voice to be loud and strong but his reply was softly spoken. She was reminded of how quickly he turned from panther to kitten last time and it felt dangerous.

'Yes, but they got what they deserved in the end.'

Louise felt she wanted to ignore this remark as although an awful thing to say, she could understand it. 'I think you said it was a car accident. Do you know what happened?'

His smile was as brittle as ice. 'Yes, I do know. It actually happened the same day that I saw them. I was furious at my mother's inability to understand what I'd been through, so when I left I went for a long walk and didn't get home until after dark. Shortly after I returned there was a knock at the door. It was the police to say that they'd been killed in a car accident. I think the car had skidded on some ice and spun into the path of an oncoming lorry.

Louise couldn't take this in. 'I am so sorry. Whatever you felt about them, it must have been awful to hear they'd died.'

She thought she caught a look of surprise as he put his head down and uttered, 'It was, it was quite awful. I know I hated them but I mean, I wouldn't have wanted them to die like that, they must have been terrified.'

Louise waited for a moment before she said, 'This has been a hard session and it may stay with you for a while, so please be careful as you make your way home as many people find they can feel slightly disorientated after a session like this, especially as you say you have never talked about any of it before'.

'Thank you, Louise, I will. You're so thoughtful and caring.' With those words he put on his coat, thrust his head up and walked out of the house and down the street.

Back in her counselling room she flopped down in her chair; totally exhausted. What a terrible, terrible story. Poor man, to experience so much abuse and trauma. Despite not particularly liking him, she hoped she could help him. When she wrote up her notes she saw next week would be his sixth session; the last one. She would normally have reminded a client and offered more sessions if she felt they needed more and was cross with herself for not mentioning it. She would need to talk to him at the beginning of his next session, she thought his work may not want to foot the bill as they had only agreed six but she was sure he could afford to pay for himself. He definitely needed a lot more sessions to deal with all he'd talked about today and then thought, clients often kept the really awful stuff until their sessions were nearly up.

Louise walked to the gym and wished she'd texted George to say she was too tired to go.

Several people waved out to her from their bikes but George wasn't amongst them. The two bikes they usually rode had been left free. They looked abandoned and she felt reluctant to get on one. 'It'll be like flogging a dead horse,' she muttered, as she hauled her reluctant body up onto the saddle.

When it had finally dawned on her he was not going to appear she stamped down hard on the pedals. She worried something had happened at first but then thought he was just up to his old tricks and felt a red fire of anger and pushed down harder still until the teacher indicated she should slow down. Damn, damn, damn. Taken for a fool again and I could have stayed home, had an early night and a hot bath and recovered from the day.

As she opened her locker she felt tears flood her eyes. She grunted angrily and brushed them away, grabbed her bag and escaped out of the building. She checked her phone but there was no message. 'I really can't do this, she muttered' as she strode up the hill towards home. She thought about her life before she'd met him. It was a sort of all right life, then a wonderful thing happened but now, I don't know. I could do without the crazy behaviour. She slammed the front door behind her, went straight to the fridge poured a large glass of wine and swallowed it almost in one go. Then paused for a moment, cursed loudly, reached for the bottle and replenished her glass.

FRIDAY 11TH NOVEMBER 2005

She'd regretted the way she'd dealt with her disappointment last evening. Her hangover reminded her drinking was not a road she wanted to go down. There'd been no further word from George since they'd spoken on Wednesday morning. He still hadn't told her what was wrong but last Sunday everything seemed to be back to normal and it was good; great even. She scrubbed herself in the shower and tried to find something positive to hang onto.

The wind almost blew her off her feet as she stepped outside the door but there was no rain and she hoped this winter wouldn't replicate the last, with endless rain and floods. She looked forward to the group session today as there were children she wanted to discuss.

When they had checked in, Katherine talked again about her husband Michael and how difficult he was at the moment. She blamed it on a solicitor who worked for him, who had the ability to upset everyone and lost his temper a lot. She added that her husband would like to dismiss him but he's good at his work so feels he can't.

This sounded horribly like Ed. Louise couldn't remember the name of Katherine's husband's firm, but he was the Senior Partner, and his name was Michael, another coincidence she couldn't discount. This could be a complicated situation if what she suspected turned out to be true and she wondered if she would need to disclose there was a conflict. However, Katherine wasn't talking about a client and if she said anything then her client's identity would be compromised and it would in essence be breaking client confidentiality which was more serious. It was interesting though if it was Ed, because clearly he still wasn't making use of the techniques she'd taught him.

Harriet wanted to talk about Tom and Louise realised this was another situation with potential for a conflict of interest.

They asked about her relationship with George. She just told them they'd hit a few snags. Katherine piped up 'It's best to find out now if it's not right' and muttered 'I should know.'

They all knew Katherine's marriage was not a match made in heaven, and Louise guessed that if Michael was under pressure at work it would make things worse at home.

Harriet shifted in her chair, then sat forward in a more upright position before she spoke. 'I would really love some input on Tom, the child I brought last time.' The rest of the group nodded. She told them the school had called in Social Services and they had spoken to the stepfather but, as can often be the case, they had then left the situation as it was. The rest of the group looked astonished.

Harriet shook her head. 'I know, it doesn't seem right, does it? Apparently, he gave a very good explanation and promised he wouldn't let his temper get the better of him again. He also promised he would seek help and so they took it no further. I'm not happy at the outcome because, from what I've heard so far, this child is very disturbed.' She sighed, 'He is beginning to trust me and since I last saw you has shared a lot of difficult stuff. There is one very positive thing though. He's found himself a friend called Max. He told me this with great excitement and so I feel this is a good thing.'

Colour rushed to Louise's face and her heart raced. It was confirmed; Tom was Ben.

'Harriet stop for a moment please. I need to disclose a conflict of interest.' Harriet frowned but did as Louise asked. 'What you've just said about Tom's friend has just confirmed it. His friend is in fact, my grandson. My grandson is Max and his friend is Ben which I now believe is Tom's real name.'

There was a pause before Frances exclaimed, 'Wow - Bath really is just a village, isn't it. Everyone knows everyone. I guess what we must decide is whether it will affect us working with this particular client and whether this knowledge could do harm to any of the people involved.'

Katherine nodded, 'We need to think about but I feel it would be inappropriate for Harriet to continue in front of Louise. I think we have two options; one is for Harriet not to bring Tom to this group and the other is we ask Louise to leave the room while you discuss him.'

Harriet moved forward in her chair and seemed about to speak, but then sat back again.

Louise turned towards her. 'I realise this is difficult for you Harriet but I'm happy to go into the kitchen and keep out of the way.' She took a sip of coffee and replaced the mug on the table. 'There have been several events since we last met which have made me wonder if Max's friend could be him but I wasn't absolutely sure until today. This is the trouble with using pseudonyms it sometimes makes it difficult to recognise a conflict of interest.'

Harriet then asked if they could hear what else she knew about Tom that might be of help when discussing him.

Louise told them the story as she'd heard it from Max and how upset he'd become as a result of witnessing the abuse.

'I'm glad he's being seen by you Harriet; he's obviously a boy that needs help. There is also another possible connection that makes me anxious, given all that we know now.' They looked puzzled but Louise continued. 'I have a suspicion a very good friend of mine has just started a relationship with the father.'

There was a silence before Harriet spoke. 'Oh, my goodness, what a tangled web. Yes, I understand why you are worried about your friend.' She fiddled with a notebook on her lap and looked unsure as to what to do. She then admitted to the group what had happened to her with Tom's father which she had told Louise about. 'I'm sorry you are involved, Louise. I would have appreciated your opinion on Tom, but I can see it wouldn't be appropriate. Perhaps therefore you wouldn't mind just stepping out of the room for a minute or two.'

Harriet's disclosure had clearly shocked Frances and Katherine and they watched quietly while Louise left them and then gave Harriet the chance to talk about Tom.

Once she had returned, they discussed a few other clients before the group ended and they all went their separate ways.

The Big Issue seller she'd seen last month was there again and this time Louise noticed she looked ill and her face was pinched. She wore the clothes she had on before and her legs were still bare. She stopped, bought a magazine and handed her a £5 note and indicated she didn't want any change. The girl turned her face away but not before Louise saw a large tear form in her eyes. She put her hand out and touched the girl on the arm. 'Are you all right? You look so cold.' The girl nodded but said nothing. 'Have you got somewhere to sleep at night?' then added 'that's safe?' Again, she gave nod and without saying more she turned and walked around the corner.

Louise's thoughts were of the girl as she sauntered slowly into Bath. She wondered what her circumstances might be and how she'd ended up on the street.

She ordered soup in the café in Waterstones and while she waited, decided she would text Caroline. She didn't expect her to want to a drink this evening, but she thought she'd ask her and made it sound jokey with no pressure.

Hey stranger, any chance of a G & T this evening or must I drink myself under my own table!! Lxx

She didn't expect to hear anything, but a few seconds later there was a ping.

'*Yeah, why not – great. Come to mine usual time?*'

Louise responded, '*:)   cu later xx*' At least something had got back to normal, she thought. They'd shared so much over the years and in a strange way, she almost looked forward to sharing her disappointment over George.

Things were not back to the normal she had hoped for. Louise couldn't believe how much weight Caroline had lost in such a short time. She was dressed in what might be called smart casual; not usual for their Friday night get togethers. She wore a short skirt with a blouse and a cardigan wrapped around her shoulders. Louise looked down, half expecting to see high heels as well but she had a smart pair of loafers on her feet.

'Come in, what on earth are you standing there for?' Caroline gave her a hug, but it wasn't the sort of close body contact hugs they'd always had, more a cursory one. She led her into the lounge and Louise saw to her relief nothing was different there and flung herself down on the familiar sofa near the fire.

Louise raised her glass. 'Congratulations to one of us who is clearly sustaining a good relationship at last'.

'What do you mean? Surely, you don't mean yours is not working for you?' Caroline's voice and look showed real concern.

Louise had to blink back a tear. 'Bit of a long story but let's just say there are a few problems on the reliability front. He keeps disappearing and then being secretive about where he's been. I don't feel I know him yet but between his vanishing acts we have a fantastic time.'

'I'm sorry, I'd hoped George would be the one. Now I feel selfish because I'm having such a wonderful time with a fantastic man.'

Louise had been a therapist long enough to suspect Caroline presented what she wanted the relationship to be, not perhaps the reality.

'That's so good to hear and don't feel selfish, I wouldn't want it any other way. Although it does sound almost too good to be true.'

'What do you mean?' A deep red colour swept across Caroline's face. She emphasised her next words slowly and Louise heard the anger in them but knew that the response to her throw away comment had resulted in far too strong a reaction for it not to have hit a chord.

'I don't know how you could say that. Everything is fine and I've met his stepson and I think we got on well. I'm sorry you haven't met John yet because you'd then know how wonderful he is. I have told him all about you and that you have a grandson, Max, who goes to the same school as Ben. In fact, he wondered if we could meet up as a foursome soon.'

Louise stood up and walked towards the fire. She put her hands out as if to warm them before she turned around.

'Honestly Caroline I'm pleased for you. I only said that because I do worry about you. I thought you were acting in a strange way when I saw you last and I'm afraid I didn't believe you stepped on a drawing pin. I came away feeling it was more than that and you'd been hurt; perhaps even by him.'

There was a silence and Caroline stiffened. Louise jumped in before she could speak. 'But, of course, if everything is going well, I'm delighted for you.' As she wandered back to the sofa, she checked Caroline's face and saw it still held a high colour. The look in her eyes told her she was going to be defensive but wasn't prepared for the harshness of her reply.

'I can't believe you've just said that! After I just told you how wonderful everything is. I hope you're not trying to spoil it for me now your relationship is not working out.'

Louise felt the muscles in her stomach tighten as Caroline continued to speak.

'I have such a lovely time with him and, as I have told you, he buys gorgeous things for me and makes me feel special. No man has done that before. I like the way he's helped me change my style, I feel good about myself, even sophisticated, which I've never done before. Obviously, people get irritated at times, you know we all do, and he always says he's sorry, if he thinks he has been hurtful.'

The ripple through her spine told her she was right; what Caroline meant was that he did hurt her but that she liked being with him and therefore was prepared to put up with it.

'I'm sorry I've upset you, but I care about you deeply and would never want you hurt in any way. I don't know what I'd have done without having you as a friend who saw me through all my difficult times and I will always support you, if you ever need me. Of course, I think you look lovely as always, but I can't help being surprised by the change, can I? After all you must see how different you look.'

Louise got up to go but Caroline remained seated with her head down and Louise thought she saw tears. 'Oh, Caroline, come here and give me a hug. You know I will always be here for you, and I'll look forward to meeting your John and perhaps will then see what you do.'

Caroline got up and reluctantly gave Louise a hug, but it was a better one than the beginning of the evening. 'I do know you mean well; you are truly a very good friend, but I am happy and that must count for something.'

Louise answered with another hug. 'I'm going to go now but hopefully we can arrange to meet up soon, even if it is not as a foursome. I may try and flush George out over the weekend - after all his behaviour is very strange. I've never been to his house before because he always came to mine, but I know where it is and he did ask me to visit him at some point, so I think it will be this weekend. What do you think?'

Caroline thought for a moment. 'I think that's a good idea and then maybe you will get some answers.'

'Right, that's what I'll do then. Thanks for that and for the gin, which if I am not mistaken was the pricey blue one!' Caroline laughed. 'Yes, you're right, John prefers it to the regular gin.'

Louise was pleased they had ended on a more friendly note, even if it had meant she'd agreed to see John but had a sick feeling and tightness in her chest. She wondered if she'd been right not to say outright that John was definitely not the knight in shining armour he purported to be.

It didn't take long to walk back to her house. In her hurry to see Caroline, she'd forgotten her torch and the dark shadows felt menacing. They seemed to dance around her like a zombie ballet.

What's that? Her skin prickled from her feet to the top of her scalp as she tried to see where the noise had come from. Damn, George and the light. She stood still, certain there was someone there in the bush on the left of the path. As if in confirmation, it rustled and shook. 'Who's there? Come out please.' She prayed an animal would appear, but nothing came, and the rustling stopped.

She peered into the darkness. Ripples of fear pulsed through her body. A wet leaf moved across her face, then shoulders and neck. She screamed and stumbled up the path. She clutched for the key in her pocket and tried to get the key in the lock, but her hand shook too much. Her heart pounded as she tried repeatedly to push it in, then realised she had her car key in her hand. Her scalp prickled and her throat tightened. She felt another scream rise in her throat and her mouth opened just as a torch shone in her face. She sank to the ground as she heard a deep voice behind her and strong hands grabbed her.

'Oh my God, Louise, are you all right?' Confused, she looked up and in the light of the torch saw Luke, from next door. She tried to speak but no sound came out.

Luke took the keys out of her hand, found the right one and opened the door. Buster rushed out but stopped for a moment when he saw Luke, then gave one bark and sniffed around in the bushes. Luke kept hold of Louise and guided her in. He found the light and switched it on as they both walked down the hall to the kitchen. He made sure she sat securely on a chair before he went back to shut the door. Louise called Buster to her in a weak voice. He rushed back, then sat and panted loudly. She heard the click of the front door, her heart gave a lurch and she shouted out, 'Don't go, Luke… are you still here?' She heard footsteps and sighed with relief. 'Stay and have a drink please, I can't thank you enough. That was such a shock - sorry if I frightened you. Silly of me, I know, but I thought someone was there watching me, then touching me.' She couldn't help the tremor in her voice and her hands still shook.

Luke touched her on the arm. 'No worries, I heard a noise and then a scream. I was on my way out but thought I'd take a look. I'm glad I did. Your path is creepy though, and in the dark even more so. You should get the builder guy to do something about the light. What do you want to drink, I'll get it; Tea? Coffee? Gin, Wine – what?'

Louise got her breath back to normal and pointed him towards the cupboard where she kept the whisky. Luke obediently obliged and poured two large ones into a couple of tumblers he found on the draining board, handed one to Louise and sat down opposite her with his. Glass in hand, Louise relaxed and then apologised for disturbing his evening.

'No need to apologise it's the most exciting thing that's happened for a while!'

She grimaced.

'Sorry. That didn't come out right. What I mean is it's been a hard week. I've been writing a long essay and not gone anywhere for quite a few days, so was due some fun. Oh no, there I go again, course I don't mean fun. Oh right, think I'll shut up now; only digging myself in but I'm glad I could help you. If you're sure you'll be all right, as soon as I've finished this I'd better go, as I said I'd meet the rest of the gang in town.'

Louise nodded, thanked him again and he left.

What a nightmare. I know I didn't imagine it. There was someone there and still could be, lurking in the shadows. She thought of a line of a rather bad poem she'd once written, which started; "Lurking in the shadows of the night" shivered and poured another whisky.

SATURDAY 12TH NOVEMBER 2005

Unexpectedly, she'd fallen asleep almost as soon as she put her head down but then a loud crash snapped her out of it. What on earth was that? She sat up fully alert. A juggernaut of fear rushed through her body. She had no idea of the time and saw nothing in the darkness of the room. She stretched out an arm for the light. It was only just after midnight and the house was totally silent. She tried to work out what she'd heard. It must have been loud to raise her out of such a deep sleep. She strained to catch a sound, any sound, but only heard her heart as it thumped in her chest. There was no sound from Buster downstairs and he would have barked at the slightest thing. The silence reassured her but felt she must investigate.

She tiptoed to the door and inched it open a crack, glad that she never shut it tightly at night and didn't need to turn the handle. She peered into the hallway which was lit by moonlight as it shone through the skylight. She saw nothing that looked untoward or different. She was about to retreat back into her bedroom when she caught a movement in the corner of her eye and a black ghost of a shadow emerged at the top of the stairs. She blinked to clear her vision but when she looked again, it had gone. Her heart galloped so fast she was afraid it might explode. Her hands felt clammy, and her throat dried. Her knees wobbled so much she felt as if they wouldn't be able to hold her weight for much longer. What should I do? Should I try and go downstairs, or would that be stupid? What would I do if someone was there and suppose they had a knife or a weapon? As these thoughts filled her head she shook from head to toe; she had to sit down. She retreated into her bedroom and closed the door without a sound, pushed a chair under the handle and rang 999.

She somehow expected the police to arrive immediately, but it felt as if she had survived a whole night and a day before there was a loud knock at the door.

Two uniformed policemen stood on her step with what she hoped were concerned looks on their faces. They introduced themselves as Constable Evans and Constable Taylor. One of them made her sit at the kitchen table while he put on the kettle. His eyebrows rose when his eyes alighted on the two empty glasses and the half empty bottle of whisky, but she couldn't find the strength or the voice to explain why they were there. As always when she felt stressed, she automatically put her hand down to feel for Buster, but her hand met only air. He hadn't stirred when the police arrived. She shouted, 'Buster…Buster. Come here boy' and Constable Evans who was making the coffee looked up. 'It's my dog, somethings not right,' Louise murmured and walked to his bed under the stairs.

He looked so peaceful, asleep in his basket, but she knew it wasn't right. She bent down, stroked his head and gave a bit of a push but there was no response. She caught hold of his body and shook him. 'Come on, Buster, what's up? You're not usually like this.' There was a slight movement in his tail and he looked up, rolled his eyes at her, dropped his head and went back to sleep.

'I think he's been drugged' she shouted to the policeman in the kitchen. 'My dog, I think he's been drugged. He didn't bark at the noise which woke me, and he didn't stir when you arrived. He's always been a good guard dog so that's unusual and now he is all floppy and tired.'

'Is he friendly your Buster?' asked Constable Evans who had moved to where she was.

'Yes, far too much sometimes,' said Louise.

He leant down and stroked him to check for himself. 'Yes, I think you're right. I have a dog myself and I agree this isn't normal. Think he'll be all right though; he just seems a bit sleepy. I should see how he is and get him checked out in the morning.'

He told his colleague who had been checking other rooms and they agreed this was a serious break in and was someone who knew she had a dog.

After a search of the house they found the back door wasn't quite closed but had not been forced at all, so they suspected whoever it was had a key. Louise told them about the key she kept hidden in the garden and they went immediately to look. The shout came back quickly. 'Yes, it's here.'

The dog-friendly policeman suggested they return to the kitchen to sit again. 'Think you look as if you need a chair.' He pulled one out and pushed it in when she started to sit. He sat opposite her. 'They obviously didn't use the key from the garden, so if they did have a key where could they have got it from?

Louise frowned. 'I really don't know. My backdoor key always hangs on the hooks under the shelf in the hallway together with the gate key.'

Constable Taylor indicated to his colleague that he should go and look. When he returned he told them that they were both there and then frowned, 'That means anyone with access to your house had access to both the keys and could have had them copied.'

'Well yes, I suppose they could, but I don't know anyone who would or could have done it.'

They asked who had keys to her house or who she could have given access to. She told them her daughter Katy had one and explained she lived the other side of Bath and was married to Dave. 'He's one of you lot actually.'

When they realised who it was, they laughed and agreed he was sound. 'What about other people, neighbours or friends?'

Louise hesitated while she thought what to say. 'Well, I have given one to my boyfriend George.' She stopped as she tried to think how to put it so it wouldn't sound strange. 'He was or rather is renovating my bathroom.' She felt her face get hot.

'Your boyfriend's renovating your bathroom?'

Louise shifted in her chair. 'Yes, he is. Well, he was a builder and then he was my boyfriend.'

'So, let's get this straight. You have only been in a relationship since he's been here doing your bathroom then?'

Louise nodded and thought her face must now match the colour of the lipstick she usually wore. 'He wouldn't have had anything to do with this. Really, he wouldn't have. He's a lovely man and I trust him. Anyway, he has been here masses of times when I have been out and could have snooped around at any of those occasions. He wouldn't have needed to creep in at night.' She was positive that he wasn't the intruder, but did she really trust him now.

Constable Evans finished writing and changed the subject. 'You say you are a counsellor. Do you work from here, or elsewhere?'

She felt exhausted and thought she needed to have another whisky or go to bed but answered the question.

'So, you work in town two days and here another two. What about confidential records? Do you keep them here or somewhere else?'

Louise told them where she kept them upstairs.

She felt blamed for all of this. It sounded as though she must be stupid to see clients here and to have given the builder boyfriend a key.

Her thoughts were interrupted by another question. 'What about clients you are seeing at the moment? Are there any you are wary of or worried about?'

She shook her head vigorously, 'No, none.'

He put his pen down on the table. 'Are you sure nothing is missing? I can't help feeling your work might have something to do with this.'

She caught her breath as she suddenly remembered what had happened the other day.

'You've remembered something?'

'Yes, I have. I'm sorry but I'd forgotten all about it. The other day, when I got home, I found my keys in the keyhole of the filing cabinet, which was strange as I've never left them there before. After I've locked the cabinet, I always put them in the jar on the shelf.'

She saw by the look on his face he thought it was a very insecure place to leave keys, but she ignored the look and carried on. 'Also, I noticed the jar had been moved. I did mention it to my boyfriend, who persuaded me it had been an oversight on my part. He thought I might have been distracted.'

The two policemen looked at each other and Louise snapped back, 'I know it wasn't him. As I told you, he's not like that. We have a good relationship, and he is a very kind and empathic man.' As she spoke, she felt a tightness in her chest and hoped what she was saying was true. Could it be him? After all he's acted strangely recently and I would have said a week or so ago, quite out of character. Could his weird disappearing act perhaps be connected? She gazed into the distance until Constable Evans coughed to get her attention.

'Don't worry, we're not accusing anyone - we are just looking to find some explanation.' He indicated it perhaps would be a good idea if she accompanied them upstairs to have a look.

Louise led the way but as she put her foot on the first step of the stairs she stopped. The events of the early evening rushed back to her, and she turned to face the man behind her, 'I'm so sorry. I don't know how I could have, as it was terrifying but there is something I'd forgotten. She told them about the incident that happened when she arrived home and about Luke. She hoped they would now understand the two glasses.

'Did your light break, or have you never had one?'

Great now they're going to think someone broke it on purpose, she thought as she replied. 'Well actually it's been broken a while. I had asked George to fix it but somehow he hasn't got around to doing it.' That sounded even worse, and her thoughts were confirmed as the policemen shared another look. Tears pricked her eyes as she thought how horribly wrong things had gone. This couldn't possibly have anything to do with George.

They made no further comments and the three of them went into her study. She quickly scanned the room but as far as she could see everything was just as she'd left it.

Louise felt the police were not convinced the intruder had come upstairs and were just about to go back down when one of them spotted it. A picture had come off the wall and now rested against the skirting board on the top stair, as if it had been placed there. It hadn't been broken but when they picked it up, they saw the glass had cracked. They then agreed she was right and whoever it was had got upstairs but perhaps gone down again when they knocked the picture off the wall.

The vibration of the phone in her pocket startled her. She looked to see who it was and saw the police were also curious as to who would phone at 2.00 a.m.

'Oh Dave, oh how lovely. How on earth did you know? What made you ring?'

'I had to be at the station because of a case I'm on and just happened to look in the log and saw your address. What's going on?' Tears started to form but she managed to hold them back while she told him what had happened. *'I'm on my way - please try not to worry. I'll be with you in about fifteen minutes.'*

She saw the question in the policemen's eyes 'It was Dave, he's coming straight over'. They grinned, so Louise guessed they must have a good relationship with him or perhaps he might even be their boss - she was never sure about police hierarchy.

Once Dave had arrived, the two policemen had a quick de-brief with him. He told her they had already phoned to arrange for fingerprints. This surprised her. 'Is that necessary? They didn't take anything, and you say they didn't break in?'

Dave explained. 'Trespass with intent to steal is an offence. Don't worry; we'll check against the data base and see if any fingerprints match any past crime. We also need to interview your neighbour who came in with you too.'

Dave made another drink and suggested they go and sit comfortably while they waited. Louise told him about the person Mr. Braithwaite thought he saw in the garden. She also told him George had disappeared again but in between that last time and this, he had been lovely and so she couldn't get her head round what had happened.

Dave listened but made no comment about George; just kept to the matter in hand. 'We'll need to fingerprint the back gate as well, if you think they came in that way.' Dave also asked about clients, but she couldn't say any more than she had already. 'Would you like to come back and stay at ours tonight? I could drop you there before going back to the station.'

Louise thought for a moment but didn't want to leave Buster on his own and so refused the invitation. She hoped the policeman was right and Buster just needed to sleep it off and could leave it until the morning to see the vet.

Fingerprints were taken from nearly everywhere in the house and hers too for elimination. They also needed Luke's and George's as well, so she gave them their addresses.

Dave told her he'd see her after his shift finished tomorrow and that as she would be considered now a vulnerable person, he would flag her telephone number so if she phoned, she'd get an immediate response.

'Is there a room in the house where you could lock yourself in if someone did get into the house? We call it a 'safe room'. I think in America they call it a 'panic room' which makes it sound alarming but is something to have in mind as a safety precaution.'

Her voice croaked as she replied; the bathroom would probably be the place as George had fitted a new door but now it had no lock.

Dave nodded, 'I don't think there would be a need tonight as I think whoever it was got a bit of a scare.' Oh my god, he thinks they'll come back, thought Louise and felt the queasiness of fear but didn't let on how badly she was affected.

'Thanks, Dave, you've been brilliant. Don't worry if I'm not here though when you call or perhaps telephone me first as I need to go to the vets and I think I will also go over to George's house and have it out with him as to what sort of game he is playing.'

Louise shut the door behind him, leaned back and placed both hands flat either side of her on the door, as if to shut everything out and to keep them from coming back but she knew nothing she did would stop someone who wanted to get in. She had worked with far too many criminals in her time to know that.

She would have liked to have brought Buster to her room but knew he'd be too heavy to carry and when she'd checked on him, he'd managed a faint wag of the tail and looked so comfortable where he was, she'd left him there. She pushed a chair under the door handle in her bedroom which made her feel safer, crept into bed and pulled the covers over her head convinced she'd never sleep for the short space of night left.

The wolves had nearly caught her. They howled and wailed at the thrill of the chase. She smelt their rancid breath and felt the rasped tongue as the leader of the pack prepared to devour her. The scream woke her. She snapped her eyes open in terror, but the tongue continued. 'Oh Buster, thank goodness.' She sighed in relief and ruffled his fur. 'I was so worried I can't believe you were drugged but you look fine now. Think we'll get the vet to look at you to make sure.' She looked at her watch - it was nearly ten and she needed to hurry if she was going to make the morning surgery.

She watched anxiously while Hugh, the young vet, checked Buster over. 'I think he's fine, but I will take a blood sample to send off to the lab just to find out what was used and if there are any side effects. My guess it was something given orally crushed in perhaps a piece of meat. Dogs will eat anything if it smells good!'

Having settled Buster at home, Louise got back into the car and drove towards the part of Weston where George lived. She spotted his car as soon as she drove into his road; at least he was there. To her amazement there was a parking space near his house.

Now she'd arrived she wasn't nearly so confident and sat for a moment while she tried to come up with a plan of what she should say. Should I knock on the door and demand to know what's going on or pretend nothing's going on and say I'd called round to see if he was all right? She got out of the car, slammed the door, muttered 'Let's do this,' strode up his path and knocked loudly. She hoped he would answer before her confidence left her.

The house was in the middle of a small terrace, much like her own. She had been past it but never been in. The door looked as if it could do with a bit of a paint. Typical of builders, she thought, renowned for not keeping their own houses in order. She knocked again but louder than before. George didn't appear and several more knocks still got no response. She prised open the letter box and shouted. 'George, it's Louise. Wondered how you are and whether you'd like to come out for a walk.' As soon as the words left her mouth, she knew he would guess that was not the reason she'd come as she hadn't brought Buster. She'd tell him Buster was still recovering from his ordeal last night.

She peered through the letterbox and saw letters and circulars spread all over the floor. They looked as though they'd been there for a long time, which was odd. She started to close the letterbox but as she did so, she heard a loud crash followed by the sort of swear words she hated. She put her lips to the opening and shouted, 'It's Louise. George, are you there?' Silence. Then she thought she heard some clanking and more words.

'For god's sake, just stop fooling around and answer your bloody door.' Her anger surprised her, and she felt uncomfortably hot. What the hell is he playing at? I've had enough, quite enough. She rattled the handle and to her surprise the door swung open.

Unable to avoid the post on the floor, she trod as carefully over it as she could and stood just inside and shouted, 'George, I'm coming in, what the hell is going on?' Her feet echoed as she stepped forwards on the tiled floor. The layout was very similar to hers, she discovered, as she walked through all the downstairs rooms but there was no sign of him. She looked up the stairs and shouted again. 'Where are you? I'm coming up now.' This was followed by another crash and then a rather feeble voice, 'No, Lou, don't, don't come up, jus donna dare. S'not safe, I mean you won't....' but she'd already reached the landing and opened the first door she came to.

'What the hell!' She looked in horror at the state of the room. George lay on a bed surrounded by empty bottles and dried vomit.

He attempted to get up but fell back, missed the bed and the top half of him landed on the floor. His legs were left behind him propped on the bed. 'Sorry, Lou, my lovely Lou, please don't be angry, it really isn't as it looks' but obviously the effort of moving had brought back the nausea and he retched and threw up again on the floor.

'George what the hell has happened? You look a wreck and are still totally smashed by the sound and look of things.'

Louise gaped. It was unbelievable that the man she had fallen for was this drunken oaf sprawled in front of her. 'I think I've seen enough. I had no idea this was what you did with your time when you weren't with me and so as of now we're finished.' She marched out of the room and shouted, 'You'd better sober up and clean up that mess or this house will stink for ever.'

By the time she reached the door tears had rolled down her cheeks and she had to stop because it was difficult to see. She wiped her eyes and tried to get control before going out onto the street. Her feet scuffed on paper, and she saw she had her foot on his post. The letters were mainly brown envelopes and most had Ministry of Defence stamped all over them. She saw one had been taken out of the envelope before it presumably got thrown down. Curiosity overwhelmed her and she picked it up. It was a summons to attend a Coroner's Court somewhere in Wales. She threw it back on the floor and stomped out. What the hell have you done and what are you involved in?

The day had become far worse than she could possibly have imagined, so she made for home as fast as she could. Once there, she grabbed Buster and curled up on the sofa with him. I just don't want to think about what just happened. I can't, and I won't. She searched through some recordings she'd made to find a movie to watch, preferably a sad one as she knew she would cry anyway but it would at least distract her or so she hoped.

She must have fallen asleep as the sound of the door being opened made her jump and her heart started to thump.

'Hi, Mum, it's only me. Where are you?'

She let out a breath in relief. 'I'm in here, Katy, on the sofa.'

'Dave called me and told me what happened, and I said I'd come over straight away, but he said you were going to the vet first thing. I hope Buster's all right.'

Louise declared she was fine, and Buster too, but her voice wobbled and Katy came over and sat down beside her and gave her a big hug.

'The whole thing sounds awful, Mum. Who on earth could possibly want to break into your house? It doesn't sound like a burglary though, unless you disturbed them before they had a chance to steal anything. I hope you've arranged to have all your locks changed.'

Louise put her hand to her mouth. 'Oh no, I forgot all about the locks and Dave wants me to make my bathroom into a 'safe room' - but what with visiting the vet and then seeing George, the whole day got so bad and all I wanted to do was shut myself in a cocoon and wake up when it was all over.'

Katy gave her another hug. 'I'll ring a locksmith now and arrange for them to come and change all the locks and do some extra strong ones on the bathroom door - but what

167

about George? You've seen him then? That's great, because you will really need his support over this.'

Louise had a picture in her head of the last time she saw him as he lay half on and half off the bed surrounded by vomit. 'Yes, you're right, it will be good.' She just didn't have the heart or the energy to explain that situation to her.

'I came to ask if you and Buster would like to stay with us tonight and over the rest of the weekend but if George is going to be here, you wouldn't want that, I guess.'

Louise hesitated but only for a moment. 'No, actually that would be good, but I'll wait until the locksmith has been and then I'll come on over. It's okay to leave me now. In the meantime, I'll get some rest, after all I didn't get a lot of sleep last night.'

She didn't manage to settle and shortly after Katy left, she wandered up to her study. The police didn't think the intruder had reached there but she wasn't so sure. She had an image of the shadow as it emerged from somewhere. She gazed round the room and tried to see if there was anything, however small, out of place but there was nothing that gave any indication of disturbance.

The locksmith had told Katy he would be there in an hour so Louise made herself some coffee and contemplated all that had gone on. Could George have possibly been the one that crept into the house; after all he did have a key? She couldn't understand it at all. What on earth was that Court Summons about and why the Ministry of Defence? There were just too many questions that needed to be answered.

She felt much safer after the locksmith had gone and started to pack some overnight things to take to Katy's. Her phone vibrated in her pocket. It was a text from Caroline. *Sorry bout last night, I know you're a true friend. Could you please, please come. I need to see you urgently. Xxxx*

Louise sighed, unsure what to do. It sounded urgent and obviously Caroline didn't know what had happened to her. She thought for a while then texted back.

I'll pop round in a bit but can't stay long - on my way to Katy's hope you alright? Xxxx

She threw on a coat and walked fast. The packing had taken longer than she'd intended, as she knew she wasn't really on the ball. She'd heard the bell ring in the house and expected an immediate answer but there was no sound of footsteps and Caroline didn't appear. She pressed on the bell again and held it for a while. She sighed and ran her hand through her tousled hair, which had not been done since the morning. My god I feel a wreck, hair not done, no make-up and no lipstick. Caroline would be sure to notice something was wrong. She swallowed a knot in her throat and her heart beat faster as she lifted up the flap of a letter box for the second time that day. 'Caroline, it's Louise, for God's sake open the door. I'm freezing, and I haven't got long.' Still no answer. When she peered in, she saw the hallway was empty but noticed her new yellow coat on the coat stand by the wall. She must be in, she thought, irritated about the whole thing. She pressed the doorbell over and over again. In the end she got out her phone and texted *I'm here, answer the door will you* and then added, *please xxxx.*

Still no response, so Louise turned away and as she did, caught her coat on a rose that climbed up and around the door. She turned back to unhook it using the light from her torch, which she'd remembered to bring this time. Something caught her eye on the same branch. It looked like a tiny scrap of material, and she thought someone else must have been caught in the same way. She stared up at the windows above the door but they were dark.

She walked slowly back towards her house. She felt exhausted and wanted to get to Katy's but something was not right. Perhaps I should be really worried she thought. If John is the type I think he is, could he have harmed her? I haven't liked what's happened to her and why did she ask me to come to her house urgently if she wasn't there. She shook her head; she didn't know what she should do. Perhaps I should phone the police she thought, but then there may be a perfectly good explanation. She hoped Dave would be at home and determined to talk to him as soon as she reached there.

At her house, she picked up her overnight bag and collected some food for Buster and went straight to Katy's.

'Come on in, Mum, I've lit a fire already and will bring you a drink. Just make yourself at home and have a rest. Max and Milly are up in their rooms playing – I've told them not to disturb you until I tell them they can.'

'That's kind, Katy, but it might be good to feel a bit of normal life around me and I know Max will want to see Buster.' The words were no longer out of her mouth when the door burst open, and Max strode in with Milly very close behind him.

'Someone listening at the door perhaps?' Louise smiled at her grandchildren and gave them both a big hug but a sigh of relief when they took Buster off somewhere and she could relax properly.

She asked if Dave was home as she needed to speak to him urgently. Katy reassured her he would be back shortly. She shut her eyes and didn't open them again until she vaguely heard someone put a log on the fire but closed them again until Katy came in and shook her slightly. 'Mum, it's supper time. Would you be happy to join us or would you rather have it here on a tray?'

A tray sounded good but thought she'd better go and join the others and her mouth started to water as delicious smells wafted out from the kitchen. She checked her phone but there was nothing more from Caroline. She hoped Dave was now home.

They didn't talk about what had happened as it would have worried the children, who had been told Granny hadn't felt well and wanted to come and be looked after. Max had taken this on board as he was very attentive and asked if she wanted some water.

When the children were tucked up in bed, Dave and Katy sat with Louise. Dave was the first to speak. 'I'm sorry my lot were unable to offer any explanation as to who got into your house. They can't do anything further about it at the moment as they haven't got all the fingerprints they need. They managed to get Luke's but not George's. He didn't appear to be in when they called. I am very glad to hear you've got the locks changed, so you should stay safe but you didn't mention the back gate or the bathroom, did you sort those as well?

She told him about the locks on the bathroom door, explained about the keycode that she'd had put on the back gate and said she'd give them both the number. 'Guess you must give it to George as well then,' said Katy.

Louise gave a grimace. 'Sadly, things aren't going too well there at the moment. Anyway, since he has at last finished the bathroom, he doesn't really need a key at all.'

Dave nodded. Katy spoke softly. 'I'm so sorry, it was obvious you liked him, and we did too. Perhaps you can work it out. I'm guessing you don't want to talk about it now as you fobbed me off this morning but obviously you can tell us more if you want to.'

Louise felt a warmth in her body. 'Thanks, perhaps I will do later. Although there is now a more pressing thing worrying me. I didn't want to talk about it with the children within earshot.' She then explained about the strange text Caroline had sent and what had happened when she went to the house. She also told them she had found out that the man Caroline was seeing was Ben's stepfather.

'What? No. Are you sure? Katy grimaced, 'We know he is not a nice man from what Max saw and Caroline is so lovely. Are you certain? How do you know?'

She told them both what she knew. 'I'm so worried that something has happened to her and when she didn't answer the door, I wondered whether I should phone the police. Then decided I'd wait and tell you.

Dave frowned and thought some more about the implication of what Louise had told them.

'I don't like the sound of this bloke at all. Had you told Caroline what you know about him?'

Louise shook her head. 'No, I haven't seen or spoken to her since I knew. I must admit I am disturbed by her message and also her non-appearance. Why would she send a text asking me to go there urgently and then not be there?'

Dave walked towards the fire and leaned on the mantlepiece for a moment, deep in thought. 'I agree with you it is odd. I'll phone it in and get someone round to her house to check. Now I suggest you try and get some sleep and we'll see what more we can do in the morning.

SUNDAY 13TH NOVEMBER 2005

'You're not leaving, Mum, surely?' Katy had a frown on her face as she spoke. 'I've just put some coffee on, do stay at least for breakfast'.

Louise apologised but told her she needed to have another look for Caroline. 'I've been awake for ages and can't stop thinking about her.'

As she pushed her buttons through the buttonholes on her coat, she explained if she did find Caroline, she would need to have a long chat, so it was unlikely she'd be back today. 'I must also try and get my head round what my thoughts and feelings are about George. I don't know if it was a one off or whether he has really been slipping off to get his fix of alcohol. I was so angry when I saw him yesterday, I just told him we were finished and walked out, but I am reluctant to just leave it without an explanation.'

Katy nodded and Louise turned to go out of the door with Buster already on a lead. 'Please say my goodbyes to the kids and to Dave and ask him to ring me immediately if he hears anything.'

Kate told her Dave had received a call from the station and left a couple of hours ago but would most likely check up on her later as he was worried about the events of Friday night and of course if he had found anything out about Caroline.

The new key to her front door was stiff and her thoughts played over the events on Friday night. Who on earth could it have been and what could they have wanted? She shivered and wondered what she ought to do now. She had been quite sure at Katy's she was going to find Caroline but without much sleep she now felt exhausted and unsure of herself. It would have been good to have someone with her just now and thought of her lovely James and what he would have made of this situation and what he would do. She felt perhaps she should have waited to hear if Dave had heard anything from the officers he'd sent to Caroline's house.

With her tired eyes the bed looked too tempting, and she lay down. She told herself she would just rest for a few minutes. When she next opened her eyes, it was two in the afternoon and the few minutes had stretched to a few hours. She'd had no messages and she texted Caroline again; *Where are you Caroline? Please let me know you're ok - am worried about you.* She gave a loud yawn, hauled herself out of bed and went downstairs to make herself a coffee and a piece of toast.

She'd just taken a bite when the sound of door knocker echoed through the house. Louise decided to ignore it and took a sip of her coffee. The sound of a key being pushed into the lock startled her. Perhaps it was the intruder returned as the police said he might and was pleased that the locks had been changed and they couldn't get in. She let out a long breath in relief but whoever it was then started to thump on the door. She noticed Buster's tail as it moved from side to side. He was obviously aware of who it was. Hmm, guess it might be George then. Buster cocked an eye at her and trotted to the front door. She followed but was in no rush to get there.

Rain dripped from his sodden hair and ran like large tears down his face and dripped onto his shoes. He had no coat and his grey t-shirt had black splodges over it. He pressed the palm of his hands together and gave a bow. 'I am so, so, sorry Lou, I can't think what you must have thought but please let me in and I'll try to explain.' She wanted to refuse but saw the state he was in, so opened the door, turned and indicated he should follow. He followed with his head bowed and muttered 'Can't believe you changed the locks though' followed by a stilted laugh. Louise couldn't be bothered to reply.

She stood with folded arms and silently urged herself to remain calm, but she couldn't help herself. 'What the hell is going on, George? You just disappeared with no explanation and when I came to look for you, I found you…

what can I say other than you were in a disgusting state. I'm sorry, but there is no way I am getting myself involved with an alcoholic. I had enough of their antics when I worked in a rehab., so you had better come up with a good explanation or you are straight out the door, and I never want to see you again....'

She paused to see whether he had anything to say but when she saw him open his mouth, carried straight on before he got a word out. 'I've had a time of sheer hell over the last 24 hours, and you just made it so much more awful.' Her anger left her and tears formed. She saw confusion in his face but when he stepped towards her she stepped away from his outstretched arms, sniffed and wiped her hands across her face, 'No. No. Don't you dare touch me, in fact don't you dare come near me until you let me in on what's happening to you and why you keep disappearing and don't you.... just don't you dare lie to me.' She flung her head up, sank into the chair opposite, folded her arms and stared at him.

His face crumbled but he remained silent. Louise stood up. 'Oh well, if you've no explanation and you're not going to speak, you may as well go right now. At least I know where I am.'

'Wait, Lou. Sit down again and listen please.'

With reluctance she perched on the edge of the chair, ready to flee if needed.

He took the chair on the other side of the table and took a deep breath. 'I do want to talk to you and you probably can't guess just how much I want to sort things out but it's not easy, not easy at all.' He put his hands flat on the table as if to steady them. 'Perhaps we could have a cuppa while I think how to put things. It is so important to me you really understand.' His face had fallen as he spoke. She could also have sworn the wet in his eyes was no longer due to the rain. She stopped feeling quite so angry and agreed to make him a cup of tea.

He'd just taken a sip when there was a knock at the door. Frustrated at being interrupted when what she really wanted to do was get to the bottom of things she sighed and got up to answer it.

It was Dave. She gave him a big hug and she whispered in his ear that George was in the kitchen and then rolled her eyes so Dave could see his being there wasn't all wonderful.

'Hi, George, what do you think about all this then? Any ideas as to who it could be, assuming it's not you of course.'

George again looked confused and Louise frowned at Dave. 'I haven't had a chance to tell him yet, he has only just called round.'

'Tell me? What have you got to tell me? What's happened, what's going on?' He looked from one to the other but before Louise or Dave could say anything, they were interrupted by the house phone and Louise went into the sitting room to answer it.

To her relief it was Henry wanting to know how she was. *'Katy told me what happened last night. What a horrible thing to happen.'*

She didn't want to upset him but felt she needed to say it as it was. *'Yes, it was. It was completely terrible and scary but Dave is here, and George too, so could I phone you back later as they've both just arrived, and I'll tell you all about it then?'*

Henry agreed and when he'd rung off, she got her mobile out of her pocket to check she'd not missed any texts and found she'd run out of battery. She shouted out to Dave she was going upstairs to put her phone on charge and suggested he make some tea.

She always kept a charger in her study, and it was usually on her desk when not plugged into a socket nearby but at first glance it appeared not to be there. 'Not surprising though, is it,' she mumbled, as she sifted through a pile of invoices that threatened to become a landslide. 'Ah there it is!' She made a grab for it and dislodged the invoices. They tumbled to the floor in a waterfall of paper together with something small and hard. She bent down to see what it was and froze. 'The garden gate key!' She exclaimed.

She felt her heart thump, sure now that someone had rifled through her desk. She picked the key up and stared at it, as if that would give her the answer as to how it got there. She realised it wasn't the same colour as the one that had always hung on the hook downstairs but it was the right shape and size, so must be a copy. The only people who had known where she kept her keys were Katy, Dave and George. She was sure it was nothing to do with Katy or Dave, which only left George. What could he possibly want with them?

All the good times she'd had with George were now overshadowed, not only by the fact someone had been in her house but also by the thought he might be the intruder. The whole thing made no sense and for two pins she would have crept into the bedroom, climbed into bed and pulled the covers over her head and pretended the last twenty-four hours hadn't happened.

She stared out at the hectic weather outside. The trees in the road shook violently, as if the wind wanted to pull them out by their roots. The rain lashed at the window, and everything felt unsettled and dangerous. She tried to think but got stuck on the thought that the only person who could have taken the keys to copy was George. She now really couldn't trust anything he said.

Dave's voice came from the bottom of the stairs. 'Louise? Is everything all right? I have to go soon as Katy is expecting me.'

'Sorry. I'm coming. Henry was on the phone. I'll be right down, perhaps you would give my cold coffee a boost in the microwave for me.'

She arrived in the kitchen just as Dave retrieved her mug from the microwave.

George got up and she so wished she'd never found the key and everything could have been as it was before. She stopped him with her hand, and he sat down again but immediately launched into concern.

'Dave's told me what's happened. It's hard to believe and I can't bear to think of how awful it must have been for you. I'm so sorry I wasn't here but I am now, and I will stay if you only let me explain myself.'

The walk down the stairs had given her time and she'd made up her mind she was not going to let George stay after Dave had gone. 'I'm sorry, George, but everything has been too much for me and I'd like you to leave. I'm not in the mood now for your explanation. Just give me a day or so and I will get in touch and then you can tell me.

George opened his mouth to argue but saw the look on Louise's face and decided against it. He got up and she turned away. 'Lou, there's just one thing you need to hear. You may not be able to contact me for the next few days, for reasons I had wanted to explain to you today. Please believe me though when I say I am not hiding from you and what is going on for me has nothing whatever to do with you and it will be over very soon.' He picked up his coat from the chair and walked out. Louise stood at the kitchen door and watched to make sure he had really gone and the front door had closed.

Dave gave her a long look. 'Wow, a bit hard, wasn't it?' Are you sure you didn't want him to be here with you? He sounded as though he wanted to explain himself.'

'I know how it seemed but look what I've just found in my study. I'm now sure I can't trust George at all.' She held up the key and waved it in front of his face.

'What's that? Where's it from? Where did you find it?'

Louise explained. 'It's the key to the garden gate or a copy of it. Since I trust my own family were not tramping through my house in the middle of the night, that only leaves George. Which is why I didn't want to be left here alone with him.'

In an instant Dave became the policeman. He spoke sternly and with authority. 'You need to check again whether anything is missing. I suppose he could have knocked the picture off the wall on his way out after he'd found what he wanted but I still think it more likely he was disturbed and brushed it off in his hurry to leave. I agree if it is George, it really doesn't make any sense at all.'

'No, it doesn't, but there's no way I can have a relationship with someone I can't trust, so for the moment I have to leave it as it is.'

Dave got up to go. 'The thing I came to tell you about was the officers that went to Caroline's house last night saw nothing untoward. There was no-one there and they shone a torch through the window and saw nothing amiss. I don't think I can do anything more now. It is still only a short while she's been out of contact but keep me posted.'

'Thank you. I do hope you're right and there is nothing wrong but I can't help being worried as it is so unlike her. I will let you know though if I hear anything. You don't by any chance have Ben's Father's telephone number as I could ring him if you did. I just wondered, as Max has visited, that perhaps Katy has a number.'

'I've no idea but I will ask her and get her to ring you. Incidentally I asked George to call round at the station to give his prints, so we can eliminate them.'

Louise touched Dave gently on his upper arm, 'Thank you so much Dave, I don't think I could have coped without your help. I'll be fine now and promise to ring if I get alarmed by anything.'

Dave was true to his word and Katy telephoned a while later with the number.

The phone rang and rang, and Louise guessed it would soon switch to voicemail. *You've reached John Jones please leave your message and I'll get back to you as soon as possible.* It sounded formal and was a message John had obviously recorded himself. His spoke with a slightly plummy accent but she couldn't form a picture of him in her mind.

'Hello John, this is Louise, Caroline's friend. We haven't met but I think you will know about me. I am rather concerned as she sent an urgent message on Saturday and asked me to go to her house. She wasn't there when I arrived, and I haven't been able to get hold of her since. I thought perhaps you might be able to shed some light. I

would be grateful if you would give me a call back if you can. Many thanks.'

She sank back on her sofa and knew there wasn't anything further she could do now. She felt a bit stupid after she'd sent the message, after all perhaps they could be away again in Cornwall. It was also possible Caroline had either lost or broken her phone. This thought comforted her for a moment but deep down her body told her something quite different.

Louise had just got herself something to eat when the phone rang with the identity shown as unknown caller. Not sure whether it would be one of those call centre calls asking her to buy a service of some sort or whether it was John, she picked it up and answered cautiously.

'Hello, it's John. Thank you for ringing, it was very thoughtful of you. I assure you there's no problem and no need to worry. Caroline developed a rather nasty stomach bug on Saturday, and I gather she rang you, as she needed someone with her. I didn't know she'd made the call and so when I called round and found her like that, I put her in my car and brought her back here so I could look after her. She's much better now but not feeling up to talking. It was only when I got your message, I discovered what she'd done. You've been very kind and I am grateful she's got such a good friend. I shall look forward to meeting you in the not too distant future. I gather my stepson and your grandson are friends so I am sure we will meet through them at some point.'

A wave of relief flowed through her, and she gave an enthusiastic reply to this news and said she'd visit once Caroline had returned home.

Louise continued to hold the phone in her hand for a while and wondered about the seemingly pleasant man who had just spoken to her and the part of him which could be vicious and violent towards Ben and Harriet. She did feel relieved though Caroline wasn't lying in a ditch somewhere and hoped she was being looked after.

WEDNESDAY 16TH NOVEMBER 2005

The last two days had been as normal as they could have been, given what had happened and there had not been any more scares. George had listened to her request to wait for contact so she'd heard nothing from him.

The weather had at last improved, and she'd managed to give Buster a decent enough walk before she had gone into her study to get her notes out and be ready for the morning sessions.

Her fingers automatically went to the slots in her filing cabinet where they should have been, but they weren't there. Her mind raced as she frantically searched. 'No, oh no, this can't be happening.' Heat spread through her body and sweat formed on her forehead. None of the files were in order, they were all over the place. She gasped, 'It's impossible.' She looked again but they were in a terrible mess, and it could only mean someone had disturbed them.

The intruder must have got in here on Friday night, found the key, gone through the files, locked the cabinet and put the key back. Her files had numbers, rather than a name, so not immediately identifiable to anyone. From the mess they were in, it looked as though the intruder had just thrown them around, trying to find a particular one perhaps. What on earth or who on earth could they have been searching for? Dave had asked her to check everything but because of Caroline she had forgotten, and she cursed her stupidity. She looked at her watch. 'Hell, I have my first client in ten minutes and there is absolutely no time to sort them before then. I need to phone Dave but there is no time now, I'll just have to carry on and see everyone and try and remember as best I can.'

Once her clients had started to talk, Louise managed better than she thought she might. As always, she found it easy to remember the history and the stories but wasn't always good at remembering names.

With a sigh of relief at having managed to get through the whole morning unscathed or caught out, she picked up her phone from the kitchen table to ring Dave. She was surprised to see there had been several missed calls from Katy and a text message asking her to phone her.

Katy answered immediately and sounded upset and breathless.

'Mum, thank goodness.   Something dreadful happened at the school today.'

Katy explained she'd dropped off Max as usual and just got home before the school rang to ask if she could pick him up as he was very upset. *'I didn't get the full story then or when I reached the school, as he was so upset Matron just told me to take him home immediately and she would phone and explain later.'* By now Louise felt quite sick as thoughts of what might have happened raced through her head.

Katy told her that Max had found Ben in a bad mood when he arrived that morning and he'd immediately taken his mood out on Max. *'He was being rude and taunting him.   Max said it was as if he wanted to pick a fight.   He tried to make him see he wasn't being reasonable but then Ben started punching him.   Max said the punches were quite hard and they hurt so, without thinking, he walloped him back.   He said it was only once but then Ben stormed off and shouted something like, "Stuff it, some friend you are. Go and die for all I care." Max was upset by his words but realised he had been wrong to hit him back.'* Katy's voice had got breathless, and she had gulped at almost every word.

Louise clutched the phone.   *'Slow down Katy, take a deep breath.'* Then heard her inhale.

'Sorry Mum.   That's better.   Now where had I got to? Oh yes, because Max felt bad about the punch he'd given, he went to find Ben to see if they could work it out and said he knew he'd be with the school pets as apparently Ben has the job of feeding them on a Monday.'

Katy took another gulped breath. '*Ben was holding one of the guinea pigs in a strange way. He spotted Max and then, with no warning, threw the animal onto the ground and stamped on it.*'

Louise gasped, hardly able to believe what she'd heard. '*How dreadful - what did Max do then?*'

'*Max said he just froze. The animal had apparently squealed loudly but then was silent and Max could see Ben had killed it but Ben didn't seem to care; he just calmly picked up the guinea pig and put it back in the cage.*'

There was another silence before Katy spoke again. '*When Max confronted Ben, he apparently muttered "Everyone leaves in the end." Max was shocked and upset and eventually was taken to Matron. She rang me later and told me the rest of the story so far as she knew it. She said the guinea pig had been found dead in the cage and been squashed by something. Ben was in his class and behaved as if nothing had happened. Matron called Ben's father and he went in and collected him. Max is extremely upset and says he can't get the noise of the squealing or the picture of the dying guinea pig out of his head.*'

Louise loosened her grip on the phone and changed to the other hand. '*It is almost too awful to believe. What a terrible thing to happen and to witness. Poor Max. I'm not surprised he's upset. Is there is anything you'd like me to do?*'

There was a large sigh. '*I'm sure you know better than me about how to handle this. I really feel at a loss. I've never heard of anything so horrible, and I am not sure how to comfort Max as he finds it impossible to believe it actually happened. All I am doing is being there for him and if he wants to talk, I am letting him, but he just wanders around aimlessly crying.*'

Louise felt the tremble move through her body. She knew she was exhausted but nevertheless offered to go over when she'd finished work.

'*Oh, would you, that would be great. Thank you, Mum.*'

Louise put down the phone and sat down before her legs gave way beneath her.

She had no time left before the afternoon session and so no time to call Dave but sent him a brief text about the notes and asked him to give her a call later.

She grabbed her diary and made it to her counselling room before the client was due. She sank into her chair to wait, shut her eyes and tried to relax. Thoughts streamed through her head, and she wondered how she would get through the afternoon. She tried to concentrate on her clients and remember what she could about them. There were only three more people to see, and she hoped she'd manage. The last one was Ed; his story had been so disquieting it was not one she'd be likely to forget.

She thought about the consequences of someone else having read the notes. She would need to tell her clients their confidentiality had been compromised but she decided to talk to her supervisor, her professional body, and to her insurers first. Oh dear, there is so much to think about and then there is also Max. I'm not sure I can cope with it all. A tear formed in her eyes just as there was a knock on the door. She wiped her eyes, put on a professional exterior and greeted the client.

Louise managed to get through that session and the next one and had forced herself not to think of the events that had happened. By the time it was Ed's appointment she had managed a quick 'cat nap' too, so felt more able to face whatever he might bring.

As soon as the session started Louise wished she had cancelled. Exhaustion had caught up with her and not having been able to see her notes made her feel 'wrong footed' and she knew she wasn't in the right frame of mind. She settled into her chair and tried to focus on all the things he had told her last time.

'Are you all right, Louise? I don't know what it is, but you seem distracted, even anxious. Has something happened?'

Is this man a mind reader as well? 'Everything is fine, but I am just wondering how you were after our last session which I think would have been quite difficult?'

A hearty laugh escaped from deep in his body, which made her jump, but she managed to put on a calm face as he answered the question.

'I see now that's how it is. You don't answer my question but turn it back to me. Very clever, very psychological but just to play along with you, I was fine after our last session, I don't have a problem with my childhood, as I told you. It is all dealt with but you seemed to want to hear it. Think it made you feel as if you were in control and wanted me to lose mine. As you know, I didn't but today there is something not right with you and so I'll go back to my original question, which was to ask whether you are all right or has something happened?'

Heat seeped up into her face and her heart started to thump. This was not going in a good direction and she wished she were in her proper 'counselling chair'. She made a promise to herself, not to offer clients a choice of chairs in the future, if choosing the 'wrong' chair made her feel like this.

'Come on, Louise, I can see my asking you questions is making you feel uncomfortable, so I'll stop but I do think you're not yourself today. Going back to your original question, I am fine and was fine. In fact, as you know, this is our last booked session, and I won't be coming again so I'm guessing you probably want to wrap up our sessions in some way?'

Louise could see all the animals, she'd imagined him to be, play out in front of her. The snake, the panther, the wolf and the gentle domestic cat and she felt more like the mouse all those animals would play with and torture before going in for the kill. She mentally gave herself a shake, shut her eyes and tried to clear the image and to focus on the years of experience she had. Her mind scrabbled to get back into a professional space.

'No, you are not making me uncomfortable but I notice you diverted the question I asked you and so I get the feeling perhaps our last session was difficult, but you don't want to continue talking about it. I was going to open this session today by suggesting you might like to have more sessions, as I feel we have only just touched the surface of where your outbursts of anger originate but....'

He leapt to his feet before she had finished, and she froze. He stared into her face then seemed to remember where he was, turned towards the fireplace and gazed at the large watercolour of some trees on a hill. She'd put it there as it was supposed to be a calming view. She saw how hard he struggled to keep his anger from erupting as he clenched and unclenched his hands. He then stuffed them in his pockets, turned around and returned to his chair.

Louise knew this was a moment just to wait, so she took some quiet deep breaths and sat quietly.

Once in the chair he sat and stared at her. She was proud she had managed to calm herself down and felt more in control. She waited, knowing she held the silence and when she glanced at him, she saw he was using the time to work something out and if she waited, he would eventually tell her what was going on.

Louise had tried to buy completely silent clocks but without success. However, she usually didn't notice or hear either of them but today she could hear the very rhythmic tick of the clock behind her as the minutes passed. She wondered how long it would be before the silence turned from what therapists would recognise as productive, to a point when the silence was no longer a useful one and needed to be broken.

She glanced across at him again. His face had changed, and she now needed to speak.

'Would you like to tell me what just went on for you there, Ed?' He put his head down and then glanced up at her with a look she thought was meant to look contrite but had the feeling he had just patted a mouse with his paw.

He lifted his head and coughed. 'Sorry, you're right it all got too much for me. I think there is a lot more there to explore and it is clever, very clever of you to realise. However, I don't want to continue after this session. As you saw then, I am learning to control my temper and so I think there will be no more problems at work, and I feel this is just not the right time for me to go deeper into the effects of my past. I have no doubt you are right, it fucked me up but I'm getting my life together with my new partner and don't want to mess that up.'

Louise took a breath and smiled. 'Just to remind you, I didn't say it fucked you up but there will have been an effect and I think some of your anger issues will be one of those'. She would have liked to have told him he was well and truly fucked up but with his past being as bad as it was, it wasn't his fault and he had seemed to have managed that angry outburst well. So instead, she said, 'Yes I do understand but even so, I would still like to offer you the chance to come back in the future if you ever do feel it's the right time.'

He agreed and said he would return if he ever needed to. He started to get up out of the chair, but she continued.

'Good, I'm pleased about that. As I can see you want to leave, even though we are only a short way into your session, there is one thing I would like to ask about before you go.' As she continued, he settled back again into the chair. 'You mentioned just now you were managing to hold your temper at work. You haven't spoken about work today so I wonder if you would like to tell me what has been going on there, as a way of ending. You also mentioned your partner, so I am guessing your relationship is going well too?'

Ed settled back but then pulled himself up and straightened his back. Louise guessed he would now tell her something that made him sound good.

'Oh well, work is great now and you would be proud at how well I'm keeping my temper. There have been no problems at all and Michael is making sure he keeps that idiot away from me and is in fact talking about a promotion as he can see what an asset I am to the firm - I don't think he'd like to lose me.'

Having discovered that, in all probability, Ed did work in Michael's firm, she wasn't sure that a promotion was something in Michael's head if what his wife said was true. She looked forward to her next meeting when she might hear from Katherine the reality of the situation.

'That's excellent, I am so glad and yes, I'm really pleased you're doing well.' She didn't feel proud of him and so purposefully didn't use the word in her response. She could see he thought the management of his anger was now sorted and he needed no further help but felt the need to explain just how difficult change can be. 'I don't know whether you've ever heard of the cycle of change but thought it might help you to understand where you are at this moment.'

He rolled his eyes as if he was already bored by what she was going to say and didn't feel whatever it was would be necessary for him to hear. She continued anyway.

'People wanting to change might start off at a point we call pre-contemplation, which is when the person knows there is something they would like to change about their life or their habits but do nothing about it.'

Louise stops for a moment to check she had his attention, which she obviously had as he protested loudly that he was doing something and his visits to her confirmed it.

Louise continued without comment. 'The stage which follows next, is contemplation. This is when a person really looks at what they would like to change and plans how to do it and decides when it is going to happen.'

She paused again and wondered whether he'd make any comment but as nothing came from him, she continued. 'Then there is action, which is just what it says, when a person starts to behave in a different way. So, for instance, if smoking was a problem, then they would stop smoking. I would say you are at the point where you've taken action.'

Ed shifted in his seat and straightened up, waited for praise, then put on a sullen face when none was given.

'However, the most difficult part is yet to come, and this is the maintenance stage. The person needs to maintain the action, or they can lapse and return to any of the stages I've mentioned. They would then need to start again at the point they returned to, if they wish to continue with the change.'

He could hardly wait for her to finish before he leapt in. 'All sounds a bit gobbledygook to me but if you think this cycle thing will make me want to see you for more sessions you're mistaken. I have learned what I need, and I've put it into action and that is how it will remain.' He banged his hand on the arm of the chair.

Louise sat for a moment and wondered whether she should challenge him on his perception of how easy it is to change habits of a lifetime. She wanted him to hear the maintenance stage is the most difficult and the one most likely to go wrong but decided she didn't have the energy and he wouldn't have listened anyway.

'That's as you wish and you have made yourself perfectly clear, so let's return to your relationship. How is that going?'

Ed stared back at her, and she couldn't fathom what animal she saw in his eyes but fancied the snake just skidded by followed by the panther and the wolf but there didn't seem to be a trace of the domestic cat. She swallowed and wondered what he was going to come out with.

'Fine, everything is fine. In fact, she is just the one for me and we are almost living together now.

'I'm glad the relationship's going well.' She felt her eyelids droop and for a moment all her own worries and fears crossed her mind. She glanced up at the clock and couldn't help a small sigh before she spoke again.

'We do still have about twenty minutes left of this session and I'm wondering how you would like to use it?'

He gave her a hard look before he replied, and she felt he'd just emptied her mind of all her thoughts both personal and professional. 'I don't really think I have anything further I want to say and I can see you're tired. I told you I didn't think you were your usual self when I came in. I do hope there is nothing bothering you. I guess if the therapist has problems, it can be difficult. What happens then, I wonder?'

Louise saw an image of a cat watching a bird. 'I'm fine, although it is kind of you to ask but I think you caught my sigh and I have to admit to being tired as I didn't sleep last night.' Oh dear, how did that slip out? He is too clever by half.

'Did something keep you awake?' Ed leaned forward in the chair and looked across at her expectantly and his eyes sparkled. She looked at him and felt a bit like the bird before she replied. She told him it was the storm and the wind outside that had caused her not to sleep.

He looked disappointed but nodded his head. 'Yes, there was a lot of wind last night and rain too.' He thumped both the palms of his hands down onto the arm of the chair. 'Right then, no point in going on further. I think I'll stop there.' He looked to see if she was going to argue with him.

'Well, if you have nothing further you want to explore, Ed, and if you are happy to finish early, then let's agree to end now.' He nodded and started to move as Louise added, I'll bill your office as agreed and I hope everything works out well for you but remember I would be very happy to see you again if things should get difficult again in the future.'

He stood up and put his hand out and waited for her to shake it. She took it and felt the strength of his muscles as he squeezed her hard before he let it go. 'I don't think we'll meet again Louise, not as a client at least,' he added and this prompted Louise to say, 'Oh yes, I did mean to say to you before now but if we should meet in town or anywhere, I will not acknowledge you unless you acknowledge me, as I do appreciate not everyone wants it known what my role is and if you choose to ignore me, I will understand.'

He moved away from her towards the door and took his coat. 'Thanks again, it has been both enlightening and entertaining.' He made a sound in his throat which Louise guessed was meant to be a laugh. 'Oh yes I have especially enjoyed meeting and talking with my red haired, freckled and rather gorgeous therapist.' As she felt her face colour, he did one of his more disturbing laughs and then the front door closed, and he was gone. She sank down in the chair and ran her hands through her hair. 'Gorgeous'! He must need his eyes tested as well as everything else.

She remembered she had promised to go over to see Max and hoped Katy would ask her to have something to eat. She decided to take Buster so Max could chase him round the garden in place of a walk.

Max's bedroom door was closed but Louise heard sniffing. She tapped gently on the door and walked in.

She felt it would be good to distract him and pointed at the large intricate Lego model of a space station which was in the corner of the room. 'Goodness, that takes me back a bit.'

Max looked up to see what she had seen. 'It's good isn't it.' He walked over to point out parts of the scene to her.

'Did you do this on your own, or did Ben help you when he was here?'

Max nodded. 'He put the control panels on. Don't think he'd ever seen so much Lego.'

'It sounds as though you got on well to start with?' Louise hoped she hadn't introduced Ben's name too soon.'

Max walked back to the bed and sat down. 'I don't know, Granny. I was scared by what had happened at his house, but I was still his friend.' He then told her what had happened at school and how Ben had taunted him until he'd punched him. 'I know it was wrong, but I couldn't help it. He shouted at me and said I wasn't a friend and could die for all he cared. He then ran off.'

Louise put her arm around him and felt the tension in his body.

Max took a large breath and then told Louise what had happened with the guinea pig. 'He stamped on him Granny. He killed him and I saw it and I don't want to see it but I can't get it out of my head.' He beat at his head with his hand.

'Stop Max, stop hurting yourself it won't help, it really won't.' She held him tight to her and he sobbed. 'You've had a horrible experience and sometimes when we see something that is almost more than we can stand, it feels as if it has burnt onto our eyes or into our brain and we keep seeing the same thing over and over. It sounds as though that is happening to you now. I can't take the awful thing away and change what you saw but we can make sure you get the help you need so you can put the memory into a different place in your brain where it won't hurt you all the time.'

He asked her what she meant, and she explained about how he might like to talk to a counsellor, just like her who would help him sort this out. 'You can tell them whatever you like, and no-one will know what you said.' He said nothing but his head came up as if he was interested.

'Tell you what Max, I am really hungry, and your Mum offered me some food, so shall we both go and have something to eat, and we can talk more, if you want, after we've finished.'

Max seemed a lot brighter after food and wanted to go and watch television.

'Think I'll make a move too Katy. I had hoped to speak to Dave, but I'm exhausted and need to get home. I left a message on his phone so I'm sure he'll ring at some point.' She gave Katy a big hug.

'Thank you, Mum, I can see you've really helped Max.'

'He will need some more help I think - some professional help. I'll have a think who might be good to refer him to.'

She was about to get in her car when Dave drew up alongside her and rolled his window down.

'Sorry Louise, I know you wanted to speak to me, but I've been held up most of the day dealing with a missing persons case. Has something more happened?'

Louise asked to sit in his car, where she told him about the notes. Dave sighed but listened carefully while she told him all that had happened. Although she now thought

Caroline was safe, she hadn't been able to get that strip of material out of head. There was something strange about that night and the SOS she'd had, but when she voiced her fear to Dave, he accused her of being paranoid and watching too many thrillers on tv.

'I'm not sure it's worth sending anyone to your house again. They told me all prints had been carefully wiped from any surfaces the intruder might have touched. There were other prints, but I guess they are George's and the student next door, and we haven't managed to get either of those yet. George hasn't called into the station as I asked, and the student has promised he will call in soon. Your number is still red flagged. I don't like the sound of the notes thing but try not to worry we will sort this. I didn't mean to say you were being paranoid, but you are distressed, and I am tired and so a bit irritable. Take care and see you soon.'

Louise walked to her car and heard Dave shout to Katy as soon as he'd opened the door.

He is right, she thought. I have been watching a lot of thrillers, but I think I am justified in thinking the things that have happened are very strange. Who on earth would want to break into my house and mix up the notes? I can't think of anything in them that is particularly sensitive or could be used for blackmail.

Too tired to sort out the notes when she got home, she poured herself a large wine, settled down on the sofa and turned on the television. She was asleep before she knew what programme was on.

A noise entered her unconscious state. Groggy and confused she looked around. Buster's ears were raised and he gave a low growl as he ran towards the window and started to bark. Louise wondered if there was perhaps someone at the door but the noise she'd heard was more off a metallic noise not a knock. She stayed still and strained to hear any more noise and when she heard nothing, lifted her feet of the sofa and sat up. Buster had stopped barking but was still by the window and had managed to push his head underneath the curtain.

Louise turned off all the lights in the room and switched off the television. She crept over to the window and pulled back a corner of the curtain. The streetlights gave a small amount of light but not enough to make out whether there was anyone out there or anything which could account for the noise. Perhaps after all it had been something on the television. Buster had lost interest and padded into the kitchen in search of food. Louise put the curtain straight and slowly followed him. She didn't usually bother with the kitchen blinds but pulled them down before she put on the light. I don't know what is worse she thought, not to be able to see outside and not have any idea what is going on out there, or to leave everything open and not know if there is someone looking in.

She looked at the kitchen clock which showed it was nearly eight; she'd been asleep for over an hour. God what a day it's been, she thought, as she dragged herself upstairs to find the notes she would need for tomorrow.

She started to thumb through her notes which she kept in individual plastic folders. She needed her code book to sort properly but could mostly tell who the notes belonged to by looking at the first session written on the page. It didn't take too long to find the few she needed for tomorrow but she was not inclined to sort through all other notes; she would have more time on Friday.

The phone rang and, in that moment, she hoped it was George. Strange she felt that, as she was angry and distrustful of him, but memories of the good times they'd had were still strong and she so wished it could be all right again. She hadn't checked who the caller was before she put it to her ear. '*Hello….*' There was no answer although she felt sure there was someone there. '*Hello, can you hear me? Who is it? Sorry, I can't hear anything.*' Louise lifted the phone away from her ear and looked at the number; it wasn't one she knew. She tried again, '*Hello, are you still there?*' There was silence. '*I really can't hear you, why don't you end the call and try again, or I will try and call you as your number has come up on my phone.'* There was still no response and the caller disconnected.

Whoever it was didn't call back and she tapped the phone in her hands while she sat and wondered what she should do. She dialled the last received number on her phone and it immediately connected. *'Hello, you just rang me, but I couldn't hear you. Who is this please*?' This time she definitely heard breathing, quite heavy breathing but no voice. Her stomach turned over and her knees felt wobbly. *'Okay, I've had enough now I'm going to end this call if you don't speak and tell me who you are.'* No answer so she clicked it off and shivered.

Could it have been George after all? He did say he was going to be difficult to contact so perhaps he just had no signal. No that can't be right, or I wouldn't have heard anything. She paced the room and thought it through. I know, I'll ring him on his own number and see if I can get him. It rang and rang and then went to voicemail. She was going to put it down but thought again, *'George, it's Louise, did you just try to ring me? Someone rang and they didn't speak and then there was just heavy breathing. If it was you, please let me know even if you are drunk, but this whole thing is scaring me, and I'd be pleased if you would just let me know.'* Bleep. Damn, why do these things never give you enough time to finish your message? Still, he should have caught the drift, if he picks it up, that is.

She tentatively opened the back door to let Buster out but didn't go out herself; instead she closed the door and shut him out for a while. She turned off all the lights downstairs but hesitated over the downstairs hall light and in the end left it on. She opened the door just enough to let him back through and slammed it shut again. She watched as he licked his lips, as though he had found something juicy to eat outside.

She was about to go upstairs when she remembered she hadn't put the chain across the front door and walked back to do it. The phone rang again. The number looked the same as the one earlier; it must surely be George, otherwise who on earth could it be? There was no-one there and she ended the call. When it rang again she ignored it and decided not to answer.

It continued to ring and she realised where the sound came from; it was outside the house. She put her ear to the door and it sounded louder. She felt the heavy pound of her heart and a scream lurked in the tightness of her throat. Her fingers fumbled as she tried to end the call. The sound outside stopped. Her hand shook but she pressed the re-dial button. Once more the phone rang outside the door. She put her ear next to the letter box and the sound was so loud she was sure the caller was immediately outside, perhaps just on the other side of the door. She gasped and leapt back. Her whole body shook as the phone she held in her hand continued to ring. She still heard it outside but it was fainter, as if the caller had walked away from the house. Then she no longer heard it. She cancelled the call, leant back against the door, gasped for breath and felt sick. Tears streamed down her face. What on earth is happening to me.

She looked round for Buster. That's strange - he didn't bark either. 'Where are you, boy? She called again and saw a dark shape in his bed. 'Gone to bed, have you?' She bent down to stroke him, 'You Ok, Buster?' It was dark under the stairs, but she caught the movement of a faint tail wag. He would normally have got up and nuzzled into her.

She went into the kitchen and found a torch and shone it down on him - he did indeed look asleep. She shook him and he raised an eyelid but no more, before he shut his eyes tight again. Oh my God, Buster, I think you've been drugged again. It must have been what you were eating. She tried to clear her head, tried not to panic. There was no way they could have got into her back garden as the back gate now has a keycode and absolutely no-one knew the number but her. She tried to be logical but in these circumstances, it was too hard. She knew he would be fine in the morning, but she was now very scared. The idea of going to bed when Buster would be unable to help if anything happened filled her with horror.

She dialled the emergency number the police had given her. A voice answered almost immediately and once she had explained was told someone would be there shortly. Should I ring Dave, she wondered, but then thought of how tired and short tempered he had been with her earlier and he would have enough to worry about with Max tonight. She expected it would be another long night and put the kettle on.

She jumped when she heard her phone again and looked at it, horrified. She left it and waited for her voicemail to kick in: *Hi, you're through to Louise please leave a message and I'll get back to you as soon as possible. If you are a client wanting an appointment, please leave your name and number and when I can call you back'.* She thought the person would not leave a message, but she heard an intake of breath and then George's voice. *'Louise, it's George. What's going on? Are you all right? No, before you ask, I'm not drunk, and I do want you to let me explain but that message you left was strange and you've worried me. Please ring me back. I would come to see you myself, even though you've said not to, but I can't because I am not anywhere near Bath. I'll be back soon - hopefully at the weekend or early next week - and then we can have a proper talk. Bye, Louise, I do love you, even if you think I don't.'*

She listened to the message twice. He didn't sound drunk, in fact he sounded fine but where was he and why hadn't he just told her? She sighed. I can't bear it. I wish I'd interrupted the answerphone; I could have told him what's happening. She'd felt a tingle in her body when he said he loved her and knew she probably loved him too. Although at the moment she still didn't trust him, she just didn't believe he copied a key – it just wouldn't make any sense. With that thought she put some coffee into her mug and filled it with water and then nearly scalded herself when the door knocker went.

It wasn't the same two this time. One was a woman who looked concerned and smiled in a very friendly way as she came in. Louise explained what had happened and particularly about the call, the dog and someone outside her door. She realised it sounded quite barmy and the man, who said he was Constable Richards, sounded quite sceptical. 'So, you didn't actually see anyone, and it could have been your boyfriend and the dog could have picked up some of the drugged meat that was missed last time.' Louise could see they had their doubts and wondered what they'd been told about her.

Richards said rather scathingly it was odd not to withhold the number. The woman who said she was, Constable Helen Ford, wasn't so sure. 'Mmm …but if it were someone playing mind games it is just the sort of thing they would do and if they used a pre-paid phone, the number couldn't be traced afterwards, and they'd probably throw it away.' They made reams of notes and had a quick look outside but couldn't see anything.

They left after making sure the bolts on the 'safe room' were in place and said to call again if she was worried.

Louise was too tense to settle in her room and so dragged her duvet into the bathroom, bolted the doors and lay on the floor alert to every sound.

THURSDAY 17TH NOVEMBER 2005

When Louise had told George she quite liked the natural wood floorboards in the bathroom, she never imagined she might end up asleep on them.

She yawned and struggled to free her legs from the duvet, which she'd wound tightly around herself to try and keep warm. Oh, my word, who or what on earth is that? She wished she hadn't caught a glimpse of herself in the bathroom mirror. I've got red eyes and a grey face and oh my goodness, my hair! I look just like some wild witch, but then I suppose I did only sleep for a few minutes at a time. She groaned and shifted about a bit to get her body moving. She listened at the door but could hear nothing. Buster would probably still be sleepy from the drugs but shouted for him anyway. 'BUSTER, here Buster. Good boy, COME.' She panicked for a moment when she heard nothing, so shouted even louder. The sound of his claws as they scrabbled on the floorboards outside followed by whining, reassured her. She unlocked the door, and he almost knocked her off her feet and she buried her face in his fur.

She pulled her dressing gown tightly around her, went downstairs and just in case she had missed any more of the drugged meat, let Buster out into the front garden. She kept hold of the door as she watched him and noticed her father's old tin bucket, lying on its side surrounded by scattered weeds.

As she set it upright and started to pick up the fallen weeds, the handle clanged down and she was reminded of the noise she heard last night. It was the noise of the bucket being knocked over! She shivered, called Buster and went back inside. As she sipped a hot coffee, she thought about the day ahead and rubbed her hands over her face, trying to clear her head. I'm so tired, I can't face clients today. I'll cancel them and go back to bed and try to get some sleep.

She'd just got comfortable in bed, when the phone went, and she wished she had put it on silent or turned it off.

'Hi, Louise, I am sorry to ring so early but I wanted to catch you before you started work.' Louise made a grim face.

'Hello, Tim. Is there a problem?'

'I hope not. I had a rather strange meeting with Paul a few days ago. I've been mulling over what I should do, then last night I thought I must tell you. I don't think there is anything to worry about, but you never know.'

'That's OK but can you tell me quickly please, as I really don't have much time at the moment.' She hoped she didn't sound as irritated as she felt.

In his usual, laborious way, Tim started to tell her again about the ex-prisoner, whose help Paul had acquired to help prove his innocence.

Louise found it hard to concentrate on the conversation as she'd heard this before. She made a mental note to turn off her phone after he'd finished. This was still in her mind when she realised Tim had stopped speaking and clearly expected an answer.

'Sorry, I got distracted for a moment, can you repeat what you just said please.'

Tim sighed, *'Paul, was talking about the guy who was going to do some detective work for him and....'*

Louise tried to cut him off there as this was just a repeat of how he'd started the conversation, but he ignored her and continued.

'...then he stopped what he was saying, looked searchingly at me and asked if I knew a counsellor called Louise Graham and he didn't tell me why he'd asked or why this guy would want to know.'

Louise's throat went dry *'What did you reply, Tim?'*

'I didn't know what to say, and although I wouldn't normally lie, I just told him I didn't and then he seemed to lose interest and talked about something else.'

The last remaining bit of energy drained from her. She tried to think if she'd ever had any connection with this man but was sure she hadn't. What on earth could have made him ask about me.

'I really can't think why your client would be interested in me and so you did the right thing to phone me. I can't remember if you ever told me the name of the woman he killed; his wife, wasn't it?'

'No, I don't think I did, but I believe her name was Julia, although he doesn't use her name much as he always talks about "that bitch".'

Louise swallowed once more, and thoughts whirled around in her head. She supposed it could just be the Julia who she'd been reminded about with Amanda the other day. But why on earth would her own name have come to the attention of Paul?

Tim's voice broke through her thoughts. *'Are you still there? You've gone silent.'*

'Sorry Tim, I was thinking - but am afraid I can't understand it. I shall look forward to hearing how things are going with Paul when we next meet.'

Desperate to finish the conversation and get some sleep she stayed silent and hoped he would be sensitive enough to realise it was time to finish.

Louise mumbled a goodbye, switched her phone off and snuggled down again. She just wanted to relax and get some sleep. She knew it would be unlikely she would manage it, as the question as to why some killer should want to know about her confused and unnerved her. Surprisingly she did eventually drift off.

It was already late afternoon and dark when she turned her phone on again. There were lots of messages on it. They were mostly from Katy but there was one from George as well; *Louise, I am worried about you, please let me know what's going on?* She shoved her phone in her pocket. Everything felt too much and she didn't want to speak to anyone, to explain anything or be faced with any new problems. She needed to clear her head and think. She grabbed Buster's lead, flung on a coat and marched out the door.

She'd only gone a few steps up the road when a car pulled up beside her; it was Katy.

'Mum why on earth haven't you answered your phone. Are you okay? I was so worried I just had to come and check. Dave was also worried but is at work and he asked me to let him know immediately if I didn't find you. I've also had George on the phone as he has also tried to get hold of you.

Louise felt bad, but explained she'd been exhausted and needed space and had turned her phone off so she hadn't been aware of their anxiety. Kate seemed to understand and tried again to get Louise to stay with them, but Louise told her she wanted to stay at home, although promised to keep in touch every day.

After that interruption she only managed a short walk. She made some comfort food and had a glass of wine but still didn't feel much better, so decided to give up on the day and try and get an early night. No matter how scared she felt, she just couldn't face another night on the bathroom floor.

She'd just started to draw her bedroom curtains when she thought she heard something outside. She peered from behind the curtain but saw nothing. Then the beam of the streetlight caught a figure by her gate. He looked back towards her house and then walked away. 'What the hell!' She exclaimed out loud. Her fingers shook as she pulled the curtains tight shut, then jumped into bed and pulled the covers over her head. She knew ought to have phoned the police, George and her family but all she wanted to do was disappear and pretend she wasn't involved in anything horrible. Just as she did as a child when her parents had terrible rows when she'd gone to bed.

FRIDAY 18TH NOVEMBER 2005

She had been sure she wouldn't sleep but exhaustion had enveloped her and when she looked at her watch it was after seven. She stretched her arms above her and gave a large yawn. Fantastic - don't think I can have moved an inch all night. I feel great. I'm sure I could deal with almost anything now, not that I want to put it to the test. I'd just like a day with no unpleasant surprises.

She plumped up the pillows and pulled herself up. I've managed so many difficult situations in my life. I've had addicted clients who challenged my every move and James dying, which was my worst nightmare but I survived. I'm not going to let this situation get under my skin. With these positive thoughts, she leapt out of bed and flung open the curtains in an exaggerated defiance. In reality she felt she'd been tossed about in the wildest of storms and found no safe harbour.

'I need to find Caroline.' She mumbled, 'She must have recovered by now and hopefully we can meet for a drink this evening.' I'll get in touch with her as soon as I'm dressed and hope she'll be free this evening.

She pressed Caroline's number into her phone. It rang but switched almost immediately to her voicemail. *'Caroline, it's me. Hope you're feeling better and being well looked after. It's Friday, in case you hadn't realised, and I could really do with a good long chat plus, of course, a large drink or two. Any chance you'll be free tonight? If not, perhaps I'll just have to come and dig you out of the palace you say you are living in, if you let me have the address or, of course, I could get it from Katy as she knows where you are. Anyway, please ring back if you can. Bye, lots of love.'*

'Now George' she muttered, 'although he probably won't be available.'

The call went straight to his voicemail. '*Hi, George, it's me. I'm sorry I didn't reply to your messages yesterday and sorry you were worried. I'm feeling better now and would like to hear what you have to say and tell you what has been going on in my life. By the way, I hate mysteries. I might love to watch them on the telly, but I hate mysterious people, so I warn you your excuse for your behaviour had better be good, and it had better be the whole truth or it really will be the end. I can't believe you...bleep*' **Damn**, well at least he would have got the gist and it would now be up to him.

She then rang Katy to apologise again for her behaviour and told her she now felt stronger after a good night's sleep. She asked if Dave had got any news on fingerprints etc but Katy said she hadn't heard.

She usually enjoyed the drive over to Jasper's with views over rolling hills and little high hedged lanes but today they hardly made an impression and she arrived at his cottage in what seemed like a very short amount of time.

Louise sunk into the chair and clasped her arms around her. She was sure Jasper would notice her body language, but he made no comment other than to urge her to start when she was ready.

She told him first things were not going smoothly between her and George. He was concerned to hear this but was even more concerned when she told him all the other things that had been happening, particularly those that related to clients. She also said the police had George in their sights as the possible intruder as he was only other person with a key.

'I was convinced it wasn't him until I found the key to the backdoor, or its replica, on my desk and then I suddenly had doubts and felt I couldn't trust him.'

Jasper stroked his beard. 'Oh, I'm sorry that's worrying and odd.'

When she told him Tim's client was possibly the ex-husband of the Julia found dead in Chew Valley lake, he raised his eyebrows, and muttered about it being another coincidence. He took off his glasses and used his jumper to clean the lens while he thought.

'I don't think we are going to get answers as to why your name came up in the prison, but I am concerned about Tim's client and his prison friend. You did the right thing in advising him to talk to the Governor. We also need to decide what you tell your clients about the breach in your security. They need to be informed that someone had access to their notes who was not entitled to see them. Maybe, once you've told them, it will throw some light on the situation. It is possible one of them might give you a reason why their notes might be of interest to someone.'

Louise nodded in agreement then told him the notes for a client who recently ended their sessions had been in the drawer, so she would need to telephone them too. 'Actually, he is someone I want to discuss today as he ended rather abruptly and unexpectedly.'

Jasper smiled. 'Let me guess, is it the chap you found a little difficult at the beginning?'

'Yes, you're right; it's Ed. Since our last session, I heard about his abusive childhood and some quite drastic and cruel ways in which he responded to this early trauma. He had been abused physically and emotionally by parents and then sexually by a teacher at his school. Later he described how his parents died in a car crash on the same day he'd had a difficult visit with them.'

Jasper sat up, 'What a host of horrible things.'

'Yes, awful. I was certain all of these things accounted for his instant rages, but he didn't want to go into it and our sessions ended almost immediately after he'd told me the whole story and I couldn't persuade him to continue.

They discussed her feelings about Ed again and how despite all that, they had managed to do some good work.

She told him more about Max and the boy Ben and the connection with Harriet and about the incident with the guinea pig and the words he had shouted at Max. She also told him that it seemed that the father of this Ben was the boyfriend of her friend Caroline. She'd wanted to warn

Caroline about him but hadn't been able to as Caroline hadn't been back home since and she hadn't been able to contact her by phone.

He was quiet for a moment and Louise saw he was thinking about all the information she'd given him. 'I'm glad, despite your feelings, you've managed to get some work done with your client and I'm sorry about your friend. I think you are wise to let her know about him as soon as you can.'

When the session ended Jasper told her to look after herself. 'It is very important to listen to your gut feelings. I don't like the sound of some of the things you have told me today, so do be cautious and not hot-headed.'

She'd just driven onto the main road when her phone rang. Agitated that she was unable to answer immediately, her heart started to race. She pulled in at the first lay-by so she could find out who it was. It was a message.

Hi Louise, Dave here. We've completed all the fingerprinting. The only ones within the house are yours and George's. It seems whoever entered was wearing gloves as there were none on your filing cabinet or the plastic folders you kept your notes in, nor on any of the doors, when we would at least have expected to find yours. There are some things I'd like to discuss with you though, so is there a chance you could ring me back this evening – I'll be home at a normal time.

She let out a huge sigh of relief. It must mean they've found George and concluded he had nothing to do with it.

Buster needed to go out, so she didn't phone immediately she got home as she wasn't sure whether Caroline would ring at the last minute and suggest they meet.

'Dave, it's Louise, you wanted to talk to me. I'm glad you got hold of George's fingerprints. Did you find him at his home?'

'Thanks for ringing back. I wanted speak to you about George.' There was silence and she heard him clear his throat.

'It's a bit awkward; I probably shouldn't be telling you this. We didn't manage to get George's from him but we found them on our database. Apparently he was involved in an investigation into a death. He was involved and under suspicion for a while.'

She gulped. *'How do you mean involved? You mean he was there? What are you saying exactly? Tell me.'* She had a sudden thought. *'Was it when he was in the army? He told me he had been involved in an accident and he suffered PTSD as a result. Is that what you're talking about?'*

'Hang on a minute, too many questions! Yes, it is about that accident. I'm sorry to have to tell you but some new evidence has been found and the case is being re-opened which means he is still under suspicion. He may have nothing to do with it, but it is being investigated as a manslaughter or even a murder enquiry.'

She blinked back tears and took a deep breath. Her knees started to feel weak, and she needed to sit down. What's going on with my life? She suddenly felt very angry and thought about the drunken mess she had found him in. How dare he come into my life and play havoc with it like this?

'Louise, are you still there? You've gone very quiet. I am sorry to do this to you when you have so much on your plate, but I thought you ought to know. Do you remember when we all met for lunch and Henry read out a piece in the paper about the body of a diver being found? It was that accident. The guy was George's buddy and George surfaced but his buddy didn't. He was never found. George couldn't give a good enough explanation of what had happened and so became a suspect. Nothing was proved but now they have the body there is new evidence and it is possible he could be charged with, at the very least, manslaughter.'

'So that's what all those letters from the army and the Coroner's Court were.'

Louise dropped the phone on the sofa, where she had sat down a moment ago. She hadn't cancelled the call and she vaguely heard in the distance Dave shouting down the phone.   She couldn't take it in.   Was he then, a killer? Hearing about the new inquiry would explain his drunken behaviour. But what about the break-in and her notes being ransacked? What could that have to do with him? She picked up the phone and told Dave she was upset by this news and had dropped the phone. She reassured him that she was all right, thanked him for letting her know and said goodbye.

Her re-gained confidence left her. How could she trust anyone every again? Her previously suppressed sobs erupted, and tears fell in a constant stream.

SATURDAY 19TH NOVEMBER 2005

Having no sleep had got her down; one good night in the last week was not enough. She'd lain awake for hours and tried to get to grips with her thoughts and feelings. She'd heard nothing more from George nor from Caroline and the idea of another weekend of feeling depressed felt too much to cope with. She made up her mind whatever else happened, she'd find Caroline and to do this she'd need Katy's help.

'Hi Katy, it's Mum and before you ask, no, I am not all right. I feel foolish and angry I let someone into my home and my heart who is clearly not the person I thought he was. I am furious he's disrupted my life and he could even be the intruder, although I cannot see why. So, all in all I am not in a good place.'

Louise heard Katy clear her throat and assumed she was about to speak. *'Wait Katy. Quite apart from what is happening to me, I'm worried about Caroline. So, all I want from you this morning is Ben's stepfather's address as I need to go and see for myself that she's okay.'*

'Mum, can I speak now. Please?' Louise grunted her agreement and Katy leapt in before she changed her mind. *'I can hear how upset you are but are you sure about this? So much has happened to you in the last few days you may not be thinking clearly. I know you're upset about George's behaviour and I'm disappointed for you too. However, Caroline is a grown woman and from what you've told me it sounds as though she has changed a lot since she started going out with this man and she may not want you to interfere. I don't like the sound of Ben's stepfather and although it's sad he's the man Caroline has chosen; he may also resent your interference. I will give you the address but please think carefully before you interfere.'* She sighed and then added. *'However, if you do go, please call us when*

209

you get back.' She paused before she spoke again, in what Louise recognised as her placatory voice. *'Look, Mum, why don't you come and have supper with us anyway?'*

Louise sighed; she hated it when she upset her children but equally hated it when they thought they knew better than her how to run her life.

'I'm sorry Katy, I never mean to worry you or Henry, but I have a bad feeling about Caroline and if I could just speak to her then I'm sure I'd be reassured. I understand what you're saying but I can't just let our relationship go; she's been such a good friend. If it hadn't been for her I'm not sure I'd have got through when your Dad died. I'm worried, so if you could give me the address or tell me exactly where the house is, then it would really help.'

Katy reluctantly agreed and said she'd ring back when she'd found it, as she couldn't remember it off hand.

'One more thing, Mum. Henry has rung me several times. He's worried about you, and you promised to return his call the night you had the break-in, and he can't seem to get hold of you.'

Louise remembered she had indeed said she'd ring him back, but it had gone out of her mind, so now she had upset him too. That would have to wait for now. All she wanted was for Katy to ring and give her the address.

Her fingers tapped on the table in a staccato rhythm, which increased in speed as the minutes ticked by. When Katy rang back, she wrote the address down and snapped her thanks. She promised she would call when she got back and said yes to the offer of supper.

The house was exactly where she had imagined it to be and very close to the school. It was a large detached and imposing Georgian house with a gated driveway. The gates were open, so she drove straight into the circular drive and parked the car outside the front door.

The beauty of these Georgian houses always astounded her. The glistening beauty of the limestone walls gave the impression of a more elegant age. She imagined finding one of Jane Austen's characters waiting inside perhaps doing embroidery by the window or reading a book. If this really was John's house, then he must be a very wealthy man and felt a little jealous it was Caroline and not her who might end up here but then remembered the type of man he was.

The lion on the door knocker was imposing but the sound it gave was pitiful and however hard she tried she could not make it sound loud enough for someone to hear. She looked for an alternative and spotted a long metal handle partly hidden by greenery. She yanked it and sure enough, a bell sounded in the distance, a sort of tinkling sound, she hoped, echoed around the house. This time she felt sure if anyone was in, they would come to answer the door - but they didn't.

It was impossible to peer through the windows as there were large flowerbeds full of roses in front of them and surprisingly, a few of them still in bloom. She gazed around her, then shrugged her shoulders and walked round the right side of the house. There she found some garages but no sign of any cars. There was a door in the large high stone wall, which she assumed led to the garden in the front; it was locked.

I guess if you parked your car in this courtyard or in a garage, then you would go into the house through the door I can see in front of me she thought. Perhaps I should try knocking on it as they might be in this part of the house and too far away from the main entrance. She walked over and rapped hard with her knuckles on the glass panel, as there didn't appear to be a bell. She peered in but again there was no sign of life. She saw a long corridor which looked like any backdoor area, with coat hooks and wellies underneath. Two doors led off it, one of which Louise assumed was the kitchen.

She returned to the front of the house and this time walked to the left side. There was an arched wall with a wrought iron gate set in it. She pushed the gate which, to her surprise opened. Her feet scrunched on the path made of small stones and wondered how she would explain herself if someone saw her in the garden. The path divided and one part led down some steps towards the main garden while the other continued round in front of the windows. These windows were more accessible, so she stood on tiptoe and peered through but there was no sign of anyone at all in any of the rooms. The house, although immaculate, looked sterile and unloved. There were no newspapers or books lying around and no flowers, it felt anonymous. More like a museum.

She smelt woodsmoke but couldn't make out where it came from. She spotted a wood in the distance, and assumed it was where Ben had taken Max. My goodness, you could get lost in there and no-one would guess where you were, she thought. She started to walk down the steps and paused, unsure what she should do. She shivered and wished she had brought Buster with her instead of leaving him guarding the house.

She continued down the steps and looked towards the wood again. She caught a movement in the trees and then a person emerged out of it. She couldn't make out whether it was a man or a woman but thought it was a man. He stopped and looked up at the house and she realised she'd been spotted. She started to raise her hand and walk towards him, but he turned around and disappeared back into the wood. How odd – I wonder who it was? Perhaps he shouldn't have been there, perhaps a poacher; I saw some pheasants roaming around.

She had just gone back through the archway when a car drove in and a man leapt out. He waved to her and started to speak as he walked over towards her.

'Hello, I didn't think you'd still be here. I thought you had already gone to your new property. I don't mean to bother you, but I just need to measure a few things before advertising the house.'

Louise chewed her upper lip. 'Sorry, I'm not the owner. I was looking for my friend the owner's partner, but I am not sure what you mean, advertising the house. Is it for sale then?'

The man looked suspicious. 'No, not for sale, it's To Let. The owner has rented another property in Somerset, and this is to be rented for a short while, possibly six months.'

Louise felt a tingle in her spine. Something didn't feel right at all and she remembered what Jasper had said about instinct. 'That's annoying, Caroline obviously forgot to tell me. Do you know where they've gone?'

'No, I'm sorry. He didn't rent through my company, but I think he said it is somewhere in the Chew Valley. Moving down there was mainly, I think, to do with her health. I saw them at the beginning of the week. Tuesday, I think, but didn't see her properly as she was rather wrapped up, which is why I mistook you for her. I now see I was wrong. She didn't even have the same colour hair as you do. He explained she was not well and said he thought all she needed was to be in some good country air. I just thought seeing you, perhaps she was better and come back to collect some things.'

What on earth was wrong with Caroline. Why hadn't she contacted me to let me know they were moving? Why would he need a house in the country? It wasn't as if this house was right in the middle of Bath and its garden and wood would be considered 'Country'. She turned to the agent. 'Thanks for telling me, I'm a bit confused as I thought this being so near to Ben's school was perfect for them.'

He tactfully made no comment about the school but added, 'It's not being let for a few weeks, and I think John said he would be coming back from time to time during that period. Perhaps if you leave a note for them, they'll get in touch.'

Louise realised there was nothing more to be learned so got into the car, gave him a wave and drove off. A car was parked just outside the gates, and she cursed. Damn it, I can't see if anything's coming with that car in the way. I'll just have to chance it she thought and started to edge out. To her annoyance when she checked her mirror, she saw the car was now behind her. What an idiot why couldn't he have moved off first. She looked in her mirror to see if she could see what the idiot looked like but saw only it was a man.

As she drove home, she concentrated on what she had just learned. The whole thing was weird. Her staccato thoughts turned to Caroline, and she blinked and bit her lip as her eyes misted up. She glanced in the mirror at regular intervals and felt certain she was being followed by the vehicle she saw as she left the house but then dismissed it as absurd.

Louise decided she would take Buster with her when she went to Katy's. It would make returning to the house in the dark feel safer, and the children always enjoyed having him with them.

The whole family sat round the table in the warmth of Katy's kitchen and had started their supper when Louise brought up the subject of Caroline. Max pushed his hair back in a way he did when he felt confused. 'What do you mean, Granny? Do I know where Caroline is? How would I know and why would Ben know? I haven't spoken to him much since he did that awful thing. The reason he did it, he says, was because he was upset when his dad's new girlfriend pushed off. He'd liked her and he feels everyone he likes just ups and leaves and thinks he must be a bad person as they don't stay. I don't understand, was Caroline his girlfriend? I didn't know. Ben never told me her name.'

The adults stopped eating and stared at Max. Dave spoke first as Louise seemed unable to find any words at all. 'How long ago did Ben say this happened Max? Louise has been trying to contact Caroline for a while.' Max hung his head as if he had done something wrong, so Dave quickly said 'No, you're not in trouble, there's no reason why you would have mentioned this but no-one has seen Caroline for quite a while so we would like you to tell us what you do know.'

Max screwed up his face as he tried hard to think. 'I dunno; she must have left the weekend before the guinea pig thing.' He opened his eyes wide. Has something happened to Caroline?' Dave reassured him as much as he could and encouraged him to try and remember when it was Ben had said this. 'That's easy it was yesterday. He came and found me and told me why he'd done it. He kind of apologised for being mean but never said sorry about killing the guinea pig. I get he was sad, but it was wrong, wasn't it what he did? I still can't get it out of my head an…'. Dave put a hand over his and said it was fine, he needn't say any more.

Louise put an arm round him. 'Thanks Max, I'm just worried about Caroline but perhaps I just keep missing her. You said Ben told you this yesterday, so do you happen to know about his new home and where it is to be? Did he mention it?'

Max again screwed up his face, 'No, not really, but he said they were moving, and it was going to be more in the country; oh yes, he said near a lake. Near a lake where he could fish and do it from a boat and everything. Can we go fishing, Dad? It sounds fun and if it was from a boat, it would be so cool - pleeeese.' Dave laughed and said it did sound fun and perhaps they could sometime. Milly, who had been unusually silent, piped up, 'Me too, me too, I wanna go fishing.'

'Wait a minute,' Louise almost shouted. 'Did you say she had left before the Guinea pig thing?' Max nodded. 'The man I saw today said she had looked unwell when he saw her on Tuesday, so that must have been after the guinea pig thing as he said it was this week. That's odd, isn't it?'

Katy and Dave both frowned at her, and Louise felt guilty she had added that last sentence; she didn't want to make the children anxious.

When the children had gone to bed Louise told Dave how worried she was. 'I think I must go back to her house in the morning and see if by any chance she has gone back there - but why would John tell Ben she had left, if she was still with him and moving with them to the country?'

Dave stretched out on the chair by the fire, 'I don't know, it is strange. In fact, everything that has happened to you in the last two weeks is strange. Can you not think of anything which might explain the break-in or any of the other stuff?'

Louise shook her head. There were so many things she couldn't talk about because of confidentiality. Could she tell Dave about Tim's client asking him whether he knew me? She didn't think she could, as she'd heard it in confidence. Could she tell him any of the things Paul had told Tim? No, again confidentiality prevented her, and it may not be connected anyway. However, if what is happening at the prison is reported to the police, she could then tell him and he could find out more through police channels.

'Sorry for the hesitation but I was thinking and I'm afraid I can't say more. I'm sorry.' She could tell by the look he gave he wasn't sure whether to believe her or not, but he left it there.

Dave and Katy both gave Louise a hug when she was ready to go. Dave told her he didn't have to be at work tomorrow and would like to go with her to Caroline's house. 'Not because of anything bad but because I think you could do with the company. With all that's happening to you, it must feel quite a lonely place for you now.'

Louise returned the hugs and gave them a big smile. 'I am so lucky to have you both and thanks, Dave, that would be great. Apart from you, my whole network seems to be in bits right now.'

The light in the window of her counselling room gave a reassuring light over the path and she was glad she had left it on and not drawn the curtains before she left. She had been calm in so many situations where her work was involved but the wobble she felt told her whatever she looked like on the surface; underneath she was paddling like mad. She'd let Buster out before she left Katy's so didn't need to take him out again and he went straight to his bed. She paid attention to each lock before she made her way upstairs and let out a large sigh of relief that, so far, nothing had happened to her this evening. Nevertheless, she kept her fingers crossed all the way upstairs.

SUNDAY 20TH NOVEMBER 2005

She was woken by a scream. She sat upright in bed and grasped wildly for the light. Sweat poured off her and her heart raced as she scoured the room for the danger she was sure was there. She saw none and took a deep breath. It was a dream and the scream must have been her own. She'd dreamt of George; a horrible dream with nooses and gallows as if he was to be strung up like a highwayman.

She just couldn't believe George could be involved in something as awful as the thing he was being accused of. She'd worked with people with psychopathic tendencies but she was certain he wasn't one of them. She had tried and tried to think whether all that had happened to her had any connection and whether all, or any, of it connected to Caroline. She doubted it; it was just another series of coincidences which made everything in her life appear crazy. The positivity she felt yesterday had disappeared but told herself no matter what, she would deal with whatever the day brought.

She looked at her watch and found it was the time she usually got up and felt pleased that, apart from the nightmare, at least she'd had a good night's sleep.

She'd just put in the last mouthful of porridge when there was a knock at the door. She hadn't expected anyone this early and she took a deep breath, made sure the door was on the chain, and opened it to find Dave.

'Hope this isn't too early for you but I have to be back by twelve to pick Max up from his match. Are you still happy for me to tag along?'

Louise smiled. 'I can't tell you how pleased I am you're here, I'm not sure I could cope with any more unpleasant surprises and I have a horrible feeling going to her house might result in one.'

The house looked just the same. The curtains were still drawn, and Louise felt certain no-one had been there since. Dave banged on the door but neither expected an answer.

'Do you know if she kept a key anywhere else? We would never advise it but so many people do in case they get locked out for any reason.'

Louise shook her head, 'No I don't think so but I often talked about client's who suffered domestic abuse. My advice was always to leave keys, money etc in a safe place so that if they needed to leave in a hurry, or were frightened to go into the house, they had access to it. Perhaps if she knew things were going wrong she might have done that.'

They searched the front garden but found nothing. Louise stood and scoured her mind for any clue Caroline might have given her. She gave a little shriek, 'I think I know where a key might be.' She moved quickly to the porch and on the outer side amongst the rose was a woven bird roost that she'd given to Caroline one Christmas. 'I remember her saying that if a bird didn't use it she could at least hide a spare key there.'

'Well remembered Louise.' Dave grinned as he poked about in the little shelter and triumphantly held up a key.

The house had a faint smell, the sort of smell which occurs when a house has been shut up and not aired. Although a bit ridiculous given the silence, they both called her name as they walked further into the house. 'Caroline. Hello … are you there? It's Louise and Dave, we've just come to check on you.' The silence mocked them as they walked down the hallway into the kitchen. There was an empty bottle of wine and a half full wine glass on the kitchen table. The chair beside the table was at an angle as if it had been pulled away rather than pushed back.

Dave stared at the wine. 'Louise, when she texted to ask you to come straight round, do you know whether she was on her own?'

Louise wrinkled her brow. 'I think so, I didn't get the impression anyone was with her.'

They searched in the rooms on the ground floor, but everything looked neat and tidy. Louise went to look in the bathroom because John had said she had been taken ill with a stomach upset but there was no medicine out or sign she'd been sick.

They moved upstairs and opened the bedroom door. They both gasped; the whole room was a wreck. There was a suitcase open on the bed, with clothes half in and half out. Some clothes were spread over the room, and some had been ripped to shreds. Shoes too, were everywhere and the red pair Louise had seen her wearing had one heel ripped off.

Dave was the first to speak. 'This doesn't have a good feel about it. It looks as if one person was packing to leave and another was angry and because the suitcase is still here, obviously prevented it happening.'

Louise shuddered. 'What can have happened? Do you think it was a row? We know he has a horrible temper so perhaps she wanted to leave and he got into a rage and stopped her. If she had a stomach upset, why would she have been drinking wine? When she texted, I felt she wanted to tell me something. Nothing felt right and I wondered if he'd hurt her. I sort of confronted her about it when I last saw her. I thought therefore she had acknowledged I was right and so wanted to leave but if that was true, it looks as though she was stopped.'

Louise pushed some clothes out of the way and sat on the bed. 'This whole thing is awful, what can we do? Where do you think she is?'

'Seeing this, we need to look at everything here more closely. Leave it up to me now. I'll send someone round to the school to ask Ben if he can tell us more about where his stepfather might have gone. He might know the name of the house but if not, surely the school office would have a new address if he'd moved?'

Louise nodded and added, 'It also won't be long before they break up for the Christmas holidays and Ben would surely know where he was going to be for Christmas.'

Dave stood and thought for a moment. 'Do you know what company the agent was from, as they would be bound to have a contact address, wouldn't they?'

Louise shook her head and said she didn't think to ask and there was no logo on his car.

Dave propelled her back down the hall towards the door. As she went Louise brushed against something soft and turned to see what it was. 'Wait Dave, this is her new mustard coat. John bought it for her and she was so pleased with it.' She looked at what else was hanging on the coat stand. 'Her old coat is here too and I never saw her in anything else, so what was she wearing when she left?' She wasn't sure Dave heard as he made no comment and continued out of the house.

He turned the key and rattled the handle to make sure it was firmly locked. Louise fiddled with her coat while she gazed around her. She saw the rose hanging over the path and again saw the piece of material. 'Look Dave, on the rose bush.' She grabbed his arm and forced him to turn to where she pointed. 'It's that piece of torn cloth I spotted when I came here before.' Dave hesitated for a moment but didn't touch it. Louise said, 'You know this piece of cloth has worried me since I found it, I had a feeling somehow it was telling me something.'

Dave nodded as he continued to look at it. 'It looks like a piece of blanket. I suppose that is a bit odd but there could be any number of explanations for it being there.

Louise sighed, disappointed at his response.

He put his arm around her and gave her a squeeze, 'Don't let your imagination run off with you, we will find her. It is still more than likely it was just a row, albeit a very nasty one, and they have gone to a new place because it will be somewhere neutral with no other memories. I had a friend whose new partner wouldn't stay in his house because his previous partner was all over it.'

His attempt at reassurance hadn't helped how Louise felt. She thought that now he'd seen the house he would be certain Caroline was in danger.

'Aren't you going to do anything more about what we've just seen?' She couldn't help the hostility in her voice. 'She's a missing person.'

'No, she's not Louise. People have seen her and the explanation the agent gave is very plausible. I know you're worried, and we'll still try to find out where she is but I don't think there is anything more we can do now. I'm more worried about what has happened to you.'

She declined his offer to go back to their house for lunch and tried to sound less irritated than she felt. 'I think I need to go home, and I think you need to spend the day with your family - I know a Sunday off is a precious thing.'

He waved goodbye. As he got into his car, he shouted she must ring or go to them if she felt at all worried.

She smiled and waved as she walked the short distance back home. As she drew near, she spotted Luke. She thought he looked like meercat keeping watch and was unable to prevent a snort of laughter.

'Hi Louise, I saw you coming up the road and just wanted to check you're okay after the other evening.'

'That's kind of you. Do you want to come in for a minute and I'll tell you?'

She wasn't sure this was a good idea; after all they were all in their late teens or early twenties and she didn't want to worry them or make them feel they were in any way responsible for her. However, it felt good there was people close she could call upon. Old Mr Braithwaite wouldn't be any help, but four strapping young men might be.

He was astonished when he heard what she had to say. It was obvious he had been aware of Caroline's existence because he said he had seen them together.

'Who was the bloke then, the one that's been hanging around?'

She stared. 'What do you mean? You've seen a bloke hanging around?'

'I clocked him a few times when I've been going in and out. He seemed to be always there at the bus stop, the one just down the road but I noticed him because when a bus pulled in one day, he didn't get on it. That's when I realised, he was always looking over at your place. I wondered if he could be spying on your builder chap, checking up on him for some reason. Anyway, I thought I'd mention it to you. Sorry if it's upset you.'

After he'd left it crossed Louise's mind, he could have been the one spying on her, after all he did seem to know a lot about her movements, which made her feel edgy.

She poured herself a large gin and tonic even though it was the middle of the day but thought of it as a Sunday pre-lunch drink. She remembered the wonderful Sunday roasts she used to cook for the family - never baked beans on toast like today.

Beans are not something to sit and savour for long and in a few minutes lunch had finished. She pushed her plate aside, put her head in her hands and tried to organise her thoughts. None of it made any sense; Caroline's disappearance; George's behaviour and his disappearance too; the break-in and search through her notes. She rubbed her hands over her face, then stood up abruptly. I just can't go on like this; I've got to take some action.

Her family had often laughed at her questionable internet skills, but she didn't care and anyway was always able to find what she wanted. First, she checked on the quarry in North Wales. There were pictures of the quarry and the surrounding mountains. The jagged landscape looked uninviting and harsh. The picture was taken on a day without sun and the lake looked jet black and menacing. She shivered. Why would anyone want to dive in that? She didn't want another panic attack at the memory of her near death in the water and tried not to think of the horror of having water over your head. The diagrams showed pictures of tunnels and ledges at different depths. There was also a piece written about the large number of diving accidents which had occurred due mainly to both the depth and the cold. With all those tunnels, she imagined it would be quite easy to get lost down there.

As she searched further, she found several articles which reported the accident at the time. George's rescue was splashed all over the articles. He'd been taken to hospital, suffering from hypothermia and was unable to remember anything. Not surprising he ended up with PTSD she thought, and that would certainly explain why he flipped out when the body was discovered. However, could he really have had anything to do with a death which would result in a manslaughter or murder charge.

Despite further searches, she found nothing that gave an indication of what had actually happened down there and no explanation as to why George was suspected of causing harm to his diving buddy. I guess the only person who would really know would be George, but if he suffered from amnesia, it might be very difficult to unlock.

The thought of death under water made her feel sick and sudden flashbacks of her near death under water mimicked tiny electric shocks. Without warning the full force of a panic attack hit her, her hands became clammy, she had pains in her arms, her breath came in short gulps, and she felt pain in her chest. She struggled to remember how to get out of it, then the voice of her own therapist came to her. *Keep calm; get your breathing under control.* She exhaled and expelled as much air as she could which resulted in an automatic intake of breath. She then focused on steady breaths until she began to feel stable. Funny that in a short space of time there had been two occasions when those early memories of being under water had surfaced.

She turned her attention to Caroline. As thoughts raced through her head, she felt she needed someone to talk to someone who wasn't involved, and she thought of Henry. With luck and his expertise in tortured minds, he might be able to throw more light on it all.

As luck would have it, he answered immediately. '*Hey Mum, lovely to hear from you at last! As you will have heard I did try to get in touch with you after that awful night, but I spoke to Katy in the end and she explained everything. I'm glad you have phoned now. Tell me how you are really?*'

Louise swallowed, knowing what she was going to tell him would upset him. '*Not good, as I'm sure you can imagine. I guess Katy has kept you up to date*'

As fast as she could, she told him everything, including anything that had happened to Max since their last phone call and about Caroline's disappearance and her suspicions about that.

Henry sighed. '*I see why you're worried. There is so much happening that is difficult to explain, and it must be frightening. If you think Caroline tried to leave and he is a controlling man then I understand your concern as leaving a controlling man can be a very dangerous time, as I'm sure you know.. As for Ben and his stepfather, I think you can leave that to social services, and I certainly am unable to form a judgment without knowing more. Although I would stand by what I said the other day at Katy's.*'

She wasn't altogether satisfied with his response but then wasn't sure what she expected or wanted from him. '*Did I tell you I saw someone lurking in the wood after I'd been to the boyfriend's house and then I think I was followed by a car when I left?*'

The tone of his voice changed, and she realised he had begun to take this more seriously. '*Mum, we all know you like to be independent but please if you are at all worried just go and stay with Katy for a while and only go to the house to see your clients.*'

Her heart started to thump but she said nothing. She couldn't explain any of it and yes, she was scared but what would be worse was just to sit back and do nothing and made up her mind to return to John's house and look further into the wood.

'*Mum, did you hear what I said? I want you to go and stay with Katy, so I know that you'll be safe. Please just be sensible for once. I would be far happier if you had George by your side, I liked him and I am sure the underwater stuff will turn out to be an accidental death.*'

Louise gripped the phone and snapped back at him. '*He is not in my life at the moment, and I don't want to be bothered with all his problems just now.*'

Henry murmured again to be careful and told her she was very precious to them all and just wanted her to take care of herself.

They both ended the call rather abruptly and Louise almost expected him to ring back as it was such an abrupt end, but he didn't.

It was too late to take any action on her plan as it would soon be dark but she started to do some research into John. She knew very little about him and it might help to know a lot more.

She pushed her hair back and scrunched it up into a tight ball and fixed it with a rubber band to lift it off her neck and then stretched her hands above her head and yawned.

It was after midnight and she'd got nowhere and hadn't a clue why. She'd thought it would be easy, but John didn't seem to have any online footprint at all. She'd been working by the light of the computer and the rest of the room was in complete darkness. She walked to the window and did a quick check outside before she put on the light. Although there were plenty of shadows, she saw no-one but as she closed the curtains she shuddered.

MONDAY 21ST NOVEMBER 2005

It had gone four when she left the practice in Kingswood. As she started to move out of her parking place, a car pulled out behind her. Her heart rate accelerated as she watched it in her mirror but once the light faded, it was impossible to say if it was still the same car that followed. When she turned into her road it carried on and so she told herself she must have been wrong - it was just her imagination.

More junk, she sighed as she picked up her post from the doormat and sorted it while she walked to the kitchen ready to throw it in the bin. She noticed a handwritten envelope stuck between the junk. She opened it quickly and held her breath.

Dear Louise,

John says you've been worried because I didn't contact you after I asked you to come to my house the other day. I'm so sorry about that. I'd contacted you both that night as I was suddenly very unwell. John reached me first and drove me straight to his house and I forgot to let you know. It was a nasty bug and I felt awful but am now better than I was. I'm now at John's other house in the country to give me a break. I asked him to post this to you when he went out today. Please don't worry about me - I'll get in touch as soon as I get back to Bath and get a new phone - I stupidly broke mine.
Lots of love,
Caroline xxx

PS I've been so lazy and not had much to do, so have been listening to music. I remembered it was this time of year when we met, and we shared our love of music. These are some of the songs I've listened to and wonder if you have too. "I predict a riot" by the Kaiser Chiefs. Particularly like the end of this one. Also, Madonna's "I'm all strung up" and the U2 one, "I can't make it on my own" really resonates. I'd love to know what you make of the latest Killers one as well. Hopefully we can meet soon and discuss.

She turned and with the letter in her hand walked over to the kettle, switched it on, then read it again. 'It doesn't make sense' she muttered. She knows I'm hopeless with titles of music and never could remember who sung what. Why would she write anyway? Couldn't she have borrowed John's phone if she'd broken hers?

She drank her coffee with the letter spread in front of her on the table and read it again. Her thoughts whirled. Did Caroline write this? If she did could she be trying to tell me something? It doesn't sound right and the music stuff is nonsense. She knows I haven't a clue and I am certain she hasn't spent time thinking about our shared love of music.

It niggled at her for the rest of the evening and when her watch showed it only to be 9.30, she put on her coat and grabbed a torch. Buster crept out of his basket, unsure as to whether he was expected to follow but sloped back when she shooed him away.

A walk in the dark was not on her 'to do' list at the moment but she needed some answers. It took at least six knocks before the door was opened by a stranger to her. He peered at her under a lengthy fringe and she wondered if the numerous piercings on his face were duplicated on the rest of his body. He was wearing a filthy T-shirt which had a logo she didn't really think anyone should display if they didn't want trouble. There was a strong smell of weed and she supposed it could be the reason his brain took a while to engage. He nodded at her and walked back into the house and shouted for Luke. He hadn't asked her in and she was conscious with the door wide open all the warm air would disappear, but the house could probably do with a bit of air. Luke eventually appeared and she wondered if he too would be in a bit of a vegetative state, but he sounded fine when he spoke.

'Hi Louise, can I help – not got another intruder I hope?' She shook her head and they both laughed.

'Actually, I would like your help.' She'd thought on her way over what she could say and it came out without hesitation. 'My friend and I are doing a sort of quiz using music titles or bands to find the answers and I'm absolutely hopeless and I wonder if you could help me with this puzzle'. She handed him a piece of paper on which she'd written the songs.

'Great, I like puzzles. Bit of a mess but do come in.' Louise followed tentatively into the hallway as he led her towards the kitchen. He cleared a space on the table and pulled up a stool. He stood against the rather tatty scratched kitchen unit, and she thought it wasn't surprising students never looked after anything if they were given such awful furnishings and kitchen equipment. He read what she'd written and wrinkled up his brows as he did, then shook his head before he looked up.

'Some of this isn't quite right. The U2 song is "Sometimes you can't make it on your own" and not "I can't make it on my own". The Kaiser Chiefs one, "I predict a riot", ends with "Sink that Ship" and Madonna's song is not "Strung Up" but "Hung up". I don't know which song she is meaning by the Killers but the latest was "Somebody Told Me". Does that make any sense to you?'

'No not really, but I'll need some time to work it out. Thank you so much Luke, you've been a star, I'm sorry if I've disturbed your evening.'

'It's fine, anytime.' He said with a raised eyebrow and a bit of twinkle in his eye. Louise felt her face grow hot. Surely, he didn't speak like that to all his mother's friends. She'd had misgivings about him but apart from his flirty manner, he appeared to be a nice enough young guy and so, when she was about to leave, she turned back.

'Luke if you're not too busy this weekend, I wonder if you'd come and help me search for something my grandson lost, when he was playing with a friend in some woods? I went the other day but there was some odd guy lurking about, and I felt a bit uneasy and a 6ft plus young man might make it less so!'

He gave a huge grin, obviously pleased to be asked again. 'Just let me know when you're wanting to go, and I'll be there.'

His enthusiasm felt a bit creepy and she wondered if she'd done the right thing. She looked back as she walked down the path and saw that he still stood where she'd left him. He was still there when she got to her gate so she turned and shouted 'goodnight' in what she hoped was a firm voice. It was only when she put the key in her lock that she heard Luke's door finally shut. Little Red Riding Hood came to mind but perhaps it was just all the talk about woods.

TUESDAY 22ND NOVEMBER 2005

She'd not managed to make sense of the musical references and had fallen asleep as she tried to work them out.

Louise was sure the letter had been sent to reassure her but the more she thought about it the more certain she was Caroline had used the music reference to make her understand what had happened to her. If she was right, then she would need to get Dave involved as well.

The microwave pinged. Louise lifted her porridge out, added some yoghurt and a few blueberries. While she ate, she played with the words in the letter and tried to put the song titles in order. It was so hard to understand what Caroline might want her to know. In the end she felt that the way she had put them was correct.

Sometimes you can't make it on your own –she wants me to help?

Strung Up – Is she tied up? Did she use the word strung instead of hung on purpose?

Somebody Told Me –more obscure but perhaps I should read it as she is telling me? *Killers*!

This makes me shiver.

Finally; *Sink that Ship* - Sounds like a directive, something she wants me to do. If you sink a ship

It's the end of its functionality. Could there be a boat involved? Ben told Max they were going fishing, is there a connection?

She pushed her empty bowl away and ran her hands through her hair. I'm sure I'm not imagining this. I'm certain she wants me to know something and can't speak to me at the moment. I'm don't believe her phone is broken but I think she's used music to hide a message perhaps because John would read it and it is the sort of thing friends talk about. However, she would have known I would find it odd - I never could remember names of bands or the title of songs.

I've so many things on my mind I just can't think and I've somehow got to go to work. Louise let out a large sigh at the thought it and wished she could cancel but if she cancelled it would mean her already stressed clients would miss out on what might be their only lifeline. She looked at her watch and saw she had time to phone Dave and tell him what she thought.

She wasn't surprised he was off hand at first, but once she had explained he changed his tone.

'Thanks Louise. It certainly sounds as though Caroline is trying to reassure you, but I do agree it is strange, if it is something you never did. I'm not sure I want to jump straight to the conclusion there is a hidden message though, but I would like to see the letter.'

She gave a slow measured breath out before she spoke. George had once told her she sounded like trees gently blowing in the wind when he'd heard her do this while she meditated.

'Dave I'm sure what she's trying to say is she can't do it on her own, that she is tied up in some way and somebody has told her they are killers, and she wants us to end it for her, in other words sink that ship. I think it is Caroline being clever and expecting me to work it out.'

Dave was silent for a moment but still only said he'd think about it and suggested she drop the letter into the station on her way back after work.

Her jaw clenched and she tried to hide her frustration. *'I think you should have the letter now. I'll drop it off at the police station on my way to work.'*

Dave laughed at her persistence. *'All right. If you're sure you've got time.'*

Louise felt work was now out of the question and telephoned the surgery and explained she would be unable to be there today and hoped she wasn't letting anyone down too badly.

Luke answered the door this time but looked rather the worse for wear and once again she wondered if she was being sensible.

'Hi, Louise, what time is it? I've not had breakfast yet.'

Louise remembered students would probably view this time of day as the middle of the night.

'Sorry Luke, I didn't think. I forgot what students are like.' She grinned as he looked down at his bare feet. 'I just wondered if you would be free later this morning to come with me to those woods, the ones I told you about?'

Louise heard bits and pieces of his student life as he chatted to her in the car. She remembered Henry used to talk like that and smiled to herself as she remembered those days with fondness.

'Wow. Does this belong to someone you know?' He gasped at the sight of John's huge house.

'It belongs to the boyfriend of the friend I told you about who is missing.' As she said this Louise felt guilty; she had dragged this boy into something which could only be called trespassing.

There were no cars in the drive but just to make sure, she knocked at the door while Luke stared at the house as if he'd never seen a house before.

'You sure we ought to be here? Your Caroline must have hit lucky with this guy, I'd say he was totally minted.'

Louise smiled. 'Come on then, let's go. I'll get Buster out of the car as I think he might be useful.' She kept Buster on a lead and led the way round the side of the house, down the path and onto the grass which led into the wood. The loud scrunch of the gravel emphasised the ominous quiet in the gardens and she couldn't throw off the feeling they were being watched. She looked back but saw only dark shadows that were the windows of the house.

The edge of the wood was surrounded by bracken and dead brambles which were still capable of doing damage, as they soon found out. She spotted the path that led into the wood and indicated Luke should follow her. She let Buster off his lead, and he immediately ran ahead down the path.

Luke said, 'What did your grandson lose? What are we looking for?' Louise again queried her decision to have brought him.

She wasn't sure how to answer. She'd got him here because she said she was searching for something Max had lost but, of course, he hadn't lost anything.

She replied, 'I think it is a football glove, but I'm not entirely sure.' She was surprised at how easy she'd found it to lie.

He shrugged and then set off to follow Buster. They came to a point where the path divided and then disappeared as the trails blended with the fallen leaves rotting beneath the trees.

Despite her reservation, she was glad of Luke's company. She wasn't sure the wood was a place to be on your own and didn't like the idea that Max had been here. She'd never baulked at adventure before, having been an independent and resourceful person even before James had died but this whole episode felt alien.

'Here, come and look at this. Buster's already gone in.' Luke's shout jolted Louise out of her thoughts and she saw he, or more likely Buster, had found what looked like the entrance to Ben's cave. He stood underneath an enormous beech tree and beside him was a dark hole which disappeared under the roots. The tree was on sloped ground, so the hole was large enough for a person to get into. Luke looked back at her to make sure she saw and then stooped down and went in.

Nettles that must have surrounded the entrance until the beginning of winter, were now dead and had been trodden into the ground. It tied in with Max's story. The hole led to a passage which ended in a large cave. There was a dank musty smell, like the smell of old socks. There were remnants of an old and dirty carpet on the floor which had been made into mats but many things Max had described were now gone. There were no photos attached to the wall, although there were some odd bits of Sellotape still stuck on it where they had been.

Buster was excited by all the interesting smells. Luke poked about in a pile of rubbish in the corner and pulled out a mud-covered exercise book. He opened it up and handed it to Louise. It was a diary or rather more a journal because there were no printed dates. A sentence caught her eye which began with *My friend came – war games like Sophie .... GREAT.* Then a few pages on

Caroline is cool... Then a little further on,...*I won't let her go... she must not go... I won't let her........* The next few pages were smudged, and she could only make out the odd word. The rest of the pages had deep cuts in them as if it had been jabbed with something pointed and sharp and a lot of the pages were ripped and torn. If this journal belonged to Ben, it showed his upset at the idea of Caroline leaving. Louise's throat constricted and she felt the prick of tears. There was no clue here as to what had happened to Caroline, but she stuffed the diary in her coat pocket and followed Luke who had reached the entrance.

She had almost reached him when without warning he stepped back, turned and grabbed her. He pushed his face close to hers and whispered in a shaky voice.

'There's someone out there. I heard them.'

Louise gasped and pulled him further back into the cave. They strained to hear the sound he'd heard and quite expected them to be found at any moment. She wondered how she would account for their presence.

'What should we do, Louise?'

It was no more than a whisper, but she was terrified whoever it was out there may have heard it. She put her finger on her lips and crept back towards the entrance. A twig snapped. But then silence. She imagined whoever was there, listened too. Her heartbeat sounded so loud she was sure it could be heard.

She looked round for Buster and saw he was still at the back of the cave with his nose pushed into something he found interesting. He didn't appear to have heard anything and she hoped he would continue to stay there. Her hands were clammy, and her arms tingled. Luke turned towards her and opened his mouth as if to speak. She slapped her hand over his mouth and his eyes widened in surprise and then fear as they heard another snap of a twig and then another.

They stayed still until they were sure there was no danger and there were no more sounds. Both let out a long sigh and Louise uncurled her hands and shook them as if to throw out the tension.

Luke had gone quite pale, and she wondered if he might faint. His voice wobbled as he whispered, 'I don't think I can do this. I'm sorry but it is all a bit weird and creepy, and I feel guilty for being here. Can we go now? I dunno what you wanted or expected but there is no sign of a glove, if that's what you were really looking for.' His head bent to the side, and he looked at her with a question in his eyes.

She shrugged; it was her turn to feel guilty. He was right, she should never have involved him but was still glad she wasn't on her own. They waited for, what seemed, a long time and until they were sure there was no-one outside. Amazed that Buster hadn't barked or given them away, she pulled him from whatever it was he had been so acutely interested in and they crept out into the wood. Louise wanted to rush straight back to the car and saw Luke had already started to walk away. She was disappointed she was no further forward in trying to discover anything about Caroline.

She hadn't paid attention to the direction they'd come in and soon realised they'd come the wrong way. The ground they now walked on was rockier with huge mounds and dips in it. Luke seemed to have regained his bounce and didn't seem worried by their mistake. 'Great place for off road biking, these jumps would be awesome.'

Louise laughed and looked around for Buster.

'There he is,' Luke shouted, as he caught sight of him in the distance.

'Come Buster; good boy. Heel, HEEL.' Buster eventually dragged himself away from whatever had taken his attention and she muttered her annoyance as she grabbed him and put on his lead. He had something in his mouth which he obviously found delicious. It looked like an old bone but as it was small, she was worried he'd choke on it and anyway she had had enough of him eating odd things. She pulled it out of his mouth and was about to throw it away when Luke stopped her. 'Hang on a minute, what's that?'

Louise held it out to him, and he took it from her and inspected it. She remembered he was doing something scientific at the University.

'Ugh, oh no. Louise, I think it's a human bone!'

Louise gasped, 'What do you mean human? It can't be, looks like rabbit, doesn't it?'

Luke shook his head. 'No definitely not. I'm doing Anatomy this term and I'm almost sure it is part of a digit of a hand, or it could I suppose be a bone from a foot.' He mused while he continued to turn it round in his hand.

Louise felt sick. She thought for a moment while she tried to get her breath. She pulled out a clean tissue from her pocket and handed it to Luke. 'Here, wrap it up, then we need to take it to the police. God knows where it came from but there is a good chance if it is human there could possibly be more in here somewhere.' At this thought she shuddered and saw the colour had again drained from Luke's face.

Back at the car, she checked her phone signal and telephoned Dave. She explained what they'd found, and he told her to go straight to the station and he'd meet her there.

'Luke I'm sorry I've involved you in this. I'll drop you home before I go to the police but I will have to tell them you were there. Anyway, I guess they might find your fingerprints on the bone, if that's even possible but if so, they already have yours from the other night, so they may want to talk to you.' He nodded in agreement, clearly glad to be going home, and only managed a faint wave when she dropped him off. 'Wait, Luke.' She shouted as he was about to go into the house. 'Can I have your mobile number so I can let you know what happens and I don't have to bother you at home?' As soon as she'd copied his number into her phone the door closed behind him.

Dave received the bone with raised eyebrows but assured her he would send it straight to the lab to be identified. 'We'll get a DNA test done, in case there is a match, but we only hold onto data if a person has a criminal conviction.' He asked Louise to sit down and then asked numerous questions. The tone of his voice made it evident he was irritated.

'I don't want to be cross with you but it is not your job to play detective - you could get yourself into all sorts of trouble. You'd hate it if I started interfering with how you run your practice.'

'I know and I'm sorry but I'm so worried and I know you do understand that. How long will it take to find out about the bone?'

'Quite quick, I hope. If it is does turn out to be human, then we'll search the woods thoroughly.'

When she heard it put in such a blunt way, she felt sick and lightheaded. In fact, she'd felt like that since they found the bone and was glad of the support of the chair. Dave must have seen her distress and was quick to say he thought there was no likelihood of it belonging to Caroline.

'Caroline has only been missing a short time whereas the bone looks as if it was part of something which died quite a while ago. I am still hopeful she is away having a good time with the new boyfriend.' Louise saw from his face even he had begun to doubt his words.

'What about the note she left me? Wouldn't that be enough to question John?'

Dave nodded. 'Yes, you're right. Once I'd seen the note, I understood your fears. We have done an on-line search on John but so far have come up with nothing about him.'

Louise sighed, 'Yes, I've done the same but also failed.'

Dave leaned back in his chair. 'To be honest, I too am now very concerned but don't worry we will do all we can to get to the bottom of what's going on.' Before she could reply he added, 'And we will find Caroline. Go home now and I promise you I will keep you posted if anything new happens.'

Louise sat with a cup of soup and tried once more to make sense of it all. If the bone was human and it couldn't be Caroline's, then whose could it possibly be?

It was gone five when she heard the ring of her landline and rushed from her study into her bedroom to answer it.

'*Louise, it's Dave. Just to let you know the bone you brought in has been confirmed as human. I immediately got a warrant and a team went over to the woods with dogs but as it is now dark they've had to stop and will resume their search in the morning. I'll let you know what we find and please don't worry - it's definitely not Caroline; forensic thinks it's quite old but have not had time to date it yet.*'

Louise let out a relieved sigh. 'That is something at least - but it does make me even more worried about Caroline. Will you be able to search the house now as well?'

'Yes, possibly but as there is public access from another part of the wood this may have no connection with whoever lives in the house.'

WEDNESDAY 23RD NOVEMBER 2005.

Any other day the frost patterns on the windows would have delighted her but this morning they made her shudder. Even her usual early morning cup of coffee offered no consolation.

By the middle of the day the feeling of anxiety had spread inch by inch through her body and she found it almost impossible to concentrate. When the client with a spider phobia appeared to have regressed since she last saw her, she smothered a frustrated sigh and hoped the client hadn't noticed.

She took a bite of apple and another of cheese, but it might as well have been cardboard for all the attention she gave to it. When will Dave pick up the phone? I just want to know what's going on. She grabbed at the kettle and burnt her hand as she tried to pour hot water into her mug. She jumped when she heard her mobile and she snatched it up and peered at the screen.

Dave was brisk and professional, so she guessed he was in a hurry and in his office.

'I can't say much, Louise, but just to let you know we did find further remains buried in the woods. Although, decayed and mutilated by animals, they appear to be female. I don't know more at the moment but thought I'd let you know. It goes without saying this is totally confidential and I ought not to be telling you. We will now get a search warrant for the house and see if we can see anything which might lead us to the whereabouts of John or Caroline. The forensic anthropologist won't have any answers for us for quite a while but in the meantime, we will go through missing persons files. Forensic think about three years ago, judging from the decomposition, but because of the disturbance by animals it makes it harder to tell.' He

promised to ring again in the evening and ended the call before she had a chance to speak.

The pain in her hand, reminded her she needed to put it into cold water. She put it under the tap and let the water run over it and wondered whether it was the water or the burn that hurt more. She had been shocked by Dave's phone call, even though it was expected. Thank God it can't be Caroline. She removed her hand from the water, wiped it dry on a tea towel and looked at her watch. She knew she had to go back into her room and spend the afternoon counselling but the idea of it made her feel ill and the pain of the burn had not gone away. Perhaps it would help to keep her focused and grounded.

The afternoon session proved even harder than she'd imagined, and she had to dig her nails into the palms of her hands at times to try to keep focused on the client in front of her.

She'd always been a person who'd taken action if there was a problem and Dave's earlier request for her to just sit and wait felt inconceivable. Surely it would do no harm to try and find out where John had moved to? After all, it would be totally normal for a friend to do this and of course any information she gleaned she would share. The obvious way would be through the estate agent she'd met at the house, even though she hadn't a clue what agency they had come from.

When she'd finished work, she sat at her computer and googled Estate Agents. There weren't many and most were open late, so she telephoned each one in turn and pretended she was someone who wanted to rent a large house in that area of Bath. She had no luck for the first two but when she got to the third, the receptionist told her she had just the property for her and gave her the rental cost, which made her gasp. She wondered how anyone could possibly afford that amount of money. She asked for further details and to her relief, it was John's address. She knew they wouldn't give out information about the owner and so asked to view the property in the hope it would give her a lead. They agreed a time on Friday at eleven thirty.

Louise had already taken Buster for his evening walk before Dave phoned. She had walked past Caroline's house but had no desire to go in, certain it wouldn't have helped any way.

'Hi, Louise, I've been through all the missing person log and there is no-one three years ago who would tie in but there is something odd. About a month ago a lady from Australia telephoned to say she wanted to register her daughter as missing. She said her daughter had been working as a nanny for about four years. It was to a man who had a stepson. She had given us all the details she had including the address. When I came across this entry, I found it was the same address we have for John. I checked with the officer she'd spoken to, and he said they'd made the usual enquiries and had been satisfied she'd gone travelling.'

Louise gasped, *'The nanny! The girl who used to play with Ben in the woods and to whom the rag belonged. Hang on, though, you said it was several years ago, so why wasn't she registered as missing then? Why wait until recently to say your daughter is missing?'*

'I asked her that and she told me she had received the occasional letter and the odd postcard. She said her daughter had never been one to write often. Then a few months ago, she had a telephone call. She said the line was bad and she could hardly hear what she was saying but gathered the job hadn't worked out and she was going travelling so may be out of contact for quite a while. She'd heard nothing more afterwards and thought it odd as in this era there was no need to be out of communication for any length of time but just thought her daughter must be having a good time and would get in contact when she wanted. When a few months had gone by she had tried to contact this John guy but had no success and so she became worried - which is when she got in contact with us.'

'You think he was the one doing the communicating to make her mother think she was still alive? What a horrendous thing to do. Surely though her mother would have noticed it wasn't her writing?'

'Yes, I agree but she said it had looked like hers and she'd never imagined that someone else might be writing them.'

'I hope to goodness he didn't write that letter to me for the same reason but no, I'm sure it was from Caroline. But maybe he was forcing her to write to reassure me, which is why she tried to send a message he wouldn't understand.'

Dave's voice dropped to a tone lower. *'I'm so sorry, I knew this would upset you but we're doing our best to find him and we do have to make sure it is the nanny buried there before we jump to any conclusions. The DNA should be back by next Wednesday or before but, for the reason I told you before, I think it unlikely that we'll have a match.'*

Louise agreed it was unlikely. *'What about the house, did you find anything in there?'*

'No not really, it was pretty much cleared out of any personal possessions. He had obviously got it ready to be rented.' He stopped and cleared his throat. *'I think I need to apologise to you. I think you were right in the beginning when you noticed how strange Caroline had become. I am sorry I didn't take notice of your genuine fears but believe me I will do everything I can to bring her back safely. She is now officially a missing person or a misper as we say at work.'*

Louise drummed her fingers on the arm of the chair as she thought about what he'd said. *'Thanks Dave, I'm glad you've now acknowledged officially that she is missing and I know you will do all you can.'* She was just about to end the call before she remembered she hadn't told him about the estate agents. *'Wait, I found the name of the estate agency John used and where the man I met came from.'*

His voice was sharp when he replied and she knew he was irritated that she had interfered again. He wanted to know why she hadn't rung him immediately with this information. '*It's too late now to follow this up. It'll have to wait until morning and that means more delay for Caroline if she is in a difficult situation*'.

She felt dreadful. She'd been so intent on finding out more herself that she hadn't really thought about Dave being in a much better position to get information out of the agency. She apologised and reminded him she had been waiting for his phone call but realised she ought to have rung immediately and left a message.

What an idiot I've been, she thought. My actions, or no action, could have cost Caroline her life. I've definitely watched too many thrillers and as for pretending to be a rental client, what on earth could I expect to get from that? I'm not a detective and Dave told me his men had already searched the house, so what more could I possibly find.

She lay in bed that night thinking, her mind full of the mistake she'd made and the possible consequences of the delay. Despite being told not to interfere further she decided she would keep the agents appointment. Just maybe another pair of eyes in the house might throw up something important.

FRIDAY 25TH NOVEMBER 2005

There was no-one at the house when she pulled into the drive. She wondered if it would be the same agent she had met before because if so, she would have had to think up an entirely different story as to why she was there. A few minutes later when the agent pulled in, she saw to her relief it was a woman.

'Hello there. Mrs Graham? I'm Margaret from Hatchers Estate Agents. Sorry to keep you waiting, I got stuck in traffic.'

Louise shook her hand. Margaret got the keys out of her pocket and suggested they go inside out of the cold. She caught sight of Buster in the car. 'Oh, what a lovely dog, will he be okay here? Only I don't think our client would like me to let a dog in; he's apparently quite particular, although I've never met him myself.'

Louise muttered Buster was fine and walked with her towards the house. It was as impressive inside as it was outside and she saw why Caroline had found it so wonderful.

The glass dome in the ceiling of the huge hall allowed the icy November light to give a blue tinge to the walls and a beige and sunny glow to the Italian tiles which covered the floor. In the middle was the start of a gracious staircase leading up to a balcony that circled the hall and there were many doors leading off it on two sides. There was a faint smell which reminded her of her grandmother's house and for a moment she couldn't place it but then realised it was furniture polish and they had probably used it on the staircase.

She tried not to gasp or comment too much. A genuine client who could afford to rent a house like this would be bound to take this splendour for granted.

There were four or maybe five doors that opened out from the hall where she stood, and Margaret walked to the back and flung a door open and indicated she should follow.

'This is the drawing room. My favourite room. Just look at this magical view over the grounds. Of course, the lawn and everything looks dreadful because there have been police here for the last two days and they've traipsed everywhere.' Louise peered out of the window and could see what she meant. The lawn beside the path which led to the woods was muddy and cut up with footprints.

'Yes, it does look muddy. I saw in the papers a body had been found in woods near here. I didn't realise the woods were so close. What a gruesome thing, I'm not sure I'm that keen on this house now.'

The face Margaret pulled allowed Louise to see she too found the whole thing unpleasant.

'Yes, I understand how you feel. This would put most people off and it should have been mentioned to you when you telephoned, but the agency's view was that until we're instructed otherwise, we should continue to market the house. The woods do belong to the owner but are not part of this rental and I am sure whatever the police were doing there, it had no connection to him. I gather from my boss he is a charming man but, of course, Mrs Graham I would quite understand if what has happened has put you off.' Then added, 'I don't think I'd be keen to rent it myself at the moment.'

'Yes, quite but do you know what has actually happened and who the body belongs to? Perhaps the owner, whoever he is, might not want you to continue with the rental.'

'It's a Mr Sheridan and as I said we have no further instructions from him. The police telephoned yesterday, and they are trying to get in touch with him but have been unsuccessful and the address we have on our books can't be the right one as they've been there and someone else lives in it.'

Louise tried not to show what she felt when she heard this and guessed that's why Dave hadn't phoned yesterday.

It was hard not to let her face droop, but she continued, nevertheless.

'That's odd. How do you get hold of him? Presumably you have a phone number?'

'Oh yes we do and he usually gets back to us straight away but in the last few days, we haven't been able to get hold of him either.' Louise knew the police would have asked them for a phone number too but she needed to ask, even if it had got her nowhere.

Margaret fidgeted with the keys as she spoke and Louise realised she was uncomfortable talking about her client. She held her breath and wondered if she would now stop the viewing but she continued to point out all the positive aspects of the room they were standing in.

Louise gazed about her. Surely there must be something that would help find Caroline but all the reproduction Georgian furniture was polished to a mirror like surface and there was no sign of anything personal anywhere.

I'm glad I'm not doing the cleaning, thought Louise and none of the chairs are ones I'd want to sink down in with my feet up and a glass of wine in my hand. It's not at all like the cosy lounge at Caroline's house; I can't imagine she would have liked it.

Margaret must have seen the look of disappointment on her face because she frowned and started to move back towards the door. Worried that she wouldn't show her the rest of the house Louise said, 'Even if he doesn't rent it in the end, I'd still like to continue seeing the rest of the house, since I'm here.'

She gave a brisk nod, turned and marched through the door. 'Follow me, Mrs Graham, but I haven't got a lot of time so it will have to be quick.'

Louise hurried after her sure that Margaret had guessed there's something odd going on. I don't care though as long as she continues to let me look round the whole house.

The next room was a large study lined with bookshelves bursting with both hardbacks and paperbacks of all different genres, fiction and non-fiction. Louise had always been fascinated by the books people chose and took a closer look, hoping it might help her know more about the so-called Mr Sheridan.

'I see Mr Sheridan has a lot of books on diving and travel books relating to places where it is good to dive. I wonder if he dives a lot?' Her raised eyebrows elicited a shake of the head from Margaret.

'I really wouldn't know. As I've told you, I've never met the man or had any conversations with him but guess you're right, looking at the number of books on the subject.'

Louise felt at last she had seen something which tied the owner to the leaflet they'd found at Caroline's, but it was strange she'd never mentioned John liked diving.

Margaret continued to lead her through all the rooms both up and down, but she gained no more information about either John or Caroline and the whole house looked as if it had been stripped and cleaned. She had a sudden thought. 'What about a Utility Room? I am guessing there is one.' It wasn't really a guess as she was sure when she'd peered through the back door there had been several doors leading off the passage.

'Oh yes, of course I didn't think you would be interested in seeing it, but it's just down here.'

Louise immediately saw she'd been right. This wasn't at all like the rest of the house and had not been totally cleared or cleaned. There were loads of discarded boots and shoes, but it was difficult to see if any of them were Caroline's size. There were walking boots, still covered in mud and a pair she was sure would have fitted Caroline but then they could equally well have fitted Ben.

There wasn't a lot of furniture, just a long rough wooden bench opposite the equally large cupboard, which held only coats. The only other things were the washing machine and tumble dryer.

Louise stared at the washing machine and thought how often small or thin items got stuck in the rim of drum; hidden until they turned up in the next wash. Without a thought, she ripped open the door, felt with her fingers around the smooth surface of the rim of the drum and had to stifle a cry of triumph when her fingers touched something soft. She pulled at it and lifted out a thin string of material, which after she'd shaken regained its shape. 'Oh dear, someone will be missing this.' She said as she held out a thin red cardigan. Without a doubt it belonged to Caroline, as she remembered her wearing it on one of their G & T evenings not too long ago.

Margaret snatched it from her and in a voice which reminded Louise of one of her old teachers rasped, 'Mrs Graham! I think you are out of order, this is a viewing and I don't think that means you can start delving about in his washing machine. He'd told us the whole lot had been cleaned and was ready to rent but this room is a complete disgrace and he'll need to come back and sort it out.' Margaret curled up her nose.

'Sorry, I probably was being overzealous inspecting the washing facilities, but I know some rental houses have very poor appliances.' She gazed around but saw no sign of it having been used for anything other than a boot room. 'It's funny though, seeing all those books about diving, I would have expected to see some evidence of that here or perhaps he kept it somewhere else.' She saw Margaret was getting tired of her inquisitive probes and had started to fiddle again with the bunch of keys in her hand. To her surprise however, she picked up on her query about his diving.

'There is an extra key on this bunch, and I noticed when I tried the handle just now, the door to the right of this room is locked. As he's handed over all the keys for this house, I don't think he'd mind if I showed you. After all, we would have to give all the keys to you if you decided to rent it.' She shuffled through the keys and produced one she thought belonged. Louise guessed this enthusiastic offer to open a locked door was entirely about Margaret's own curiosity.

It was more of a large cupboard than a room. There was no window and was pitch dark and felt cold and damp. It smelt a bit like rotting seaweed. Once the light was on, Louise saw peeled paint on the walls and thought if this had been a scene in a film it would be the place where they'd have found a body. It could also be a good place to imprison someone and felt goose bumps on her body. What on earth would it be like to be locked in with no window?

A large cupboard ran almost the length of one of the walls. She opened it up and exclaimed, 'Here they are, the wetsuits.' They both peered in and saw rows of pegs on which hung bits and pieces of wet suits. On the bottom of the cupboard was a selection of diving boots and in the corner a couple of air tanks and harnesses. He obviously took his diving seriously. They shut the long cupboard, and both started to leave.

They had nearly reached the door when Louise noticed something white under the long wooden bench against the opposite wall. It was half hidden under material of some kind, and she pulled at it until a bunch of old rags and a crumpled piece of paper emerged. Margaret leant over her shoulder to look and tutted so loudly Louise felt her breath on her neck, as she told her not to pry and to put down whatever she had in her hand. Louise thought perhaps she now felt guilty for taking her in there.

Definitely flustered she fiddled with the keys even more as she spoke. 'I don't think he intended us to come in here at all. He probably forgot he'd left the key on this bunch. I think, now you've seen the whole property, we should leave.' She turned and marched out of the house via the back door.

As her feet hit the gravel, she turned a red face towards Louise and in a voice of a much higher pitch than she'd used before, said, 'You don't want to rent this at all, do you? You just wanted to snoop around. Tell me, just what exactly do you want?' Her hands flew up to her face. 'Don't tell me you're a reporter.' 'Oh no please. I could lose my job.' Without waiting for an explanation, she put her hands out and shooed and manoeuvred Louise around the house to the cars. Gone was the smooth estate agent's voice as she growled, 'I should leave now, Mrs Graham. I hate being used and this whole thing has been most irregular. I'll tell my boss how you hoodwinked me into showing you around and don't even think of ever renting through our agency.'

Louise tried to think what to say. She felt mean having lied to her, she was only doing her job. She opened her mouth to speak but Margaret had already reached her car, started the engine and begun to pull away.

Louise drove a short way from the house and stopped the car on the side of the road. She felt a lump in her throat and tears formed in her eyes. She reached in her pocket for a tissue and found she had the crumpled paper she'd scooped up with the rags under the bench. She opened it out and found it was the same diving leaflet she and Dave had found at Caroline's house.

The canal wasn't far away, and Louise decided to take Buster there for a walk. There was now no doubt in her mind Caroline was in danger.

The footpath was soggy and made squelchy by fallen leaves. She crossed the bridge and left the canal to walk beside the river, which was high, but not high enough to flood Max's school playing fields, which lay behind the river. She stopped and watched some boys as they played hockey. She loved the way they rushed about the field with such enthusiasm and their breath sent up clouds of steam in the cold air. The game came to an end and one of the boys broke away and ran towards her; it was Max.

'Hi, Granny, what are you doing here? Did you come to watch me? Did you see the goal I scored it was awesome!' He looked disappointed when she told him that sadly she hadn't seen it and hadn't realised it was him playing. She noticed the other boys about to disappear off in the corner of the field. 'Think you'd better go and join your group, but I'll see you soon.' Max started to run off but turned back, 'Yeah right! Granny you are funny - you'll see me tomorrow - my birthday tea.'

She stifled a gasp. Not only had she forgotten it was his birthday tomorrow but there was no present for him yet. She couldn't believe it; she was usually great at birthdays.

She felt so guilty but pleased she'd been given a chance to put it right and Max would never know.

The Duty Sergeant was on the desk when she asked if Dave was in and he contacted him immediately.

'You OK, Louise? I haven't really any more news for you. As I already told you, we went to the house yesterday and didn't find a thing. It was all cleared out and clean.'

Louise shuffled her feet, not able to look him in his eyes. 'I know, I saw. Sorry Dave, I know you said not to get involved but I met the Estate Agent just a short while ago and she showed me around the house.' She told him about the jumper she'd found in the washing machine. 'Did you go into the room where the all the diving gear was? I found another leaflet there, the same as the one we found at the house.' Louise handed it to him so he could see it was the same one.

Dave sighed as it took the leaflet and replied in an angry voice. 'I thought I told you to leave it to us. We obviously did miss the jumper in the washing machine, but it only proves she was there with him, which you knew anyway. Yes, we did find the diving equipment, but it only proved he's into diving and quite seriously by the look of what we found. Go home now and just let us do our job here. Please Louise.'

Louise pursed her lips together; her little expedition had done nothing to move things forward and there had been no evidence of anything untoward. Dave had already turned away, but she couldn't resist a response. 'I know she's in trouble, even if I can't prove it and I can't bear to think of her trapped somewhere or worse.' He didn't look back.

She'd parked near the police station and Buster, who'd been made to wait in the car, gave a little yelp in delight at her return. The light had nearly gone and she had to put headlights on. As she pulled out into the road she was aware another car followed. She felt a chill run through her body. She was certain it was the same one as before. She wished she could have seen the number plate but all she saw were headlights. She was certain she hadn't imagined it but it had disappeared by the time she reached home.

SATURDAY 26th NOVEMBER 2005

It had been a bit of a dash to the shops to find something Max would like. She hadn't asked Katy or him what he wanted, so just had to take a guess. Eleven years old, I can't believe it. He's growing up too fast. She smiled at the thought and remembered how much it had lifted her mood when she saw him yesterday.

She found a small flying remote-control helicopter in a shop which sold all sorts of gadgets and she walked home happy - sure she'd found just the right thing. At least, she would have liked it at his age!

Max hadn't wanted a party and instead had planned to take some friends somewhere exciting as soon as the term ended, so a family tea was all he had asked for on the day.

'Wow, Granny, fantastic! Thank you – awesome.'

Louise laughed; glad it had been a success.

Katy called them to the table and they watched as Max blew out the candles on his cake. Unfortunately, Dave had not made it home which was not surprising given he was in the middle of a murder enquiry.

'How's Ben doing?' Louise wondered if this was an insensitive question, but tea was over, and Katy had started to clear away.

'He's OK, I suppose.' Max looked away and made a face.

'Doesn't look like you think he's really OK,' she said.

Max grinned. 'No, s'pose not. I'm staying away from him. He's always in a nasty mood. I've tried to talk to him, but he just brushes me off.'

'He's probably upset because he thinks no-one wants to be his friend.'

'Mmm, but Granny, I think what he did was so bad – really bad and don't think I can be friends with him.

'I wasn't asking you to be a friend but try not to let him feel he is totally isolated from all of you. Being on your own in a crowd can be a very horrid place to be.'

Max nodded his head and she saw he understood what she'd said and felt a pain in her chest at the thought that he had already experienced something similar. 'Does Ben know where he is going when term ends? You said it was somewhere near a lake. I wonder if you know which lake?'

She felt bad to probe but it was an opportunity she felt she couldn't miss. Max shook his head and told her he had no idea other than it was a lake where Ben could fish.

She settled herself down on her sofa, glad to be home. It hadn't been the best of birthdays for Max but it had been good to be with all the family.

She carried her laptop under one arm and a large glass of Sauvignon Blanc in the other. She searched first for information about Chew Valley Lake as it was the place the first estate agent had mentioned. She'd heard about it but never been there. She scanned through the amenities - there was a sailing club and fishing either from the shore or on a boat. She smiled as she took a large sip. This is very likely the place then, but it is very large with several villages on various sides, and she imagined other more remote houses as well. That's as far as I'm able to go with this now, she thought, but at least it could be the place.

The next thing to do was perhaps easier. She smoothed out the leaflet she'd rescued from the floor in that horrible room found the website and put it into Google. The place was not far away from Bath or Chew Valley. She Googled other diving in the area but there was nowhere else offering lessons or a place which had such interesting dives. She shuddered at the thought of diving and just couldn't imagine how anyone could see it as a fun thing to do. Her near drowning experience had coloured any thoughts she'd had about going underwater. She worked out that it wouldn't take much more than half an hour to reach from either Bath or Chew Lake.

The last thing she did before going to bed was to find a photograph of Caroline just in case there was anyone at the dive centre who might remember her. She tripped on the bottom step of the stairs and realised she'd ended up drinking more than she'd meant to. Perhaps it's a good thing. I'm sure I'll sleep better and whatever might be going on outside I won't know or care about it. She immediately felt her chest tighten and wished she hadn't had that last thought.

SUNDAY 27th NOVEMBER 2005

The drive to the quarry took a bit longer than the half hour but that was because she was unsure where she was going. Despite the glossy leaflet, it turned out to be a rough and ready sort of place, with a few shed buildings that looked as though they had been cobbled together by inexpert hands. It reminded her of the garden shed James had once put up for the children to play in and she hadn't the heart to tell him it would probably not last a winter, which in the end it didn't. She parked the car and found her way to the building with a large sign propped up against the door saying Office.

There was a young lad at the desk with his head down and a pen in his hand. He didn't look up as he wrote something in the large book in front of him. She guessed it some sort of a log of who was on site and what they intended to do. When he still didn't acknowledge she was there she coughed as politely as she could.

'Yeah, can I help you?' he mumbled as he raised his head. 'You a member?'

Louise smiled as warm a smile as she could manage. 'No, I'm not. I have a friend who would like to join and as I was in this area, I said I would find out some details about your centre.'

He reached behind him to a shelf where she saw piles of leaflets, like the one she had in her pocket, stacked up against the wall. He handed one to her, put his head down and picked up the pen again.

'Thank you, that's great. I'll give this to my friend.' She didn't get an acknowledgement.

She coughed again. 'Actually, I heard about this place from a friend of mine called Caroline Meyer, who I think came here with her boyfriend who dives.'

The young lad still didn't take his eyes away from the log but when Louise pulled Caroline's photo out from her pocket and put it in front of him, he stopped and looked at it. 'No, don't think I've seen her here - would've remembered.'

Louise sighed and pushed the photograph back in her pocket. 'Would it be all right if I had a wander around? I've come quite a way and it would be good to say I'd seen what you're offering.' The young guy just nodded and waved her away.

The weather was bright and clear and the air had a sharp edge of ice and leaves on the trees had edges of frost. She caught a glimpse of the flooded quarry through the trees that edged it and thought it looked menacing, although some people, she was sure, would have described the scene as enchanting.

The leaflet showed there were quite a few different dive sites in the lake. It also indicated the places where various objects like old cars, a helicopter, several old boats and a lorry had been sunk. She supposed it made for more interesting diving, like wreck diving in open water.

The people on site were mainly dressed in wet suits, either ready to dive or had already done so. A few people were grouped round another rough sawn timber shack with mugs in their hands. A sign made out of an old piece of board propped up against the door advertised the building as a café. There was an old wooden table to the side of the door where another group of people appeared to be deep in conversation. No-one took any notice of her as she walked inside.

The light in the room was dim and it took her a minute to adjust to her surroundings. So much for those low wattage eco bulbs, she thought. The smell reminded her of the aquarium at Bristol Zoo which she always tried to avoid if she could. It was dark, damp and musty. Now she thought about it, more like the smell of forgotten clothes left wet in the washing machine than the aquarium. She guessed this was probably because people came to sit there between dives in their dripping wetsuits.

There were bare wooden trestle tables with some old chairs and in the corner at the back of the room, a sink and bits of kitchen equipment. In the middle of one of the walls was a large cork notice board with notices fixed with coloured drawing pins, giving information about the dives.

At a table in front of the sink was a notice which suggested she should help herself to a coffee and give a donation of a pound to cover any beverage and one biscuit. The tin of biscuits did not have a lid and she suspected they were probably stale. She put the required money in the tin, carried her chipped blue mug outside and stood close to the group of people. A young woman smiled at her. 'You're new here?'

Not sure if it was a statement or a question, Louise smiled back and nodded.

'I'm Sally. Come and meet the Sunday gang.' She beckoned to her and made the others make a space for her on the end of the bench. There wasn't much room and she had to squeeze herself onto it but it still left her teetering on the edge. 'Actually, I haven't come to join for myself but..' She hesitated, they seemed a pleasant group and they'd welcomed her so she didn't think it would do any harm if she told them the truth. They must have noticed her hesitancy because they went quiet and turned towards her.

She cleared her throat before she spoke. 'Well actually, the situation is this. My friend started coming here, or I think she did, with a boyfriend and now she's disappeared, and I came to find out if anyone had seen her.'

It all came out in a bit of a rush, and she saw several of them frown as they tried to grasp what she'd said. She put her hand in her pocket and rummaged around for the photograph. She held it up towards the girl, 'This is my friend, Caroline. Have any of you seen her?' Most of them shook their heads but an older man who was standing on the edge of the group walked over to take a closer look.

He studied the photo in his hands and Louise watched his face to see if there was any sign of recognition. She knew immediately, he did. 'Yes, I think I've seen her. I didn't see her dive and I haven't instructed her but I'm sure she came a few weeks ago with a man who I've seen around, but is not a regular diver; at least not on a Sunday.'

Louise could feel her heart beat faster and her hands went clammy. This was her first real lead. 'Do you know when it was exactly?' She tried not to sound desperate and gave a smile which she hoped covered her anxiety.

The man shook his head in a slow thoughtful way. 'No. I'm sorry, I don't think I can remember but was probably around the beginning of November sometime. Wait a minute, yes, that's right, I think it could have been the day after Bonfire Night, as it would have been a Sunday and I was at my nephew's house watching fireworks the day before. I noticed her because she had a thick padded jacket which looked expensive and very warm and I thought it would have been good to have had a thick jacket the night before when I was watching the fireworks.'

Louise's gratitude and excitement at having heard something definite made her reach forward and grasp the man's upper arm as she thanked him.

He shrugged his shoulders and looked down at his feet, 'I'm glad I could help and I do hope you find her. As I said, I don't think she was a diver. She came with this guy but it was the way she looked at the water, not exactly frightened but wary and I thought it was unlikely she would want to go into the water.'

Louise remembered discussing her own fear of water with Caroline, who then disclosed she too had a fear connected with water. 'Yes, she wasn't keen on going underwater. Do you remember what the guy looked like? I know you said he wasn't someone you recognised from any Sunday diving.'

He laughed. 'I dunno. I suppose I wasn't really looking at him. She was pretty and I think I was looking more at her. Although, I'm sure he had light brown or blonde hair and he was quite tall, taller than her anyway. Sorry, that's all I can remember.'

Louise felt she had got all she could from this helpful guy but asked if there was any way she could find out what the man's full name was, as she only knew from her friend his name was John. She remembered the estate agent had called him Mr Sheridan but she doubted it was his real name.

Sally, who had been listening to what they'd been saying, leapt in and told her it would all be in the daily register. She explained they had to sign in when they arrived in a book with space for name, address, date, time, intended dive length, buddy's name or instructors name and then when they checked out there were columns to enter the completed dives and their time of departure.

Louise hesitated before she spoke again, not sure if what she wanted was more than they would give out. 'I don't suppose one of you could look in the register for me and check his name? If he was here on the 6th November, then surely his name would be in the book and if I ask to see it, it might look odd as I'm not a member.'

There was a moment when no one answered but then the man called Jim, who had helped her originally, handed her his mug and muttered he would go and look.

She hadn't waited long before he came back smiling. 'His name is John Barton but he hadn't left an address, just a mobile number.' He handed her a scrap of paper with his number on it.

Her hand shook as she took it. 'Thank you, thank you so much. That's really great. I can now ring him and see what she's been up to and why she hasn't contacted her friends for a while.' She said goodbye and as she walked back to the reception hut, Jim shouted good luck. She turned and waved back at him; something about him reminded her of George. It was the way he stood, straight and confident.

She signed out in the visitor's book and as she walked back to her car, peered at the piece of paper she'd been given. I'm certain that's not the name Caroline told me; nor is it the name the agent gave me. The number seemed familiar though. She remembered his description of

Caroline's coat. It wasn't a coat she remembered, as she didn't think she had a padded one and it certainly wasn't the new one she had worn at the café. I guess he must have bought it for her, which is why perhaps both her coats were at her house.

When she was home she looked again at the paper with the number on it. Even though her stomach flipped at the thought of it, she decided that she must find out more. Dave would probably think she was interfering again but she'd come this far and wasn't going to let it go, after all Caroline could be in danger. It rang a few times and then she heard the cultured voice she recognised from her last phone call with him.

'*Hello, John here. Who is this?*' He sounded puzzled. '*Hello, are you there? I don't recognise your number. Are you the agent?*'

Louise swallowed and took a deep breath before she made herself speak in as strong a voice as she could manage. '*No, John, it's Louise.*'

There was silence but she caught the intake of breath. '*I just want to know where Caroline is. You both seemed to have dropped off the face of the earth and I'd love to speak to her if that's OK?*' Then added lamely, '*She must be better now surely?*'

There was another silence and then he cleared his throat several times. When he eventually spoke, his voice had a wobble and he didn't sound nearly as confident or calm as when he first answered.

'*I'm sorry, Louise, but she can't come to the phone right now.*' He paused and then, as if he'd suddenly found the story he wanted to tell, said with much more confidence. '*Actually, this might be difficult for you to hear but she'd rather you didn't keep calling. We've decided to start our lives completely afresh, which is why we've left Bath. I expect she'll see you at some point as she will need to sort out her house but, in the meantime, I think we'd prefer it if you didn't continue to call.*' He ended what he was saying with a bit of a flourish, as if he was a magician and he'd just pulled a rabbit out of a hat.

She took a deep breath; she didn't believe a word of it but his lies showed her he didn't know the police were searching his premises and she certainly wasn't going to be the one to tell him. *'Well, John, if that's what you both want then I'm sorry. Caroline and I have been special friends for many years now and it seems an odd way to end a friendship.'* This time the only sound was silence as he cancelled the call. I can't believe the audacity of the man. There was no doubt in her mind now Caroline was either dead or trussed up somewhere and a prisoner and she resolved to contact Dave immediately and tell him what's happened.

She felt it would be better to talk to Dave in person rather than phone and so made her way to their house.

'I didn't think you were coming, Mum?' Katy ushered her in but looked puzzled.

'I haven't come for lunch but I needed to speak to Dave and thought I'd come in person. Of course, if there's any lunch left over, I'd love some but if that's too cheeky please don't worry.'

Katy gave her a big hug and said they'd only just sat down and there was plenty.

Louise was once again pleased to be amongst the family although it meant she wasn't able to talk to Dave until after the meal.

'What have you done now?' Dave tried to look stern but Louise knew his worry was more for her own safety than irritation for interfering.

She related her day and his eyebrows shot up several times before she'd finished. 'Wow. What a mother-in-law! Although I'm angry that yet again you've taken no notice of what I asked of you, you have done some great detective work and we've now got his number. It's a pity you rang and spoke to him though; he'll almost certainly be more wary now. You said you didn't think the number you rang was the one he spoke to you on before?'

'I'm not sure.' And she got her phone out to check. She confirmed it was different. It's funny though because I thought I'd recognised it, but so many mobile numbers are similar I'd obviously muddled it up.'

'We were going to the quarry today but then we had a report of a possible sight of Caroline, which seemed highly plausible so we followed that up instead. By the time we'd established it was a false lead the quarry had already closed but we will go tomorrow first thing. Thanks to you, I now know the date he was at the quarry, and I will arrange to get a trace on the number you've given me now. Maybe we'll be lucky this time.'

Louise didn't return until late evening. She fumbled for the lock and as she turned the key, she caught a waft of cigarette smoke. She felt a now familiar crawling sensation on her skin and sensed a presence behind her. She flung herself through the door and slammed it shut. She ran to the counselling room window and peered out. She saw nothing at first then as her eyes focused on the far side of her road, she could have sworn a face looked out of a car directly at her. She couldn't make out the registration from where she was and felt too anxious to go outside.

MONDAY 28th NOVEMBER 2005

'Mmm, at least you're dependable and huggable.' She ruffled Buster's coat and he wagged his tail at the attention and then padded over to wait at the back door. The rush of fresh air did nothing to help prevent a large yawn escaping from her. She hated these mornings when she had to get up before dawn.

I must go to work today, she thought as she idly pushed the toaster down. Life's so crazy at the moment I need to feel grounded and work might help. She flung open the door of the larder cupboard and then slammed it shut almost immediately. What a mess. I can't even remember the last time I went shopping. She opened the fridge and she was met with the cold and emptiness of it. It's bad enough there's no porridge but there's not even any jam, marmalade or marmite.

Having given up on breakfast, she walked into her therapy room. She'd never liked the thought of curtains being closed all day while she was at work, even though it was dark now and would be dark when she returned from Kingswood. She flung them open and the light from the streetlights were bright enough to make out vehicles parked on the road. She saw the frost on the windows and guessed that all the cars she could see had been parked there all night.

She shivered and thought how much she hated having to clear frost from the car windows before she could get going. She had always meant to buy a proper tool but had an old CD case in the car which served as a scraper. She blew on her hands and stamped her feet after she'd cleared the frost as best she could. It would have been better if I'd let the engine run while I cleaned the frost off the windows, she thought. However, the many police warnings about people nipping in and driving off while you were still scraping, prevented her. She started the engine and set the heater onto the highest temperature.

'Oh, who's that trying to get me now', she murmured as she heard the ping on her phone. She'd left it in her briefcase and the briefcase had slipped behind her seat, so with a large sigh she reached back for it. She saw the message was just labelled client, which is what she did to preserve anonymity but it meant she didn't know who it was from until she opened it.

Hi Louise, Ed here. Just wondered if I could take you up on your offer of seeing me again. There are things I think I need to talk through with you.

Well, that's a surprise. I hadn't expected that, at least not after only a couple of weeks. What on earth could have happened? She pulled her diary out of her briefcase and texted back, *Hi Ed, there is a free spot on Thursday at 8.30 a.m. if you want that. I know it's not the time you like but it's all I've got.*

Once on her way she thought about Ed and wished he'd waited a bit longer before returning but then perhaps I would feel the same about all my clients at the moment. I'm not sure I'm in a good enough place to be working. As if to emphasise this statement the brake lights came on in the car in front. 'Hells bells,' she shouted as she missed his bumper by a thumbnail.

As soon as she arrived at the surgery and checked her phone, she found she had a message from Dave who wanted her to ring him. She logged onto the surgery system, got everything ready for her first client and thought she had just enough time to return his call.

He picked up straight away and she realised that he had something important to tell her as there was no social preamble.

'I just wanted to let you know straight away the bone you found definitely belonged to Sophie. We managed to match her DNA from our data base because at some point she'd been involved in a demonstration and had been temporarily arrested. We've informed her mother who was obviously

distressed at the news, but was also relieved that she'd been found.'

She could hardly take in what he was saying. She had known in her heart the bone would prove to be Sophie's, but it was still a shock to hear it. Louise knew the mother's reaction was not unusual and felt for her. When she discovered that the postcards had not been from her daughter she must have feared something awful had happened to her and not knowing must have been agonising. She realised Dave was speaking again.

'We managed to find most of the remains of her skeleton and the hyoid bone was fractured which tends to indicate she died by strangulation. We are definitely treating this as murder and John is high on our list of suspects. Louise, please would you now leave all the detective work to us. I'm saying this for your own safety because none of us could bear to lose you.'

Now that her fears had been realised Louise shuddered when she thought where Caroline might be and what could be happening to her.

She thanked Dave for letting her know, especially as he probably shouldn't be telling her. He started to talk again but she stopped him and apologised for not being able to talk more because she was at the surgery and had a client in a few minutes.

'Right. Of course. There was something else I needed to tell you about which was really the main reason I rang, but I guess it can wait. Ring me when you can though.'

She agreed, turned off her phone and walked to the door ready to get her first client of the day. Then realised she didn't want to wait to hear what Dave had to say, so put her phone back on and rang him back. It went straight to answerphone so she had to be content to wait.

The day proved harder than she'd hoped and when she arrived home, she was exhausted. 'I'm absolutely beat, Buster, so only a short walk this evening.' Perhaps it's not just Caroline and all that's going on; perhaps I'm just getting too old for this job, she thought but then felt a chuckle emerge when she remembered the energetic sex, she'd enjoyed only a week or so ago.

There'd been nothing from George since Dave revealed what he was involved with in Wales. She had found that whole story almost impossible to believe. Surely, I couldn't have got his character so very wrong. Her mind felt consumed by images of him and the time they'd spent together. As hard as she tried, she couldn't equate the man she thought she knew, with the liar he'd turned out to be, nor the one she'd found drunk and the one who may be a killer. He appeared to be so charming and gentle but many killers had proved to be charming and gentle. She shuddered.

She'd reached the brow of the hill and stopped for a moment by one of the gates which led down the path to the church. The dark and ominous shape below reminded her of a French film she'd seen where children from the village were kept in captivity in the vault of a church by some evil man. She couldn't remember the title and she'd been quite young when she saw it. Perhaps it was because it was in black and white and the buildings around the church and the church itself were all black and the sky was a dim grey. She shivered and cursed her overactive imagination.

She had her hand on the gate ready to go in, when a movement caught her eye. She peered into the gloom and at first saw nothing but then saw that at the side of the porch stood a man. The movement must have been his hand as he lit a cigarette and she saw a small glow in the dark. She grabbed Buster's lead, wound it tightly round her hand and marched with him as fast as she could back down the hill the way they'd come.

Louise looked back over her shoulder several times but saw nothing untoward. Despite this, she had the feeling she was being followed.

WEDNESDAY 7th DECEMBER 2005

Once Tim was seated in the chair, she gave her usual greeting which today felt robotic, and she hoped it wasn't how it sounded. He looked even more dishevelled than usual and he had already run his hand through his unruly hair several times. He was wearing a jumper which ought to have gone to a jumble sale a long time ago and his corduroy trousers could have done with a wash. His doctor wife was obviously not keen on domesticity. His scarecrow appearance irritated her today. Somehow it felt disrespectful and she hoped he made more of an effort when he saw clients.

'I'm fine, and everything is good at home too. I'm glad to be seeing you today though, as these sessions with Paul are beginning to trouble me greatly.'

'Right, perhaps you'd better start with Paul then. I must say I have felt slightly uneasy since your phone call. I can't think why he would have asked if you know me. Has he said anything else about it since?'

He ran his hands through his hair again before answering. 'No, not about you, but he says this guy is very near to finding the man Paul wanted him to find. The thing worrying me though, is I'm not sure what he is going to do when he does find him. I thought Paul wanted to prove his innocence but it is beginning to sound more like a man hunt than a search for justice.'

Tim picked at something stuck to his jumper and then sighed before he spoke again. 'Do you think I should do something about it? I mean, should I inform the prison?'

She gazed out of the window while she thought, then asked, 'What has he told you exactly? Has he asked this man to do anything other than find the guy he's looking for? Has he said he's asked him to assault, injure, or even kill him? If the answer is yes, then you do need to let the prison know. But if not then I'm not so sure.'

She was always surprised by how easily she talked about violence and couldn't help wondering whether she was on the way to being burnt out. She'd been to a workshop on Therapist Burn Out and the signs to watch out for. One warning sign was when the abnormal starts to sound normal or when empathy dies.

She thought carefully about whether the Governor should be informed. Breaking confidentiality was a very serious thing. If Paul had told Tim he had specifically asked this man to injure or even kill, then this would necessitate informing the prison, but if not then it should remain confidential.

Tim explained Paul had said this man was going to find the guy he held responsible, investigate him fully and try and find evidence that would prove his innocence. The thing that worried him though was he had said things like 'he'll get his just desserts' and 'he deserves everything he's got coming to him.'

'I don't quite understand. How would hurting or even killing this man help Paul to prove he was not Julia's killer?'

Tim shook his head. 'I don't know but it worries me, as you should see the look in his eyes when he talks and I still haven't forgotten what it was like when he turned on me.'

Louise felt her head begin to whirl. 'I think what you are saying is your gut instinct is telling you this man they are chasing is in some danger.'

The rest of the session was spent deliberating what, if anything, needed to be brought to the attention of the Governor.

'Based on what you've told me, it seems clear that although you feel there is no immediate danger, there is potential danger to the man who is being followed. I think you need to remind Paul of the confidentiality clause you told him about at the beginning of your sessions and tell him that because of what he has told you, it is no longer possible to keep it confidential. Tell him you will now be talking to the Prison Governor. It will then be up to the Governor to do what he feels is right.'

Tim nodded his head, shut his eyes and let out a long sigh.

While she waited for him to collect himself, she was aware of the tick of the clock behind his head and hoped she could end the session soon. She pulled her hands through her hair and realised she had mimicked Tim's anxiety, so laid them back in her lap. Tiredness overwhelmed her and she tried to keep her eyes open and pay attention to Tim.

'I suggest you continue your work on his anger and it might be worth reminding him, he would be responsible for any violence this friend of his causes and it could elongate his time in prison.'

She gazed out of the window after she'd spoken. The wind moved the skeletal fingers of the bare branches. It was as if they waved and pointed at her and she shivered as she turned back towards Tim.

She couldn't help returning to the question which burned in her head but Tim again said he had no idea why Paul wanted to know if he'd known her.

'I'm sorry Louise as I said, I just didn't ask. I was shocked when he mentioned your name but we didn't talk about it this time.'

Louise tried to stop her irritation showing. If it had been her who had been asked this, she would have wanted to know why and would have pursued it until she knew.

She ended the session but asked Tim to ring her once he had spoken to the Governor.

THURSDAY 1st DECEMBER 2005

It wasn't obvious at first but by the time she'd eaten a bowl of porridge, the cold had seeped into her bones; the heating had not turned on.   She cursed and checked the oil tank; she'd run out of oil. Bloody hell, how did I let that happen, she thought, but knew the answer.

She telephoned the oil company she had used for years but they said there could be no delivery until the weekend. As she pulled a thick sweater out of her cupboard she realised she'd need to switch on the oil filled heater for clients and that was expensive.

She opened her now rather worn and ragged diary and ran her finger down the list of names written on the page. She matched the names to the notes in her filing cabinet and put them in a pile on the desk. She'd realised Ed's would need to be retrieved from the file labelled 'Ended 2005' and opened another drawer where it was housed.   I still don't get it, she mused. It's very unusual for anyone to return so quickly. Something must have happened and something pretty drastic as he was so sure he'd never need to see me again. She smiled as the thought 'I told you so' came into her head.

There was something different about him when he arrived. Between meeting him at the door and being seated Louise tried to work out what it was. Was it the way he was dressed, the way he looked, his manner, what?   He behaved in the same way he usually did. He'd thrown his coat over the chair, in a way that could only be seen as possessive and smiled as he did it. She again wondered what you'd need to pay a dentist to get teeth as white as the keys on her piano, that she hardly ever played now.

'God, Louise, bloody cold in your house today. Heating not working then?' He glared at the heater sitting in front of the fireplace and reached for his coat and put it back on.

'No. I'm sorry it's not. I was going to tell you when you walked in but you got there first.'

His lip curled and Louise wondered if it was a smile or a sneer. She studied his immaculate suit and wondered who kept the trouser creases so razor sharp and was glad she wasn't responsible for anything similar. She'd always been hopeless at ironing but perhaps he had a trouser press.

'So, how are you? I was surprised you asked to come back so soon and wondered what could have happened to make you change your mind. Perhaps you'd like to tell me about it.' She searched his face for a clue but got none. She thought she caught a glint in his eyes when he answered but it was no more than a flash.

'Right, I'm fine really but after I'd finished our sessions, I realised there were a few ends I ought perhaps to have tied up. Silly of me to have left them undone. I thought it would work out but it hasn't so I realised I needed to come back.'

This was followed by a definite smirk and Louise couldn't help the thought there was some sort of double talk going on. It took a while but then she realised what was different. He had a confidence of the sort you have when you feel in control. She could see he felt comfortable in how he was and it did feel much more real.

'You want to be here to finish some issues left undone. Perhaps you'd like to start with the time you came to the realisation you've just talked about and tell me what exactly the loose ends are?'

He gave an enormous and charming smile but said nothing.

Her breathing slowed and she sat quietly waiting for whatever he had to say. He held the smile for a while, then clutched his upper arms and shivered.

'Sorry, Louise, this cold is affecting my bladder, can I use your loo again?' His asking was a formality as he was already out of the chair and had started towards the door.

She nodded and remembered what happened last time and wondered how long he'd be today but he appeared again in less time than she expected and seemed to have upped his mood even more than before. She'd worked with many clients who took drugs and noticed his pupils were now smaller and suspected he'd taken some substance, perhaps a line of coke. She saw he could now hardly contain himself as he shifted about in his seat and again, she got the sense he was going to divulge something of significance.

'Before we begin, I just want to say something. I was looking at those photos again in your loo and realised I recognised one of the people in the montage you have.' She cursed inwardly and wished she had taken it down after he'd last mentioned it but with so much going on, she'd forgotten.

'Really, who do you know?'

'No, I don't know any of them but I recognised one. The woman, the one in red with her arm around you.

Louise held her breath. He could only mean the one Dom took of Caroline and her, all those years ago when they first met. 'What do you mean, how do you recognise her?'

'I think I saw her in a pub I go to sometimes and not long ago. She was with a man and they were leaving as I was going in with my girlfriend. She was a very striking woman, so worth a look. What's she called?'

Before she could stop herself, she uttered her name. Could he possibly have seen her and when was it? She swallowed and her chest felt tight. She tried not to sound too eager when she spoke.

'When was this? Which pub was it?'

He smiled. 'I think it was a couple of Sundays ago. It's the pub by Chew Valley lake called The Fisherman's Catch. They do great Sunday lunches and I sometimes drive out from Bath with my girlfriend. We walk round the lake and end up there for lunch it's the lake where I fish.' He grinned and sat there watching her. 'You look worried. Is something the matter?'

Louise needed to know more even though she knew she wasn't being very professional. 'She's a good friend but she's gone missing.'

Ed stared at her. 'How dreadful. Looking at the picture, it seems she is a good friend. It must be awful to not know where she is but now I've told you she was fine two weeks ago perhaps she's not really missing.'

Louise tried to think what was happening two weeks ago and remembered it was when she and Dave found mayhem in Caroline's house. She tried not to let her voice wobble when she replied.

'Thanks, you've been helpful. I've had no contact with her and so I'm worried. Have you been there since? To the pub I mean.'

Another grin and she wished she could stop him doing that. He hadn't been like this in other sessions.

'No, I haven't but I will certainly be going again at some point and if I see her, I'll give you a ring, shall I?'

Louise managed a smile and thanked him. She thought, I must get him back into the session. She'd allowed herself to be diverted and was not being professional.

'Thanks again Ed but let's get back to you and why you came back.' Have you had more trouble at work?'

'No, I haven't, in fact it's all been going well. I haven't got into an argument since I last saw you and I think Michael is pleased.'

'What is it about then? Take your time and tell me what is worrying you?'

Louise settled back into her chair and waited to hear about the issue that troubled this man, who had suffered so much as a child. She imagined he might want to explore many of the things he had talked about. The abuse, the relationship with his parents, their death and many other things.

What he brought in the end was something so minor, she could hardly stifle her surprise. It reminded her of a time when a sex addict came for six sessions before he was able to tell her what his fetish was and by the time he did, her imagination had worked overtime and she had conjured up awful and depraved sex acts so when he finally disclosed what he did, she had almost laughed at how lame it sounded and chocolate and feathers seemed ridiculous and funny.

'Well, there you have it. Can you help me, do you think? I really do need to be able to get into a boat without feeling sick and yet it is what happens every time.'

Despite her underlying feeling this was not the real issue, she reassured him and told him she worked with anxiety and phobias of all kinds and was sure she would be able to help him as long as he really wanted to change how he felt.

'Oh, but I do, it is really important to me.'

Not convinced she continued to question him. 'Have you always felt like this, or when did it start? Do you remember?'

Ed told her he had been fine until about five years ago when he had gone in a dingy to fish and felt sick almost immediately and since then the same thing has always happened and it was so unpleasant, he had to return to the shore immediately. 'I like fishing, you see, and especially from a boat but it is out of the question for the moment.'

The tension she had felt at the beginning of the session and the talk of Caroline, had faded a little but she was glad when the rest of this very mundane session came to an end. They booked a few more sessions and he left.

She stretched her legs and arms and with a loud yawn wandered over to the window in time to see him walk to his car. As he drove off a car pulled out from behind him and followed him up the road. She was sure it was the same one that had followed her.

She tried to reach Dave but only got his answerphone. She left a message to tell him about the sighting at Fisherman's Catch and to let him know what she had just seen.

FRIDAY 2nd DECEMBER 2005

The frost hadn't left the grass as Louise scrunched her way across the park and she pulled her scarf tighter around her neck and walked as fast as she could. It had certainly been a hard frost last night and the trees still looked as though they'd been dipped in sugar. She was glad she'd put on her warm insulated coat and boots.

Once out of the park she passed a few shops showing evidence of the Christmas yet to come. It made her stop for a moment; she'd almost forgotten it was only a few weeks away. She felt a tightness in her chest and tried not to think about it. Her eyes welled up at the thought of the wonderful time she'd had last year with all the family. Caroline had joined them in the afternoon, as she was on her own then, and they'd played stupid games with the children and had so much fun. She dabbed her eyes with a tissue and walked on. She hesitated for a moment when she reached the café where she had seen her a while ago and automatically glanced inside, although she was certain she wouldn't be there.

At Frances' flat Harriet opened the door, gave a smile in greeting, caught hold of her arm and whispered, 'Is there a chance we could meet for coffee after?' She didn't get a chance to reply because Frances appeared and started to talk, so she only had the opportunity to nod at Harriet before she engaged in a conversation with Frances.

She told the group what had happened since she last saw them and they were aghast. A horrified Harriet almost shouted, 'You mean you had someone break into your house?'

When they had finished the meeting, Harriet moved quickly to leave at the same time and again asked if they could go for a coffee. They made their way down to the café on the corner as they had before.

Harriet put her hand on the latch and before she fully opened the café door, she turned back to Louise, 'Thanks for doing this. I need to share some things with you. It might not be totally ethical but I've decided it's important you hear what I've got to say.' Louise hesitated in the doorway, 'Are you sure? It is not like you to be in any way unprofessional.' By way of an answer Harriet walked in and went to order coffee and cake and Louise found a seat.

'It's about Ben (I'll call him that now since you know his real name). I need you to hear something and it's something I didn't share with the others just now.' Louise was glad she'd managed to secure the table in the corner which was furthest away from everyone and checked to see there was no-one close enough to hear what they might say.

'Okay, go on. What is it worrying you?'

Harriet struggled out of her coat and hung it on the back of the chair.

'I think you know about the incident with the dead guinea pig?' Louise nodded and Harriet continued, 'I don't want to talk about it now, even though I know it was horrifying and extreme behaviour. I am sure you will have guessed it was all about being left again. What I want to tell you is….' Louise felt her throat constrict. Whatever he'd done this poor lad was going to discover at some point soon his beloved nanny was dead and a possibility his stepfather killed her. It was too awful to think about and with Caroline still in danger too. Why on earth hadn't they managed to discover his whereabouts.

Harriet continued. 'What I want to say is, in a way, more relevant to you. He told me how much he had loved having a young nanny; she was called Sophie. Then she left and he felt sad and upset. He said it made him think of his mother.

When his stepfather introduced Caroline into their home, Ben was delighted. He said she was great fun and she reminded him of Sophie. He said he felt happy again. Then something happened, he didn't know what but his stepfather became worse tempered and Caroline changed too. He was at school most of the time but on the occasions when he went to visit, he noticed how different she was; not so much fun and he was reminded of how his mother was sometimes, although he wasn't able to be specific.

'He told me there was a room in the house which was scary and horrid and he remembered his mother made him promise never to try to go into it. This room was mentioned by his stepfather when he and Caroline started to argue one day. His stepfather got really angry and shouted something like, '*Remember the room. You don't want go back there, do you?*' Ben was frightened more than he'd ever been before because suddenly he remembered Sophie had talked about a room when they'd been playing in the woods and he knew it scared her. Caroline had turned and shouted at him but Ben couldn't remember what she'd said but what he did remember was what his stepfather said next. He said, "*And don't think your lefty friend Louise will help you because she knows now what a terrible friend you are and I'll make sure you never have the chance to meet again.*" I have put this sentence into the words I think Ben said, although he knew he may not have remembered them correctly.'

Louise could hardly breathe; she felt heat rise in her body and felt faint. There was so much to take in. She took a large gulp of the water she'd asked for.

She thought about the room behind the kitchen where they'd found all the diving kit and remembered the thoughts she'd had about it when she first went in. The idea of being locked in there with no windows and that awful smell horrified her.

Harriet continued, 'The thing is, Ben never saw Caroline again. He did go home again but his stepdad just told him Caroline had gone. In his words, she'd pushed off and he told him it was good riddance too. Ben was upset and immediately after that weekend, he came in and killed the guinea pig.'

Louise sat quietly for a moment while she turned over all this information in her head. 'Harriet, I'm going to have to pass this information to my son-in-law, who is a detective in the local police. He is searching for John now and we suspect something awful has happened to Caroline. What you don't know is the body that has been in the news, was found in the woods adjoining his property in Bath. They haven't released information as to where the woods are as they don't want all and sundry delving about. You must promise to keep this to yourself as it is not general knowledge but they have confirmed the body belongs to Sophie, the nanny who went missing a few years ago.'

Harriet gasped, put her hands up and covered her face. 'That's dreadful. I can't believe it. The man's a monster, an absolute monster.'

Louise agreed with her. 'I'm sorry to upset you but this whole thing is going to affect Ben in a drastic way when he eventually learns about it, and he will need a lot of support. No wonder he was so cruel, it was a way of dealing with his huge unmanageable feelings. Thank you for sharing what you did and as I said just now, what I have said is absolutely confidential. As Caroline is at risk, the police need every piece of information they can.'

Harriet looked shaken, her face had lost its colour and Louise noticed her hands shook.

'I think I'll get us another coffee,' murmured Louise as she got up to go to the counter. When she returned Harriet looked a bit better but clearly had questions.

'I just can't take it in. Are you saying the man might also have killed Caroline and he might be a serial killer?'

'I think you have to kill three people at least to be called a serial killer but who knows, there may be more.' Louise screwed up her face as she thought about what she'd just said.

After a morning like the one she'd had Louise felt she needed to snatch some rest before going to see Jasper. He'd moved the date forward a week as he was busy when they should have met, which was really fortuitous as she had so much to tell him.

She'd tried to phone Dave again but once more only got an answerphone and so left a message to ask if he had any news following the information she'd left yesterday. She also told him what she had heard from Harriet about the room.

She felt completely drained by the time she got to Jasper's and when he asked if she was alright, she asked him for one of his famous bear hugs, which he gave her without hesitation.

She used the whole session to tell him what had happened to her since he last saw her, leaving no detail out and expressing her panic about the situation now and Caroline still missing. She added the part she had learned today. She also told him about her session with Tim.

Jasper thought for a moment then he said, 'I have never liked coincidences, in fact as you know I don't really believe in them. I always feel there is a real connection. Perhaps we're missing something but I can't think what.'

Louise sighed. 'I feel totally adrift. I've never had to deal with anything like this before and I am not sure which way to turn.'

I know' he said and leaned forward again. 'This is an extraordinary and terrible situation you find yourself in and it's not surprising you feel adrift; anyone would. I will give you any support that is within my power to give. In all the years I've known you and through all your personal grief, I've never found you lacking in courage or the ability to put your life aside and give your full attention to your clients. However, this may be a time when it is necessary to look after yourself and take time off from your work. Whatever the outcome of all this is, I know that you will come through it with the strength you have always shown you have.

'Thanks Jasper I appreciate what you've said but I want to keep working if I can. I think it is helping to keep me sane at the moment.' She paused for a moment and then said, 'Talking about clients I remember I haven't yet talked about Ed.' She told him how he had asked for more sessions and her surprise at that, particularly when she heard what it was about. She quickly gave him a resume of the whole content of the session including how he had spotted Caroline's picture.

Jasper told Louise that he thought she needed an extra session to talk about clients and agreed a later time of five next Friday.

Driving in the dark often highlighted how alone she felt and the drive back that night was no exception. How she would have loved to have been meeting Caroline tonight, as they always had done before she met John. She drove the long way around, which brought her into her road from Caroline's end. As she drew near to the house, she thought she saw a light. She parked the car and dashed towards the house.

She thought the light she'd seen was in the bedroom but once she reached the front door the house was in darkness. She opened the door, with the key that was still in her bag and shouted but no-one replied. She put the hall light on and walked through to the kitchen. It took her only a few seconds to see someone had broken a pane of glass in the door. She shuddered and felt her skin crawl. She retraced her steps, careful not to make a sound.

She rang Dave as soon as she got home, and unusually he picked up straight away.

'Thanks, we'll go and search the house again and see if we can see what they wanted. You say you think you are still being followed and whoever it was appeared to follow a client of yours?'

'Yes, I do. I could be wrong but it looked as though it followed him; it certainly pulled out just after he'd left. I am finding everything creepy at the moment though, so could be imagining things. Are there really no more sightings or news about Caroline? Did you get any more leads using the information about the pub?'

Dave cleared his throat, *'No, I'm afraid not. I went to visit the pub but no-one seems to remember seeing her and of course, he could have been mistaken. Please try not to worry. By the way, the thing I wanted to say before was... Um has George been in touch with you?'*

'George? No, should he have? We are not together anymore, although I would like to think he hadn't done

anything dreadful. However, it's difficult to know what to think in all that's happened. I can't help thinking about the insinuation from your officers that he was implicated in the break-in.'

Dave cleared his throat again. *'I just wanted to tell you that the case he was involved in over. No charges were brought against him and the verdict was an accidental death.'*

Louise let out a long breath which sounded like relief. *'What does it mean exactly? Were they sure he wasn't involved?'*

There was a delay before Dave answered, *'It means there was no evidence to suggest he had any involvement in his death. I think it's more than likely to be true. It was a quarry apparently known to be dangerous and it appears he somehow got himself caught in a mine shaft and couldn't get out or lost his direction. If George does get in touch, why don't you give him a chance to explain? I liked him and you were good together.'*

Louise mumbled a reply but wasn't going to commit herself to anything.

She stretched and an image of a hot bath and some lavender essence came into her head. She had been so excited by the new shower she hadn't had a really good soak in a bath for a long time.

She tried hard to keep her eyes open enough to read the book she'd bought the other day, but it was no use. She'd just turned out the light and settled down in bed when her phone pinged. Typical, she thought, just as I want to sleep and looked at the text in irritation. *Hi, Maybe Dave has told you but I'm off the hook - desperately keen to meet up. Can you ring tomorrow please? There is so much I need to say. George xxx*

She threw the phone down and wished she hadn't looked at it. Her head hurt and knew it would now be impossible to settle and the benefit of the bath seeped away. I can't cope with him as well. No way. There's too much going on to even think about it. She turned the phone off, plumped up the pillows, turned off the light and pulled the covers over her head. She ignored the feeling of excitement and the accelerated beat of her heart.

SATURDAY 3RD DECEMBER 2005

Determined to have a relaxing start to the day she brought her breakfast back to bed. She didn't turn on her phone until she was up and dressed and when she did, saw she had several messages. She decided not to read them and got into her outdoor clothes, clicked her fingers at Buster and reached for his lead and left.

The frost glistened on the branches of the shrubs and as she took deep breaths of the cold air, she felt energised and perhaps even a bit free. She saw the beautiful and unique patterns of ice on the windscreens of the parked cars as she walked by. Then came to one with no ice at all. She looked more closely, took a sharp intake of breath and her knees wobbled. It was 'the' car; the one that had followed her and there was someone inside it. She kept her eyes down and walked past as fast as she could and hoped she hadn't been spotted.

Her joy of the morning disappeared, as did her interest in doing the intended longer walk with Buster. Instead she did the short loop round the church and approached her house from Caroline's end in order to escape being seen. This gave her the opportunity at last to really look at the number plate. She had no paper or pen with her so tried to memorise it. She repeated the number over and over until she was in the house, where she wrote it down and hoped she'd remembered it right.

There were three messages from George and two from Katy, each of them urged her to ring them. Katy was the least difficult so rang her first, but she only wanted to check up on her and reminded her that Dave was concerned she was getting over involved.

George's texts told her nothing other than he desperately wanted to speak to her. If he is drunk when he answers, that's it, she thought, as she put in his number.

'George? Hi, it's Louise, you wanted to speak to me?' She didn't add she was sorry not to reply sooner. She was going to wait for him to make the first move.

'Thanks for ringing, Lou, it's so good to hear you. I've missed you and I want you in my life. I don't know whether you want me in yours, but I'd like to see you and hopefully we can work all this mess out.'

He talked fast. She guessed it was nerves and couldn't help a smile but she wasn't going to let him off the hook immediately. 'George, my life is in chaos at the moment. I can't cope with anything extra on top but Dave told me the case you were involved in found your diving buddy had an accidental death, so you're not guilty of any crime. I still don't know what happened exactly but it probably explains your behaviour but doesn't excuse it. So, for now I'm not sure about meeting you let alone even thinking about a relationship.'

She'd expected big argument but there wasn't one. He said he understood and put the phone down. She immediately felt she had been too hard on him, so rang him straight back.

'Sorry. I didn't mean to be hard, but hopefully you do understand. Perhaps Dave will have explained a bit about Caroline and all the other things. I don't want to talk about any of it at the moment, but how about I see you next week in the pub and we can have a chat and see where we go from there. Would Friday at six thirty be any good for you? I'm seeing Jasper at five so it would give me enough time to get back to the pub afterwards.'

She'd picked the day at random as she didn't want to make it sound as though she had forgiven him or was eager to see him. She heard the hope and excitement in his voice when he agreed.

The next call was to Dave and she left a message giving him the registration number of the car that she thought had followed her.

During the night when sleep just wouldn't come to her she'd planned her next course of action. She was sure Dave wouldn't object to a small amount of sleuthing.

'*Hey, Luke, it's Louise. Just wondered if you by any chance free tomorrow mid-day?*' She heard the snort and realised he was thinking about their last expedition. '*No, I don't mean we will go hunting for bones or bodies, but I wondered if you fancied coming out to a pub and having a proper Sunday lunch, as a sort of thank you for helping me out?*'

'*Wow, thank goodness, thought you had meant we should go on another investigation. The last one really freaked me out you know, so I'd have refused but a Sunday lunch is another matter. So yes please. What time should I be ready?*'

She agreed to pick him up at twelve and would book a table for twelve forty-five, which should give her enough time. She felt a little guilty as she put the phone down because she knew she hadn't been entirely truthful.

SUNDAY 4TH DECEMBER 2005

'No dog today then?' Luke peered into the back seat as he got into the car.

'No, not today. Thought he might get bored while we are in the pub.'

She glanced across at him as he fastened his seat belt and noted he had obviously made a bit of an effort. His jeans were clean and although he was wearing the same scruffy jacket he'd worn to the woods, she caught sight of a clean light grey sweatshirt underneath it. He'd also managed to get his hair under control enough for it to look relatively tidy. She smiled to herself, pleased he'd dressed as if he was going somewhere special.

In the first few miles he told her more about himself. He'd come from Liverpool to do a degree course at the University of Bristol. He'd decided to live in Bath as his aunt owned the house he shared with three other students and it meant he could live relatively cheaply. He didn't have a car and once she'd driven further into the countryside, he spent a lot of time telling her how lovely it was, not at all like Liverpool at all. She'd only been to Liverpool once and she told him how she'd gone across The Mersey on the ferry and done a tour of all the places connected with The Beatles. He laughed and said it was quite a naff thing to do. She agreed and laughed as well.

Louise had never been to The Fisherman's Catch but the journey took them through stunning country. The fields and hills in the distance glistened in the sharp sunlight and the country lanes seemed to beckon towards something magical. After a few more miles the road broadened out and ran alongside Chew Valley Lake where the light danced and the pale blue water sparkled like diamonds on a shimmering dress. It was magic and for a moment she forgot her worries.

As they caught a view of the island in the middle of the lake, Louise thought of Julia, Amanda's client and a shiver ran up her back. It didn't look sinister today though; it was beautiful and calm. Probably a bit too calm for the many sailing boats, static as chess pieces waiting for the game to start. There were fishermen too out in boats, who chose to be still so they could stop and fish in isolation and peace. She knew the lake was a reservoir and she'd read somewhere that when it was built whole villages had been flooded and were buried underneath.

The pub's focus was very much on fishing. On the walls there were pictures of fish that had been caught by the happy grinning fishermen and a pair of pale vacant eyes stared out from an enormous fish captured for ever in a glass case.

They were shown to a table by the window which looked out over a garden, where a climbing frame was festooned with children of all sizes and shapes. They shrieked with joy, which Louise thought was probably the freedom they felt while their parents stayed in the pub.

Luke continued to chatter and by the end of their meal, she felt there could be nothing left of his life story to be heard. His voice relaxed Louise and she sat back and enjoyed the food. When they'd finished their main course, she excused herself while Luke interrogated the sweet menu.

'Excuse me.'

The young waitress stood at the till her hand about to press the buttons but looked up when Louise spoke.

'I wonder if you've ever seen this woman?' She handed the girl the photo who frowned and shook her head, 'No I don't think so. I don't think I have. Do you want me to ask the others?' Louise nodded. 'Why do you want to know though, it's nothing bad is it?'

How bad could possible murder be? thought Louise, but said, 'No, I hope not but she's gone missing and apparently she had been seen here. I wondered if it were true and if so, how long ago it was?'

'Ooh - is it the woman who was in the papers then?' Louise nodded again. 'Okay, I'll be back in a min.' She turned and pushed a swing door behind here and disappeared through it. Louise looked over to where Luke was but he seemed only interested in the pudding menu.

The girl came back with a young lad about the same age, 'Yeah I did see her.' He said, then added, 'I liked what I saw which is probably why I remember her.' The girl shoved him and he blushed.

'You idiot, she doesn't want to know what you thought. You'll get complaints if you carry on like that and then you'd lose your job.'

The boy apologised and looked sheepish. 'It was at least two weeks ago. She was with a bloke, he was quite good looking an' all, though I guess I'm not allowed to say that either.' And he gave the waitress a nudge. Louise guessed there was probably something between them.

'Thanks, that's really helpful. If you do see her please ring the police but I'll also give my mobile number and I would be grateful if you would also phone me. They nodded and said they were happy to help.

Luke managed to put away a large portion of sticky toffee pudding before it was time to leave. 'I'll catch you up,' he murmured as they were just about to go out of the door and disappeared off to the toilet.

Louise stopped in the entrance and looked through a stand of leaflets advertising local amenities. She caught sight of another diving leaflet. She picked it up and saw it was the same as the others. She opened it and looked at it intently, so she could pinpoint the exact location.

Without warning, a sharp blow landed on her arm. Knocked off balance she fell to the floor as a man pushed past her and ran out of the door. She was stunned for a moment and couldn't believe whoever had pushed her over hadn't hung around to apologise or to see if she was all right. She was helped to her feet by the young waiter she'd talked to just as Luke reappeared.

'You Ok? Luke laughed. 'Seem to be making a habit of falling over in front of people or is it just men then?' Louise took no notice of him and he saw her focus was on the car park and looked to see what she was staring at.

Louise watched as the only man in sight rushed up and down the lines of parked cars. He stopped and stared at a 4x4 which had started to pull out; turned and ran towards a car parked in another row. For a moment she couldn't breathe and her hands felt clammy; it was a car she knew only too well. The man leapt into the car, started the engine and roared after the other car, which had just turned onto the road. She hadn't been able to see the driver of the first car clearly but it was a man.

THURSDAY 8TH DECEMBER 2005

From the top of the stairs she spotted a note pushed through her letter box. She bit her lip as she picked it up; it could be another from Caroline but let out a long sigh of relief when she saw Luke's name scribbled at the bottom of it. It was a thank you for lunch on Sunday – unusual for a student she thought. He'd added cheekily on the bottom, *I hope you got the answers you wanted at the pub!!!* She felt heat as blood rushed to her face. Not so unaware as she thought then.

Her anxiety about Caroline felt like a rat gnawing at her guts. She'd not seen any sign of her stalker and hoped he had found some other person to go after. Not what stalkers normally do though. It was strange as he had pursued that other car and also a client of hers, so if not a stalker what was he?

Buster came to her side when she called but looked a bit forlorn, which she guessed was the lack of good walks recently; hopefully she could plan one for the weekend. She'd nothing organised apart from Christmas shopping, which as the festive season appeared to have crept closer she must at least attempt to do. She thought of the festivities held in her house when James was alive, and all the family Christmas meals; a part of her yearned for the return of those early years.

This year was already different and she wasn't sure how she'd manage to function with the worry of Caroline's disappearance if she hadn't been found by then. It would be so hard trying to be merry while her mind was elsewhere. She wiped her eyes, blew her nose and told herself that being like this would not help anyone. At this moment she would have given anything not to be alone. This led to thoughts of George. She really didn't have the time or mental capacity to deal with him at the moment yet she'd said she'd meet him the day after tomorrow in the pub. 'Just concentrate on the here and now' she murmured.

She only had two clients before she was due to see Ed and as she got his notes out and glanced through them, she remembered his strange behaviour last time. Was his worry really about getting into boats?

He was not so exuberant or unnervingly jumpy this time and he actually hung his coat up in the right place and sat in his chair in rather a meek way, she thought.

'How are you, Ed? Not feeling so great today?' She often sensed a client's mood when they arrived and usually brought it to their attention so they could explore what they were feeling.

He raised his head and looked at her. 'Sorry I'm fine. Just the cold weather, I think, and I might be starting a cold and that always makes me feel low.'

He didn't sound as though he was starting a cold and the wolfish smile he'd given, didn't fool her. Something was definitely not right and she wished she could understand this man better.

He leaned forward in the chair. 'How are you though, Louise? You didn't seem yourself the last time we met? Glad you've got the heating going though, perhaps that's why I caught this cold. I do hope you're not running short of money?'

He laughed and the way he did it made her feel like a little woman who couldn't manage to run her own life without getting into a muddle or debt. She flushed as she thought this. How dare he? She took a deep breath and ignored how he'd ended his question.

'Yes, I apologise for the cold last week. My oil delivery hadn't arrived on the day I'd asked for it, which was unusual as the company has never let me down before. However, it is fine now and so am I.' She felt it might not be a good idea to bring up Caroline again but knew she needed to ask. 'It was a bit of surprise to me when you talked about my friend and I was a little taken aback you'd seen her.'

'Yes, I understand that. I can't imagine how you must feel. I guess she's not been found but have you any more news about her?' He turned towards her with what she read as concern in his eyes and she instantly lost any irritation she'd felt.

'No, there's been no more news and I was going to ask whether you'd seen her again. I went to the pub you mentioned, just on the chance she would be there but sadly no luck.' There was a slight change in his eyes and there it was again she thought; the snake. Was he lying?

'No. I haven't been there since. It was a while ago, when I saw your friend. Don't worry, if I see her again, I will let you know straight away. In fact, I might even go there on Friday, as I have the afternoon off and may go fishing with a friend. We nearly always end up at there and it may be the last chance I get for a while because the school holidays will soon be upon us. Have the police found out anything more, do you know?'

His concern almost tripped her up but she didn't disclose anything more. 'Thanks, I appreciate your help but let's focus on you now. Let's start working on the anxiety you have about going out into a boat and the nausea you feel.'

He seemed to be receptive to her ideas of how to reduce his anxiety and change his thought pattern. She suggested if he did go fishing this week, he could try out some of the strategies and see how they worked.

As the session went on his mood shifted up a gear and by the time the session ended he again appeared quite hyper, but he hadn't had any opportunity to take drugs, so Louise supposed it was excitement at seeing the girlfriend he said he was now exceedingly close to.

FRIDAY 9TH DECEMBER 2005

Buster finally got the walk he'd been whining for all week and Louise felt infected by his enthusiasm as she watched him gallop up the hill. It was always a bit of a slog, but she loved it up here at the top of Lansdown.

The weather still produced lots of frosts but with them often came these glorious days with clear blue skies. She managed to put her troubles out of her mind for just a short time she felt positive and hopeful things would work out.

Perhaps it was the clear air, but when her thoughts turned to George and meeting up with him tonight, she felt she knew what she wanted to do. In her heart she wanted to put it right and get him back, possibly permanently but then her head told her to be cautious because so many unexplained things had happened.

All she could do, she supposed, was to give him the chance to explain and then see. She thought about what she would wear - she hadn't been to the hairdresser for ages. He seemed to like her rather unruly mane though, so that probably wouldn't matter. These thoughts awakened a deep longing to be loved, to be cared for and of course some half decent sex! She felt the colour rise in her face at the thought.

When she reached the stile at the bottom, she lent down to attach Buster's lead and felt her phone vibrate in her pocket. She didn't recognise the number but answered it and was surprised when she found it was Ed.

'She's here, Louise, I've just seen her. I'd been out fishing and then went around the lake to the café by the car park. I saw her go in with a man only a moment ago and I bet she'll be there a while. People often walk around the lake between the two visitor areas after they've had their tea, so if you get here soon you might even catch her.'

It was too good to believe but didn't doubt it for a moment and in an instant lost any irritation she'd felt towards him. 'Oh, Ed, thank you so much I'll get over there as quickly as I can – it will be at least forty-five minutes, but thank you, so much.'

She ended the call and pulled a reluctant Buster after her as she ran.   It took ten minutes to get home where she changed her shoes as quickly as she could and got into the car.   She tried to phone Dave, but his line was engaged and didn't have time to go through all the inevitable questions his colleagues might put to her if she rang the general line. I'll do it when I get there and when I've found out if it really is her, she thought.

She hurried inside the café, stood by the door and surveyed the tables set out in small groups within a large vaulted room. She wasn't there. Hell, she'd missed her. She spotted the sign for the toilets and headed towards them. There were only two cubicles and both were free.   She rushed straight out again and bumped into a woman who was on her way in. She mumbled an apology as she hurried past and vaguely heard the obscenity hurled at her.

There was a queue at the counter but Louise couldn't wait. 'Excuse me,' she shouted across to where a young woman was making coffee. 'Sorry to interrupt, but can you tell me where the walk starts that leads to the other car park?' The machine hissed as coffee spluttered into a cup and her question was ignored until it was handed to the customer.   Louise felt she might scream.

'Sorry, what did you say?'   The girl looked towards Louise and raised her eyebrows.

'The other car park - where is it?'   She realised she'd shouted her request and she saw the girl push her jaw out and knew she wasn't going to help her. She rushed out of the door and with a stroke of good fortune, a woman in the café had seen it all and pointed in the opposite direction to where she'd parked the car.

She caught sight of a group of people in the distance as they disappeared down a track that ran through some trees.

She ran as hard as she could but had to stop and bend double to get rid of the stitch in her side before she ran on.

The path wound its way around the side of the lake and eventually came out into another car park. It was fairly empty but at the end there was a car and a white van. Beyond the vehicles was a grass path that disappeared into another group of trees. She stopped for a moment and scanned the area but saw only a woman with a small child and dog in the distance. As she came near to the car, a man stepped out and waved at her. She felt confused when she realised it was Ed but then thought how kind of him to stay and help her find Caroline.

'Hi, Louise, well done for getting here so quickly. It must have been hard as you do seem to be quite out of breath. Perhaps not as fit as you appear.'

'What? Oh yes, hello, Ed, thanks so much for your phone call. I got here as fast as I could but I think I'm too late; I must have missed her. Have you seen her? Did she go down there?' Louise pointed vaguely in the direction the path went.

'Yes, I'm sure I caught sight of her and yes I think she may have gone down there.'

Louise went to follow but Ed stopped her. 'Wait, I know that walk. She won't be long as it's a circular one, so if you wait here then you'll see her as she makes her way back. Tell you what, why don't you come and sit in my car and have a cup of coffee? I've got a spare cup and I was just about to open my flask.'

This was an unusual situation and Louise would never have dreamt of getting into a car with a client normally but she was exhausted after the run and a coffee sounded good especially if it was certain that Caroline would come back this way. 'Thanks. I think I'll take you up on that.' She was aware he was in one of his excited moods, almost hyper, and she nearly changed her mind but he gave her such an engaging smile as he opened the passenger door for her that she allowed herself to be ushered in.

She knew very little about makes or models of cars but knew this one was a posh one, with all the gadgets that most men loved so much. He got in beside her, unscrewed the top of a thermos, poured coffee into a mug and handed it to her. 'I always carry two mugs as my girlfriend and I often go for a walk and have a coffee afterwards.' Louise thanked him and sipped the rather bitter tasting coffee. She knew why women fell for this sort of guy as he came across as charming, educated and she imagined great company.

'I think you said Caroline was with a man. It's the boyfriend we're all concerned about. Was he with her?'

'Yes, there was a man with her, he looked all right to me. Sort of good looking. They made a good pair actually.'

'I wouldn't be so sure,' murmured Louise. 'He's turned out not to be what he seemed at all.'

'Really! That's a shame. Perhaps people interfered. It so often happens, then everything is ruined and there's no way of going back. It ends, which is sad, but the end is my happy place, a place where I finally get to where I want to be, to experience the thrill I always want.'

Louise's eyelids felt heavy and she could no longer see clearly out of the window. A mist had come down in the time Ed had been talking. What Ed had just said didn't make sense. He'd talked about Caroline, about her relationship. Then suddenly related everything to him, as if it was his relationship.

She felt goose bumps on her arms; something was very wrong. Her gut instinct told her to get out and run but she couldn't move her legs. The coffee mug fell out of her hands and she gasped. She turned her head and he moved his face close to hers. 'Not so sure of yourself now, are you, Louise? What technique or tool should I be using now, do you think?' The tone of his voice had changed; he had lost his charm and all the animals she had ever seen in him were there, released from their cages and hunting for blood.

'You thought you were so clever, with your questions. Thought you knew the answer to everything but you hadn't a clue. Not a clue! You don't even know now, do you? I can see the question in your eyes. Well, let me introduce myself. I'm John, Caroline's one and only, truly marvellous boyfriend. To be specific my name is Edward or John something or other, depending on what I'm doing. Oh, it was such fun, pulling the wool over your eyes. Sometimes I could hardly stop myself laughing. Even at the beginning when you asked what made me happy, I didn't tell you the truth but don't worry you'll find out. I'll let you know when it's the right time and then you'll know.'

The laugh was like the howl of a wolf, with its prey at its mercy and although she could no longer move her lips Louise's whole body stiffened. Everything made sense now. Her feelings about this man. Deep down she'd known he was dangerous but she hadn't let her unconscious thoughts rise to the surface. He had all the classic traits of a psychopath, but she'd missed it.

'That idiot Michael just gave me your number and it was your bad luck I came to you. I had no idea Caroline was a friend of yours but from the start, she couldn't shut up about you; couldn't stop telling me what a good friend you were. This woman down the road who was older than her but you got on so well. It was sickening but at the beginning I thought I'd get away with it, after all I've always called myself Ed for work. John is the name I use for playtimes.'

Louise shuddered as she tried to speak but couldn't get any words out.

'I thought it added to the fun at the beginning and then it started to get a bit dangerous. I decided I needed to find out what you had written about me, whether you'd guessed. I know you said at the beginning of our sessions, I could ask to see the notes, but I thought it might make you suspicious and it was more fun finding your keys and making a copy. I used a bar of soap you know; an old- fashioned way, but it works.

'I came into your house a few times and after the builder bloke left it was easy. Sorry I broke that picture; hope it wasn't expensive.' He laughed again and Louise turned her head and looked in his eyes and saw the maliciousness.

He shunted his seat backwards as far as it would go and stretched his legs as he lounged back. 'It was incredibly funny. You were scared, I could see, but brave enough to come out onto the landing but then when I moved, you rushed back into your room. I had a hard job then to keep quiet, it was quite hilarious. Your notes confused me though. Why on earth couldn't you just write a name on the front of them? It took me two searches to find mine and then they weren't worth the bother. You didn't say much of interest, so don't think you're much of an expert actually.' He paused as if to make sure she'd heard.

Louise could do nothing but listen as he revelled in telling her how clever he'd been.

'It was fun scaring you in the bushes by your house. What idiot doesn't get their light fixed? Some handyman you've got there, I don't think! I could almost have bottled your fear when you got to your front door. I anticipated more fun but that young git came by and pretended to be your knight in shining armour.'

Louise's thoughts rampaged through her head, all that time he was the one doing everything and she'd blamed everyone but him. She'd thought it might be George and, in the beginning, had even thought it might be Luke. George, who she was supposed to meet tonight, was innocent of anything that had happened to her. Oh heavens, she'd been so stupid, she hadn't even let Dave know where she was going as she had intended doing as soon as she'd got here.

Ed stopped talking for a moment and stared out across the lake. 'It was here, you know, just near here. She was special – Julia. I enjoyed every minute of being with her. I even married her and took her kid as well. She'd been with such a bastard before me so I tried to stay true. I really didn't want to harm her but, in the end, I needed my fix and I couldn't hold out any longer. Anyway, I made sure her ex got what he deserved.'

Louise's eyes widened and then the horror of what he had said hit her. Of course, it was all connected she thought.

He was the one who had killed Julia and now he's told me there is no doubt as to what he has in store for me.

He started speaking again. 'It's the watching, you know. Watching life drain away. Julia was beautiful, she died with flowers all around her. She didn't deserve a bad death so I was glad it was a perfect death. It was quick, unexpected; just perfect. Hell, now I've given the game away but never mind, you'd know in the end anyway. That's the addiction, if you like, watching them die. Course, I sometimes have a bit of fun first. There's no drug I know of gives me that kick.'

Louise would have liked to have held her hands over her ears but nothing worked in the way she wanted it to. She felt disconnected from her body watching what was happening; like the first horror film she'd ever seen, when she had taken refuge under the seat to distance herself and peered out when it felt safe to do so. Here she was a captive and had no choice but to sit and listen.

He put his hand out, patted her knee and made a sound of endearment. 'There, there, you'll be fine. I've thought of a good way for you both to die. Never done two before. I was going to do my parents but in the end they did it to themselves and robbed me of the special death I'd prepared. No, your deaths will be a breath of fresh air.' He rolled about in his seat with laughter. He's mad completely mad, she thought. She tried to scream but no sound came out. All she could do was stare at this evil man. 'Oh yes, breath of fresh air, that's good, very good, I'm cleverer than I knew.' He'd said two deaths; could Caroline be still alive? My brain is fuzzy but who else could it be?

When he had mentioned Julia all the various links fell into place. It was horribly clear now but what stood out for her most was, like many narcissistic psychopaths he wanted her to know how clever he'd been. He had a definite plan to kill her and looked forward to it.

'I will give you one thing though; there are a few things you are clever at. You did notice when Caroline changed and you guessed something was wrong. She was more stupid than you; she was so desperate to please me, she'd do anything, wear anything, be any way I wanted - stupid cow. It wasn't fun at all. One day, though, she got desperate or brave enough to decide to leave. Your idea was it?' He peered down at her. 'Mmm, guessed it was. Thought I'd better get her away from you then, but my god you were persistent. All the ringing and threatening to come to my house. I had to do something and so I sent the letter and we moved out of the house.'

Ed paused for breath and Louise noticed a dribble of saliva escape from his mouth.

'I know you've tried to get Ben to tell you where I live but he doesn't know, poor little sod and he won't know until this is over. Had to resolve it before the end of term, don't want him involved. Killing children. Ugh, definitely not my thing. He's a complicated one though. Hear he killed a guinea pig. If he was mine, I'd say he was a chip off the old block, wouldn't you? Have to watch him though, keep him in line as I don't want any social workers sniffing around. I've found a lovely young girl to look after him, another au pair; easier to hide when I get bored of her. Think you found Sophie though, must find somewhere better to put this next one.'

Ben of course! She'd never heard Ed call him by his name. She tried not to let the horror of what he was saying get to her. No-one knew where she was and the drugs he'd obviously given her were strong. She had to try and clear her head and think, but as hard as she tried she couldn't prevent the mist that enveloped her.

'Think I've brought you up to speed for now and for the next bit you'll get a ring side seat, for sure.' He patted her knee again, put his seat back into an upright position and pulled it forward as he put the key in the ignition. Let's go, it's Friday night – gin night!' He laughed loudly. 'Think of me as your fairy godfather - here to grant your every wish.' The wolf howled and all Louise saw were his pearly white teeth.

The engine drowned whatever he said next and she caught the smell of his expensive aftershave as he leaned over, fastened her seatbelt and moved out of the car park. She smelt it instantly, the faint flowery smell which had always lingered in the room after a session. If only Caroline had mentioned his aftershave, maybe I'd have put two and two together. She cursed herself for not recognising it when she came back the evening she'd thought something was wrong.

Her head hurt and all she thought of was how stupid she'd been. All the time it was the same man and all the same boys. Why had she never asked Ed the name of his son. If she'd known she might have put it all together and she wouldn't be in this mess. Jasper was right, coincidences are often not what they seem.

The area was unfamiliar to Louise and everything looked blurry anyway, which made it difficult to know where they were going, but she thought it was mostly through open countryside. Her head felt heavy and difficult to turn so only saw what was directly in front of the car.

Quite a while later the car pulled into a gravelled drive and stopped outside a large house. 'Home sweet home,' sang Ed as he walked round to the passenger door and asked her to get out. 'Oh of course, you can't, can you?' She could see the smirk on his face as he bent down and picked her up. 'Not a lightweight, are we, Louise? All that sitting about pretending to listen to people not helpful, was it?'

He carried her into the house, through a long corridor and down some steps to a cellar. He opened the door and, with blurry vision she managed to make out two mattresses on the floor. On one of them, there appeared to be a bundle of rags. Ed flung her down. 'Have a good time, girls.' He left the room and locked the door.

Louise had no energy to lift herself up but the drug must have worn off a little because she found she could move her head slightly. Her throat was dry and she tried to moisten her lips, as she looked around her. Just beside her mattress she saw there was a bottle of water. It looked new and she unscrewed the unopened top and drank it down in almost one go. Then turned towards the other mattress and saw the bundle of rags move. Could it be Caroline? If it was, could she really still be alive? Her thoughts were slow and despite the water, her throat still felt raw and dry so when she spoke her voice only managed a croak. 'Caroline?' There was no response so she tried again and much louder. 'CAROLINE? Please, please, let it be you and please don't be dead. It's me Caroline, it's Louise. I've been trying to find you.'

The rags moved again and a tousled mess of blonde hair appeared. Then Louise saw two eyes peep out. 'Oh god, it is you. Speak to me, Caroline. Please. Just make a sign if you can hear me. I've searched everywhere for you but now I've messed up and been caught too. I was so stupid I didn't see him for what he was. He's drugged me and I can't move but I'm here, you're not on your own.' She hoped Caroline was reassured by her words even if it changed nothing.

The rags shifted and this time a whole head appeared and Louise saw her friend more clearly. She was painfully thin, bedraggled and obviously ill. She looked almost dead and Louise trembled at the sight of her. Caroline opened her eyes wide and then shut them. Eventually she managed a small whisper. 'Louise! Thank God. What's happened, how can you be here?' She tried to raise her head but it fell back onto the mattress. Where is he?' she whimpered.

Before she could answer a mist enveloped Louise's brain and she realised she'd fallen for an old trick and the water had been laced with something after all. She tried to fight it but when she closed her eyes, floated away to a place far from reality.

FRIDAY 9TH DECEMBER

George

He'd planned all day what he would say to Louise, but now in the pub all he thought of how wonderful it would be to see her again. See her smile, see that glorious hair and those luscious red lips. He thought she'd be on time, but maybe not if she was still angry with him. She might make him wait as pay back, or to make a point. He knew he had a lot of explaining to do but hoped she'd give him the chance to say all he needed to.

He looked down at his empty glass. He'd got there early because he wanted to be ready and to have their drinks on the table when she walked in, so there would be no interruptions, but her white wine sat there untouched and for a moment he felt mocked by it.

The old guy at the bar muttered as he pulled George another pint. 'Been stood up then? That's tough.'

'No, she's often late.' George tried to make it sound as if there was no problem at all.

His stomach churned and he didn't really feel like anything more to drink. He made sure the barman looked away before he checked his watch again. She'd said 5.30 and it was now nearly 6.00. Perhaps she wasn't going to come; perhaps she'd never meant to come. He knew she'd been having a hard time because of what Dave had told him and Caroline's disappearance must eat away at her.

He reflected on all that had happened over the last few weeks. It had been hard to stay calm and not disappear again into those horrifying moments in the dark depths of the quarry but Dave's phone call when he was still in Wales had lifted his spirits and given him hope. He could never thank him enough for that and he had started to believe there might be a chance to explain it all to Louise and then, he could hardly dare hope, they might get back together again.

The sound of his fist as it hit the table reverberated over the pub and the couple on the table next to his, stopped mid-sentence and stared at him. The barman started to come around from the bar but he held his hand up. 'Sorry, didn't mean to cause a disturbance, everything's fine.' He hadn't realised how frustrated he was at his inability to help her when she needed him most. If only he had been there to help and protect her. He'd fallen for her almost immediately but it wasn't until they really started to go out that he'd realised what a very special person she was.

His thoughts made him anxious; where on earth was she? He looked at his watch again and at his beer glass which was empty once more. It was no good, she wasn't coming. He thought for a moment, pushed the chair back, put his coat on, walked towards the door and waved at the barman, who put his arms out either side of him and raised his shoulders in a large shrug. George gave a grimace and strode out of the pub.

He'd managed to park his car just outside. The windows were already frosted and it took a while to clear the windscreen enough to see. It was only a couple of minutes to Louise's and the car was hardly warm by the time he got there.

There were no lights on in the house and no curtains drawn. He stood for a moment as he wondered what he should do. It was difficult to see and he felt guilty he hadn't fixed her light. He felt his way to the door and gave a large knock. He knew from the way the house had looked it was unlikely she was at home but felt he had to try. On the second knock he could hear Buster, who sounded distressed and he knew he must get into the house. She'd changed the locks so even if he'd had a key he wouldn't be able to use it. The Yale lock appeared to have been replaced with a mortice bolt and so there was no chance of picking the lock, or at least not with his lack of expertise. He moved to the window at the front. It wasn't double glazed and after a slight hesitation he broke the pain. Buster's snout appeared through the hole the broken glass had made and he pushed him back as he put his hand through and fumbled around for the window lever. Once it was open he climbed in.

As soon as he was in he stroked Buster, opened the back door and ushered him out. He gave a small yelp and rushed past to the garden. He was sure if Louise had been in the house, the sound of the glass breaking would have brought her there immediately but he still shouted. 'Hello, Louise, it's George.' The smell of dog was overwhelming and when he walked into the kitchen, he could see Buster had obviously not been able to contain himself. He became more uneasy; Louise had clearly not been home for a while.

'Hey, Buster, where's your missus then?' George bent down and gave him a reassuring pat. He cleaned up the mess on the floor, found some dog food and put it down. It disappeared in a second. 'Whoa, you're mighty hungry. Wonder when you were last fed?' George walked slowly around the house to see if there was any indication of when she'd last been here or any indication of where she could have gone. He spotted a cereal bowl in the sink, so assumed she'd been there at breakfast time. He searched the whole house to make sure she wasn't lying injured or ill but there was no sign of her or any sign of anything unusual.

In her study he stood by her desk and picked up her large diary which lay open at today's date. There were only two entries, one at three thirty to see Jasper and another at five thirty where she had written his name. It certainly looked as if she had intended to meet him.

He opened the back pages of her diary and there was a loose typed page in the back with work names and addresses and he didn't have to look very hard to see the one he was looking for.

The phone was answered straight away and George checked it was Jasper he was speaking to.

'I'm sorry to bother you, but I'm a friend of Louise and was due to meet her this evening but she didn't turn up. There are a few odd things going on in her life at the

moment and I am very concerned about her. I know she was due to see you this afternoon and wondered if you could tell me if she kept her appointment.'

Jasper knew who he was and George guessed Louise had told him about their relationship. George explained he'd waited over an hour before going to her house to see if he could find her. 'I am phoning from there now. I had to break in and I found a very distressed dog who had obviously been shut in for a while, possibly by early this morning, and I know Louise would never leave him for a great length of time.'

Jasper gave an instant reply. *'Yes, I agree with you. I know how much Buster means to her.'*

There was a long pause and George checked he was still there.

'Sorry, yes, I am. She didn't turn up for her appointment with me and I have been ill at ease ever since. She's never let me down before and there were things she said in her last session which have caused me concern and I was going to speak with her about them today.'

George gripped the phone hard and urged Jasper to continue.

'She mentioned various coincidences in her client work and actually I don't really believe much in coincidences. I guess you know she was being followed by a man who she thought also followed one of her clients after his session. The client he followed was someone she'd never felt comfortable with and it made me think.'

George shook his head. *'Actually, I don't know much but none of that sounds good. I was about to phone Dave her son-in-law who, I expect you know, is in the police, and I think he needs to know what has happened as soon as.'*

'Yes, I do and agree you should let him know what's happened. I would also like to investigate this client of hers and that is something you can't do because her notes are confidential, but in these circumstances and as her supervisor there would be no problem in my looking at them. I'd like to see if there is anything to indicate that he

has any involvement in the things which have been happening to her and throw any light on where she might be now. If it is all right with you, I'll drive over to her house now.'

George felt relieved Jasper had taken it so seriously and gave him directions.

Dave was shocked to hear Louise was missing and said he'd get onto it straight away. *'Let me know what Jasper finds out, if anything, won't you. I'm so glad to hear you're there, George. I've been telling her for ages to leave the sleuthing to me and not to pursue this John guy, who I think in all probability is very dangerous.'*

George noticed her wardrobe door was open but there was nothing else out of place upstairs that he could see, so returned downstairs to wait for Jasper. As he came down the stairs, he caught sight of her walking boots by the front door, which he'd hadn't noticed because he'd climbed through the window. It looked as if they'd been flung off in a hurry. One was upright and the other was a little way away on its side. 'That's odd,' he muttered, knowing she always put them back in the hall cupboard under the stairs. I'm guessing she must have left in a hurry. Perhaps she'd been out for a walk when something happened to bring her home quickly. He remembered he'd seen Buster's lead on the kitchen table which was not where it was usually kept.

'Damn I didn't check to see if her car was in the road.' he muttered. He didn't fancy a return climb through the window so searched in the place in the hall where he knew she kept her keys and spares. 'Great' he exclaimed when he spotted a door key that looked new and to his relief it opened the door. He walked up and down the road but there was no sign of her car. I'm right, she must have been out with Buster when for some reason she rushed home and went straight out again.

Buster had disappeared into his basket, presumably in a sulk as he didn't come to him even for a biscuit. He made himself a mug of tea and sat in the kitchen to wait for Jasper. He'd just taken a sip when he heard a knock at the door.

George was tall himself but Jasper was a giant, with an enormous stomach and George had the impression that a large bear had turned up on the doorstep. He led him up to Louise's study and showed him where she kept her notes and where the key was kept.

Jasper rifled through them for quite a while before he gave a satisfied grunt as he pulled one out of its plastic sleeve. George watched the frown deepen on his face as he read but then he gave a loud 'Ah'.

'What is it? What have you found? Whose notes are those?' George had to resist the impulse to wrench them out of his hand.

'Sorry, I know you're anxious. These belong to the client she never felt sure of. At first, I couldn't see anything other than what I would expect to see. Then I found a more personal entry.'

George could hardly hold his frustration and felt his fingers clench and unclench and his jaw tightened. 'Go on then. What does it say?'

Jasper read out what Louise had written; *"Amazing! Ed recognised Caroline from the picture in the loo. Saw her two weeks ago leaving a pub - The Fisherman's Catch, by Chew Valley Lake. Told him I was worried - should have been more professional. Not said anything. Now feel guilty. Will tell me if he sees her again. Ed was weird today - hyper – probably using."* That's all she says that's relevant.

'Why did she feel guilty, not sure I understand and why do you think this is significant?'

Jasper explained it was not professional for a therapist to disclose things about themselves or their life outside their work to clients and it is significant merely because it shows a connection.'

'Mmm I see. Listening to what you've just said, I am guessing she went to look at the pub. In fact, wait a minute.' George had flicked back a few pages of her diary. 'Yes, look here, in her diary on Sunday 4th December, there is a note which says Luke – Fisherman's Catch.'

Jasper raised his eyebrows and George explained Luke was a student who lived next door, though he wasn't quite sure why she'd gone with him.

Jasper thought for a moment. 'There's more perhaps you ought to hear. Through her work Louise heard some disturbing things about John. I know she has already given this information to Dave but I'm going to tell you in confidence, in case it helps.'

'What are they, what's she been told? Please, Jasper, anything that will help us find her.'

He told George what he knew about John and added, 'The last thing she'd heard which disturbed her was about was a room in his house which all the women connected with him had been frightened of. This information came from his stepson who was very distressed when a Nanny of his left and later when Caroline was no longer around. I gather when Dave heard about it, he was going to have a look.'

'I can't believe all this has happened while I've been out of contact. I knew she was concerned about Caroline and about her new relationship but I was the one that kept reassuring her. Poor Louise, I wish I'd been around, particularly when I knew she was being stalked but I'm afraid I've not been her favourite person since my life went to pieces for a while.'

Jasper made no comment but added, 'Something else, which might not be relevant, is Louise supervises a man who counsels prisoners and is, at present, seeing someone who was convicted of murdering his ex-wife. The prisoner insists he is innocent and told his counsellor he's hired a mate of his to investigate. The odd thing is, the prisoner asked his counsellor whether he knew anyone of Louise's name, which makes little sense. He believes his ex-wife's husband is the one who killed her. Louise and I couldn't see a connection but by coincidence it turned out, Louise also supervised the counsellor who was seeing the wife before she was killed.'

'What has any of this got to do with Louise's disappearance though? I don't understand.'

'Just hear me out. As well as those coincidences there is a further one. During her supervision Louise mentioned two children called Ben. One of them was a friend of Max's and client to one of Louise's supervisees and the other the son of Caroline's boyfriend, John.' At first she assumed they were different children but then discovered they were in fact one.'

Jasper cleared his throat and went on before George could speak. 'As I've already told you, I don't believe in coincidences and there are rather a lot of them in this story. When I last saw her, she told me that Ed has a stepson who is around the same age as the boy Ben and is also at a boarding school. She didn't mention the boy's name and so I can only assume she hadn't ever asked it. Too many coincidences altogether. I wanted to explore this week, the possibility of them all being the same child but she didn't turn up as you know.'

George hadn't taken his eyes off Jasper. 'So, if you're saying all the children are the same? That would mean that John, Caroline's boyfriend, and Louise's client are one and the same man?'

Jasper nodded. 'I think it's more than possible.'

It was George's turn now to put his head in his hands and he groaned. 'This is the client she told me she found disturbing. If it is the same man that is also Caroline's boyfriend, Louise could be in a very dangerous position and, of course Caroline too. We must give Dave this information at once.'

Jasper agreed but said he also needed to explain the leaflet she'd found in John's house. 'It was a leaflet for a dive centre at an old quarry in Somerset. It appears from things they found at his home; John is a keen diver. Louise visited and discovered from an instructor that Caroline and her boyfriend had been there. I am sure Dave already knows this but you might mention it when you speak to him.

George watched Jasper leave and wondered if he'd seen the effect that the mention of the quarry and the diving had on him. His hands still shook and he tried to collect his thoughts so he could give a coherent message to Dave. Stuff whirled around his head but was clouded by a mist of fear which slowly spread throughout his body which trembled as he lifted his phone to speak.

Dave listened to what he was told and made only the occasional grunt as the story got more and more complex but did not interrupt.

'*So, Dave, I think the quarry is where we must start and I think we should go now.*'

There was a silence on the other end of the line for a moment and George wondered if Dave had already ended the call.

'*George, there is no 'we'. I want you to leave this to me and my team. We have been watching the guy who has been stalking Louise and if he is connected to all this; if he is the man who has been hired by the man in prison, then he may well know more than we do about where Caroline is and therefore perhaps where Louise is.*'

George pursed his lips but said nothing.

'*Believe me, George, we will do everything we can to find her. I could never face Katy again if I let anything happen to her. Anyway, it is unlikely we'd find anything at the dive centre tonight but I will send a couple of men out there to take a look just in case. Now the best thing you can do for Louise is to go home and let me do my job and I promise I will contact you the moment I have any further information.*'

George started to speak but Dave had ended the call. Buster crept into the sitting room and put his head on George's knee, who automatically put his hand out to stroke him. 'Yes, you are right, boy, I can't just sit back and do nothing.' His thoughts went to the quarry but the vision he had was of the one in Wales and the dark waters that covered and concealed all those twisting hidden passages where he had searched desperately for his missing buddy.

His skin crawled as he remembered the feeling of panic as his tank emptied and the desperation and agony as he made the decision to stop searching and to save himself. He had no other memories because he'd blacked out.

His hands became clammy as he re-lived these memories. He lost control of his breath, started to fight for air and felt a remembered piercing and sharp pain in his chest. Buster whimpered and pushed his wet nose against his face and licked him. This brought him back from the dark depths enough for him to know he must take control again. He purposefully slowed his breath and counted as he had been taught to do.

While he sat and recovered he thought through what he should do. Once he'd decided, he let Buster out of the back door, poured a mound of food into his bowl and checked he had water. He then texted Dave and said he was going home and could he pick Buster up later for the family to look after him until Louise had been found.

Adrenalin started to course through his body and he felt more like the soldier he used to be. As he drove to his house he formulated a plan. Once at his house, he grabbed a few things he might need; a rug, a thermos of coffee, some snacks and a torch.

SATURDAY 10TH DECEMBER

George

It was just after midnight when he reached the quarry and guessed if Dave had sent the officers when he'd promised, they would be long gone now. He suspected they had found nothing untoward or he was sure Dave would have phoned him. If Caroline or Louise were prisoners it was unlikely to be at the dive place but it was connected somehow and the only thing he could do was watch and wait, although for what, he had no real idea.

He saw a security guard walk towards the gate so he reversed and pulled the car into a layby he'd spotted a bit further back. It was far enough away for it not to look suspicious; probably if anyone saw the car they would think it was a couple having a some fun. From his position the gate was still within sight and he watched as a police car pulled out, then the security guard shut and locked it before he walked away again. Either they'd been there for a long time and given the place a good search or Dave hadn't been able to send them straight away.

It was too late to attempt entry to the premises, so he pushed his seat back to give more leg room, lowered the back of the seat to make it comfortable, pulled the rug over his knees, poured himself a coffee and settled down to watch in case anything happened during the night. He must have drifted into a sort of dream state as, before he knew it, the night had passed and nothing untoward had happened. It was nine thirty before people started to arrive and the gates were finally opened and he could drive in.

'Really, I only saw her once when she came looking for a friend, but then some of the members might be able to tell you more as I know she went to talk to a few of them.' George thanked the lad who was at reception and headed over to where there were a group of people who had just changed into wetsuits. Unfortunately, they couldn't give him any more information either, except she had spent time with an instructor who was only there on a Sunday.

Although it frustrated him, there was little point hanging around so he decided to go home, get some sleep and return for another night vigil later. God, I feel so utterly helpless, he thought. I haven't got any of the power the police have and with no more clues there's literally nothing more I can do.

After a bit of a sleep his head felt clearer and he had an idea it might be helpful to speak to Luke who, according to her diary, she appeared to have taken to a pub. Perhaps he would have some ideas.

'Yeah, I'm Luke. What you want me for? Hang on, aren't you the builder bloke of Louise's? Haven't seen you around for a while. What's going on then?' George explained Louise was missing and knew she had been to a pub with him near Chew Valley Lake.

'Missing! No way. Oh, that's bad, really bad. I have only just got over finding those bones – that was more than creepy I can tell you, but I didn't know she was in any danger. What can I do? I'd like to help, we all would, I know.' He looked back into the house and waved his arm in that direction as if to include all who lived there.

'Don't think there is anything much to do at the moment, Luke, but thanks. I saw from her diary she went with you to a pub by Chew Valley Lake the other Sunday. Can you tell me why and perhaps what it was about?

'Yeah that's right.' George noticed Luke's face coloured. 'It was a bit of a laugh, as she thought she'd deceived me. I knew it was to do with her missing friend but I didn't let on. After all, wasn't going to pass an opportunity for a free meal, was I? Very good it was too.'

'So, you don't know if she found anything relevant?'

'No, I don't think so but she spent quite some time chatting to one of the waitresses and I could see she had told her something of interest, but I don't think it helped much as she wasn't in particularly good spirits on our drive home.'

'Thanks, I will look into it and I will be sure to let you know if there's any news.'

Luke scribbled his number down for him on an old cinema ticket he found in his pocket.

Dave didn't sound too pleased when George phoned him to say he intended to keep watch at the quarry again but George told him he needed to keep occupied, he couldn't just sit and do nothing. He would then be able to speak to the man who had spoken to Louise as soon as they opened in the morning. Dave emphasised the necessity of reporting to him if the slightest little thing needed further investigation.

Dave also told him that they were uncertain about how the man who had been following Louise fitted in or whether he posed any danger. She'd never seen him clearly and had no idea why he might be following her or her client.

Still on the phone Dave added. *'Incidentally we do have a little more information about this Ed guy but still do not have an address, so we are still trying to find out where he might be holding Caroline and Louise.'*

George groaned and ended the call.

SATURDAY 10TH DECEMBER 2005

Louise

Something poked her; poke poke; poke poke. Hell, it was annoying. She tried to open her eyes but when she did, she saw only blackness and shut them again. Then there was a voice, it was very faint but it sounded familiar. 'Louise, wake up, wake up, Louise. Please wake up, he'll be back soon.' Then an internal voice, pleading with her to make an effort, to wake up. She shook her head, where had the voices come from. Were they real? No not real, inside my head. She held her head then; it was pounding and she couldn't think, couldn't make any sense of anything, yet she knew she must.

Something shook her hard and this time she opened her eyes wide and made out a shape beside her on the floor. On the floor! What am I doing on the floor? She put her hands down and felt the hard ground but she was on something soft. The shape moved; touched her. She recoiled in fear and confusion. The shape poked her again and she grumbled. 'Stop. Stop it, what are you doing? Who are you? The mist in her head cleared and she remembered. She remembered Ed. What had he got to do with anything? Why was she thinking of him? She'd been looking for Caroline. Caroline! Caroline was here on this mattress with her on the floor of a room. Why? Where? Where was here?

With a loud sob, a skinny arm wound around Louise's shoulders. Confused, Louise returned the hug but still couldn't quite work anything out or remember what had happened. She tried hard to make sense of images that rushed through her head. She saw a car. Yes, think Louise think. I remember I got in a car to go somewhere fast. Where was I going? Oh god, my head hurts.

How long have I been here? Why am I even here?

Gradually it became a clearer and she pulled Caroline closer. 'I was looking for you everywhere.'

Caroline hugged her again. 'I know. At least I didn't but I do know now. He said, he said you'd come, that he'd bring you here but I didn't believe him. Louise, he's evil; evil. I was so happy, so pleased to have found someone at last. Like a fairy tale, a dream come true but it wasn't, it was a nightmare. He hurt me, made me do things.'

She shuddered and stopped for a moment. 'He's clever though, you'd never guess. He's such a charmer when people meet him, they think, how wonderful he is but that's not a word for him. He's killed people and he said he'd kill us both. He was just waiting for you. We'll die, we won't be able to stop him.' She was so weak the sobs sounded more like the mewing a kitten might make as it searched for its mother.

Louise heard what she said but struggled to make sense of it; her brain had fogged over again. 'Keep talking, Caroline, I think it's helping me. I just can't quite get out of this feeling, this feeling of being in a dream where everything is unclear, hazy.'

'It's the drugs, Louise, don't you remember? He drugged you. He drugged me too, but not for the last two days, I think.'

Yes, I remember now thought Louise. It's why I can't think but I must, I must. Oh hell, I just can't remember anything. Did I tell anyone where I was going? I don't think I did but I can't remember. 'How stupid.'

Caroline shifted. 'What? What's stupid?'

Louise realised she'd said the last words out loud. Even her thoughts were not thoughts anymore.

The sound of a lock as it turned made them both jump and Caroline pulled herself over to her own mattress as fast as she could.

'Morning, girls. Had a good sleep, Louise? Thought you might have.' The laugh was cruel but with the light shining through the door Louise saw he was smiling and showing those 'all the better to eat you with' teeth. He carried a tray with bowls of something and she could smell coffee.

He put the tray down on the floor between the two mattresses, walked past them and pulled up a blind. The light immediately illuminated the dowdy room. The walls were bare and there was nothing in it but the mattresses she and Caroline lay on and there was a bucket in the corner.

'Think everyone deserves a decent last breakfast, don't you? Yes, a good Sunday breakfast just like my mother used to make.' He laughed again. 'Didn't know it was Sunday, did you? Think you may have just spent yesterday lazing around sleeping Louise but then you've no dog to walk, nothing to do, so you might just as well sleep.'

Buster! Poor Buster, he'd have been shut in all this time. Was it Sunday today? Had she really missed a day? She turned to Caroline. 'How long have I been here, what day is it?'

Caroline didn't answer she just stared at Ed or John, or whoever he was - perhaps neither. He stared at them and said nothing. A snake ready to strike, thought Louise and shivered.

'Right, ladies, this is your special day. So exciting. You just won't believe all I've got planned. It'll be a treat for us all.' He rubbed his hands and his eyes danced with excitement. Suddenly he took a giant step forwards towards Louise, bent down until his face almost touched hers and whispered, 'You know I could kill you just like that' and he snapped his fingers - 'if I wanted to,' he added, and stared into her eyes before he let out a shriek of laughter.

She knew she mustn't show fear; she'd been in similar situations with clients. She just had to remain calm and didn't let her eyes drop for a moment. 'Yes, you could I suppose,' and held his eyes until, not getting what he wanted, he backed off and muttered, 'I don't want to now anyway. That's not what I do, I have to do it in the right way and I'm saving that part for later.' As a parting shot when he got to the door, he shouted, 'Enjoy your breakfast; not good to dive on an empty stomach.' The laughter reached them through the locked door and got fainter as he walked away.

Louise wasn't sure what she'd heard. Did he say 'die' or 'dive'? She remembered the room in his house with all the diving equipment and knew. He had said dive but he might as well have said die. She shook so hard the blanket she'd wrapped around herself fell off. It was almost laughable because there was no possibility he could have known the fear she had of water. Whatever his plan she'd probably die having a panic attack. She said nothing to Caroline, who hadn't appeared to have heard what he said.

The breakfast was just a bowl of cereal and a cup of coffee. She looked at it longingly but didn't want to risk it in case it contained more drugs. Louise watched as Caroline wolfed hers down and drank the coffee despite her warnings it was probably drugged.

'I don't care Louise, I'm so hungry and thirsty I'm prepared to take the risk.' Then continued to eat what was left.

Louise moistened her lips with her tongue. She inspected the room and looked for ways to escape, but nothing was obvious. The small window was too high and she couldn't see out of it. It let in some light but she couldn't see sky, just a few bits of a dark green shrub or perhaps ivy, so guessed the room was mainly below ground and the window was probably at ground level. There was nothing in the room they could stand on to reach the window.

Caroline didn't seem to be any the worse for the food and the coffee, so perhaps it hadn't been drugged after all. Louise asked her to explain what had happened the night she'd been taken. The sigh Caroline gave before she answered tore at her heart. She'd been so happy with this relationship and that it should turn out to be such a cruel betrayal was dreadful.

'Things began to get really bad. John started to behave in a strange way and all the things you said to me made me really think hard about my relationship. I'd decided enough was enough and I would leave. He frightened me and I think you realised he had started to hurt me too.' Louise got up, moved over to her and put her arm around her.

'I left his house when he'd gone out to get something but needed to go to my home to get some more things. I knew he'd come after me and realised I must go right away for a while; leave Bath. I was going to ring and tell you what had happened but I didn't get a chance. I know at this point I was finding it hard to think straight. At home, I put some clothes in a suitcase but felt so exhausted I went downstairs and poured myself a glass of wine. I just sat there, at the kitchen table while I thought what I was going to do and where I should go.' Caroline stopped and rubbed her arms as though she was cold or had remembered something which was difficult to talk about. Louise hugged her tight and urged her to go on.

'I should never have done it, I ought to have left immediately but I was so tired and he said he wouldn't be back for a couple of hours. Now I keep going over and over it and wishing I'd gone. I knew he would look for me, but when the door crashed open and my chair was yanked away I was shocked he'd got there so quickly. He then transformed into Mr Nice Guy once more; helped me up off the ground, sat me down then topped up my glass and poured himself one. He said if I was leaving him, we ought to have a glass together first. I could feel my heart pounding but went along with it as I thought maybe he would then let me get my case and go.

I didn't see him slip the drug into my glass, but that is what he must have done. We sat for a few minutes and then he turned. You should have seen him, Louise - he looked quite mad and I was really frightened. He shouted something about him being in control, and he wouldn't allow me to ruin his plans. He pulled me up the stairs to the bedroom. When he saw the suitcase, he picked it up and threw all the clothes about the room in a rage. He went into every drawer and the wardrobe and anything he found there he threw down on the floor. I was so frightened I couldn't move. I started to feel really woozy and thought the wine had gone to my head so I sat down on the bed.

I didn't know what was going on and I pleaded with him to tell me. He switched into Mr Nice Guy again, told me I was obviously not well and should lie down. I knew he'd put something in the drink. I tried to get up and push past him but my legs wouldn't work. That was when he picked me up and carried me downstairs to the lounge. He put me on the sofa and wrapped a throw around me. It was so tight I couldn't have moved even if I'd been able to. He carried me out to the car and took me back to his house and shut me in the room.' Tears were rolling down her face and she started to sob.

Louise held her tightly and tried to comfort her. 'It must have been terrifying, you poor thing. I wish you'd come to me. You know, I found a scrap of material on the rose outside your door, so it must have come from the throw when he carried you out. I was there searching for you and just happened to see it but didn't know if it was important or not until I learnt from the estate agent you'd been carried from his house in Bath wrapped in a blanket.'

'It's hopeless. He'll kill us both, won't he?' Caroline didn't bother to wipe the tears as they dripped from her eyes onto the mattress and Louise gave her another squeeze.

'I rather think he is going to try, but don't let's make it easy for him. We must try and survive; fight to stay alive.' She said this in as positive voice as she could manage whilst her whole body was rigid with fear.

He didn't visit again for many hours and they shared all they knew about this man; this killer. Louise told Caroline all about George, as she was unaware of what had been going on with him and the trouble she'd experienced. Caroline frowned, 'But I think you love him, right? You still love him?' Louise stopped to think for a minute but she already knew what her heart told her. 'Yes, I think I do, but we have a lot to sort out before then and we have to stay alive.' She sighed and turned away.

Caroline dozed on her bed, weak from lack of food and sleep. Louise too lay on her mattress and tried to deal with nightmare thoughts. He had said 'dive' so she suspected he intended to do something horrific under water. She knew nothing whatever about diving and she'd never ever contemplated it because of her fear. She did know there were canisters which contained what she thought was air, and there was a tube connected to them through which the diver could breathe. She knew divers wore wet suits and masks but that was about the extent of it.

It hit her without warning and she could only blame the drugs as to why she hadn't realised before. She shouted across to the inert body a foot away. 'Caroline, wake up. I know where he's going to take us - I've been there and you have too. It's the flooded quarry with the diving club. I found a leaflet in Caroline's house and there were more in his house in Bath.

Caroline murmured and curled up into a tight foetus position. 'No, No. I'm definitely not going there, it was horrid - I'm not going anywhere. If I'm going to die, then I want to die here, not underwater or playing one of his vicious games. I want him to kill me here, not somewhere else. I may not know how to escape him but I do know how to make him angry and hopefully he will kill me quickly.' She sobbed and curled up even tighter.

Louise shook from the bottom of her feet to her neck but tried to hold her hands steady so Caroline wouldn't see. 'Come on, we mustn't give up, otherwise he wins in every way and we can't let that happen.'

She had no idea of the time, just knew she was desperately hungry and thirsty and wished she hadn't refused the cereal and coffee. The thought of food made her stomach rumble but her main problem was thirst. She licked her lips over and over, but they were dry and beginning to crack. She saw from the small window above them it was nearly dark, which meant it must be after four in the afternoon.

They'd not heard or seen Ed since the morning when he'd come in to collect their plates and mugs. He'd sneered when he saw she hadn't touched hers, grinned and said, 'It wasn't even drugged you know.' So, when the key turned in the lock again, it made her jump in fright. He had another tray in his hands and the same cheerful grin, 'Ladies, it's gin time. Afraid you missed your Friday night slot but am sure you can make an exception and drink it on a Sunday. No crisps or nuts, I'm afraid, but then you can't have everything.'

Louise watched him walk towards her. He had the same look he'd had when he'd taken up his sessions again, when he'd talked about the ends he needed to tie up. She'd known then it felt wrong. It was as if he had a secret, one he couldn't yet disclose but whatever it was it made him feel superior. It had irritated her at the time but now it made her angry and her body tensed and her heart pounded.

She knew adrenalin had started to flow and her body was getting ready for a response. Would it be fight, flight or freeze? She hadn't frozen, so gave a kick and the tray flew into the air and the drinks with it. As all three items crashed to the floor, she kicked again and managed to hit Ed in the groin. He doubled up but quickly recovered from the shock of her sudden attack, grabbed her, flung her to the floor and kicked her hard in the gut. She lay not able to catch her breath and felt as if she had been smashed into a thousand pieces. She clasped her stomach to try to ease the pain.

He stood above her, brushed down his clothes and said, 'You should have said if you hadn't wanted gin. Was it the wrong make or perhaps the wrong tonic? Never mind, there's plenty more, just hang on for a minute and I'll get it. Oh yes, but of course you have to hang on, don't you?'

Bile rose into her mouth. The burst of adrenalin had worn off and try as she might, she couldn't control her body. She felt pain she'd never experienced before and her muscles responded to the kick by cramping. Each contraction felt like a knife wound. She almost missed the click of the lock as he left the room. Caroline hadn't moved through the whole thing; just lay and whimpered.

The key turned and the sound roused her from a pain befuddled state. He held two bottles of water. 'Sorry, girls, no more gin but thought you might be thirsty. Particularly you, Louise, after your splendid display of, well, what was it do you think? Bravery, idiocy? Whatever - I just thought you'd need it.' He threw a bottle at each of them and Louise winced as she put up her hands to defend herself.

His pupils were like pin pricks and his voice had an excited tone. 'Oh, but this is fun I haven't done this before, at least, not quite like this. I've thought about it a lot, what you might say pre-contemplation, followed by contemplation and now I'm into the action Louise. You see I was listening. I took it all in and I think you said maintenance would be the hardest part, but I don't think it will be at all. I think from now on I will make sure all the fun I get from killing will be slower, much slower. I will take more time, so watching the final gasp of death will be much more exciting and much more satisfying. I really think your therapy has helped me enormously. I am changing my behaviour, which is what you wanted, wasn't it?'

Louise gasped as he left. She had it all wrong. She had made him feel powerful and strong and tried to remember what Jasper had once told her about working with the psychopathic mind. Try to keep your emotions in check, don't show you're intimated, don't buy into their stories and turn the conversation back to them but none of it applied to this situation. They had been trapped by a psychopath. There was no walking out or talking herself out of this. Louise made up her mind to deal with him in a different way, even if it made no difference to the outcome.

She turned towards Caroline and saw she had unscrewed her bottle and already drunk half of what was in it. 'Stop Caroline. Wait. No don't, please don't drink it.' Caroline slowly lifted her head, her eyelids already drooping, already disappearing into the hazy world of what Louise guessed was Rohypnol or perhaps GHB.

'Is good, Lou, this,' and she waved the practically empty bottle at her, 'but he got it wrong; s'not fizzy water, it's gin.'

Louise's heart lurched; the only other person who called her Lou was George. If only he was here. She was sure he'd know what to do. 'It's OK Caroline, don't worry. Glad the gin tasted good. Go to sleep now'. Words to reassure but Louise knew Rohypnol taken with alcohol gave a stronger reaction and could be dangerous taken with GHB. She'd learned this after working with clients who had been given it before being raped. Like most drugs taken to abuse, it was originally designed for legitimate use. In this case an anaesthetic. She had no intention of drinking anything, even though her mouth was watering at the thought of it. She focused on the bucket and started a slow crawl towards it. Every muscle screamed with pain and a cry escaped her as she clutched her stomach with each move. Once there she emptied the bottle and in the same painful way returned to the mattress.

The sound of the key as it turned in the lock alerted her and she sat back against the wall to give her support. Her body desperately wanted to fall and she wanted to hold her stomach again but resisted the urge as she didn't want him to think she had been weakened by his kicks.

'Hello, Ed, what delicacy have you brought us this time? I thought the water was not up to your usual standard at all. I'm a bit surprised, I must say. In fact, I would have thought you would have gone for something much classier than the Co-op's own brand. Then Caroline told me it was gin, not water at all, but we both know, don't we, it was so much more.'

Ed peered at her and screwed up his face, this was clearly not what he was looking for in his victim and Louise could see he wasn't quite sure what to do for a moment, so she continued.

'I must say I am amazed at your deceit; but you are right you know. I didn't guess or see your deception. I knew something wasn't right, but then you'd had such a terrible childhood, such abuse from parents and teachers, I couldn't help but feel sorry for you and wanted to help you.' She paused for a moment to check he was still listening.

'That's your gift, though, isn't it? Your innate ability to control and coerce people to do what you want, to only let them see what you want them to see and like many people similar to you, you have the ability to rise to high places, get important well paid jobs. However, it can also go disastrously wrong if you go too far too soon, like you did at your work. Poor Michael, he didn't know what he was dealing with. He knew how good you were at your job, but he was beginning to tire of what you were putting colleagues through. I think if you hadn't come to see me, he might even have sacked you and you couldn't let it happen, could you? That wasn't your plan at all, so you curbed your natural tendencies and toed the line. I wonder how you managed it. I now know it wasn't anything I did, you did it all on your own. It must have been so hard putting up with that idiot, as you called him, but you managed to control yourself and impressed Michael.'

He held his head to one side as he listened and she was reminded of a puzzled bird. She continued to talk, gave him praise and she watched as he preened his feathers and puffed himself out.

'You're right, Louise, it wasn't easy, but yes, I did manage it and actually it was quite fun for a while but then it got tedious. Anyway, enough. I am glad you realise there is nothing I am not in control of and nor will there be, because it makes all your fighting and plans to outwit me redundant.' He stopped for a moment. 'I am thrilled you now see me for what I am and I can see your admiration. You know I told you about my early years, at home and at the school. Well, it was there I learned killing was such fun, not the actual killing but watching them die.'

Louise couldn't help an intake of breath as she imagined him killing his peers but surely, he couldn't have got away with it without being caught.

'Animals Louise, animals.' He roared with laughter. 'You thought I meant the other pupils or staff, didn't you? That would certainly have been good but no, just animals at first. Rodents mainly, but there was a pet rabbit, which was much better and then a cat I think belonged to one of the teachers. I can't remember now the name of my first human but I realised immediately I could never go back. Like drinking good wine and then knowing you can't ever go back to plonk.'

Louise tried not to let her imagination conjure up faces of these poor creatures and people as he so casually talked of their deaths. He was worse than she even imagined and could not understand how he had never been caught. This time it was different though, because Dave was on to him and they'd found Sophie, so they knew what he was capable of, they knew about Caroline and they would soon realise about her. So, whatever happens to us, he will get caught and this knowledge gave her some satisfaction.

She was so deep in her thoughts she hadn't noticed he had taken something out of his pocket until it was too late. Her eyes widened in fear.

'I knew you wouldn't drink it, Louise, and if you had you would have been like that bundle of rags in the corner. You're smarter than the rest, I'll give you that.' And he glanced in the bucket as if to confirm what he said. 'But you must know, I can't have you like this or my plan just won't work and it would be so much worse for you, so much worse.'

The snake uncoiled and its eyes fixed on its prey as it slithered towards her. It's hypnotic stare held her in the moment – entranced. He struck so fast the needle was in her arm before she knew it. Her muscles relaxed and she collapsed backwards onto the mattress.

'You bastard, you utter bastard - you won't get … away… with it… this time.'

'Oh, but I have, Louise, I have,' and with half-closed eyes she watched him almost skip out of the door.

SUNDAY 11TH DECEMBER 2005

George

The sound of a bird as it landed on the roof jolted him awake. He snapped open his eyes, puzzled as to where he was. It was dark but not as black as when he went to sleep. His watch showed him he'd slept for a good four hours. He cursed his incompetence but was sure his army training would have jolted him awake if a vehicle had come by.

He'd been better prepared than last time and had brought a sleeping bag to keep warm and turned on the car heater for short bursts. At the start of the vigil he'd tried to keep awake and by midnight he'd drunk almost a whole flask of coffee. However, once the flask was empty and with the warmth of the sleeping bag, exhaustion got the better of him.

Ghost-like shapes of trees emerged as dawn made its presence felt and the branches glistened white. He tried not to think of Louise because, when he did fear gripped him so hard he couldn't breathe. I must stay focused he thought. Perhaps I am on a wild goose chase; maybe this guy has no intention of bringing her here, but my gut instinct tells me I'm right.

He worked his legs to ease the stiffness then gradually unbent them and placed them on the ground. Glad circulation had returned to his toes, he walked round to the back of the car, opened the boot and pulled out his camping stove and kettle. There was no point trying to get into the centre until it was properly open and he could do with a good strong cuppa and a snack. He couldn't see the quarry from where he was parked and he was glad, as his near panic attack yesterday worried him. It was better not to contemplate the dark water.

When the gate finally swung open and the same security guard had fastened it to a post and walked off, almost immediately a car arrived, followed by another. With the help of his binoculars he saw the young man in Reception he had spoken to yesterday and another man who he didn't recognise. He hoped this was the instructor he wanted to see.

George spotted the man he hadn't recognised go towards a cabin nearby. He got out a key and unlocked the doors. It must be him, he thought and hurried towards him, anxious to catch him before he disappeared inside.

'Hi. I'm sorry to disturb you immediately you're open but would you mind if I asked you a few questions?'

The man swivelled round in surprise but smiled. 'Er, yes of course, what's the problem?'

As succinctly as he could, George explained the situation and added he knew it was a long shot but was really concerned about Louise. The guy nodded and introduced himself as Jim.

'Yeah, I met her the other week. Lovely woman, very anxious about her friend. I wasn't able to help her much but I liked her and we had a bit of a chat. How strange she is also missing. Tell you what, why don't I finish opening up and then we'll go to the café and have a cuppa and you can tell me exactly why you think this is the place to look for her.'

Once they'd got themselves a drink, George introduced himself properly and told Jim all he knew about the situation.

When he'd finished, Jim sat for a moment as if he was trying to take it all in. 'Phew, what an awful story. You say this man's already killed and maybe more than once already?'

'Yeah, I believe so. I think he has planned to get rid of Caroline, if he hasn't already, and now also Louise. There seems to be a connection with diving. Leaflets advertising this place were found in his house and it is possible this is a place with some significance to him. Although it is a bit of a long shot, I have a feeling he might turn up here.'

Jim was silent again for a moment, then patted George on his arm. 'In a while this place will be full of my Sunday diving group.   They're all quite experienced divers who come in all weathers, even when it is as cold as this and the water is pretty icy.   I think if this guy had planned to do anything here it would be very difficult with all this activity going on, both above and below the water.'

George nodded. 'Yes, I agree with you. I used to dive myself and those are my thoughts exactly. I think, if I am right and if he's going to come here, it will be after dark when the centre is closed, which is why I have been keeping watch in the lay-by just outside your gates for the last two nights.'

'Blimey, you must be exhausted, but I guess you haven't seen anything or you wouldn't be here now.   Are you sure this is the place you need to be watching? There are quite a number of other flooded quarries in the area and probably a bit quieter.' He paused as if he wasn't sure whether to ask the next question but went ahead anyway. 'What sort of diving have you done then?'

George chose to ignore the last part of his question. 'Yes, I've looked at the map and seen the other lakes but because your leaflet was found in his house and also in Louise's friends, it seems to be too much of a coincidence. If he has dived here before, he would know what it was like and where everything was. And if he is someone who likes to plan ahead, then knowing the site would be important.'

'You think he's a member of this club then?'

'Yes, we think so, as I guess you can't just come without becoming a member, can you?'

'No, you're right you can't. I recognised the man, as I thought I'd seen him around, but couldn't tell your friend much more but did find out his name and telephone number from the register, which I gave to her.   I told her I had the impression her friend would not be going diving as she looked at the water as if she hated the idea of it. I remember roughly when I saw them though. It was at the beginning of November as I'd been to a bonfire party the night before and got very cold and she was wearing a garment which would keep anything warm and I envied her. Anyway, you didn't tell me about your diving?'

George shifted in his seat; he hadn't wanted to get into a discussion about this but understood Jim was only being curious. After all, he was helping him and deserved an answer, even though the knot in his gut tightened. He kept the explanation short.

'It was many years ago now when I was in the army and diving was my job. I've been out of the army for a while and I don't dive anymore.' He hoped Jim would leave it there but saw there was another question forming on his lips, so reluctantly he continued.

'Yeah, it was all a bit of a mess really. I was involved in an accident and I lost my buddy. He never surfaced and afterwards I found I really couldn't cope with it anymore. As a consequence, I left the army and have not dived since.'

He'd said more than he'd meant and for a moment he found it hard to get his breath back to a steady rhythm. He rubbed his clammy hands together. He saw the look of concern and knew Jim understood even before he spoke.

'That must have been dreadful, am not surprised you didn't want to dive again It's a shame as it's a great sport, but definitely not without danger. Hang on, you're not the guy are you who was in the papers? The one who was diving in Dorothea, or Old Dotty as it's known?'

George didn't reply, so Jim continued.

'I lived in Wales for a while and dived there once. My god it was an exciting experience – quite challenging though, all those tunnels. So, they found your buddy then? That must have been hard and then having an inquest, after all this time. Well done for being exonerated, what an ordeal and now this to happen as well. This Louise, she's your girlfriend?'

George nodded. It felt good to talk to someone who understood what it was like to be literally lost in a dark place.

The café started to fill up as people came in to make a hot drink before going off for their dive and Jim said he'd have to go as he was leading a group to explore one of their more unusual sunken relics; an old helicopter. It was at a depth which was quite challenging for some. He suggested either George hung around or came back later and then he'd have time for a longer chat and they could make a plan.

As he'd managed get a good bit of sleep and it was a longish drive home, George decided he would hang about for a while, have a good look round and then go off and find a pub to get himself some lunch and come back, as Jim suggested, later in the afternoon.

Although it wasn't close, he plumped for The Fisherman's Catch, where Luke said he had been taken to for his Sunday lunch to see if he could chat to the same waitress that Louise had spoken to.

It wasn't hard to find but it was already full of people and most of the tables had been taken. He went to the bar and asked if they could squeeze him in as he was on his own and had heard what great Sunday lunches they did. The waitress smiled and took him to a tiny place at the other side of the room away from the general restaurant and told him what was on offer. He plumped for the roast beef and Yorkshire pudding. He thought he really ought not to feel hungry at all but anxiety had always made him want to eat more, not less. He could see why the pub was called Fisherman's Catch. The wall near him had four or five old rods arranged in a pattern and there was a chalk board at the back of the bar which showed how many trout had been caught during the day or perhaps the previous day.

The food was worthy of its good name and George made it last, as he had time to kill. He even ordered an apple crumble for dessert followed by a coffee, which he made last a long time as he wanted to wait until the waitress was less busy before asking her any questions.

Once the place had thinned out, he saw his opportunity and asked her if she remembered talking to someone about a week ago and gave Louise's and Luke's description. She hesitated and went a bit pink but when he had given reassurance she wasn't in trouble and he was searching for his missing girlfriend, she relaxed.

'Funny, 'cause she was looking for a missing friend. She brought a photo with her but I wasn't any help as I hadn't seen her - but Harvey had.'

George raised his eyebrows.

'Yes Harvey, he was on shift then but he's not here today. He said he remembered what she looked like. I think he thought she looked hot, even though not young like him. Your friend gave me her phone number in case we ever saw her in here again or the bloke, but we never did.' She turned to go and then obviously had another thought because she came back to his table.

'Something was a bit off though. Harvey thought the whole thing odd. Watches too many crime series on the box, if you ask me. He watched as your friend left. He said the young guy went off to the gents and she stopped and looked at the leaflets in a stand at the entrance. Apparently, as he watched, a bloke charged out of the pub and knocked her over. Harvey went to check she was all right and said she was really shaken. It looked to Harvey as though the man who'd bumped into her had jumped into his car and followed another one. He was excited by it, thought it all a bit suspicious and made up stories as to what it could all be about. As far as I know, none of them have been back since.'

George thanked her and asked for his bill. He hadn't really learned anything much, except there had been something which had worried Louise.

By the time he got back to the quarry, Jim had finished his diving and changed out of his wet suit and was in the café surrounded by, what he assumed to be, his pupils. 'George, hi, help yourself to a drink and come and join us.'

He sat down on the edge of the group and listened to their excited chatter about the dive they'd done. One girl described it as 'truly awesome' and he smiled to himself, as he remembered there was a time when he would have felt the same sort of excitement by a new dive experience.

After a while they drifted off one by one and by the time it had started to get dark, they'd all left apart from Jim. 'Just got to go and check Ross has locked up Reception and see everything has been left as it should be but help yourself to more coffee or tea and I think there might even be some cake left.'

With the dark came the cold. He shivered and thought of Louise and wondered if she was warm wherever she was. He tried to get hold of Dave but he didn't answer and he felt despair at the hopelessness of the situation. Jim returned with a fan heater and some rugs and he instantly felt better.

'You really don't have to stay with me, you know. I could be wrong and nothing will happen. But we've got no other leads and at least I feel as if I'm doing something even if nothing comes of it.'

Jim smiled. 'I wasn't doing anything this evening. So, as I see it, you're doing me a bit of a favour in rescuing me from a rather boring night in. Nothing better than a night in a dingy dive school waiting for a psychopath.'

George laughed; it was good to have someone to share this with. It reminded him of the camaraderie of the army he'd missed dreadfully. Working on your own could be isolating and he immediately felt a pang of fear for the one he loved and what she might be facing while he sat here.

Not having anything else to do, they sat and talked and found they had interests in common. Jim was a member of the Territorial Army and had been for many years; so at least understood the stresses and tensions of being in the services. Like George, he had always preferred the outdoor life and as well as being a diver, enjoyed rock climbing too. They wondered if their paths had crossed without knowing. There were many good climbing spots around Bristol, like Avon Gorge or Cheddar, or if the weather was bad, at the wall in an old church in Bristol. They'd both been there and agreed their strong tea was the best there was.

Jim was interested to hear George was now a builder and said the Club might well be able to use him in the future as the buildings here were pretty much on their last legs. Jim said he lived locally but had originally come from Wales, which explained his knowledge of the quarry. He was aware of its reputation as being a bit of a death trap and the rather high number of deaths which had occurred there, but for him and many other divers, it still held huge appeal.

George found Jim to be a good companion and easy to talk to, so wasn't particularly surprised when he found himself telling him more about that terrible dive and the loss of his buddy. It was helpful to be able to explain the terror of his frantic search down the many passageways and caves to someone who knew exactly what he was talking about. Only another diver could understand the despair and panic when air runs low and there's a need to surface, when you haven't finished what you're doing. Jim would even understand the reason he made a bad judgement call, which meant he didn't make it in time and blacked out himself.

As George finished the story, he could feel the cold as it seeped into his bones just as it had then, and he felt himself start to fall down the black hole where panic attacks lay.

He again saw understanding in Jim's face and dreaded the sympathy which would follow. But all Jim did was give his shoulder a squeeze.

'Hey, mate, think it's enough reminiscing for one night. How about us having ourselves a bit of a fry up?'

George felt the warmth of Jim's hand and the upbeat voice and forced himself back into the here and now. His breath returned to normal.

'Could do with a hand in here, George.' Jim peered out from the kitchen door and gave a wave.

The smell of the frying bacon reached his nose before he saw what Jim was cooking and his stomach felt as if it smiled. Jim was obviously a man after his own heart. Jim showed him where the butter and the bread lived and they didn't speak again until they had a large bacon butty each and a mug of tea.

'Ah, that's better,' sighed Jim, wiping the grease from his chin with his hand.

'Yeah, you're so right,' agreed George.

The noise of a car approaching made George jump, but Jim put out a hand to reassure him. 'Just Ian, the night watchman. He comes on at eight and sits in his little sentry box place by the gate and does a round of the property every so often. I can't see the point myself but our insurance would be sky high without him. Not a person I take to particularly, but then it's a horrible job. I'd better go and tell him we're here and ask him to give us a warning if he hears anything.'

George could just make out their voices as he cleared away the plates and mugs.

Jim shook his head as he came back. 'That was odd. He's always a bit of a surly fellow but he was even worse this evening. Wanted to know how long I'd be here and what it was all about. I bet he was angry at me for upsetting his routine. I reassured him we wouldn't get in his way. Makes me wonder what he does get up to when we aren't here.

They spent a while trying to imagine what Ed/John could have planned for his victims which would involve bringing Louise and Caroline here.

Their talk turned to other things for a while, both conscious they needed a break from the dark thoughts which accompanied their morbid speculations. They were interrupted by the sound of George's phone. He saw it was Dave and immediately answered. It was to tell him the mysterious car following Ed had been spotted on the outskirts of Radstock.

'*I think you may be right George, there's a good chance it's heading for the quarry, which means in all probability he is following Ed there but for what purpose I have no idea. Two of my men are following and I've put a dive team on standby so if your guess is right, I can activate them very quickly.'*

'*Right, thanks, Dave, Jim and I are in the café keeping watch and I'll let you know if we see anything.'*

'*Yes, but please don't do anything stupid, leave it to us. I'll tell the guys following where you are. We'll get her back, George, believe me.'* Despite Dave's emphasis on the last sentence, George did not feel reassured one bit.

Jim got the gist of what had been said and got out of his chair. 'I think I'll go and let Ian know what's happening and tell him to keep an eye out for anything unusual.'

George nodded as he grunted an acknowledgement and continued to look out of the window. He frowned; 'mm,' could be a problem, he murmured to himself. The security light in the car park cast dark shadows over a large part of it, which left an area of blanket darkness around the shower block.

SUNDAY 11TH DECEMBER 2005

Louise

In what felt like seconds later, Louise heard the key again but Ed gleefully told her she'd been out for a night and almost a whole day. She hadn't even woken when he'd given her another shot a few hours ago. Her head felt as though it had been split in two by an axe. She knew her responses and reactions were slow but no longer felt anxious - the only advantageous thing about these drugs.

Ed leaned over Caroline and whispered with maleficence in her ear. 'Time to wake up my dear. You've had quite enough beauty sleep. Get up now!' She was still curled up but when he raised his voice at the last command, she uncurled herself and without looking at Louise, got up slowly from the mattress. He yanked Louise's arm and pulled her upright. She groaned and clutched at her stomach as her body was reminded of his kick. In a voice that made Louise shiver, he demanded they move. He caught hold of them both of and dragged them with him through the cellar towards the steps and then up and out of a door to his car.

Louise felt her mind had left her body and from afar, now watched a person who looked like her, comply with everything the voice asked. The voice in her head urged her to rebel; Fight, Louise; run; get away. This is your last chance. Please don't get in the car but in her drugged state these thoughts were powerless, unable to connect with her body enough for her to take any action.

Ed pushed Louise into the back seat and she saw he'd already put Caroline in the front. She stared meekly ahead of her. The car smelled different than before, it had a sort of dank smell, which seemed to come from a dark shape on the seat beside her. She tried to think what it could be and with an effort moved her head to try and see. She put her hand out and realised it was a wet suit. She shuddered, knowing it must connect to what he intended to do but in an odd way she didn't feel the intensity of fear she would have expected; definitely the drugs.

The drive seemed to go on for a long time but as it was dark, she couldn't see the direction they went in. At the beginning there were a few streetlights but very soon they were deep in the country where the dark outlines of hedges and sculptured ghost like trees were thrown into the spotlight by the cars headlights. Not even shaking her head cleared the mussiness she felt and she blinked hard, as if doing it might bring things more into focus. She pushed down on the door handle but as she guessed, it didn't shift. There was probably a child lock. Could she hit him with something? She felt about her but there was nothing she could use as a weapon.

She guessed they had probably travelled for about half an hour but in the drugged state she was in, wasn't sure, knowing she'd drifted off at times.

A sudden jolt interrupted her thoughts and was alerted to a change in the road surface. The car suddenly pulled to the left and turned in another direction. The seat belt cut into her sore stomach and she let out a cry of pain. The movement of the car told her he had driven onto a road with no tarmac. She was certain now; they were on the road to the dive centre. Surely there'll be someone there to help us, a security guard or something she thought, and despite not being religious, a prayer came to her from a distant religious childhood.

SUNDAY 11TH DECEMBER 2005

George

'Bloody man, nowhere to be seen. Clearly, doesn't think much of the job. It's not going to be his for much longer.' Jim returned with a couple of wet suits, fins and diving gear.

He shuffled his feet, as if he was unsure of himself. 'Look I know this might be difficult for you but I think at least one of us ought to be prepared in case one of the scenarios we were thinking of gets played out and people end up in the lake.'

George's stomach churned and hoped Jim couldn't see the tremor in his hands when he reached to take some of the load from him. 'No, you're right, but there's no way I'm letting you get in alone, Jim.' Brave words. If only he felt as confident as he sounded.

The familiarity of the feel of the neoprene against his skin surprisingly didn't give him a problem but he wasn't sure what might happen once he had the regulator on.

It was nearly midnight when they heard the scrunch of gravel and the sound of a car approaching quite fast. Jim leapt up and turned off the light and they peered out of the window and saw what looked like a black Range Rover driving towards the lake.

'How the hell did it get in? The gate was locked when I checked just now.'

'Damn, I knew those lights might be a problem,' Whispered George when he saw the car had stopped on the edge of the lake and was almost completely hidden by the shadow caused by the shower block.

Jim eased the window open so they might perhaps hear, even if they couldn't see properly. It was a frosty night so, in all likelihood, sound would carry.

A car door opened and closed, followed by the scrunch of gravel. Then another door opened and was slammed shut. From the sound, it was a weighty door and George guessed the boot had been opened. This guy was certainly not worried about being heard by anyone, which probably meant the security guard had made himself scarce, perhaps after he'd let the car in.

They heard nothing for a moment and then once more the scrunch of gravel as a figure emerged from the darkness and walked towards the changing block.

'God, this guy is confident. Clearly knows his way around. It must be Ed.' George's whisper came out louder than he intended and he worried the sound might have carried across the car park. If that's Ed, then where is Louise? Could she be in the vehicle, perhaps a prisoner? He started to move and whispered to Jim he was going to investigate. Jim pulled him back. 'No. I think we should wait until we know what's going on.'

He was desperate to go but thought perhaps Jim was right and sat down again. It was no good to rush in but after what seemed like ages, he decided he couldn't wait any longer. He'd just got to his feet when Jim pulled him down again and they saw the same figure emerge from the changing room. When he got into the light George gasped; he was now in full diving gear. More car doors opened and then slammed shut and then nothing.

They peered into the darkness. George started to move, 'Damn. Wish we could see what's happening, think we should try and get nearer. Use the shower block as a screen.'

SUNDAY 11TH DECEMBER 2005

Midnight

Louise

The engine stopped and Louise put her hand on the handle of the door and gently pressed it but it was still locked. Ed laughed as he opened the driver's door, as if he had known what she'd tried to do. He whispered, 'Stay right there, my lovelies, I'll just get the gear out and make sure the security guard has gone. Be good.' This was followed by another laugh.

Louise heard the click of the lock and knew there was no way out. She heard Ed walk around to the back of the car, open the boot, then slam it shut. Footsteps scrunched on gravel and then silence.

'Oh god, my head feels so muzzy.' She shook it to see if it would help. 'Caroline, talk to me. Caroline, wake up. We've got to get out of here. There's two of us so it should be possible. We need to clear our heads, get our bodies under control.'

There was still no reply. Louise leant forward and tried to squeeze between the driver's seat and hers, but the gap was too narrow and could only manage to put one arm through. She tried to shake her shoulder. 'Caroline, please talk to me. Can you reach the front pocket? Is there something we could use as a weapon?' There was no response, so she shook her as hard as she could but was couldn't rouse her. She heard the scrunch on the gravel again and with a scream of pain twisted back into her seat just as her door opened.

MONDAY 12TH DECEMBER 2005

Just after Midnight

George

'Ello, 'ello, what's going on here then?'

'What the fuck?'

They spun round and faced two men in police uniform with large grins on their faces, clearly amused by the discomfort they'd caused and their caricatured police greeting. George and Jim had been so intent in their observation of the scene around the changing block they hadn't heard them.

'Sorry we scared you - the Gov told us you were here.' They introduced themselves and then one of them described what they'd been doing. 'We followed the guy we've been after all the way from Bath. He turned up the track which led here and pulled into a rough lay by and parked. The car was empty when we reached him - he must have then set off on foot. We hurried after him but he'd disappeared. Don't know what the hell he's doing but think he's somewhere in the undergrowth round the lake. It's impossible to track someone there as the scrub is dense and we had no idea what direction he took. We thought it best to come and find you before pursuing him further, as our orders were only to observe.'

After this length description, the policeman who'd remained silent, nodded in agreement.

They were interested to hear about the car partially hidden by the shower block and while one of them contacted Dave, the other stared out of the window and tried to see what they'd been looking at. George wished he'd phoned Dave himself but it had all happened so quickly.

'The gov said to make sure you didn't do anything but watch, but seeing you dressed like that it looks like you intend to do more than just watch. He also said to stop you doing anything stupid, so I don't think you ought to be going anywhere and therefore I'll ask you to sit down, sir.' He seemed to have returned from his phone call with Dave in a more assertive frame of mind and was less friendly.

A sharp anguished cry echoed across the lake. 'What the hell's that? Sent shivers down my spine. unnatural - spooky.' The distracted policeman turned towards his partner and by the time he'd turned back, George and Jim had already got to their feet with diving gear in their hands.

'Now what have we just said? We need to ask you to remain here, sir. Sirs.' His words were lost as the two men sped through the door before they could be apprehended.

They tried to avoid the brighter areas of the car park and kept in shadow as much as possible until they reached the protection of the shower block.

MONDAY 12TH DECEMBER 2005

Louise

There was a movement to her left and Louise looked round. Illuminated in the light of the moon she saw Ed, now dressed in a black wetsuit. Her body shook - he was ready to go underwater. Before she could process this, he'd flung open the door, yanked her roughly out of the car and pinned her against the side. He stretched past her and picked up the suit beside her on the back seat. Her eyes turned to look towards the lake; the water was jet back with an oily and dangerous glint to it.

Ed caught her look and giggled. 'Yes, that's right, that's where you're off to my dear. You'll love it. Nothing like a good dive and this one will be good, believe me.'

She tensed her muscles and tried to push him but he was like solid granite and her attempt only resulted in his landing a hard punch to her stomach. Nausea threatened to overwhelm her. The pain was almost intolerable and her resolve to escape left her. She expected him to get Caroline out, but he locked the door again and she was left in her seat as unresponsive and immobile as a statue. Ed shoved the suit into her hands and indicated she should put it on. She stared in horror, unable to move.

'Put it on NOW.' His shout shook her. He then muttered in a low voice she was only just able to hear. 'Don't want you to die too quickly, do we.'

Still with a firm grip on her, he stood behind her and pushed one leg and then the other into the legs of the suit, just as a mother would dress a child. He directed, pushed and pulled as she tried to resist but finally got the rest of the suit over her body and her arms into the sleeves. She had seen how tightly his wetsuit fitted him but hers was way too big. She guessed he had planned this so carefully and it was intentional. Guess it made it easier to put on someone who might resist, she thought.

The drugs in her body had made her compliant but they restricted her movement and the pain where he'd kicked her caused her to shriek. He slapped her across the mouth and hissed she should be quiet. He rested his hand on her lower spine and, in a slow and measured way, zipped her up at the back. When he reached the base of her neck, he gave it a light caress and pulled the attached hood over her head.

Droplets of sweat ran down her face and she shook from the effort and fear. He made her put on boots and gloves. When finished, she looked down at her body, reminded of Kipling's *Just So Story* and 'How the Elephant Got his Wrinkly Skin', For a second she felt removed from what was happening until he grabbed her wrist and roughly clamped a handcuff around it.

He pushed her forward in hard short sharp bursts. When she almost fell, he caught hold of her waist and half-supported, half-dragged her. Even in her drugged state she still couldn't understand her compliance when all she wanted to do was run.

At the water's edge, he squeezed her into a jacket which held the air tank and handed her a mouthpiece attached by a tube. He picked up the mask, spat into it and wiped the moisture round the glass. 'Want to make absolutely sure you can see everything, Louise.' His voice resonated with glee.

Her body shook so hard she was reminded of how a dog shakes after being in water and her head throbbed. She knew her muscles were too weak to swim and she was aware he hadn't given her flippers. I guess it won't matter though, as long as I can breathe. With that thought her legs, which had seemed to be frozen, melted and collapsed under her. She clutched wildly at Ed and just avoided tipping herself into the water.

He put on fins, his own mask and air tank and fastened a weighted belt around his waist and then another on hers. The weight pulled her towards the ground but his grip held her upright. He manoeuvred her around to face him. Fear enveloped her and she struggled.

'Don't, Ed, No. Please don't, this isn't the way.'

He silenced her and pulled her tight against him. The whisper came sharp as glass. 'Don't worry I'll watch you die.'

She gasped at the menace in his words and felt her heart accelerate but before she could take a breath, he pulled the mask roughly over her face and pushed in her mouthpiece. Then caught hold of her free hand pressed it against it and hissed 'hold it.'

How could this have happened, she thought as hands grasped her shoulders and pushed her backwards. She expected to fall but he pulled her towards him again; he was the cat and she the bird. His eyes danced with excitement; it was all a game to him. He held her there for so long that the push when it came, was unexpected and shocking.

She hit the surface and sank down into the water, spiralling around and around on her back like a struggling turtle. The weight of the tank pulled her further and further down, through the cold and dark towards the unknown. His menacing words still danced in her head as she eventually managed to right herself.

Fear gripped her now rigid body and she pleaded with an unfamiliar God. Let this be a dream, let me wake up at home, safe in my bed. I don't want to die. She felt a scream in her throat and took fast anxious breaths as she peered out of her mask into the slippery dank water that surrounded her. She saw nothing but the blur of bubbles as they rose up to the surface and the darkness of the water increased.

Without warning fingers closed around her arm and a bright light shone in her face. She'd known he would be there somewhere waiting but hadn't been prepared. She tried to pull away and kicked out but he didn't loosen his grip; just held tight and pulled her deeper and further into the lake.

She tried to disassociate from where she was, to feel she existed only in some surreal place where there was no danger but the beam of his torch caught an outline of a large dark shape ahead and the terror of it all overwhelmed her and tears pricked her eyes. This was a man who had sat in her house; had been a client.

Something touched her legs and from the light of his torch saw it was a mass of weeds which almost covered the dark mass behind. It wasn't clear at first but then saw it was an old car with no doors. He yanked her close to a door frame and despite her struggle to resist, attached the other part of the handcuffs to the steering wheel. Horrified she continued to struggle and her heart raced and her breath became fast and heavy. This caused an enormous amount of bubbles which limited her vision more.

Ed flapped his arm up and down in front of her, which she took to mean calm down. Calm down! I'm screaming in my head. Is this it? Am I to be left here to die? What's he going to do next? Her imagination gave her a hundred different ways he could kill her and each was more terrifying than the last. She screwed her eyes tight shut but the horrendous images wouldn't leave. She opened them again, but now it was inky black and all she could see was a pin prick of light from his torch as it disappeared up towards the surface and she was alone.

Silence and darkness engulfed her. The only sound was her breath as it passed through the tube in her mouth and all she could see were the bubbles rising in front of her. All sense of reality or time left her. She continued to try and wriggle her hand free from the steering wheel but it was firmly fixed and not as old and rusty as she'd hoped. Her heart still pounded at what she thought was twice the normal speed. The cold hadn't got to her yet but the water was icy and she was sure she'd feel it soon.

Something brushed against the leg of her suit and she pulled herself away. She wanted to scream and took short sharp breaths. I've always hated horror films she thought and now I'm in one.

She wasn't sure what might happen if she hyperventilated but guessed it wouldn't be a good thing, so urged herself to stay calm and used the mantra she helped clients to use. Breathe slowly and evenly, count as you breathe in and out. Don't let your thoughts take you away with them, stay in the present. Ridiculous! Is that really what she said? She thought staying in the here and now was the last thing that was helpful and she struggled and yanked at her tethered wrist again.

Dreading an onset of a panic attack, when she felt the change in her breath and knew what might come, returned to the slow breath count, in and out. The voice in her head continued; deal with each worry as it comes along. Don't let it escalate, just ask yourself what action you can take, because it is the action which will resolve the worry, not the worry itself. If there is no action to be taken, (for instance if you are bloody handcuffed to a car at the bottom of a flooded quarry) then you need to put it aside, as worrying won't change anything. By putting it aside, you have taken action and accept there is nothing more you can do. At this last thought her body went rigid again. She clenched and unclenched her fists aware her fingers had started to tingle; another sign panic was not far away and continued to talk to herself.

I have to try and remain calm, not get angry and stay alive as long as I can. I want to live; I want to see my children again and grandchildren. I've got to fight. She tried harder than ever to get her breath under control. She thought about Caroline. Where was she, what did he do to her and what will he do to me? Anxiety crept like a snake around her body, so she concentrated again on her breath. Stay calm; in and out. Not fast - slowly. Don't, don't think.

She had no idea of time but it seemed hours. Oh my god, how long does air last in this tank? Goose bumps spread and crawled over her skin inside the suit. That's what he's doing, isn't it? He was going to leave her here until the air runs out. She felt a swift blow of terror and her breathing rate increased again. Stop it, stop it, she shouted to herself, slow down - you're using your air. She forced herself to go back once again to her slow regular breaths. If only it wasn't so dark.

Thoughts of being shut under water in the dark until death were what nightmares were made of and she tried to focus to prevent herself from going there. If only I had a torch. Damn, why didn't I think of that before. He had a torch so perhaps I've got one too. The jacket is heavy and there could be one, perhaps on the belt. She used her free hand to explore. There, what's this? Her fingers rested on a clip with something that hung down from it. With difficulty she managed to release the clip and held the object in her hand. Fearful she would drop it she rested it on her arm attached to the wheel while she felt for a switch. There! Her predicament was now illuminated in ghastly reality.

MONDAY 12TH DECEMBER 2005

George

They peered round the building but it gave them no further answers. All they saw was the car and some movement beside it but it was too dark to make out more. George glanced towards the lake and the tension in his body was like a steel band clamped around his chest. He turned away, not wanting to look at what he saw as the evil glint of the mercurial dark water.

Jim's hand landed on his shoulder and it helped him focus. Where was Louise? Was she in the car? Was Caroline with her and what was Ed up to, because it had to be him there in the wet suit.

There was sound as if something was being dragged or pushed across the gravel that lay on the path. This was followed by a splash, then almost immediately another and then silence. They peered round the building but saw nothing.

'Quick get the gear on, I think we need to get down there.' There was an urgency in Jim's voice and George focused on following his orders. After they'd each put on their BCD and regulator, they used Jim's torch to do a quick buddy check, then with their fins in their hands moved as fast as they could towards the lake.

A ripple broke the surface followed by a head. Just in time they ducked behind the building before the diver appeared on the bank, pulled off his fins and walked towards the car. They heard a door open and shut. Then he reappeared out of the shadow and in the dim light they saw he had a body in his arms. Hair hung down over the face but it looked like a woman and by the way her arms and legs flopped about while he walked, she was either unconscious or dead. When he reached the edge, he stood for a moment

MONDAY 12TH DECEMBER 2005

and then threw her like some refuse into the lake. As the body hit the surface the light of the moon caught the glint of blonde hair before it disappeared under the dark mass of water. The diver quickly slipped his fins back on and jumped.

'My God. That was Caroline; he's thrown her in' shrieked George as they moved fast towards the lake. They had only gone a few yards when something hit the gravel with such force the small stones ricocheted into the air. Another burst of noise echoed round the quarry and more gravel flew.

'Gunfire! We're being shot at.' Yelled George. There was no cover and they were too far from the lake so they retreated in a zigzag fashion and took cover in the shelter of the building.

'What the hell is going on?' Whispered Jim. They recognised the danger they were in but had no way of defending themselves. 'Where did it come from? Who is it?'

'I don't know but I'm guessing it's the man who has been following Ed and Louise, who the police lost earlier. Why he would want to kill him or her I've no idea.'

MONDAY 12TH DECEMBER 2005

Louise

She caught sight of movement ahead of her. The water was being churned around and there were figures. She shone the torch beam on where she thought they were and saw something being dragged in her direction, presumably by Ed. She took a sharp breath, No. No, it's got to be Caroline. Is she dead? She narrowed her eyes and tried to clear her vision. Caroline's hair flowed ethereally in the water and she was still fully dressed.

As Ed swum towards Caroline, her body jerked and she struggled to swim. She's alive Louise thought as she willed her to fight but Ed wouldn't let go. Bastard. He's killing her and loving it. She watched as Caroline continued to struggle. He wants me to see; to watch her die. Transfixed by this horror she didn't want to see; she screwed her eyes up tight. When she opened them again, Caroline's limp body lay on the bottom and Ed circled like a vulture around her. He then moved down beside her and for one moment Louise thought he might take her back to the surface but he just caught hold of her and dragged her inert body further away into the darkness, until she was lost from view. Louise watched in horror and something died inside her.

Ed returned quite quickly on his own and swam towards her. He held up ten fingers and pointed at the watch on his wrist. Ten what? What's he trying to say? He then pointed up towards the surface. What did he mean? He repeated his actions and she watched as he and his light disappeared. Would he be back in ten minutes? Did she only have ten minutes of air? Where had he taken Caroline? She shone the torch wildly around but there was nothing to see and tears filled her eyes and dripped into her mask.

MONDAY 12TH DECEMBER 2005

George

The two policemen had almost reached them. 'Get back,' George shouted. 'We're being shot at. Radio for backup NOW.' He was certain they'd heard but they seemed fixed to the spot. He guessed they couldn't believe what had just happened. There was another burst of fire which spurred them back towards a safer place.

'I've got to go Jim. I've got to dive. That was Caroline he just threw in. She might be dead and so might Louise, if she's down there. We don't know what the hell is happening but we know we heard two splashes at the start.'

Jim nodded and George took a step forward just as a head emerged from the lake and the diver hauled himself onto the shore. He stood for a moment and looked at his dive computer.

George hesitated, 'What's he doing now for God's sake? What's happened under water? It's no good, sniper or not, I'm making a run for it.'

'Not on your own, you're not.'

They both moved forward but just as the diver was about to jump he turned and saw them. A loud crack reverberated around the quarry and the diver jerked to the right, clutched his side and fell back into the water. 'He's been hit' shouted Jim. At the same moment George heard police and ambulance sirens and the night was illuminated by blue strobe lights. He rushed to the water's edge and pushed his feet into his fins as fast as he could. They'd hardly come to a stop when Dave leapt out of one of the cars and ran towards him. He shouted something indecipherable but George didn't wait to find out what it was. He waved back at Dave, indicated to Jim he was going in and jumped.

In an instant George was back in the that death quarry in Wales. He struggled to breathe; his body rigid with fear. It was pitch black and the cold seeped through his wet suit into his bones. A primitive survival instinct spurred him to swim back towards the surface; he needed to get out, get out of this place away from the dark, away from death.

A beam of light shone in his face and a hand gripped his arm and yanked him round. Jim's eyes were kind and he smiled as he patted his shoulder and George calmed. This was no time to lose his nerve; he must just conquer his fear and find Louise. He reached on his belt for his torch, put the lead around his wrist and gave Jim a thumbs up. They swam slowly as they moved the torches from side to side and systematically scanned the bottom of the lake.

When they first caught sight of it they thought it was a rock with white weed attached to it but when they drew nearer, saw it was Caroline. Jim instantly scooped her up in his arms and with a jerk of his head, indicated he would take her up.

MONDAY 12TH DECEMBER 2005

Louise

Louise strived to wrench her arm free but it held tight. Her breath accelerated and she tried hard to get it under control. It would be good if words helped but it doesn't matter how many times I say 'be calm' it doesn't work and with these thoughts and frustrated by her ineffectual efforts, she turned away from the wheel.

Something was spiralling down towards her and she saw it was a light swirling around in the water. That's strange. The way it's moving - it's weird – oh no now I can see, it's a diver – is he dead? She watched as he sank to the bottom in front of her, where Caroline had been a while before. From the light of her torch she saw a dark cloud emerge from his side. What could have happened who is he? Then another light and another diver came into view.

The second diver had nearly caught up with the first when the first diver, clearly not dead, pushed off from the bottom and grabbed him. They whirled about in front of her and stirred up debris which made the water cloudy and impenetrable. When it had cleared slightly, one of them had disappeared. The remaining one swam towards her in an awkward lopsided motion, one hand pressed against his side. He was either too injured or hadn't the energy but didn't manage to reach her and she watched as he sank, landed on his back and lay still. Was it Ed or perhaps someone who might have rescued her?

Please God, let it be Ed lying there. He no longer had a torch and she guessed he must have lost it in the struggle but from the light of hers she saw the cloud ooze from his body and darken the water around him. She tried to make out what had happened to the other diver but beyond the beam's reach it was inky black. Caroline was dead, the other diver must be dead and this one, who she hoped was Ed, was going to die soon too. Then she whimpered in horror. There was no-one left who knew where she was. She would definitely die down here and the irony was, no-one at all would watch her die.

With this thought she made a desperate attempt to free her hand but the metal on the handcuff cut into the suit and into her flesh. A vice like grip of terror overcame her and again her breathing became faster. She tried to take a slow breath in; nothing. Nothing to breathe. Her lungs and her mind screamed. The tank was empty. No air, no air. Panic rushed through her body and instinctively she went to rip out her mouthpiece but knew the only thing she would breathe then would be water. She hit the steering wheel violently with her torch but it stayed firm. In one final attempt she smacked it so hard that her hand, now ice cold, loosened its grip and the torch slid away and disappeared into the darkness.

Time stopped and tears ran into her mask. She recollected Alice in Wonderland who nearly drowned in tears. Images floated in front of her; her children, her grandchildren, Buster and surprisingly, George. Loss overwhelmed her as she sank into oblivion.

MONDAY 12TH DECEMBER 2005

George

George watched the stream of silvery bubbles as they rose up ahead of Jim and his burden. He knew he ought to go with him and help take Caroline back to the surface but there was no way he could leave with the possibility that one of the splashes had been Louise. Images of the search he'd made in a not dissimilar place, flooded his mind. He'd been on his own then too and he had lost him and didn't want it to happen again.

He pushed these thoughts away and used his torch to pierce the murky darkness. The beam of light caught a dark shape in the water ahead of him. He watched as it wriggled and writhed towards a large dark mass and he saw it was the injured diver they'd followed into the water. He writhed and clutched at his side with one hand and used his legs and the other arm to propel himself forward. It was made more difficult because he also held a torch in his free hand, which whirled madly around as he swam.

George followed but moved his torch away, as he didn't want to be seen. Where was Louise? What had he done with her?

Gradually the dark mass ahead made sense; it was a car with no doors. As Ed moved forwards a random movement of his torch swept over the car and for a split second showed a figure clipped to the steering wheel. No. Not Louise, please no. He threw himself towards Ed and had almost reached him when Ed twisted round and lunged with his torch. The blow hit George with surprising force for an injured man and for a moment he fell back stunned.

Thoughts of Louise urged him on; he wasn't going to let her die. Certain that Ed would have been weakened by the effort of striking such a blow, he flung his body towards him with as much energy as he could. When he was near he pulled his arm back and using his torch like a dagger thrust it as hard as he could into the site of Ed's wound. There was no retaliatory response and George's breath returned to a steady rhythm as he watched Ed fall towards the bottom; sure he'd caused further damage and pain. Let's hope that's done it and I see no more of him, he thought as he turned and headed back towards the car.

He'd swum quite freely for a few strokes when without warning something wrapped around his foot. He shook it and tried to get it free thinking it was caught in weeds but it was held in a tight grip. Ed!

George arched his back, swung round and smashed his torch as hard as he could down on Ed's head and he released his grip. Once again George watched as Ed sank out of sight and then moved as fast as he could towards the car.

He shone his torch on Louise's mask and saw alarm spread over her face as she clutched at her regulator and wrenched at the handcuff in a frantic effort to break free. Her tank must be empty. The bastard had planned this - she hadn't been down long enough to have used a full tank and it wouldn't be long before she lost consciousness. Yes, now she's gone limp. Without hesitation he pulled out his mouthpiece and almost simultaneously took hers out and replaced it with his. He shook her and when there was no response, shook her again and when she opened her eyes, indicated she should breathe.

She took a breath and the look of relief was unmistakeable. He searched around on his jacket for the second hose. He used the technique he'd been taught and swung his arm up and around to find it. Ah, there it is and with relief took a breath. He tried to free Louise from the wheel but it was impossible. He didn't know how long it would be before any rescuers would get to them and Louise needed to be released quickly. There's only one thing I can do and with this thought he slipped his tank and jacket off, indicated with his hand he was going up and would be back. He took a deep breath, released his mouthpiece and swam slowly towards the surface, mindful of not surfacing too quickly.

He was only just out of sight of the car, when there was a turmoil in the water and once again fingers locked round his ankle and held him down. He knew he couldn't hold his breath for long, his lungs already screamed for air. Using the same manoeuvre as before, he twisted his body around and sank the torch as hard as he could into Ed's side. He released his grip and sunk once more to the bottom. George gave a silent prayer that this time he really had seen the last of him but this man seemed indestructible.

As the lake edge, a hand caught him and hauled him onto the shore where he lay gasping for air.

'I told you to wait, didn't I? You're an absolute idiot.'

'She's still down there Dave - handcuffed to a car and Ed may not be dead, he may still try to harm her. Got to get back down.' George pulled away from Dave and got to his feet but Dave caught hold of him. 'Don't be ridiculous. You're in no state and anyway the divers will have reached her by now.'

'They don't know where she is, it will take them ages to find her, but I know, I know.' He tried again to pull away but was pushed back down. 'They'll find her, you can be sure, George, she'll be Okay.'

MONDAY 12TH DECEMBER 2005

Louise

She'd hit that wheel with what remained of her strength when she knew she couldn't breathe but then almost immediately had drifted into a dreamlike state. Fear left her and she felt peace. Then with no warning she was shocked out of oblivion; her mouth wrenched open and something pulled out and immediately something pushed in. She kept her eyes tight shut and wanted to return to that dreamlike place.

Her body shook - something or someone had shaken her. She opened her eyes and was blinded by a bright light. Through her mask she saw a man in a dive suit. He pointed at her mouth and then at his. She took a breath – air. She took another and another, then looked to see who had helped her. She saw he'd given his mouthpiece. Tears formed; was she really saved? Mesmerised she watched as he took another tube from his equipment and started to breathe through it. Then he lifted the tank and his jacket and slipped it over her shoulder and her free arm.

He put his hand up, pointed towards himself and then up towards the surface, then down again. When she realised what he meant she couldn't believe it, she had to make him stay. Please don't go, I can't be here on my own again. Please, please, don't leave me. Her thoughts went unheard and she no longer felt rescued. Any feeling of relief left as she watched the diver and his light move away.

The light stopped moving and for a moment she thought he was going to come back but then he jerked to one side. The beam of his torch showed another diver had grasped his ankle. The torch whirled and the figures stirred up so much mud and weed she saw nothing, just weed and debris in a whirlpool. Darkness engulfed her.

Her heart raced and she knew her breath was too fast but couldn't help it. What had just happened? Had either diver survived? Her rescuer would be desperate to breathe. Please, please, let him have got to the surface. Her body shook. I don't think I can hold on much longer. It's so dark and Ed could be near if he's not dead. He might still grab me. These thoughts fuelled her feeling of panic but she knew she must keep focused, breathe slowly and try to think positively. She banged on the wheel with the cuffs and hoped the sound would carry. She'd read somewhere you attract people underwater by banging on something metal. She banged again and again but her fingers were numb and it hurt her wrist so had to stop.

She had no idea what might be happening maybe only a few feet from her. She shuddered. Her eyes closed and again felt she was being lulled into oblivion.

A movement in the water alerted her and she feared another attack but when she opened her eyes it was a vision of angelic lights. Perhaps I'm really dead now, she thought but as the lights moved closer and almost touched her, she saw not angels but divers. One of them shone his torch in front of her and made a thumbs up sign. Another diver cut her free with some tool and then a third diver appeared and two pairs of arms clasped her round her waist. They lifted her gently and supported her as they rose to the surface in a slow and steady pace.

Hands reached out and helped them from the lake onto a landing stage. She blinked, dazzled by the light and was helped to a sitting position. The jetty was brightly lit from various sources; car head lamps; large lamps; torches and security lights. An ambulance pulled away with lights and the sound of sirens as two pairs of strong arms lifted her up, carried her to the café and lowered her onto a chair.

She shook, her muscles screamed and her wrist hurt. Was she alive, she wasn't sure. Someone wrapped a silver survival blanket around her and helped her take off her mask, pulled back the hood and removed the gloves. She knew it was one of the divers but it wasn't until he pulled her gloves off so gently, she looked into his face. 'George.' The face grinned. She flung herself forwards and sobbed in his arms as emotion and fear flooded out of her. They squeezed each other so hard the slippery suits gave off their own burst of sound and they laughed and the tension broke as others joined in.

'Dave. You're here too and …' She also recognised one of the divers who stood next to George.

The man grinned 'Hi, I'm Jim. Yes, we've met before and I am so pleased to see you back safe but am sorry about your friend. I know she was the one you were looking for.'

Caroline. She couldn't bear to think of what she'd seen. She didn't want to ask, to make it real, but had to know.

'George, where's Caroline? I know she's dead but where is she? I couldn't see her.'

He explained she'd gone in the ambulance, the one she'd seen with the siren. Louise, shook her head, 'Why the siren? She was dead. I saw her die, it was horrible. He was watching. He wanted to watch us both as we died.'

George put his arm around her. 'I know, but don't think about it now'. He told her they thought Caroline just might have a chance. The water was so cold her body temperature plummeted as soon as she touched the water and she'd only been in there for possibly seven or eight minutes and no longer, which was apparently significant. It is why they didn't wait for you, they sent for another ambulance as they wanted to get her to the hospital as soon as possible. He also told her about something he'd learned, which was about a primitive reaction believed to occur on occasions when under water, which might have kicked in. It is apparently an automatic mechanism in our bodies which somehow allows breath to be held for longer. 'I don't understand it, but they thought there just might possibly be a chance they could revive her with a specialist team.' He told her not to get her hopes up.

Louise enjoyed the feel of his arm around her. She was still confused; it was hard to make sense of what had just happened.

'You know George, he wasn't John, or rather he was, but he was also Ed who was a client of mine, the one I told you about. But he was John to Caroline. Ben is the son of one of his victims whom he married and…'

Dave put his hand out to stop her and George gave her a squeeze. It was clear Dave was in charge here and he said, 'Don't talk now, we'll take statements later. The main thing is to get you checked out by the medics and then home and into the warm. I expect you'll want to take care of that, George.'

George nodded, pulled her to her feet and with his arm around her waist to support her led her away towards another ambulance, where the crew were waiting to check her over.

A shout reached them across the car park 'Hey George just make sure you get yourself a good cooked breakfast once you've got her home – you deserve one.' Jim laughed and then mumbled under his breath, 'Sure it won't match mine though.'

WEDNESDAY 14TH DECEMBER 2005

A pale wintery sun shone through a gap in the curtains and with reluctance Louise forced her eyes to open, terrified of what she might see after so many confusing and frightening night images. The clock showed it was two in the afternoon and she was safe in her own bed. A faint waft of something cooking reminded her of an evening she'd shared with George when he'd cooked beef bourguignon - his speciality.

She swung her legs out of the bed but winced; for some reason her stomach muscles hurt. She knew there was a reason but as hard as she tried, could not remember. In fact, she remembered very little except she had gone to look for Caroline at the lake and met Ed. His name triggered a flash of an image of a diver and she shook her head. Don't know what's the matter with me, everything feels odd. I don't know why but I know when I go downstairs I'll find George.

He was lying on the sofa by a roaring fire in her sitting room. She watched him for a moment. He looked so at home and it was good to see him there.

She was right, the smell had belonged to his beef bourguignon and she'd enjoyed every moment of it. She then felt ready to attempt to unravel what had happened to her over the last few days which was still a blur to her.

'What day is it now?'

George hesitated, then told her it was Wednesday. He let this sink in.

'You mean I have somehow lost some days?'

George nodded but said, 'I think there are some things I need to tell you about me before you start worrying about missing days.'

Louise turned the corners of her mouth down. 'I think I know most of it from Dave. I know he made contact with you.'

'Yes, he did. I think when he knew I was in the clear, he wanted to keep me up to date. He was worried about you and perhaps your over involvement! It was a good thing he had because when you didn't turn up on Friday night, I was alarmed as I was certain this time you had definitely meant to be there.'

Louise nodded, 'Yes I remember, I wanted to meet you even though I was still unsure about some things.'

George filled her in with his side of the story. When he'd nearly finished, she gave a large yawn but as her eyes started to close, she jerked them open. 'Tell me what's happened to Caroline, I remember you said she had a chance.'

George told her there was no news yet but Dave promised to let them know as soon as he heard anything. Louise lay back again and closed her eyes. A few seconds later she opened them again. 'Where's Buster - what happened to him? George told her he'd dropped him to Katy's before going to the quarry and he was still there. He put another log on the fire and settled back on the sofa.

She couldn't quite take it all in, this man sitting with her now had gone to so much trouble to try and find her and without him she would be dead. Tears formed in her eyes and George, ever watchful, pulled her closer.

THURSDAY 15TH DECEMBER 2005

Louise didn't appear until mid-morning when Buster alerted George to the sound of her feet on the stairs.

'Morning, sleepy head. Fancy a coffee?'

They sat at the kitchen table and once she'd had one refill Louise asked him to continue with the rest of the story.

George pushed his chair back a little so he could stretch his legs out under the table and continued to tell her about the events she wouldn't have known about.

When he got to the part where they were being shot at he stopped talking, reached over and caught hold of her hand. 'How're you doing? Just tell me if you want me to stop.'

Louise shook her head and squeezed his hand but felt bile in the back of her throat. 'Who shot at you? I don't understand. Ed was the villain and he was in the water with us.'

'I know but the man who had followed you and then Ed was also involved. It seems he was intent on killing or hurting Ed. Dave's men caught him as he emerged out of the scrub at the side of the quarry and tried to get back to his car. It turns out that he had just got out of prison and...'

Louise stopped him, 'I know now, of course I do. He was the man that Tim told me about. The private detective asked to investigate the man Paul thought had killed his wife. He was right. Ed had killed her.'

George frowned, he didn't recognise any of the names and didn't know who Paul was. 'None of it matters now Lou. You saved yourself; you let the other divers know you were there.'

'I don't understand - I didn't do anything.'

'I think you may not have realised it but one of the divers said they knew where to come as they heard banging in the water. You must have known that was important to do.'

'Yes, I did. I hit my handcuffs on the steering wheel. What I don't understand is what happened to Ed - because he was shot, wasn't he?'

'Yes, he was. He was shot in his side, which sadly did not prevent him trying to carry out his plan.'

'I know but I think he died eventually. What happened to him? Did they fish him out of the quarry?'

'Yes, they did, the police dive team went back for him while we were in the café. He was dead.'

'Jasper always said he didn't believe in co-incidences and he was right. I'm so glad you met him, he's a great man. Although even he didn't spot that I was working with a man with that particular personality disorder.'

'No, he didn't but from what I understand now, both psychopaths and sociopaths are often really hard to spot.'

Louise nodded. 'What has happened to Ben? I feel sorry for him, he's already a very disturbed child and this will make him even more so. It must be the end of his school term now. Ed told me he didn't want this to happen with Ben around. Odd he felt something for the boy, when he has no compassion for others.'

By another coincidence, it was at this moment Dave turned up at the house wanting to know if Louise would be strong enough to go to the station so they could take a formal statement.

'I have some amazingly good news though.'

Louise looked at him expectantly, 'Is it Caroline? Tell me quickly. Is she alright?

Dave grinned, 'She's alive.'

Louise gasped and put her hands up to her face in disbelief. 'I thought she was dead. I didn't dare believe. How wonderful. Tell me, how can it be? What happened what did they do?'

Dave grinned. She's in a controlled coma at present, but she is breathing and they think has a very good chance of recovery. They won't know yet about her brain function but they are hopeful. Amazing what they can do now. It was all down to the temperature of the water.

Louise let out a long sigh. 'That's amazing and wonderful news. Thank you. I feel I can now relax just a bit. Tell me, I had just asked George, do you know what has happened to Ben as he would have broken up from school today?'

'They've taken him into foster care. Apparently, it's with a lovely couple who are happy to keep traumatised children for a long stay and he will get therapy eventually but it means he does have a chance of a good Christmas perhaps.'

'Christmas!' yelped Louise. 'I can't even think about Christmas, it seems so unreal after all that's happened. Thank you so much Dave. You really are a truly an amazing son-in-law.'

'Kind of you to say, but you Louise are the stereotypical, irritating and disobedient mother-in-law.' Then before she could say anything he laughed and added 'But we wouldn't have you any other way.'

Louise wiped the frown off her face, joined in the laughter and put her arms round George and squeezed him tight. She whispered in his ear. 'I owe you my life and hope we have the rest of our lives together in which I can repay you.' There was so much of what happened that she couldn't remember but she knew, though didn't say, the drugs she had were very likely to cause unpleasant flashbacks of all the unspeakable things she saw and felt over those few days. At least now she had someone close to support her.

Buster bounded into the kitchen just as Katy, Max and Milly arrived. Katy wanted to hear the whole story but Louise made a face and suggested Dave tell her when there weren't so many little ears around.

MARCH 2006

Louise heard the house phone ring while she was seeing a client off just before lunch. It was Dave.

'Great news Louise. I've just spoken to the hospital and Caroline's come out of the coma and they think her brain is working perfectly. I am now allowed to get a statement from her but thought you'd want to know immediately.'

Louise's knees had weakened as soon as Dave had mentioned the hospital. 'Thank you Dave, that's wonderful news, I can't quite take it in. It's been so many months and I feared she'd never come out of it or be alright if she did. It'll still be a long road to recovery for her as she will have to deal with the trauma of it all but perhaps eventually, we will be able to put all this behind us.'

DECEMBER 2006

The social worker led the boy away from the house and walked towards her car. She was aware of his stiffness as he walked alongside her, apparently disengaged from what was going on. She stopped and spoke directly to him. 'You do understand why you can't stay with Mr and Mrs Morgan don't you, Ben?'

His head was down and he made no acknowledgement he'd heard her but continued to trudge towards the car.

She had been a Social Worker for years but had never met a child quite like this one. When she had first engaged with him, she found him to be a really charming young lad with excellent manners and a lovely smile, and he had seemed to settle into his new home well. When she received the phone call from Mrs Morgan, she thought perhaps she had exaggerated things but agreed to remove Ben and arranged some temporary foster parents.

It was only when she arrived to collect him and was shown to the shed in the garden, she understood their distress.

The wall was covered in photos, mostly women. She recognised one of them from the court case and there was also a picture of a child. They all had crosses drawn on them; done quite roughly with a thin pen or even a knife but it was what lay on the table which filled her with horror. How could anyone torture a cat? She feared for him and wondered, as she asked him to get into her car, what his future would be.

The End

ACKNOWLEDGEMENTS

I'd like to thank all those who supported me through the months of the pandemic lock-down when I planned and wrote this novel. With special thanks to Sian who was always ready to join me for a coffee over the garden fence; Sarah and Kirstie, from my writing group for their encouragement and suggested amendments throughout the whole process and without whom I would never have begun; Barbara from Cornerstones who helped in the very early stages and tried to put me on the right track; A big thank you to readers who ploughed through various drafts and who gave helpful and encouraging feedback; Jane L, John, Sue, Lucy and Linda and those that gave me help with police matters. My brother Peter for his editing advice and encouragement to make the final push to publish it. Finally, to my family for just being there.

Milton Keynes UK
Ingram Content Group UK Ltd.
UKHW010123210224
438187UK00005B/372